The Echoes

MW01484427

\----

Rod Keys

\----

To Jen, Christmas '18

Rod

To my wife Diane

and

To the forgotten tens of millions of millions

Preface

".. for it was the offspring of happy days, when death and grief were but words, which found no true echo in my heart."

Mary Shelly

"Some things are unforgivable."

Back in 1972 friends might stop by my little rented house. My place was just a short drive from work and it was cheaper than going to a bar. When it was warm, we could sit on the back porch and look out on nearly a mile of abandoned farm land.

One September Friday evening we were out on that porch. The man who had spoken was older than most of us. He was an engineer from our east coast home office and he was in town for a couple months to work on a big industrial project. The man was stuck in a hotel, away from his wife and family. So naturally, he was welcome.

The truth of it is was he had arrived early that evening with a half gallon of vodka and by now enjoyed the advantage of several cocktails. He gazed out at all that vacant land, "Some things are unforgivable," he said a second time.

We usually talked about college football or the Detroit Tigers baseball team which was in first place that September or the election that was just two months off. We might even talk about work. Unforgivableness was not our usual fare. Faces turned to the gentleman with quizzical expressions

"When I was a kid in Hungary they threw us all out. Anyone who spoke German was a Nazi to them. They came to our house with guns and put us in an army truck. Then they loaded us into a boxcar with a bunch of other families. We rode

in that boxcar most of a day. When the train stopped, they told us we were in Germany. They pushed us out and I fell onto the ground below. It was gravel down there under the train tracks and when I landed I bloodied my knees. There was nothing around, nothing, just a big unused field." He waved his hand toward all the land behind my place. "Not even a house was in site. And there we all were. And we had nothing. We lost everything. We only had the clothes on our backs. We had nothing. Even my mother started to cry."

When he came to the part about being pushed out of the boxcar, he looked down at the palms of his hands like they still hurt and then he rubbed his knees.

Nobody else spoke for an awkward moment, so I said, "How about another one János, that was a vodka martini, right?"

Then another older guy broke the tension and spoke up, "Hey János, you were lucky. The Russians occupied Lithuania. That was when I was a kid. They wouldn't let us out at all. They figured we were their slaves or something. My Mom and Dad and brother hid under boxcars and when the train started to move we climbed onto some narrow board-things down there and we grabbed the undercarriages and held on for life. We went over a really tall trestle that was way up high over a river. That part scared me to death. We went all the way to Germany like that. Lucky you! You got to ride inside the train."

Then both men laughed heartily. They both seemed to think this conversation was uproariously funny.

That conversation was the real beginning of this book. Or I should say, a while back I decided to write a murder mystery and try to weave it around memories of terrible things that happened to people. Then, as I thought about my murder mystery, that short and odd, but to me, intense conversation came back.

Oh yes, the scene for my story; Suburban Detroit is my home. The scene is only half fiction. Time-wise, the scene is some years back when everyone's dad was a

World War Two veteran, but not so far back as to be before laptop computers and cell phones.

I had plenty of help writing this book. The first help came from the two gentlemen above, neither of which was really named János. My cousin and best-selling author Rodman Philbrick suffered through the first draft of this book and was polite enough to find a couple nice things to say. Then he offered some blunt advice. Then Rod, whose first name is, by the way, is the same as mine, wisely insisted that we adjourn to his private club in Portsmouth, New Hampshire, drink scotch and smoke foul smelling cigars. Others who read and reread and offered valuable input included Mrs. Claudia Swink, and Mrs. Emily Barberry. Neither of these ladies suggested we drink scotch and smoke malodorous cigars, but the cheer and enthusiasm with which they gave their time and input is greatly appreciated. My brothers Richard Keys and Andrew Keys read and corrected much also. Friends Jim Graham and Mark Thomas read later drafts and helped out plenty as well. Then my wife's cousin Jim Petix jumped in and eradicated numerous typos and errors. To all, thanks.

My wife Diane graciously put up with all of this and gave me encouragement. She was the source of many good ideas like Jane's General Tso's Chicken and the Feine's family hug.

This, dear reader, is a first try at novel writing, so be nice. It is, if nothing else, honest.

The Echoes

Schmidt

"None are so old as those who have outlived enthusiasm."

Henry David Thoreau

Günter Schmidt had eight hours to live. Not that he knew. He stood at the front door of his big house and had thoughts not of his end, but thoughts of the clouds and skies of a pretty September afternoon and of the campus nearby where he had worked for so many years. Today, the campus would be filled with students just starting another year. The old man remembered decades of new students arriving on campus, full of hopes and excitement and foolishness, but also full of the quaint, childish trepidation of leaving home. This was a beginning for young people.

Günter Schmidt had paused while entering his front door. He turned feeling a warm breeze rush into his house.

For a very old man he was healthy and strong still, but Schmidt also had a growing enjoyment of things he used to ignore, things like good weather and naps and warmth. Here, near Detroit, September held the last of the dog days. September was warm, at first anyway, but later it brought the first days of the Great Lakes' winter overcast with its humid, penetrating cold. It was the beginning of rain and more rain. Then, the rain would turn to snow. On campus, it would cover lawns and there would be tracks were students had taken shortcuts instead of sticking to the sidewalks. The campus goldfish ponds would freeze and the outdoor statues of

4

naked women and men would don odd white clothing made of snow. Sometimes a pond was cleared of snow for skaters, but few students skated these days and none were graceful figure skaters like he and his friends used to be. Snow would cover the outdoor benches by the ponds and outdoor courtyards and make sidewalks sloppy and slick and make feet cold, even through shoes inside rubber boots.

New students at the campus made pretty thoughts for Günter Schmidt, but they were mixed with melancholy too. To Günter Schmidt, it seemed, September was an ominous warning that winter was not far off and an end to yet another year was near. September, it seemed to him, was full of contradictions.

How many years had he been retired? For that matter, how long ago had it been when he himself was a new student? That was very long ago, far away, another time altogether. That was in cold, dark Danzig. Danzig, on the cold Baltic Sea. Danzig, 'The Free City.' Some free city! It should have been German. The people were German. But the insufferable Treaty of Versailles took it away from Germany. Danzig was ruled by ambassadors from other countries who were not elected, but assigned by The League of Nations. The League of Nations spoke about President Wilson's 'self determination,' and about democracy and freedom, but the only people with no say at all in ruling Danzig were the Germans who lived there. Danzig was a 'free state' starting in 1920, before Günter Schmidt's earliest memory, but he remembered the results under The League. Free? Hah! In those days, the Poles had special rights and were given much German private property. The German population was handed nothing but difficulties and penalties, as if Germans alone were to blame for the first war, as if every single German speaking person was personally responsible.

Günter Schmidt did recall the first day of September in 1939 when the next war began. He was a young man by then. The German army obliterated Poland in days and Danzig was united with Germany once again. At first that seemed to be a relief, an improvement.

How life and events corrupt and dash youthful hopes. It all leads to the bitterness that only old men really know, men who strived and, against all odds, who persevered and succeeded only to find the end of it all empty.

Günter Schmidt pictured today's young people showing up for their first classes. They were not polished or polite or well prepared as his generation had been.

Really, they were rich, spoiled, naïve and they had no manners. They knew no discipline or respect, were slow to learn and they were impossible to teach. By spring, some would have failed their classes and gone home to their parents. That, he supposed, was for them, the first step on the road to disillusionment and bitterness that all people, spoiled and stupid or not, must travel. What did today's children know? So many let themselves be stopped and crushed over trivial, self-made trouble. What did they know of hardships and real terrors like those that he had seen? Had he not managed against all horrors? Horrors these spoiled children could not even imagine? Had he not helped people in real trouble? And indeed, he had overcome it all, but for what?

He had shared successes with Natalie. She was a good, kind, obedient woman and strong too. Long ago, she would have been called as tough as they come and crafty too, but now, and for many, many years, just happy would be a better description. She lived well, better than she could have imagined in the old days. But she could never be one with him. Not really.

Günter Schmidt was bitter. He felt old and alone, unappreciated and forgotten. He felt too old to do anything about it. Günter looked toward the afternoon sun. Soon the sun would slip behind the tall trees in front of his house. They were still green and full. But days were shorter now and soon, the leaves would fall leaving only stark, bare branches. Perhaps, in the back of his mind, he knew this, in its way, reflected himself.

Günter Schmidt stood up straight. He was suddenly annoyed with himself. He knew downcast thoughts were just weakness. He did not allow himself self-pity. There was to be a house party tonight plus new students were coming to live in the gate-house. He was wasting time with this maudlin nonsense. Günter Schmidt snorted at himself out loud. He closed the big front door firmly and walked briskly to see what help he could be to Natalie with preparations for tonight. He thought of Disraeli's quote, "Never complain, never explain." Disraeli was right, no complaints, no explanations, not even to yourself.

Perhaps, had Günter Schmidt known his time left on earth was not years or even days, but just hours, he might have allowed himself to be more philosophical. But perhaps that knowledge would have made little difference to him at all.

Feines

"Ye've got to weep t' make it home"

Edgar Guest

Things were perfectly normal at the Feine house today. But that would not last.

Lois Feine, had her laptop computer open on the kitchen table.

Lois's mom, Sylvia, said, "Look, I'm not mortgaging the house to pay your tuition and buy books and pay for your car insurance so you can take classes in remedial knitting and cosmic Zen positions. You're supposed be getting a degree. And a degree that starts 'Bachelor of.' Quit changing your classes and major all the time. You'll never finish."

Lois knew her mom's mock-angry voice and she replied in her version of it. "Mom, Conversational Spanish 201 just opened up. I was locked out of it yesterday, but now it's available again. Somebody dropped it. I'm going to grab it. You gotta have a two semester foreign language sequence to get a BA and a semester more's required for an English major."

Sylvia Feine said, "You need extra foreign language classes to get an English major? What's that? Show me that in the school catalog. Where does it say that? And what happened to teaching?"

"Teaching's not a major, it's a certificate, so c'mon Mom, I'm doin' it. I have to get a foreign language sequence to graduate. That's what you want, right? Like, otherwise I'll be old and gray and I'll still be sitting here at the kitchen table, right? I'm doin' it."

"You can do this on a computer? When I was in school, we went to the field-house with the list of classes we needed and we pulled cards out of boxes that were on tables all over the place. It was a circus with everyone running around trying to get the right classes. Upper classmen went first and I was a year ahead of your

Dad, so I pulled his stuff for him too. In a real college, that day in the field house was a rite of passage. Now you punch a computer? Ah, what you kids miss. And Spanish? Why Spanish? Why not .. Yiddish?"

"Funny Mom."

Lois's cousin Swan was there too. She looked up from a day-old newspaper. "German! Take German! It's the same as Yiddish. Then the old Kraut next door can coach you."

"Right Swan. He's probably Heinrich Himmler himself in disguise. He's old enough. Sure, he'll want to teach me German so I can finally understand Bubbie's Yiddish. Anyway, these days, half the world speaks Spanish."

"No they don't. Half the world speaks Chinese or Mandarin or Cantonese or whatever it's called. "

"That half doesn't live here. The half that speaks Spanish lives here." Lois typed something, "There, I've got it. Now I should drop something. I'm dropping Art History. It's an elective anyway."

Then Swan said, "Hey, look Aunt Sylvia, here's a cool apartment for a winter sublet. And it's furnished. It says sublet, so maybe I can work a deal. I've been in that apartment complex for parties and stuff. It has two pools and an exercise room and all these cool people."

Sylvia Feine moved behind her niece and read over her shoulder, "Looks cool alright, but where are you getting that kind of money?"

"Why don't you have Lois go in on it with me. She's twenty. It's time for her to move out. Half each isn't that bad."

"Yeah, just run out back and bring in a bushel of money from the money tree. That'll pay Lois's rent for her. But until the money tree blooms, Lois will get her bachelor's degree living here. After that, she can get more school and I'll even pay some of it, or she can get a job and move out, or, how about both, or she can get married, if she ever finds anyone who amounts to anything. It's her choice. As a matter of fact Swan, why don't you forget this apartment idea of yours and stay here too? That'd save my dear brother-in-law some money. Then maybe he'd even send me some of his money leftovers. I'm not so bad a room-mate you know. You seem to have survived the summer here."

"Aunt Sylvia, you are a cool house-mate, and the summer's been great here. But I was on my own every school year since my folks moved up north. That's three years ago. And I seem to have gotten a 'bachelor of' in spite of it and gotten into grad school in spite of it. I've kind-a gotten used to having my own place. And be fair, remember that summer job in Parks and Rec? I've worked that job five summers running."

"Mom, are we making honey-cake for New Years?" Out of the clear blue, Lois suddenly started to cry. "Oh jeez! I'm sorry. I was just thinking about Daddy and you in college and then I thought of putting that little bit of honey cake on his grave this time last year .. I'm okay. I'm sorry." Lois sniffed and then recovered herself as quickly as she had cried.

Sylvia regarded her daughter. "That's okay baby, I know the feeling. I cry too. Do I ever miss him. I was younger than you two when he first took me out on a date. I look at you two and have a hard time imagining it. Oh my, now I'm going to cry too. But being buddies here in this house, the house he got us, is being true to him. In that way, he's still with us. He's still with us in lots of ways. We'll make honey cake in the round bundt pan again this year. Keep the circle unbroken and all that. .. Remember that song about it? Some folk group used to sing it. We'll do honey cake in a Bundt pan again and put a little piece on his grave. We'll do that every year."

"Aunt Sylvia, isn't that song some Christian thing?"

"Yeah, maybe it is. Now that you mention it, I think it is. But it fits. Rosh Hashanah is only a couple days. New Year's stuff is supposed to be round, like a year, it comes back. It fits. Rosh Hashanah is about repentance and sounding the shofar for a new start once every year. It's like a circle."

The room was silent for a moment.

Silvia spoke again, "Then, Yom Kippur's next. That's atonement. That's part of it too. … Swan, who will you call on Yom Kippur?"

"Aunt Sylvia, that's a couple weeks away isn't it? I have to think. Probably call my Dad. We had words, nothing bad, but we had a little argument and that bugs me. And I never got up to Charlevoix to see either of my folks this summer. I'll phone my folks I guess."

"Lois?"

"Oh, probably you, I've been a pain now and then. I'll talk to you. Mom, who will you call?"

"Hmm .. maybe Swan's Mom. We didn't get along so well at first. But she's been good family for so many years. She's been a great wife for your uncle. I'll call her and tell her that she has been wonderful all these years. I should tell her that."

After a moment Lois spoke again, "Mom, are you going to start dating men some time? Daddy's been gone a couple years now. And, I mean, you're pretty and stuff and kind-a well off and you're not that old."

"Oh, I guess some day I will. But it's not time for me yet. I'm not ready. I have my own clock. Inside, I'm still all wrapped up with your Dad and you guys. I'm way not ready. Some day, I will. Long ago, your Daddy told me to go on if he ever died. Isn't that funny? Like he knew. But not yet. Somehow, I'll know when."

An older lady entered the kitchen. "Bubbie, you look wonderful! Are you ready to go? Look guys, it's time to scoot. We can't keep the old Krauts waiting. But I think we need a big all-around family hug. You too Swan."

Jane

"We live as we dream – alone"

Joseph Conrad, Heart of Darkness

It was Jane's birthday. Jane entered her little house, the one she grew up in, the one her mom left her. Cancer got her mom just a year ago, on this very day, on Jane's birthday. It was five years and a month earlier that a bad heart got her Dad. Besides a few thousand dollars in a checking account, this house was her inheritance.

The door closed behind Jane and clicked its old familiar click, and she gazed at the familiar bright yellow kitchen with its white metal cabinets, white enamel sink and her mother's old kitchen stuff. Jane deposited mail from the mailbox and a box of carry-out Chinese on the kitchen table. Then Jane noticed the sound of the window air conditioner in the back bedroom. She had forgotten and left the air on all day. 'Not good for the electric bill,' Jane thought.

In September, Washington DC was still stinking hot, so Jane slept in the back bedroom addition with her father's humming window air conditioner. It sounded like a cheap motel room, but it put her to sleep. Her Dad had put that room plus a bathroom on the back of the house. That was when his bad heart would not let him climb the stairs anymore. That back area and this kitchen were pretty much the range of Jane's movements in the house these days.

Jane hadn't even been in the living room for a month, much less gone upstairs. Her folks' old bedroom and her childhood bedroom were upstairs, in fact, right over where Jane was now. It loomed up there, some ghostly place from the past. The last time she actually went up there was to clear her folks' old stuff out. Now, the upstairs rooms, each with their ceilings bent down under the roof's slope, seemed very small, even claustrophobic. The stairs were narrow and steep. It had been awkward to carry boxes of clothing and other stuff down. She liked her childhood bedroom when she was little, but now the second floor's grungy old bathroom tile and footed tub and every other part of the second floor just seemed old and small. It was dusty and small and hot up there. Jane did not like going up there anymore.

Jane thought back, she should have sold the old place as soon as she got it. Moving in, like becoming a school teacher, had been a mistake. She could easily have stayed in her cute little rented suite of rooms a little longer. That flat had served her just fine through the days when she worked as an elementary school teacher and rode all night in police cars to get credit for a new degree in criminal justice. It served her fine during her night classes and when she pounded out a master's thesis on conflicts of interest in police investigations that were due to administrative political agendas. Teaching little brats had definitely not been for her and getting that second master's, this time in criminal justice, opened the door to the FBI, or rather, not exactly the FBI, but 'The Office of Independent Investigations.' Jane had wanted to be an FBI Special Agent. That had sounded exciting. But her master's thesis brought a job offer that bypassed the FBI academy. This job, on the face of it, was more prestigious than an FBI agent, her co-workers included lawyers and even a former federal judge, but the new job lacked what Jane thought was the down-and-dirty grit and excitement of the real thing.

Jane resolved, for the hundredth time, to sell the house and buy a new condo in a trendy part of town. Her new income was quite good and it paid the bills and more. She could afford it. She'd start looking into real estate companies by way of the internet this very night. She'd see who had sold the most places in this part of town.

As far as her new job, Jane was pleased with herself for that. It turned out to be more bureaucratic and political than she had hoped. In that regard, it was as bad as teaching. And there were few, really no handsome, smart, athletic, romantic, dashing men available. Oh, there were self possessed divorced jerks, or even worse, overly forward and self possessed jerks who were not yet divorced, and there were a couple whiny weaklings of men and men who drank too much. Unlike some women, she did not feel like a mother toward weaklings or men who thought being drunk was cool. She did not imagine that she could fix them. She tried to remember who said, 'Women marry men hoping they will change. Men marry women hoping they will not. So each is inevitably disappointed.' Whoever said that was onto something. Anyway, welcome to adulthood. Life is not what teenagers hope for. Yes, the Office of Independent Investigations was another disappointment, but it was way better than snotty little brats and their over-indulging Moms in PTA meetings, Moms who were either totally blind or blamed their misbehaving kids faults on the teacher. She wondered if now she might, some fine day, have the pleasure of throwing a few of those kids in a federal penitentiary.

And there was John Mill at the office. Mill; after the hot chicks had gotten all the hot men, maybe he was really just some kind of a left-over. Or maybe he didn't like chicks who thought themselves hot. Maybe he didn't like Jane that much either. Who knew? Mill was the office nerd. Mill was a walking encyclopedia of knowledge in a sports coat and bow tie. Outside of that, he was stoic and unreadable, inscrutable, except for a temper that flashed once in a while. He never apologized for that temper either. He just resumed what he was doing. Maybe that temper was the only window into the real man. Maybe inside he was really mad as hell. Maybe he was mad because hot chicks seldom like nerdy men.

Jane had just gotten a promotion. She got a raise too. At least that part put a positive spin on things.

Inside the carry-out box some odd tubes of browned chicken were swimming in an unknown sweet and brown sauce next to vegetables in cornstarch gruel plus a ball of rice that looked like it came out of an ice-cream scoop. Jane had ordered it because something with a power-name like 'General Tso's Chicken' might buck up her dreary mood. Besides, it just had to be better than something named 'Bang Bang Ji' or 'Happy Family.' But General Tso's chicken had a remarkable ability to break the tines of the plastic fork. So Jane got real silverware from a drawer.

Jane spread the mail out; a couple bills, lots of junk mail and a hand addressed card sized envelope. Inside was a note written in big script that said, "Happy Birthday Jane, John Mill". That made Jane smile. How did Mill find her address? Weren't addresses of employees secured? And how'd he know it was her birthday? Gee, however he did it, that was nice of him.

There were two fortune cookies. Jane broke one open; 'Fact, Facts with Dignity.' Now that's appropriate, thought Jane. She broke the other one. It said, 'Your smile will tell you what makes you feel good.'

McIntyre

"No man ought to looke a given horse in the mouth."

John Heywood - 1546

Every year, September was a new beginning. There were new students, new teachers, and then everything went into high gear. And every year, there were unexpected problems.

Dean of Students James McIntyre sat in his office. It was in an old building that was precariously close to the street. In 1911, when the building was built, little thought must have been given to either sidewalks or new-fangled autos. Outside of being way too close to the road, the building was unremarkable. McIntyre's office was small and had just one widow and that window looked across a narrow drive at the wall of the next building. But McIntyre felt comfortable here.

This year's big problem was a screw-up that double-booked all the classrooms in one of the buildings. Changing classes to after-hours would, no doubt, mess up schedules of teachers and students alike. Even now, Miss Gordon in the front office was checking the schedules for spaces like the school's little theater, music rehearsal rooms, a cafeteria and a couple administration meeting rooms. There was to be a meeting in one of those rooms on what to do about this mess in fifteen minutes. Thank goodness for Miss Gordon.

McIntyre sat back taking a short break. He thought back over the last year. A huge gift to the school had surprised him. It had been so unusual that it made him rather uncomfortable. Big money does not just come from the sky like that. Had he missed something?

A simple letter of inquiry about the school came from a German consortium of some kind. McIntyre replied with an out-of-date brochure. Then, in short order, there was a grant for a new modern-art wing that was to be added to the school's art museum. Colebrook School did not even know it wanted a new wing for modern art. The art museum's architecture was famous, an 'International Modern' style building built in 1933. It was an architectural gem. In front of it was a fountain with statues of unnaturally long-legged, naked ladies and men all standing on pedestals. The building and the statues were striking. The last thing it needed was an incongruous wing pasted on the side. The money would have been better spent for art to go inside the museum or, if the donors insisted on a building, it should be separate and at a respectable distance from this gem.

But when twenty-million dollars fell out of the sky into McIntyre's lap for a 'modern art wing' and Colebrook's president took a public bow for it, that was that. This president seemed to think that a college dean's sole job was fund raising. The gift suddenly put McIntyre's sleepy and possibly endangered career on a fast track.

McIntyre knew good publicity could bring more good stuff. Grants brought better faculty, better students and usually, more grants. It was a vicious circle, a good vicious circle. So McIntire went to work preparing press packets featuring artistic drawings of the new wing. He had a series of un-copyrighted public interest video pieces made about the school and sent them to television stations for free use. He hosted luncheons and worked to line up art by famous artists for exhibitions. All the action and publicity did indeed bring more outside interest to Colebrook and sure enough, employment feelers came from artists whose names McIntyre actually recognized.

Colebrook, half prep school, half college, was, after all, mostly noted for Art. In the old days a number of celebrated artists and architects had taught here. Graduates from the old days usually enjoyed good careers, even fame. Recovering some of that momentum would be good.

But the grant did not come the way things usually went. There was no politicking, no receptions, no playing up to rich old ladies and putting their dead husband's names on buildings. It made no sense. It was too easy. And it was way too much money. What was he missing? But there was no doubt that it was true. The construction was already under way.

Then another uncomfortable surprise, a Miss Dorman who said she was a secretary for that well-endowed but mysterious German consortium had phoned McIntyre and asked for his 'assistance' with two German art students. They were a young couple named Hans and Helga Hoffman. Their last name, the same as the name of the head of the consortium, was not explained. They would be in the U.S. for the first time and would attend Colebrook School. Colebrook's policy was to associate each new student with a faculty mentor and the same mentor would guide them throughout the student's time at Colebrook. Miss Dorman already knew who they wanted, old, retired, Professor of Fine Art Günter Schmidt. McIntyre thought this was rather presumptuous, but twenty million dollars was twenty million dollars, so he just said "Of course." He bypassed the admissions staff, waived any and all admission requirements and enrolled their names. This was all very irregular, but twenty-million said it was the right thing to do. McIntyre wondered about European wealth and etiquette. Was this how it was done over there? Was it just understood that money bought a place for wayward kids? But when the two Hoffman kids sent information about themselves, they were both well qualified. That was a relief. On the other hand, they were married and a bit older than most other students. But that part need not be a real problem.

Then McIntyre wondered about that word, 'assist.' Assist with what? Just getting the kids into the school? Or would there be more? Married students were rare at Colebrook and there was no married student's housing. So McIntyre decided to assist with housing. Twenty million bucks said this was a good idea too.

Coincidentally, old Günter Schmidt had just phoned to let him know that he might welcome a student at his home. Schmidt admitted that he had just lost his driver's license. He had run into a parked car at the grocery store. The police had ticketed him and ordered a driving test because of his age. He had failed the eyesight test, twice, and that was the end of his license. He might trade use of spare rooms for driving his car and a little other help. So McIntyre made a phone call to the long retired Professor. Dr. Günter Schmidt agreed at once. "Two students? Named Hoffman you say? From Germany and married? Perfect! That is good." That came out, "Dahss east goot."

But now it was time for that meeting.

Hoffmans and a Party

"Welcome the coming, speed the going guest."

Alexander Pope

Dean James McIntyre personally drove to Detroit Metro Airport. The young German couple was good looking, polite and spoke good American-style English. They seemed almost American and quite at ease.

A twenty mile ride took them to Bloomfield Hills, one of Detroit's wealthiest suburbs. Bloomfield Hills had winding residential streets with curbs and sidewalks and groomed lawns in front of expensive houses. But there were other areas nearby that were wooded and had roads with no curbs or sidewalks. In these areas trees stood close to the road and made it dark. Here the woods were old and natural and houses were hidden back among the trees. Here, foxes still scampered up the roads, owls still hooted in the night and after dark, deer's eyes reflected headlights and made people drive slowly. McIntyre thought it was much prettier here.

McIntyre passed a drive that led into a Catholic seminary and a quarter mile further, turned down a wooded road. In another quarter mile he spotted an odd slant-topped redwood column. It held a back-lighted address cut into a piece of heavy metal. The column also held a mailbox. It was, perhaps, an attempt at modernism but McIntyre thought it just looked odd. The contraption marked a brick-paved drive that curved through a treed acre or two and then made a loop around a groomed yard with a fountain in the middle. The loop passed in front of a huge house and then it curved by a long garage that looked, to McIntyre's eye anyway, more like a horse stable. McIntyre counted nine garage doors in three sets of three. The house itself was long, low and made of brick, concrete and redwood. It had an incongruous rustic porch stuck on the front loaded with Adirondack chairs and tables. In fact, the house was incongruous all over. The house sat low on a slope that ran sharply down from the drive so that the entrance porch looked, to McIntyre's eye, like a medieval drawbridge over a moat. There were oversized, arts-and-crafts style doors from the porch into the house. The doors were at least ten feet tall, of finely finished and heavily varnished wood and were out of place on the rustic porch. The house was modern, arts and crafts, and rustic and Tudor styles all thrown haphazardly together with no regard for the natural setting at all. And the fountain out front looked like it belonged in a Roman piazza. The effect was chaotic and disagreeable. McIntyre thought any real architect would have apoplexy.

Even fifty years ago when Schmidt built this place the land and the construction must have cost a fortune. Today's property taxes must be absolutely deadly. McIntyre thought to himself, .' 'Money doesn't guarantee taste, and this guy headed our art school ... holy cow!'

McIntyre wondered where the old man's money had come from. Some big-name artists had worked under Schmidt. But Schmidt was not a noted artist himself. Besides, Colebrook never paid anybody, department head or not, noted artist or not, enough for a place like this.

The young German couple sitting in his car had been quiet for most of the ride, but they stirred now. Hans pointed at the mixed-up house and the over sized garage next to it. His eyes betrayed amazement, but the two spoke in German and McIntyre could not make out what they said.

Someone was moving a minivan that had 'Kuhn's Catering' painted on it. It moved from the front of the house, where it had apparently been unloading, and stopped by the garage. A mature woman got out. She wore a remarkably short skirt that betrayed robust thighs. McIntyre stopped where the minivan had been. The lady with the short skirt reached the front door first and opened it, and there, as if on cue, stood Günter Schmidt and Natalie. Dr. Günter Schmidt looked tall and hale, but older than McIntyre remembered him. Natalie was old too, perhaps older than Schmidt and she looked very small next to him. Schmidt's steady sky-blue eyes were still as penetrating as ever and he still sounded German. "Please follow me. I am glad you are here. Hans? Helga? Welcome." Schmidt led the way through a dramatic, high ceiling foyer or entry hall or whatever this big front room was. That room was open to another even bigger room with a low ceiling. The second room had windows looking out the back of the house. "Soon, we will have a little neighborhood cocktail party. We arranged it before we knew you were coming so now it is a party as much for you as for our neighbors. What a nice accident." The young couple's replies were obviously polite, even deferential, and in German. The conversation continued in German.

McIntyre noticed the woman in the remarkably short black skirt again. She wore a white pleated, tuxedo-style shirt. It had long sleeves, big cuffs and oversized cufflinks. She had a bow tie and her hair was sprayed in place to stay. She hurried about spreading white cloths on little tables, and pulling wine glasses from a box. She worked very quickly. All the while, she barked instructions to some unseen person who must have been in a nearby kitchen.

McIntyre tuned the conversations out and walked to a wall of metal framed casement windows. The windows had metal hand cranks and gears that looked like they had not been operated in a decade. McIntyre looked outside. Below, the yard was big indeed. Part of the yard was sunken like a conversation pit in an old 'modern' style house. The square pit was surrounded by a short brick wall with steps in the corners. It had several concrete park-bench style seats and they looked like they would make very cold seating in the winter and uncomfortable seating year-round. McIntyre wondered what kept heavy rain from making the sunken area into a swimming pool. He supposed there must be drains of some kind. Beyond that area, the yard was very big indeed. "Campus" or "grounds" might have been better words than "yard".

A little stream passed through the yard and disappeared into the woods. There was an arched wooden foot bridge over the stream. It was painted white. McIntyre thought that little bridge was the nicest touch in the whole yard. Well to the side of the yard, there was another bridge over the stream, this one was flat and gray. Maybe the flat one was for a yard mowing tractor. You certainly couldn't cut all this grass here by hand. McIntyre tried to imagine shrubs hiding that bridge. In fact, he thought the yard needed more plantings all over. He wondered if a hedge maze with seats in the middle might help. There was certainly enough room for one.

The back of the yard was wooded. McIntyre could make out an outbuilding back there; perhaps it was a guest house. There was a second building too. Maybe a gardener's shed. It was nearly hidden by the woods.

'What a spread!' he thought to himself, 'and when Schmidt dies and they knock this ridiculous place down and chop the property up, how many houses will they stuff in here?' He tried to picture a cul-de-sac with big houses all around. Five with big yards could fit here with ease.

"Come Dean McIntyre, help show our guests their quarters." McIntyre started and turned. Günter Schmidt waved toward a metal stairway headed downward that was much too narrow and steep for the scale of the house. "Please go ahead of us, we are old and much too slow on these steps."

The Hoffman kids led the way followed by McIntyre. Below was a small room with a sofa facing more of those metal windows plus a door. Neither windows nor door looked very weather-proof. 'The heating bill for this place must be fabulous,' thought McIntyre, 'the old man must be made of money.' McIntyre turned and saw Günter Schmidt descending. Schmidt held a skinny metal tube of a hand rail and descended one step at a time, but he stood very erect and this made his descent look dignified. Natalie was behind him.

When Schmidt arrived below, he spoke, "Hans, Helga, when Mrs. Schmidt and I came here, it was a different time. It was not good to be from Germany then. You are too young to understand how it was. We had lost the war and the question of the Nazis and their concentration camps was on everybody's mind. Even so, the Americans were kind to me and helped me get a new start. So I told Mrs. Schmidt, 'We are American now, we have left the old behind. All Americans came from one place or another in their own turn and like them, this is our home now.' I said to Mrs. Schmidt, 'We will speak English here because now we are American. We must leave the past behind and close the door.' That meant a great deal to me then. I think I was right to insist. Things have gone well for me here and Americans who were kind to us allowed that to happen. So I will ask you to respect a request of an old man. It is a wish that is left from another day perhaps, but it is still my wish. We will speak English in this house."

Hans paused and looked at Helga for a moment, then nodded, almost bowed and said, "A good practice ."

McIntyre thought of the time years ago when he saw Schmidt's framed diplomas on his office wall. The diplomas had swastikas and pictures of Stuka dive bombers and Messerschmitt ME 109 fighters flying around on them. Those diplomas were framed and on display. Schmidt was not so ashamed of his German roots then.

"Also Hans, I spoke to your uncle. He wants you to learn about America. We will talk about some travel for next summer so you can get acquainted with this land and its kind, honorable people."

Hans looked at Helga again, but McIntyre could not read what the look meant.

Schmidt spoke again, "There are several autos in the garage. You may use the older Lincoln as your own. The newer Lincoln you will drive for Natalie and me. You will need some practice, they are bigger than autos you are used to. The other cars are antiques for investment or for my fun and we do not drive them so much. We would also like some modest help around this big and old place, help making meals perhaps, not real work. It will be just as if you are our family. For a little help with things I can no longer do as I would like, you may stay without charge. You will become the family Natalie and I do not have."

Natalie opened the outside door, "Come Helga, your rooms are behind the garage. We call it the gate house, but there is no gate. Two bedrooms and a small study are upstairs and there is a door into the garage from the study. There is a living room downstairs and a kitchen. It is comfortable and private. Dr. Schmidt and I lived there for a year while the rest of this house was finished. It is more than enough for two. There is a hall and stairway that leads to the laundry and kitchen in this house so in the winter, you need not go outdoors. I will show you how to unlock it. It is probably dusty and full of spiders but a little of your young energy will perk everything up. I will help with the linens and other things. We must check everything because they have been stored too long. If anything is bad, we have many more extras here in the house."

It was warm outside, as it can be in Michigan's September. The grass was cut and neat, but cement walks were old and, in shady places, black with mold. Planters no longer held the shrubs or flowers for which they once must have been intended. Still, it was quiet, warm and pleasant.

McIntyre thought 'gate house' with a hall to a laundry room and kitchen and located behind the garage? This must really be servant's quarters. He wondered about the guest house he saw back in the woods. The Hoffmans, he thought, would be happier back there. Why in the servant's quarters? Is that what Schmidt thought the kids were? Servants?

Then Schmidt squinted at his watch. "Oh Hans, you will excuse me, we expect our visitors now and I should be upstairs to show them in. Please get your things from Dean McIntyre's car while Mrs. Schmidt shows Helga your quarters. As soon as it is convenient, you and Helga please come to our living room. You will meet some neighbors. Dean McIntyre, please go up in front of me. I am too slow. Natalie and I will take care of everything here with our new family, our new son and daughter, and I will be sure that they are at your office at school at nine tomorrow morning."

McIntyre thought, 'Germans and specific times! And he's dictating the time to me. And Germans are always prompt. You can set a watch by Germans.'

"I thank you for thinking of us in this matter. I am slow on the steps, so please go ahead of me and let yourself out."

The none-too-subtle and repeated invitation to leave was welcome. It was the end of a full day and McIntyre wanted to go home. But upstairs he found it was already too late. The lady with the remarkably short skirt and bow tie carried a tray of hors d'oeuvres and an old man in a tuxedo, apparently the man on the receiving end of those barked instructions, carried a tray of wine in glasses. He repeated, "Merlot, Cabernet, Chardonnay" with a thick unidentifiable accent. Another man in an expensive tailored gray suit was mixing cocktails at some sort of sideboard that served as a bar. People turned to McIntyre as he topped the stairs so he smiled and moved quickly for the front door. But his escape was blocked by a lady. She spoke with another accent McIntyre did not recognize, "Dean McIntyre, how nice to see you. I am Mrs. Hubchic, I am Natalie Schmidt's best friend, except for Günter of course. I live in Grosse Pointe, but I was at your school's fund-raiser last month and gave a hundred dollars."

Then another lady pounced on him, "And I am Sylvia Feine, I was at that fund-raiser too and we spoke, you remember of course. My daughter Lois and my niece Swan are here. That older lady over there is my aunt who everybody calls 'Bubbie.' I know your school's president. Do you know the mayor of Detroit? I do, and he wants his youngest boy to go to Colebrook. Would you like his number? That's Mr. Webb making his special rum drinks for us. Isn't he a gentleman? Mr. Webb was a neighbor of a US representative once. We always just let ourselves in here. We all seemed to get here at once today didn't we? That young attractive lady near Mr. Webb is his wife Sally. I'm sure she knows important people too. Isn't this nice of Günter and Natalie?"

McIntyre thought he'd met the attractive Sally Webb somewhere but he wasn't sure. He also thought slinky might be a better term than attractive. Then he gazed at the youthful Lois and Swan with curiosity. He noticed a decided similarity between Swan's costume and the cocktail waitress with the remarkably short skirt. In fact, the short skirts were almost identical. Above that, Swan had no bow tie. Instead, her blouse had ruffles and was very low cut, but it had the same long sleeves and big black cuff links. In fact Swan looked angrily at the waitress. She obviously noticed the similarity in costumes and that did not seem to please her. Swan's blouse was so low cut and skirt so short that McIntyre suddenly felt he should look away, which he did. He also felt his eyes should not dawdle on the evident trophy wife Sally Webb.

McIntyre turned back to Mrs. Feine who was saying something about the mayor of Detroit, or the mayor's wife, or knowing the governor and a senator, but by now Günter Schmidt had managed the stairway and came forward. "Thank you Dean, these are my neighbors."

McIntyre was glad that Schmidt had cut in and he took the pause to say, "Good evening ladies, and thank you for that generous gift Mrs .. Hubchic." He had nearly forgotten her name. "I'm afraid I must rush right off." He repeated to himself, 'Hubchic, Grosse Pointe, claims to be Natalie's best friend, first name, Mrs.' McIntyre had learned remembering such stuff often comes in handy in fund raising. He repeated, 'Hubchic, Grosse Points, first name Mrs.' under his breath.

Outside, Hans already stood by the car. He must have come out through the garage. McIntyre opened the trunk. "Can you manage all this yourself?"

"Sure, I carried the whole works through customs at Kennedy. Thanks for the ride Sir, and thank you especially for setting this all up. Old timers in there, eh?"

"Yeah, it's a regular geriatrics ward, except there's a couple poor twenty year old girls trapped in there with them. They'd probably appreciate someone under the age of eighty to talk to."

Hans smiled. "Really, this is all very good, sir. The quarters are much better than we had hoped. Much better! We only expected a room or two and a shared kitchen. This is great. Helga and I will make the most of it and keep the old folks at ease. Thank you for making this excellent arrangement. Really! And we'll be sure to rescue those helpless young ladies inside. Good night!"

McIntyre thought to himself, 'Hans has suddenly found his tongue and he speaks just like an American.'

Too pat. Was he missing something? But he really just wanted to go home. Tomorrow was going to be busy.

Washington

"I see you stand like greyhounds in the slips, straining on the start. The game's afoot:
Follow your spirit"

William Shakespeare – Henry V

-

"It was Holmes. The candle in his hand shown upon his eager, stooping face and told me at a glance that something was amiss.
'Come Watson, come' he cried. 'The Game is afoot'"

Arthur Conan Doyle, Sherlock Holmes - The Adventure of the Abbey Grange

Jane looked at herself in the ladies' room mirror. She smiled her big wide smile. She did a little skip and a goofy wiggle. She thought she was cute and curvy, but she was not sure. Maybe her butt was really just a little fat and she was a bit too old to be exactly cute. Vanity had never been her problem, but her birthday had come last week. Nobody noticed except Mill who sent a note and it just said. 'Happy Birthday.' That was it. She was now thirty, still single and with no romantic prospects. If she wanted a successful husband and a suburban house with little Dicks and Janes scampering about, time was getting short. That knowledge displeased her. Today she had dressed a little better than usual. She wore nice black dress-pants and a floral blouse and a bright scarf, but she wondered if it helped at all.

Last week she had been moved up a pay grade. That did please her. Now she was officially senior to .. to who? Mill? Mill was the office nerd. He was hardly ever sent into the field for real detective work. But then, she was seldom sent out either.

Jane thought Mill was actually the brightest, or maybe hardest working agent they had. His work had led to several arrests and even classified reports that went to the Secretary of State and maybe the President. Few could say that. He was a walking encyclopedia too. He knew everything. And he scored the best in the office on the pistol range. But he was still a nerd. He actually carried a magnifying glass in his pocket. A magnifying glass! Evidently, he thought he was Sherlock Holmes. He over-dressed and always sat at his desk as straight as an arrow. He was not burly like some of the guys, he was just .. slim. No wonder she got the promotion, not him. Jane wondered about that too. Was it because Mill was a nerd or because she was a woman? Was this really a quota thing, an Affirmative Action promotion? Well, she liked the promotion regardless.

Jane left the ladies room and headed down the hall toward the office. Behind floor to ceiling windows and a glass door was a small foyer with a desk. The desk had little plaque that just said, 'Reception.' Behind the desk on the left side was a door with a big round FBI symbol. On the right of the desk was a door that said 'Office of Independent Investigations.' Under that, in smaller letters it said 'Department of Justice' and smaller yet was a miniature FBI emblem. That, Jane was told, meant agents in this office had more freedom of action than the real FBI agents. They were not limited to just grinding out evidence for prosecutions in politically motivated or news-headline grabbing cases. But if that was so, she'd hate to see what happened next door in the regular FBI office. Mostly, in her office, things were micromanaged. Tasks were assigned, but getting results was not. Next door it must be terrible.

And there at the reception desk, overwhelming his chair, sat the big lummox of a summer intern, Patrick O'Neal. He was not just big, he wore thick glasses that never quite seemed to do the job for his myopic eyes. He bumped into things and never seemed to be entirely sure who was talking to him. Most of the staff had long since become impatient with Patrick and that landed him here on the reception desk assigned to do almost nothing except wait for his thirteen week summer internship to end. But Jane thought he was a nice kid, he had figured the out office file system and he could find almost anything. He was useful in his way, but yes, he was ill suited for this place. This morning O'Neal sat holding what was obviously a ladies lingerie catalog. It was very close to his face. He had put his glasses on the end of his nose and he was looking over the tops of them with his eyes party crossed. The effect was comical.

27

Jane said, "Good morning Patrick."

Patrick O'Neal jumped. He quickly folded the catalog up, then pushed his glasses back to their normal place, then he sheepishly unfolded the catalog again and said, "Umm, just looking for a present for my girlfriend. You know .. umm .."

Jane said, "I see. You must know her pretty well."

O'Neal said, "Umm, well, you know." Then he turned a picture frame toward Jane and smiled. It was some kind of studio photo, a graduation photo perhaps. Jane thought the girl was attractive, in a superficial way. Jane also though she had the top of her blouse unbuttoned at least three buttons too far.

"Cute," said Jane, "Say, isn't your time here about up?"

"Yup, I got permission to leave the office at three p.m. today. I have a flight home at six thirty. I'm packed and have a cab coming." He jogged his head at a couple suit cases against a wall. "That's why the present you know. Heading back home and back to good old Oakland U."

"Okay then, bye if I don't see you later. It was nice to know you. You were a big help to me."

"Thanks. Ya-know Dorsey didn't renew the internship for next summer. That kind-a bums me out. But you were nice. So thanks. And, bye!"

Jane couldn't think of anything more to say so she went through the door on the right. Behind that door was a bull-pen full of desks. There were no cubical dividers. And there, as always, at his desk, sat Mill with his white shirt, bow tie and an un-stylish plaid sports jacket. He was alone. Jane flopped into a chair facing Mill. She slouched down in the chair and put her feet up on his desk. She knew that bothered Mill.

"Say, I was just in the can looking at myself in the mirror. Am I cute?"

Mill looked up and at her with a puzzled expression. He looked like he had never considered the question. Then he rocked back in his chair still looking. Then Mill seemed to reach for the pocket in his jacket. For a second Jane thought he was going to pull a magnifying glass out and inspect her. But he didn't.

Then Mill sat up, turned his eyes back to his papers and said. "You have a great smile and feminine curves and you dressed attractively today." He paused, then said, "Women who think they're pretty, are pretty. Women who might, in fact, be pretty, but don't think they are, aren't pretty. It's all in the lady's attitude. It's all in how women present and project themselves. It's all in how they see themselves. Jane, you are cute, but sometimes you look like you need a little vanity. You should smile more and be more confident of your looks. Dress flashier. Have fun. If you like your own looks, then you'll be cute. It's in how you present yourself. And stuff like feet on my desk makes you look uncouth."

'Vanity,' thought Jane, the same word that was in her head in the bathroom. Is vanity good? She did not take her feet off his desk.

Then Jane regarded Mill. His was slim and overdressed and an obvious nerd. "Mill, why do you always wear a tie?"

"Men shouldn't dress out of vanity like women should. Vanity is for women. Men who dress for vanity's sake are children. Men should dress to show respect to people around them. Under-dressing is self centered and insulting to people around you."

Jane slouched down in her chair a little more. "Hmm ... Are you pissed that I got moved up a pay grade and you didn't?"

"You're qualified. Congratulations."

"Are you pissed?"

"Sure. But not at you. For you it's congrats."

"I'd be pissed too."

Mill did not react.

Then Mill said, "Look Jane, somebody's moving money. A guy I know at the Fed sent me a tip. Every time a big cash withdrawal is made in Washington DC, like a hundred thousand, the next day, the same amount is deposited in a Bank of America branch in Miami.

"The same day, Herb Able flies from Dulles here in Washington, to Miami. It's always the first and the fifteenth of every month. On the third and seventeenth, Herb Able flies back to Washington. But sometimes Herb Baker goes down, and then Herb Baker comes back,"

Jane eyed a mountain of paper on Mills desk. "Are those airline manifests? You went through those?"

"Right, it was a pain. Anyway, I mean they really book the tickets as Able and Baker. I told Dorsey and he thinks it's financing for terrorists. But he always thinks that."

Jane raised an eyebrow. "A little ahead of yourself aren't you? Someone's depositing lots of cash in Miami and without anything else, you guys say it's terrorists? And Able and Baker? Able, Baker?"

"Looking at these manifests was a hunch. It took some phone calls and persuasion to get all these print-outs from the airlines, but in the end, they handed them over without being subpoenaed. It's all paper copies, no computer files, so it was hard-copy all the way. It was a pain."

Jane wondered if Mill used the word 'pain' so much on purpose. Paine was her last name.

"If it isn't terrorists, it's drugs or something else we should know about."

"You plowed through those manifests on a hunch?" Jane picked a coffee cup up off Mill's desk. That was tricky with her feet still there on his desk. She considered the cold stuff inside, a day old at least.

"At least the Fed reports that gave me the money movements also gave me the dates to look at. But get this, on February first, the flight diverted to Jacksonville because of a heart attack on board. It was three hours late into Miami. That time the bank deposit was a day late. That confirms it. This guy's flying and moving money. Plus, I've checked train schedules and common carrier truck schedules and stuff like that, but nothing pops out like this Able, Baker airline thing."

"Christ, don't you sleep? You checked truck drivers?" Jane sipped some cold coffee. "Mill, you usually wash this cup before you leave. Were you just thinking of me last night?"

"Hey! That's my cup!"

Jane took another sip. "So why move the cash to Miami? There's Bank of Americas in Washington isn't there? Why not just deposit it there. What are you reading in this Mill?"

Mill ignored her drinking cold coffee from his cup. "Dorsey says terrorist about everything. But something's up we should know about. I asked a couple guys I know at IRS and Treasury about your question, why not just deposit in Washington? Why move cash to Miami and then put it in a bank that has a branch here? I don't know why. My guess is there's a cooperative teller or something that knows it's funny-money but does the deposit anyway. Or maybe they think it's to miss-direct someone about something. Maybe it's an accounting scam of some kind to make it look like more money than there really is. Maybe someone actually wants us to notice. I don't get it .. yet."

"But Able, Baker? Too obvious."

"Unless, that's a way to track things or something."

"Okay, okay, what do you want to do?"

"I need to figure out where the money comes from and where it goes and not tip them off that we're on to them. Like is it going around in circles and coming back here again. I don't know yet. For one thing, I want to observe the airline boarding, I mean let's put someone, or me on the plane, or in the jet-way dressed up like the jet-way operator or something. And I want to know if he's actually carrying the cash or if it's already in Miami somehow, like shipped UPS or something. I mean how does he get it past airport security? I bet the airline will co-operate letting us look in this guy's bag. If not this might this enough for a warrant. That is, if he checks a bag. And how about we set up cameras in the bank. I already checked and the bank's security cameras are old and need to be tripped by an alarm button. I want to replace them with our cameras and have them record all day. I suspect an inside accomplice and I don't want him to know, so I want to have the branch manager think they were ordered by his own headquarters. I bet Bank of America headquarters will cooperate with us."

A phone rang, "Paine here," Jane put her feet on the floor and pulled herself up straight. "Now? ... On the way."

"Jim Dorsey's wants us both in his office. Give me a list of what you need, this sounds expensive for just a hunch. Dorsey'll want a plan, action steps and a budget. I'll have to work it all up. I'll need to say what we expect to find to justify it. But right now, Dorsey wants us." Jane wondered if Mill noticed she had just horned in to get part of the credit for his work. But everyone did that. Everyone took credit for what Mill did. But Jane just said, "Oh yeah, thanks for the birthday note. That was thoughtful."

Jim Dorsey's office had a real door and outside windows too. Dorsey was a big man and he sat at a big, garish, carved walnut desk. Behind him were plaques and awards and a photo of a younger and more slender Dorsey with a longer hair and sideburns standing in front of some flags with Jimmy Carter. Dorsey usually wore a suit and tie, but today he was in baggy jeans, he had not shaved and he looked tired. Another man was in the office too. He was old, broad shouldered, and he wore a flashy sports coat. He was older than Dorsey but he looked more fit. The older man was pacing. "Christ!" he said, "You call me in the middle of the damn night, as soon as I get here your goons at that new metal detector take my gun, the next thing you want is for me to disobey a direct order from the President of the United States and now you invite these guys in to hear all about it! Dorsey, I'm supposed to be retired and damn it and two Presidents of The United States told me to keep my mouth shut!"

"Smitty, this is Millnose and Jane Paine."

"What? What the hell kind of names are .. "

"My name is John Mill. These guys think it's funny when I say my name is not Mills, it's Mill no 'S,' so they call me Millnose. Mill, no 'S.' Then they call me grindstone because I usually work late. Nose to the grindstone ... supposed to be humorous."

Smitty stared for a minute, then roared a horse, short laugh. "Millnose? And Jane Paine too. Oh no! What's next Dorsey?"

Dorsey said nothing. Jane glared. She disliked this guy at once.

"Okay, okay, don't act so sore Paine, the name's Smith. My folks had a sense of humor too. It's Deasmumhnach Smith. That's Irish for 'from Desmond Ireland.' That's where my Mom was from. I never saw the place myself. They thought with Smith for a last name you needed a special first name. Ya like that nose-stuff? Ya like that Paine? Fair enough? We're all funny one way or another."

Jim Dorsey said, "Okay children, very cute. Everybody here has funny names. Me too, but I never played a saxophone. Now look - last night a call came in."

"Jim!" said Smith, "This is a White House level secret."

"Look Smitty, you were told to keep a secret, I wasn't. And these two are on our team."

"Dorsey, damn it!"

"Okay you guys, Smitty already knows about this. There's a secret phone number that rings downstairs. It's been there since World War II. When we used to relocate agents or counterspies or witnesses and guys like that, we'd give them the secret number and code words that we used to identify them. It was so they could cry for help if their cover sprang a leak."

Jane and Mill looked at each other in surprise. Smith looked at both of them then he said, "Jim! When did that happen? I don't remember that."

"C'mon Smitty, you were here. I thought you knew about the phone contact thing. Okay, maybe you were on other stuff by then. But it goes way back, way before me. But look, the phone and the staff have been on the budget hit-list for years. We'd just like to get rid of it. It's expensive and really a waste. It's never used. But some of those old relocated guys are still alive and even Washington has ethics now and then. So we haven't cut the phone off yet. We still staff the phone around the clock with expensive ladies with expensive top-secret clearances. We tried giving the phone ladies other work besides answering, but that doesn't work out. They spend most of the day answering guys who want to clean the furnace or give free trips to Las Vegas, but they still have to listen to it all for code words. They have to answer every call just in case. But there's only a few of those guys left so it won't be for long before we axe it.

Smith cut in. "We got a slug of secret identity changes and relocations when Wild Bill Donovan and Harry Truman had a pissing match in forty-five. Donovan thought Truman was a joke. So Truman returned the favor and shut down Donovan's OSS. That was just after the war. He gave Donovan about three days to close down. So Donovan tossed his operatives, really orphans, to us. And we had to save some of their butts by relocating them."

Jane said, "Wild Bill Donovan's politics were somewhere to the right of Curtis LeMay." History was not Jane's strength, but she did know that Donovan was an aristocratic pal of Franklin Roosevelt, He was in charge of foreign intelligence during the Second World War even though his Conservative politics were at odds with Roosevelt. She also knew that by all reports, Donovan got the job done.

Smith turned to her, "Yeah, but Donovan knew how to get stuff out of Stalin's underground and if Truman had listened to him, we could have saved China from the commies and saved about fifty million people Mao murdered and skipped wars in Korea and Viet Nam in the bargain. Donovan won the Medal of Honor and every other medal we had to offer, Truman was just a damn crooked county clerk who threw road building money to his political boss. He should have been indicted, not made President. You know how many good men he left hanging in the breeze when he shut the OSS?"

Jane glared again.

"Cool it guys! We have work." said Dorsey, "Last night a call came in at 11:45. The man dumped every code word in the book. The words were oldies, assigned in 1946, but the operator picked them up off an old list just the same. She will be recognized for that little miracle. The caller used words 'Institute of Art' which told us who he was, 'old friend' which means actual, confirmed enemy contact, not just suspicion, 'polite' which means assistance requested, and 'airmail' which means emergency. He repeated all the words in case we missed them, then he said 'Please rush, this needs action now.' He said that in plain English. We have it all on tape. The man had never called before except to respond to communications checks.

"Smitty was involved in '46. He was a rookie then. But Truman himself ordered Smitty and his boss to keep their mouths shut, even to other agents."

"Jim, how did you even learn that much?" asked Smith.

"Smitty, you're the contact name on the secret call list. It's right next to the code words and so is an old photocopy of the secrecy order signed by Truman."

"Oh."

"Anyway, Smitty's all we've got. We don't know what the big secret is. Everybody else connected with it is dead."

"Not just Truman. Eisenhower confirmed the secrecy order," said Smith.

"Smitty, sit down damn it. I haven't even given you the punch line yet."

Smith stood with his hands on his hips, "Punch line? This isn't enough?"

"The operator called me at midnight and I called that O'Neal kid and we both came into the office."

Jane said to Smith, "O'Neal's an intern. You'd call him a summer student secretary back in the dark ages."

Dorsey went on, "So no bitching Smitty, I've been up all night. It took till one in the morning just to find the man's file and when we did, it only had about three pages. It says nothing I could use, not even where he was, it gave a 1950 phone number. There weren't even area codes in 1950. That's when I called you. I mean I didn't even know where he was. You wouldn't tell me and it took till two to even figure out what state he was in. I called Detroit FBI at two thirty. They called back at three. After faxing some stuff to them, they decided they couldn't get an agent to the scene till morning so they called Bloomfield Hills cops asking for assistance. The local cops hadn't a clue what to do, but finally dispatched a car to park out in front of the guy's house. Here's the part you don't know Smitty. At seven, or a little after, the guy's wife called the cops. The guy had been shot dead in his dining room."

Smitty sat down like a sack of concrete. "Shit. Ohhh shit!"

"Smitty, I've asked the White House to reverse your silence order so you'll tell us everything you know. I sent the request by channels marked urgent. But I'm not holding my breath. I mean the guy's dead, so what are we protecting now? I also requested a disclosure of everything they have. Till we hear from them, you're it Smitty. You gotta coach us. And Smitty, the outside agents are all up to their asses in terrorist stuff, so these guys get the assignment."

Jane said, "Oh! So Grindstone and I are the third string huh? We're it .. "

Dorsey turned to her, "I didn't say that. I want you and Millnose working here because you guys get results here, but for one like this, I have to spring you. You two guys are going to Detroit. I found a King Air that the Army's running back to Oakland County Airport where they base it. They're holding till you get on. They're waiting now. Grab your toothbrushes and stuff on the way to the airport, or expense new stuff when you get there. Don't pack much, I don't want this to take long. But I want you to get there now, so go! Go! The Detroit FBI office has an agent on the scene right now with the local cops, he'll meet you at the Airport. They're finding a hotel for you too. I want resources on the ground the minute the White House tells me what's going on. I want you there. You need to go."

Smith stood and said, "I'm going too."

"Smith, you're retired. Just give us some clues, okay? I can't ask you to break a presidential directive, but tell us which rocks to kick over. We need something."

"I'll just kind-a ride along with these guys, okay?" His voice was rising, "I put that guy there and now he's dead. I'm going to Detroit if I have to hitch-hike. Dorsey, where's my gun?"

Jane said, "Dorsey, I say we just picked up a hitch-hiker. I want him to come with us. Smith we'll do everything, just tell us what to look for. Play 'Clue' with us. Okay?"

Smith looked back and forth between Jane and Dorsey.

Dorsey sat back for a minute, "Okay Smitty. Okay, you'll be on expense too. Until Smitty talks we treat it like the dead guy was one of ours. I'll phone the lobby and they'll give your gun back on the way out. But cooperate with these guys Smitty. Coach 'em, don't get in the way. Policies are all different these days and you don't know new procedures, so it's their show. You're retired."

Smith leaned forward, and spoke in a strained voice, "Get me that white-house release, make me honest, okay? Now look guys, I don't know much. It was just a war-end relocation. That's all I know and you know that much already. In those days every lightweight ex-Nazi or SS joker or Gestapo thug without the clout to get himself to South America wanted to trade everything he knew for his own hide. There were millions of dislocated persons too. They all wanted to get out of the east and away from the Russians and they tried anything to get out. The usual trick was they'd claim they had secrets and they would inform for us. But they really just wanted to escape the Russians. Russians would murder anyone who so much as spoke German right where they stood. Mostly we could care less about them. They really had nothing for us."

Mill said, "Except maybe Reinhard Gehlen."

"What? You know about that? That's secret. Who is this guy Dorsey? Okay, okay, but his guys really were big shots in German intelligence. We probably should have hanged the SOBs, but I heard they did good work for us. But not every turkey or sucker who ever wore a swastika arm band was worth it."

Dorsey said, "Smitty, you've been asleep. Gehlen's no secret these days. He wrote a memoir book all about it. Now get on with it, tell us where to start on Schmidt. We're blind, we're losing time and we need a clue what we're looking for."

"Okay, okay, this guy, Schmidt, let's see here, let me remember, he wasn't on any level with Gehlen, not by a freaking mile, I could tell that, but somehow he got through to Truman. I can't guess what Truman wanted him for. Truman was a sucker. I thought it was a bad joke. Schmidt was just one of ten million Krauts trying to save his own hide. But I got an order to move him, so I dragged this guy's butt out of the Russian zone. I just drove a staff car with a big American star on the side into the Russian zone, just like I belonged there. I waved my American papers at anyone who stopped me and they all just let me go. It was a long ride. I picked him up at an address, Konigsberg I think or maybe not quite that far, it was someplace in that. Ya-know, that chunk of Poland that used to be Germany. After the war, Russia never gave the place back to either of 'em. I found him hiding in some office, and I drove him back out, simple as that. Filling the gas tank was the biggest problem. It was that long a ride. But again I waved American papers at some Russians with a gasoline truck and they filled me up. Then we flew him here on an Army transport and we parked him at some artsy-fartsy prep school in Detroit. I named him Schmidt, that's German for Smith, for myself. It was a joke. Then I personally faked his credentials. I even put ME 109's on an Engineering Degree and then I made him a Phd in Fine Art. At first I wanted to name him Kunstler. Germans know that name means artist, like Schmidt and Smith means blacksmith. I almost got away with it too, but my boss caught on."

Dorsey said, "C'mon Smith, enough with names. What's going on?"

"I never even knew the joker's real name. He just had a code name, 'The Danzig Kid' I think was the code name. Something like that anyway. And the joker knew less about art than my dog did, but maybe he studied fast. He did okay teaching art I heard. He had a lady with him too. He wouldn't come without her so I 'married' them. I faked German marriage papers complete with an affidavit that she had no

38

Jewish blood. I thought it was all BS so when Truman quit, I requested a new review from the White House. They actually did it I guess. That's because I got a reply that said they looked it all over and Truman's order stood. I was told keeping it quiet, it was a matter of national security and that it could put people or property at risk. It was initialed by Ike himself. I was told, talk to nobody!"

"Dorsey, get that release because I've said too much already. One other thing, I was told they were Krauts. Maybe he was, but she was no Kraut. Her German sounded all wrong to me and her accent, when she spoke English, was all wrong too. She was Russian or Polish or Lithuanian or something. That's what I know. I don't know what Truman's dark secret was all about. I was just told to go get him. That's all I know. C'mon Dorsey, it was a while ago. I can't remember much more."

"About what I figured," Dorsey said. "Look, for now the job is get out there then stand-by till we know what's up. Develop rapport with the cops out there, learn what you can, so when we get data, we can jump on it. Report whatever the hell is going on to me and put it all on paper. I don't like surprise ghosts from the past. I don't like dead friends, if he really was a friend. When we learn what's up, I want everything put in a box with a bow around it so we can write a report then close it all out. Then I'll decide what's next, if anything. I'll personally chase the White House. The murder case is for the local cops. Don't get in their way. Okay, go. The plane's waiting. And tell me what you find."

"C'mon!" said Smith, "We'll talk more on Sky King's plane."

Bubbie Feine's Story

"Many and sharp the num'rous ills

Inwoven with our frame!

More pointed still we make ourselves

Regret, remorse, and shame!

And Man, whose heav'n-erected face

The smiles of love adorn, -

Man's inhumanity to man

Makes countless thousands mourn!"

Robert Burns

Yesterday had been sunny and warm. Today, it was raining and cold and when Sylvia Feine answered the front door to her house chilly air rushed in.

"Oh! Mrs. Hubchic, Natalie, come in out of the rain! Please hurry right in!"

The unexpected guests put an open umbrella on the flagstone floor and shed hats and raincoats. "I'm afraid we walked. What a soaking we got. We were foolish."

"Oh my! You're all wet and it's so blustery out there. Please sit, you look like need some hot tea! But, well, I'm glad you came here."

Mrs. Hubchic spoke with an accent, "I asked Natalie to come out of her house while those police do their work. My house is too far. I thought you might like to have us wait here. We should have called. I think Natalie should sit and relax."

Natalie Schmidt said. "Yes, may I?"

"Please come in. Please come in." Sylvia Feine repeated. "Lois! Swan! Put water on for tea before these ladies catch their death of cold. There are cookies in the pantry too! Bring those too." Then Sylvia said, "I am so sorry to hear, if the rumors are true. Please come in Mrs. Schmidt, here is my favorite chair. Come in Mrs. Hubchic, you did the right thing coming here. Thank you Mrs. Hubchic."

Natalie Schmidt. Said, "If the rumors are that Günter is gone, I'm afraid they are true."

"Oh, I am sorry, I am so sorry. I had hoped it was only talk. I hoped otherwise. What can we do? Do you have family you would like to call? There's a phone in the kitchen."

"I'm afraid not. You know we have been alone a very long time."

"I am so sorry. How can we help?"

A small elderly lady entered the room. "Bubbie, I'm afraid it's true, Mrs. Schmidt has lost Günter and Mrs. Hubchic brought her here to sit until the police have gone."

Bubbie Feine silently sat down with her head bowed. She remained quiet.

Natalie seemed to look out the room's big front window. Now and then, rain pattered loudly against that window, then, when the wind shifted it was quiet again. Looking out the windows, most of summer's gay flowers had gone, only some fading geraniums remained by the walk and even they were sparse, their leaves losing their green. It was dull, colorless, gray and raining out there.

Natalie broke the silence, "I found Günter this morning. He shot himself I think. He has been dejected recently and one of my old guns was there. I called the police and they took me to their police station and asked me about everything. They are being very thorough, I am surprised how thorough. They even brought some kind of laboratory-on-wheels truck to our driveway. They asked all about the new students and your visit last night. They took me to the police station and we spoke for more than an hour. They just brought me home now and Mrs. Hubchic was already there. She suggested we sit here in your house for a while."

Mrs. Hubchic said, "Mr. McIntyre from the school called me. He said the new students called him and he had just picked them up. He said he remembered me from last night's party and knew I was a friend of Natalie's and it was good thing my phone was listed. He felt I should come right over. That was thoughtful of him don't you agree?"

Lois Feine appeared with cookies on a fancy dish and china cups. "Swan will have tea in a minute."

The old lady they called Bubbie finally spoke, "Natalie, you have been a good neighbor. Perhaps it is finally time."

Sylvia said, "Aunt, Mrs. Schmidt has lost her husband just now, time for what?"

"Natalie knows I think. Yes, she is even older than I. She was there I think. I can speak to her now." The old lady pulled up her sleeve. There was a faded tattoo, hardly visible, numbers.

Natalie Schmidt gazed at the tattoo and said, "Yes, I knew, or guessed."

"Natalie, you are not German are you?"

Natalie Schmidt said nothing.

Silvia said, "Bubbie, you have never spoken of this. We respected your silence. Is now really the time for this? Please, Mrs. Schmidt has just lost her husband."

"Yes. I think it is the right time."

Swan brought a wooden box of tea bags and hot water into the room. She wore the tight clothing of young people. Her blouse was low cut revealing her large chest and her jeans showed her curves.

Lois spoke, "Bubbie, Mrs. Schmidt is, well, why speak of this now? The subject is awful. Let's have tea and speak of nice things."

But Bubbie Feine spoke, "Mrs. Schmidt, my father helped the farmers. He lent money to them at spring planting time so they could buy seed and sow crops and he took his money and a fee when the crops came in. I suppose we should have left our home long before the war, many did, but even under the Nazis we lived well. I think we could have left easily at first because my father sent my brother to Canada for school and he said I would go too in a few years. My brother was Sylvia's father and grandfather to Lois and Swan." The old lady regarded Swan's outlandish clothes for a moment. "We lived well in spite of losing privileges, but I was a child, what did I know? Perhaps things were worse than I knew. But after the war started, even a child knew there was bad trouble. The Nazis barred my father from collecting his money from the farmers. Next our house, our furniture, our auto, even our best clothes, my mother's jewelry, almost everything we had was taken. We were given receipts for some of it, but the receipts were worthless. We lived for a time openly with a nice Catholic neighbor, but after a year or more, my father said we must hide. Then we lived in a factory storeroom. Then came the arrest."

Natalie Schmidt gazed with a far away and nearly blank expression, "yes, arrest," she said.

"We were taken to a rail siding then herded like swine with many others into a boxcar and rode for more than a day. I do not know where even now. We lived in a camp without food for days sleeping cold outdoors on a handful of hay. Then they moved us all into a single room. We were allowed a cup of thin soup and a crumb of peasant bread some days, other days we had nothing. This lasted, I think, three or four months, but I cannot really say how long. Then we were moved again, and the next place we stayed even longer. We knew certain buildings were death chambers at this place because those who were led there never came back. Some went there, many more just walked into the woods and we heard gun shots. Certain among us were told to remove gold teeth from the dead and do other awful work. One day we were all put in two lines, children in one line and mothers and fathers in the other. I knew at once I would never see my parents again. I have not forgotten. My mother and my father put a finger to their lips as if to say 'stay quiet.' My father smiled and did that gesture again. I think I was perhaps twelve years old. Then they were moved to that death building with all the others."

Swan knelt on the floor next to the old lady. "Bubbie, you have never said this. We knew it, it is a common story with us, Bubbie, why now Bubbie?"

"I was moved by train again. We were thrown out of the boxcar at another camp, but I was lucky. A guard grabbed me by the arm as I fell from the car and he took me to a kitchen. That was very, very lucky for me. I was to work in the kitchen.

"Soon I saw that it was a work camp and those who could not do as much as others were shot. Those who resisted in the slightest way, or tried to run away were horribly hanged with their feet kicking and their tongues coming out, their eyes bulging. We were all made to watch this.

"One cold day in winter I saw a work-group come back from the forest. They had not cut enough trees which was their work that day. Some refused to work and some had run off. That group was made to bathe in water then stand naked until one by one, they died of the cold. It was sadistic! Sadistic!

"But a few of us wore berets. The beret meant they were 'political prisoner' and they got double food rations, and less work. We hated them.

"Some prisoners were kapos. The Germans had too few guards and kapos were the police inside the camp. The real German guards only watched from outside. They watched for escape. They did not come inside the camp. The kapos were picked from among us and were guards inside the camp and they got special treatment. They formed the work parties and assigned the work and were brutal to the rest of us."

"Bubbie, that is not so! We studied this in school, and the Jewish people stuck together," said Swan.

"Child, the kapos were given clubs and they beat the other prisoners. We did not know who was Jewish and who was not."

"Kapos were not Jewish!"

"Listen to me!"

"You only saw a little. We studied in school!"

"Ha! Listen to me! We only wished to live. But one by one, if a kapo was ever alone, we took care of him. Others cooperated with the guards too, but in secret. They spied on us. They got special treatment from guards and so we knew who they were. If someone was fat, or not beaten, he was a spy. It was death for them too. We learned to keep ourselves alive however we could, but to be a kapo or spion, sooner or later, that was death from us!

"The kitchen let me steal enough food to stay alive. Raw potato peels or bread crumbs from a cutting board at first. I was a lucky one. If I was caught stealing, I would hang, yes they would hang children. I saw it. And kapos would flog even children, even for impolite talk.

"There was a loose panel on the outside of the kitchen. Behind that panel was a big space. Later, when I learned how to do it better, I stole food for others and left it there. One time I got a whole loaf of bread and a guard took the blame. The guards, even the Obersturmbannführer took what they wanted from the kitchen, so shortages were blamed on them. They would accuse us, of course, but they knew it was the guards. A whole loaf was good work. A man named Hiram knew the hiding place and would get what I left for the others after dark. But he ate most of it himself. When I told the others all I had taken, Hiram was killed with a kitchen knife. I took that knife from the kitchen and gave it to a man, then, when the work was done, I put the knife back and so guards did not know how Hiram was killed. The guards did not care because he was not a kapo or spion.

"We learned to stay alive and care nothing. 'Death is our friend,' some said, but others, like me, learned how to live.

"Always more, always more the others wanted from me, for I worked in the kitchen and was not as thin as the rest. When they threatened me, I stole less, not more, and I told them why. I could control them and have my way because I could get scraps of food. I was only a child, but I was the queen. Behind that loose panel was our hiding place.

"Some days the Obersturmbannführer would have supper for officers and I would serve them. On those days, the Obersturmbannführer gave me a pretty dress to wear that had been his daughter's. I hated myself when I wore it, but it helped me stay alive. If the others had seen me wear such a thing they would call me kapo and spion or berichterstatter and maybe kill me. I learned even the German officers did not eat so well as we supposed. The supplies must have been short all around. And as the supplies got worse, and sausages, even for the officers, were mostly sawdust. Then I knew the Germans were losing the war. Then the Obersturmbannführer gave me a beret to wear as if I was a 'political prisoner' and not Jewish and he increased my food ration too. I knew others might kill me for this and so I told them I had tricked the beret out of the Obersturmbannführer and that it let me steal more food for them. That it helped me steal more food, at least, was true."

"Bubbie, what place was this? There are records of all the camps! The Germans at least kept good records. I can look."

"Hush! After many months, we could hear the thunder and some said it was guns. At dinner the German officers eyed each other as the thunder grew louder and they looked worried. The next day, an outside German guard came to me in the kitchen when others were not near. That was remarkable. He said to me, 'Tomorrow we march the prisoners away. The front has come too close. I think few will survive this march. Perhaps it is a trick to kill you all. For your life, hide. Hide in the wall where you hide the food you steal and do not come out till you hear Americans speaking English.' So that guard had known the hiding place all along. And so I hid behind the panel all the next day. The departure was organized in haste and I could hear shouting and footsteps till it was quiet. Then I came out.

"But when voices came again, they were German still. I could see from a window it was Schutzstaffel! I hid again and could hear them search for those who did not march away. I could hear shouting and orders to line up. Then I heard guns fire and groans and screams. I knew they had killed all they found. Later I saw where they tried to burn the bodies with too little gasoline.

"The next day I heard English. With much fear, out I peeked. And I came out finally. An American soldier saw me at once. He came to me fast and knelt by me

46

and held my hands. Then he wept. He wept! He took a chocolate bar from his pocket and gave me water from his canteen also. Then he wept like a child bowing his head next to me. An officer came then. They argued terribly and he shouted at his own officer! That soldier picked me up and said 'No! No!'with tears in his eyes. He trembled so terribly. The officer put his hand on that soldier's shoulder and then he cried too. I do not know that soldier's name, I spoke no English then. He did not like the dead all around and seeing a child in rags. I did not understand then. I had no feelings then, except to live. But I remember that soldier today and I know his passion. Perhaps he had a fifteen year-old at home, for that was my age then. He was my first meeting with humanity, but it would take long for me to understand. Today I would give much to know that soldier. He was a man.

"I could write books about that time. It was not so simple as they say. We learned to keep ourselves alive, that was all, and we trusted nothing but the next moment.

"There were more of us left that day than I thought. Perhaps twenty had survived. Soon the Red Cross came with better food and some clothes and a Nurse. Still, we stayed in the camp till one by one, a way out was arranged. I told the Americans of the Red Cross my name and that my brother was in Canada. It was a difficult time, even then food was too little, they did not expect how many we really were and they were not ready. At first I had only rags to wear with the stripes of a prisoner, but the Red Cross lady gave me clothes and even a hat. It took a year, but finally my brother arranged for me to go to Canada and five more years till we could come here."

Swan said, "Bubbie, why do you tell this now? Why now? This is for our family. And you saw so little. The class I took is a bigger picture."

"I was a child, but I learned how cheap life is. I saw death. I knew death. Today I would still kill every German I met if I could. It made a joke of the word 'civilized.' Death? Who cares now. I am old now. What I saw was the devil's work. Nobody should see that. And I was a child. I would kill the Germans, one and all and any man who cooperated with them, even today. But Natalie, you are not German are you."

Natalie Schmidt looked blankly at the wall.

Uncomfortable moments passed. Finally Mrs. Hubchic said "Mr. Hubchic was very much older than I. He was Ukrainian and there was Stalin."

"Ohhh, yes, 'Hubchic' Yes, Ukrainian."

Another pause.

Then Natalie Schmidt said, "Mr. Hubchic must have escaped, did he get out through Poland?"

"Hmm, Polish." said Bubbie Feine.

A Short Flight

"Isn't it astonishing that all these secrets have been preserved for so many years just so we could discover them!"

Orville Wright

There was a little fold-up staircase near the rear of the King Air. Jane figured the last person to climb on would end up sitting in back, so she hustled and climbed aboard in front of the men. Inside there was a little closet to stow coats and maybe a little luggage. To the left, it looked like the world's smallest airliner, or maybe the world's biggest private plane. There were eight seats, that is, besides pilots' seats in front. An aisle down the middle was so narrow the men turned half sideways to move. Jane said, "I want a window seat." That got a laugh.

Then, the one and only pilot climbed aboard, pulled the steps up and closed the door. He said something about weight and balance and asked who wanted to sit in the co-pilot's seat. Jane smiled and said "Sure!" Jane had to wiggle by a center console and over levers that might be throttles or something and into the co-pilot's seat to the right. She wondered how bigger men fit in the seat, much less got into it, yet the pilot got into his seat with reasonable grace. 'Practice,' thought Jane.

The engines, when they started, did not sound like regular private plane engines. They had propellers but the sound was more like jet engines. Jane vaguely knew that turboprops were, in fact, small jet engines, that drove propellers. The pilot started jabbering numbers and words like "eight five uniform" into his headset. The King Air taxied and turned through a maze of pavement and lights, then turned onto what was obviously a runway. There, the plane paused for a moment's dramatic view of a very long stretch of pavement straight ahead. Then the pilot pushed levers forward and the plane started to move. Jane was surprised that the take-off run was so exciting, and when the earth fell away below them, it was a thrill. Maybe she should look into getting a pilot's license herself.

Now the pilot flipped some switches and a picture of wheels lit up. Jane figured that meant the landing gear was coming up. A clunk and the lights changing confirmed her idea. Numbers in displays on the plane's instrument panel changed and gauges moved. An illuminated green graphic that looked like an airplane seen from behind caught Jane's eye. It tilted as the plane banked and retuned when they leveled out.

Out the windshield, buildings and cars on roads grew smaller and, as they climbed, the horizon, took on the look of a broad, downward curve. After a time, the pilot pulled the throttles back. The climb was apparently over. Clouds below were ahead, and soon, to Jane's disappointment, the view below was lost. Only white cloud tops could be seen. Still, the white clouds and their slow parade under the plane were pretty.

The pilot turned to Jane and said, "Good luck! We're cleared to Motor Intersection via direct. That never happens. Usually we have to fly to Timbuktu and back. We'll be working Cleveland Center most of the way." After that, mostly, the pilot just jabbered into the headset now and then except at one point he said, "We're about over Pittsburgh now, too bad you can't see through the cloud deck. There's pretty hills and lots and lots of bridges over the rivers."

Mill made some noise so Jane looked back. Mill had opened a book. Jane made out the title, 'Ivan the Terrible's Wars with the Teutonic Knights of Lithuania.' Smith was asleep.

An hour later and the pilot pulled the throttles back more and adjusted a couple other levers. The plane obviously started down. Soon he said something into the headset about "back-course for nine right." Entering the clouds made visibility zero, just gray in the windscreen and then it started to rain .. hard. The rain made a terrific din on the King Air's windshield, much louder than in a car. The pilot seemed unperturbed by the racket as he pulled levers, adjusted dials, then flipped switches which Jane figured lowered the landing gear. There was a satisfying whine then 'clunk' as the lights worked again. Then they broke out of the clouds and below, a gray landscape appeared. There was big lake with an obvious lakefront park. Near the park, houses on the lake had docks sticking out into the water and boats by the docks. Wet looking roads had cars with lights on. They seemed to move slowly. Jane was surprised at how hard it was to identify the airport that she knew must be ahead. That took till they were almost on top of it. Her first clue was a multitude of parked airplanes. Then the landing happened much faster than Jane expected. The pilot seemed very busy manipulating controls and adjusting things as they rushed toward the runway. Then a thump announced that they had arrived. Only then did the pilot start windshield wipers. Jane Paine thought they were surprisingly like automobile wipers, except they were smaller and they worked much faster. As they slowed, the noise of rain subsided to a more automobile-like drone and the pilot was jabbering numbers and jargon into his microphone again. They taxied, and then stopped in front of a low building.

The pilot dropped the steps then Mill made a move to take Jane's overnight bag, but Jane said, "I've got it." On the ground, a cold, stiff breeze seemed to announce that here in Michigan, summer was over. The raindrops were coming fast and they were the big fat kind, the kind that soak clothes in no time. Jane hurried across the tarmac for a door with a sign that said 'passenger lounge.' To Jane's surprise, Smith stood in the rain and held the door open as she, then Mill rushed into the warmth inside. The pilot, evidently, had business to finish inside the plane.

A sullen, even unfriendly man was waiting in the lounge. He said, "Clarence, I'm Detroit FBI." He read their names from a little note pad. Jane wondered if Clarence was his first or last name. Then Clarence tilted his head toward a door. The car ride to Schmidt's house was not long. Clarence popped the trunk with a button inside the car and said, "Close the trunk when you have your stuff." He did not get out of the car. Jane, in her annoyance, didn't close the trunk but Mill did. Then man drove off without any arrangement to pick them up later. So Jane Paine, Mill, and Smith dashed through the rain for the porch of the big and very odd house.

The dash required a wet detour around three police cars and a big van that said, 'Michigan State Police Mobile Forensic Lab.' A police barricade consisted of a single piece of yellow plastic tape stretched across the front of the porch. There was a uniformed policeman with a fur collared police jacket sitting, gloved hands folded, out of the rain in an Adirondack chair on the porch. As the three stepped over the yellow tape, the policeman, glanced at their badges without standing, or at least he glanced at Jane's badge since she led the way, then he gave the obviously older Smith a double take. Then he made a wordless gesture at the big front doors.

The First Murder Scene

"For murder, though it have no tongue, will speak"

William Shakespeare - Hamlet

Dry and warm inside the big house was welcome to Jane. She looked around. This was the biggest house she had even been in. She said, "Wow!" As Jane looked around she imagined herself here at a fancy gathering. She pictured herself in a puffy shouldered evening gown with an orchestra playing 'So This Is Love' as she waltzed with a handsome prince. Or maybe she hummed a couple bars of 'Some Enchanted Evening.' Jane imagined seeing the big double doors to the dining room swing open as a uniformed butler rang a little bell and announce, 'Dinner is served.' Jane pictured a table set with white cloth, fabulous gleaming silver and crystal filled with amber and red colored wines. A roast wild boar with an apple in its mouth was in center of the table. There was a great chair at the head and a smaller great chair, for her of course, next to it.

Then Jane noticed Mill looking her way. He wore a bemused expression. Jane wondered if she had done that humming out loud or just to herself. She looked around again. This was not Cinderella. Jane remembered she was here about a murder. She said to Mill, "Wow, big place!"

The dining room's doors were really already open and the table lacked roast boar or even a table cloth. Instead, some men were talking. A couple more men plus a woman were looking closely at the back wall of the room.

One man turned to Jane and said, "I'm Henderson; State Police." Jane showed her badge then bluntly asked if he was in charge. "That's how it looks, for now anyway. Bloomfield Hills has had exactly one murder in its whole history, Bingham Farms none. The county would normally be here but they're swamped and short-handed. They called us requesting assistance. Our forensics van was only a couple miles away anyway. So here we are. You're the guys who phoned the local cops last night?"

"Our boss Dorsey phoned. I'm Paine. This is Mill and Smith. Dorsey sent us out here."

"I gotta be quick, a couple TV reporters are headed this way and I have to stop 'em out front and think up something to say. Anyway, the victim was in the dining room over there, looks like he was sitting at the head of the table and fell out of the chair, or maybe he was standing. The yellow tape'll show where. The gun was on the table, we marked that position with tape too. We'd call it suicide and maybe it was, except for your midnight tip. So we've called out the first team to do a real crime-scene thing. It's turning into a regular Agatha Christie complete with doors locked from the inside. That might say suicide too. But okay, what's this all about? You tipped the Bloomfield cops. What's going on? We don't know what we're looking for yet and we need to know. This is a lot of resources to be poking around what looks like suicide. What's really up?"

Jane spoke again, "We think the victim might be the same guy as a secret identity change and relocation from 1946. Someone made a coded phone call for assistance on the emergency line just before midnight. We think maybe it's something from the distant past, maybe he saw someone. That's all we know. Our files on the relocation are long gone or taken away for security reasons. We hope maybe there are still files on him at the White House. We've requested a release of anything they have. But we don't know if they really have any such old files. Nineteen forty-six is a long time ago. Whatever you do, don't tell the news guys even this much. The relocation and the real I.D. definitely remain secret. The three of us don't even know the real ID."

Henderson raised his eyebrows, "The White House? And we don't even get to know who he was?"

Mill pulled a big magnifying glass from his pocket and started for the dining room's double doors.

Smith said, "The man carries a magnifying glass? What next! Okay Sherlock, what are you looking at?" By then, Mill was looking at the handle on the double doors to the dining room then handed the glass to Smith who looked too.

Mill said, "These doors don't lock automatically when you close them. They had to be locked by hand."

Smith said. "This has already been dusted, let me guess, no prints, wiped clean."

Mill, looking through the glass again, paused and said, "Right no prints."

Henderson looked annoyed but said, "Right."

Smith said, "Let me guess, Mrs. Schmidt had a key and opened the doors. She opened it because they're normally left open and she hadn't seen her husband."

"Right." Said Henderson.

Mill said, "How'd she do that and not leave a print? And you looked behind that false panel across the room?"

Henderson looked surprised, "Yeah, it took us an hour to notice the fake panel, and a half hour more to figure out how to open it. There's file cabinets and papers in there. Nothing else. How did you .. "

"And that swinging kitchen door has a bolt on the ceiling or floor, maybe both, and they were set." Mill went back to looking at that door with his glass. Smith looked again too.

Then Smith said, "Henderson, that's Millnose. Mill no 's.' He's good, really good. Don't sweat the Sherlock act. Believe me, he'll find some useful stuff."

Jane was a surprised by that remark. Was Smith warming up? Was he going to be a real team player?

Henderson stared at Mill and his magnifying glass, then said "Agatha Christie and Sherlock Holmes. Maybe I'll just go home. Look you guys, it's our case. We'll cooperate with you, but tell me something I don't already know. What's going on? I really need to know. We can't play games. This isn't a murder and I've got half an army wasting time here. This isn't the only suspicious case in Michigan and we're losing time. What's going on?"

Jane felt annoyed at the pressure. She said, "We request your assistance in a Federal investigation and we promise to cooperate with your investigation as far as federal law allows us. Soon we hope to know more than we do right now, but we need to have the White House release any secrets, plus there have to be secrets still there to release. It's more than fifty years ago and who know if they kept anything."

Mill said, "This door has every print in town, right? Except here by the knob. Wiped clean ."

Henderson scowled, "Yeah, right. Now look Ms. Paine, maybes and cooperation are not the same thing. They didn't send you three here for fun. There's a reason. What the hell's going on?"

Jane said, "Henderson, Smith is retired, but he was slightly involved in 1946. The relocation was done then. His knowledge is very incomplete, but at least he was there at the time. He pulled a man and woman out of the Russian occupied zone and relocated him here. We think this might be the man. We don't even know that for sure and we don't know why he was brought here and we don't know why it's all a secret. Smith doesn't know either. And what I have just said is classified. We have requested more information from the White House and we have already requested permission to share anything they give us with you. Right now, Smith's the only connection we've come up with."

Mill asked, "Footprints outside the windows?"

"None, no footprints. Okay Ms. Paine." Henderson still sounded annoyed, "I want all you can give us and as soon as you can. And yes, we will do the same for you. But if you ask me, this is BS."

Jane said, "We're on the same team Henderson. We've already told you we think the man is not who he appeared to be all these years. That's a start. We think the White House is looking for some old files. Smith here was connected with the case back when. Mill is a bulldog, he finds stuff. You'll like him soon enough. We'll do what we can, but we really don't know any more than what we I just said. And we'll try not to get in your way. Okay?"

Mill turned to look at the pistol on the table. "Wow! Smith, is that a Radom? Collectors look for these things. Good gun. Design ripped from American guns, Colt 1911A1 and a Browning High Power. Polish nine millimeter. Heavy American frame with only a medium sized round, made recoil lighter so it's steady. That makes it accurate."

Smith said, "Sure is, I must admit I haven't seen one of those in a while. Radoms were good guns. Krauts used tons of 'em in the war. Mostly they liked them better than their own Lugers or Walthers."

Henderson turned, "A Radom .. war era huh? Does that fit with this relocation thing?"

Smith said, "Radom's the Armory where they were made, name of the city too, about fifty miles from Warsaw I think. They started makin' 'em in the thirties I think. Used by the Poles at first, then by the Germans after the invasion. The Krauts really prized them. I don't remember that the guy I relocated carried a gun but maybe. Hell, everybody did. But it's the right time and place all right. Prints?"

These scraps of information seemed to melt Henderson a bit, "Only the victim's prints. It was on the table where the tape outline is. But I have a hunch it's not a suicide weapon. The wound in the victim looks too small for nine millimeter. And the gun doesn't smell like it's been fired lately. The clip wasn't full, but that doesn't mean it's been fired. My guess is this is no suicide. I bet he had it out for defense."

Smith said, "Schmidt. The victim I mean? Where?"

"At the morgue. His outline's over there like I said, the tape's on the floor. You can see the photos on my laptop if you want to look."

"I would" said Smith. "In fact, can I see him at the morgue? I want to confirm he's the same guy I knew, if that's even possible this many years later."

"Right! I'll set that up. No, better yet, meet me there in an hour. I need to go over there anyway. If it's him, I want to talk. Hell, if it's not him I want to talk anyway. I'll give you directions or get a cab or something and meet me there in an hour."

While Henderson wrote an address, Mill walked to the kitchen door and swung it back and forth. Then he turned a floor bolt away from its catch and toward the dining room, then he slowly closed the door. The bolt dragged along the floor as it went. An arced scratch on the wooden floor's finish showed this had happened from time to time in the past. The bolt missed its hole on the first pass, but with a couple more passes and some jiggles and taps on the door, it dropped in.

Henderson turned from Smith and watched, "We noticed that too, could be an answer to the locked doors," he said. "I need to tell you guys that a couple students arrived yesterday, Germans. They're staying in the servant's quarters. Access to their quarters is that way, through the kitchen. But they're not old enough to be your voice from the past. And there was an old-folks neighborhood party here last night."

"Germans? Maybe this is going to be simple." said Jane.

"Nothing's easy." said Henderson. "This one's an old fashioned 'Who Done It,' suspect party and all. Agatha would be pleased. The victim had a house party last night, but nobody says they heard anything and there are no clear clues yet except your call in the night. We really need your secret dope. Everybody's meeting at the Bloomfield Hills cop-shop at four this afternoon to talk and wrap up the day's work. You should be there. Try to get your White House dope by then.

"Mrs. Schmidt, the victim's wife, is at a neighbor's house. The Feines I think. The students called the school and a Mr. McIntyre, the Dean picked them up. Some welcome to the U.S. huh? I got his card and I have a list of those at the party, at least those Mrs. Schmidt remembers. We're interviewing some of them now. I have to make a statement to those reporters right now, so I have to cut out. Have a good time, see you later."

Smith just said, "Millnose, what an act! Do you always show up the local cops like that? Where'd you get that magnifying glass? I about laughed my ass off. Jane, I'm starting to like this guy."

Mrs. Hubchic's Story and Natalie's Story

"If misery loves company, misery has company enough"

Henry David Thoreau

Natalie was still very quiet but Mrs. Hubchic said, "Mr. Hubchic seldom spoke of it. It was very bad and he was only a boy. He was a good deal older than I. In those days our Orthodox Churches had been closed, so were the Catholic churches for the Poles in our midst.

"Mrs. Hubchic went on, "Even before he was born, Ukrainians fought the Bolsheviks to the end. The last stand was in Crimea. When that fell, the Bolsheviks simply murdered everyone. They shot ot hanged everyone, even civilians. That was 1920. A few had joined the White Army and they fought as they retreated all the way across Siberia. Then, after the lost at Vladivostok, they got the same treatment. Muslims, well, they kept up the fight in the east into the thirties.

"In his childhood but before my memory really, we had our fighting men. There were also Tar Tars, Cossacks, Muslims, Jews and they all had their militias too. That is, any of them who somehow escaped the Bolshevik slaughter in 1920. After that, all those forces wanted to kill each other and kill us too. What a mess it was.

"Worst by far, of course, was the starvation campaign. It is hard to understand that Stalin wanted a whole Ukraine dead from starvation. He said it was to make our farms communist collectives. But why then kill us all? That started in 1932. After the war someone asked Stalin which was worse, the war, or Ukraine. He said Ukraine. Seven million at least starved, some say twice that.

Swan said, "The Jewish suffered the most!"

"Hush!" Bubbie hissed. "Silly girl, listen to this nice lady and learn!" Swan looked amazed.

"In school they said .. "

"Hush! Look at you! Just look at you! Spoiled child! They know nothing and you know nothing!"

"Lenin always said we could have our way if we just would become part of Russia. When Lenin died, Stalin ignored Lenin's promise and he was ruthless. He killed the kulaks, he killed the teachers and intellectuals. The Jewish militia had been with Lenin, his family was Jewish after all, but when Lenin died, they sided with Stalin. I'll never know why. They did much of his worst work in Ukraine."

"That's an anti-Semitic lie! Are you a Holocaust denier too?"

"Silence!" Bubbie stood and raised her hand as if to strike Swan. "Silence you little fool! Learn!"

"My husband's family had a farm and Stalin's militia came for all their grain, cattle, everything. Everybody knew they were coming so they hid what they could in a shed in the woods. They even dug a great pit and hid a cow under sticks and straw and dirt, but the militia found the shed and the cow and took everything.

"The secret police said you could not travel even to town without a passport and papers. In 1932 Stalin ordered farm quotas. He required more than had ever been made. And it must all be given to Russia. Then he doubled the quotas. No food could be kept, even to feed your own family till the quotas were filled. It was impossible. To eat a handful of grain meant hanging. The police and militia took everything, even the seed for next year's crops.

"And there was no escape. The borders were sealed."

Natalie Schmidt spoke, "In Poland we were afraid. We had fought two wars with Russia not so long before. We won both. But we did not want another war. And Ukraine had been with Russia, at least in the second war. We helped a few escape death at the hands of Stalin, but we did not help enough. Not as we should have."

Bubbie Feine said, "Ah, Poland, I thought so."

Mrs. Hubchic fell quiet as Natalie Schmidt went on, "In Poland we had been our own country since the end of the first war. Lenin sent an army west to invade Estonia and invade us, but we beat it off. Then we fought again over where the border with Ukraine should be. Lenin said we'd have peace if we joined Russia, just like Ukraine. We said no. And when Stalin came, we learned his idea of peace with us was slavery. Stalin had his underground inside Poland. Their centers were mostly in the colleges, but Stalin's Bolsheviks were no scholars. They were thugs and murderers. They said they spoke for working people. Ha! They were just like Lenin and Stalin. They just wanted revolution so they could be dictators themselves."

Mrs. Hubchic sat back and listened to Natalie.

"But there was more than one underground! I was a courier for, um, in English, 'The Nationalist Militia.' We fought the Communists and handed them death for death. They murdered us, some say two-hundred thousand of us, and we fought back. And a good job we did too."

"Bubbie!" said Swan.

"Hush! I will hear these nice ladies."

"Bubbie, nothing is wrong with Communism as Marx explained it. Stalin was a perversion. We studied Marx and his philosophy of history. His ideas are now how scholars see history. Imperialist and 'Great Man' history is out. History is the people, just like Marx said."

Bubbie said, "And these ladies are not people? Child, hear the real voices of real people. And child, if you speak again, you must leave this room."

"Thank you Ma'am, now I understand," Swan said with sarcastic politeness. Then she rose bowed slightly and left the room. But Lois remained.

"But the Germans invaded in September, 1939. Our army fought them. Yes! Our good young men from the universities, our heroes, were made army officers in only days of training and our working men signed on to be new soldiers. We were proud of our heroes, but then we were stabbed in the back by Stalin. He invaded next. He invaded with a militia called in from The Ukraine. But, ha! We counter-attacked with our own militia! We fought like madmen and died as heroes! It was glorious! We actually drove the Russians and the Ukrainians back over the borders. We invaded Russia itself! But then, Stalin sent his regular army. There were just too many of them. Then we ran out of ammunition and supplies. By then the cities were in turmoil. Communist cells from the universities, those cowards who refused to fight invaders, organized revolt and actually helped Stalin. Finally, it was too much. Our government escaped to Paris first, then later to London. And they carried on till we were double-crossed at the end of the war and Poland was handed over to the Communists."

Natalie paused for long moments. "The man I was to marry did not come back. I was told he was shifted to the east when Stalin invaded. I was told he would not surrender and was shot, but another said he was captured. If so, he was certainly shot in the Katyn Forest as with all of our young men and officers. Stalin murdered all of our officers there, even young college students who joined the militia only days before. Tens of thousands were murdered. I do not know what happened to the man I was to marry. I will never know the truth. I hoped for a time, but it was no good.

"Then, Polska was cut in half, half to the Germans, half to the Russians. But we kept up the fight in secret and kept up secret communications with our government in London too. That is when we became 'The Polish Underground State.' We were the ones loyal to our legal government.

The Germans were brutal. The Nazis put Jewish people in ghettoes and concentration camps to die. They packed the Jewish people into ghettos then killed them in Warsaw for fighting back, just because some fought not to go to the concentration camps. And the Nazis murdered many more of us just because they wanted our land or just for no reason but being Polish.

But more and more they saw that we were heroes fighting the Russian animals. The Nazi SS men were murderers and killed even innocent civilians, but the Russian rapists and murderers were not human. Over time, some Germans, at least those who were not Nazis, came to respect us for fighting the Bolsheviks. Oh, after the war, any record of that time was destroyed by Russian SMERSH and NKVD. Our leaders, those loyal to Poland, were carried away to mock trials and murdered. All trace is gone now and nobody knows. Russia only allowed a made-up version of that time, a version invented by their Bolshevik thug friends. Pah!

"Well, in 1941, Stalin was ready to invade Germany, but Hitler struck first. Then, like the Finns before us - 'the enemy of my enemy and all that' - sometimes Poles had to be allied with the Germans Wehrmacht, that's the German army, but surely never the Nazis or SS or Gestapo.

"After the Soviets took over at war's end, after their fake 'Three Times Yes' election, you got murdered by SMERSH or sent to the gulags just for keeping a record of what happened or even talking about that time."

Natalie Schmidt fell quiet again.

Bubbie, in a tender voice, as if to a child, said, "Natalie, there is more. I see it. Tell me please."

"I have never spoken of it except to Günter."

Natalie Schmidt looked blankly at the wall for a long time. Then tears came and her voice trembled.

Bubbie said, "Natalie, speak at last. Tell me. Tell me."

"I was Natalia Paderewski. I was, and I suppose, I am still." Natalie paused as her shoulders shook. "I am Natalia Paderewski, 'Das Mungo, The Mongoose' .. Oh, that none of it had ever happened."

Then Natalie recovered herself with a deep breath. "Very well, perhaps it is time after all. I was an inspector of women's working conditions in factories and so I traveled the country. I looked at the width of factory aisles for fire escape and if there was a sanitary bathroom and talked to women about their treatment and wrote reports. I could even order certain corrections to bad conditions. That was before the war. And because I could travel officially, I was also a courier for the underground. I carried messages and sometimes parcels, although carrying parcels was very bad if one was caught. How odd it is to think nationalists had to hide what they did, but the murdering Communist animals had great influence and were in the open. Then after the Russians came ..."

Natalie paused yet again, then spoke in a firm voice. "When Stalin had taken our lands and murdered our young men, I was arrested and taken to a building and locked up in a dark room. There was another woman in that room as well, Maria. Mostly, the two of us were left in the dark in that small room. But there was another more terrible room down a flight of stairs. They interrogated us in that room. 'Did you meet so and so at such a place on this date? Did you not carry a gun to this man?' But I said I knew nothing. I said I knew only that women must have a dressing room in any factory and a separate bathroom. I said I was an inspector of working conditions and I said nothing more.

"I was imprisoned in that first dark room with that other woman. She called me Natalia of Nicomedia, that saint was from the time of Roman persecution and she cared for doomed Christians awaiting death. She was Maria and I called her Święta Maria.

"Sometimes days would pass with our waste stinking in a bucket in the corner of that windowless room, and sometimes they would take me to that other room down that flight of stairs for more questions. Some days they made us stand for hours. Sometimes they would threaten me and show me a gun. Sometimes they would try to be kind and offer good food or a shower with good towels and clean clothes. Sometimes they would give me an electric shock. But I said I knew nothing. A single crack and they would torture me for more and more and more. I knew that. Maria and I gave our tormenters nick-names. 'The Devil,' 'The Briber,' 'The Savage,' and 'The Animals.' They were the Communists we had known before, not the same men, but the same kind. And now Stalin had put them in charge.

"'The Animals' .. I .. I cannot tell this part."

Tears came again and Natalie sat silent for several moments looking down into her lap, her face unreadable.

"Months more and then one day 'The Devil' came and unlocked the door to our room. He pushed us both out of that building onto the street and without a word went back in alone. That was all. They no longer wanted us. We had survived.

"If the man I was to marry, by a miracle, came back, would he still have me? And my family was all gone. My underground contacts all gone, mostly shot in the woods by the Russians, I am sure of that, but the torment of that prison had ended. I was out of that dark room at last. I was still alive.

"Bubbie Feine, you would kill Germans, yes I know." Natalie's voice grew harsh, as if a wild person spoke. Her face reddened and she trembled, "But I would dice the Communist animals like so much bad pork and feed them to dogs in the street! What they did to me .. the murder of our young men .. the world is barbarous. I .. I .." An avalanche of sobbing overcame the woman, she shook from head to toe, and she spoke no more.

At length, Bubbie Feine said, "You have been a good neighbor Natalia Paderewski, and in our hearts we have both known all that we have we have both just said." Bubbie Feine looked into Natalie's teary eyes and at length tears come into hers too.

Finally Natalie Schmidt spoke and voice was again steady, "It was another person's life, but it was me. I cannot bear to think of it. I will think of it no more. I must leave it now. With Günter gone, it is all over."

Bubbie Feine said, "I did not cry until my brother's children were born, then, somehow, I knew what was lost. Then it all finally came out and I wept every night. No, it cannot be got rid of. No, not ever. Some things cannot be forgiven or forgotten. But we can, perhaps, still live.

"Lois, never forget what you have heard this day. You have just been given a great, great gift. A gift of profound knowledge. Keep and save what you have just heard and seen. We must never see such times again. Never! Never! Learn from what I have said and what these ladies have told! And tell your fool of a cousin and your friends too."

Now Swan retuned with some papers, "Bubbie, I found this on the Internet, Stalin's Ukraine Militia was not really Jewish. See only some captains … "

"Swan, I do not care what men say who were not there. It does not matter. Jewish? Perhaps some of Stalin's captains of the Ukrainian famine were. Perhaps the first militia he sent into Poland was. But they acted for Stalin, not for our faith. Their faith does not matter. This lady has told us the truth. She told what she saw with her own eyes. Do not argue! Learn! These ladies have given gems bigger than all of your college holds. Learn and one day you, with your college and wealth and luxury, might write real history, not the storybook nonsense I hear from you now. Instead of looking at that computer box full of hear-say, you should have been here for truths deeper than you may ever in your life grasp!"

Then Bubbie Feine turned to Natalie. "My neighbor and friend, for now we are real and true friends, what Jewish blood do you have?"

Swan's mouth fell open.

Natalie turned to Bubbie Feine, "Bubbie, I do not know. My name is Paderewski. That was my Mother's name. When I was little I was told that my father had died in the first war. I suppose illegitimate children were all told their father had died. But we did not live so badly. And I went to school too. Money came by mail once a month. I now suppose it was for my support. I do not think there is Jewish blood on my Mother's side. But I think my father may have been a Jewish merchant my Mother knew. I have never really known. I hate that some men never have courage to tell. And I hate that it so degraded my mother."

Bubbie Feine turned and looked at Swan with fire was in her eyes, fire that was far beyond Swan's comprehension.

Swan said, "But .. " then she fell silent.

Rain pattered on the window again. It was dull and gray outside, but headlights in the drive attracted attention. Then a lady with a clear plastic rain hat and a windbreaker moved quickly up the walk. Lois was already opening the door just as the doorbell rang.

Sally Webb entered. "Oh, thank goodness! Here you are! I saw Mrs. Hubchic's car but you weren't in the house. I thought another terrible thing might have happened. You scared the daylights out of me."

The Guest House

"There are no secrets better kept than the secrets everybody guesses"

George Bernard Shaw

Jane was in the secret room looking in file drawers when Mill appeared. Mill jogged his head to one side as if to say 'let's leave,' then he said, "These guys don't need us, let's do some exploring."

Jane and Mill paused in the dining room. Smith was there and he seemed totally absorbed in the tape on the floor and the photos on the computer.

Mill said, "Let's scoot," and he led the way down the narrow metal stairs as if he already knew the way, then outside in the chill and drizzle.

Jane said, "Mill, it's raining and it's cold. What did you see to drag me out in this for?"

Mill pulled his sports coat off, "Here, jut put this over your head and we'll scoot."

Then Mill gestured at the grass. A path was worn in the grass and it led across a little white foot bridge over the small stream and on to what was apparently a guest house. From where they stood, the house was almost hidden in the woods. Mill led the way quickly around the depressed and wet area in the yard, across the little white foot bridge and off toward the little house. Jane felt like a little child hurrying after her parents. After shoe-soaking walk, they were there. But the path didn't end at the guest house. Mill pointed. The grass was also worn in the direction of the neighbor's house.

"You noticed this from inside the house? You brought me out in the rain to see that the neighbors walk over when they visit? So what? You really brought me here to look at this? I'm getting soaked and the rain isn't improving your jacket either. You'll need to get it cleaned and pressed, your shirt and tie too." Jane then thought better of her words, she wasn't really angry and she wondered if she had been too blunt.

Mill said, "Yes I did, and yes, and maybe and I'm more soaked than you are so quit complaining. Now, let's snoop around."

Jane thought to herself, that this was mild as Mill's temper outbursts got, but it really was cold and wet. So this better be worth it.

Steps led up to a Swiss chalet style front porch that was, at least, dry. But there on the porch, for some reason the wind seemed stronger and colder than in had been in the open. It felt downright blustery here. Jane stamped her feet to shake water off.

Mill produced a handkerchief and tried the door. It was unlocked and he and Jane entered. Inside, it was surprisingly warm. That was welcome. It also smelled faintly of pine. The patter of rain on the windows and the sound of wind outside lent a cozy feel. Inside the door was a row of big pegs, obviously there to hang coats and hats. Jane hung Mill's damp jacket on one of them.

The inside of the guest house was Alpine style, just like the outside. Unlike the main house, it was not incongruous at all. It all went together. The small entry hall opened to a big room with an open fire place in the middle. There was a copper hood and a pipe or flue reaching up high to a cathedral ceiling. Furniture was simple and wooden. Chairs and a sofa were of wood with simple leather cushions for seats. They had small wooden tables between them. There was a bar, much over sized for the scale of the place and it had many bottles behind it. That bar looked very much like the kind Jane had seen in expensive hotels. There was a bottle of expensive-looking scotch and another fancy looking bottle of Luksusowa vodka on the bar's serving area plus two glasses that seemed to be waiting for someone. The two glasses were in front of barstools that were turned invitingly toward each other. A small balcony sort of space projected out over the bar area with a couple tables and chairs up there. Beside the bar was an open stairway with a hand rail on one side only. The stairs led to the little balcony. There were two closed doors behind the tables up there too.

Jane thought, by the look of the place, there should have been a long vestibule outside with a racks full of snow skis and inside, a much bigger entry hall with outdoor wear hanging to dry. There should be young people in ski costume, hot drinks in hand, milling around. There should have been a big picture window with view of a long, snow-covered downhill ski-run and an old style, t-bar ski lift clunking slowly along. There should be a ski lodge far below and barely visible through gray of falling snow. But, of course, there was none of that. It was just a rainy day outside and a snug warm feeling inside. No young skiers, just Mill with a bow tie and a wet shirt.

Jain said, "Wow! Cool! I could live in this place. This is cool! And everything's spiffy. But look Mill, somebody's been using this place. It's not musty. It's not been closed up too long or anything like that. Everything's dusted and cleaned and stuff." In fact it seemed to Jane likes a good cleaning crew had just left and the place was ready for guests to move right in.

Mill moved quickly opening and looking behind a few doors. There was a small kitchen, sodas were in the refrigerator. A second refrigerator, this one behind the bar, held beer and mixers. He looked in a little store room and a bathroom. There was short hall to a back door that he opened and looked out. Then he looked in a rather large closet near the back door, a washer, dryer and shelves full of linens and cleaning supplies were there. Next, he rapidly climbed the steep and bare wooden stairs that led to the balcony directly over the bar. Jane followed.

"Mill, what are we looking for? Why are we butting into this place? We don't have a search warrant or anything."

Mill was silent.

Behind one door was a bedroom with a small bath. The other door was locked. Mill muttered, "What a pain," he dropped to a knee and pulled an odd piece of metal from a shirt pocket. Jane remembered his pocket-filled sports coat that held the notorious magnifying glass was still downstairs. How many pockets does Mill have? Mill quickly picked the lock. Then he said, "Bingo. Jane, come in here, no hundred mile rule for Schmidt I guess."

"Hundred mile rule?"

Mill said "Oh, old traveling salesman talk. Salesmen chase women when they're a hundred miles or more from home. Their wives catch them less often that way."

By then Jane had come in, she looked around and said, "Don't explain, I get it. Mill, Geez! Look at this."

The room was outrageous with lacy pink curtains, mirrors on the ceiling and all over the walls, except for a suggestive Art Deco painting of a nude lady over the head of a huge bed. Furniture was glossy and black with even more mirrors on top of a chest of drawers.

Another dressing area held a vanity with enough lights to satisfy any Hollywood starlet and closets ran the full length of the guest house's eves. Beyond the dressing area, a bathroom had pink tile with more nude ladies inlayed and there was a garish oversized footed bathtub with flowers made of some kind of colorful shiny stone ornamenting it.

Jane said, "C'mon, it's just for Natalie," but in truth, she thought otherwise. "You men always see creepy motives." But Mill was rummaging in a dresser just then and held up ladies underwear of the skimpiest kind, obviously way too small for Natalie's mature behind. Jane opened a closet door and found a variety of sheer things hanging there too. It was obviously for a much younger woman than Natalie.

"Hard for me to picture Natalie Schmidt in this stuff," Mill said. Jane need not have been told.

"Expensive," Jane said. She was holding a sheer garment of some kind. She did not even recognize what it was. Jane held the garment in front of her and started crossing her legs back and forth in a goofy side to side dance. "Poop-boob-a-doop! What do you think Mill?" She was rolling her eyes back and forth like Betty Boop.

"Geez Paine! Cut that out!"

"Yeah, then quit staring at me like that you voyeur." Jane returned the sheer thing, whatever it was, to the closet. She stood quiet for a minute then looked at Mill. "Really, I feel like I'm the voyeur with all this stuff. I guess we better get Henderson to look at this and look for fingerprints and stuff. I see murder motive all over the place in here. On the other hand, you never know, maybe Schmidt just let the neighbors or friends use the place, I mean you can see the neighbor's house from here, it's actually closer than Schmidt's house and you remember the wear in the grass?"

"And what, Schmidt decorated like this and went to this expense to be nice to neighbors? Nah .. Schmidt and someone, who? Or .... "

Jane said, "I dunno, men are weird."

"Women too."

"I guess."

"Expensive underwear and stuff?" said Mill. "Expensive enough that the buyer can be traced if it comes to that?"

Jane said, "Well it's not Fredrick's of Hollywood. There's some Eres and La Perl. Those are fancy brands. Maybe we can see what stores carry this stuff around here. But I don't think it's all the way to rare or anything. Even the big-bucks brands like this probably make tons of this stuff. I wouldn't be hopeful. Some jerk I hardly knew tried to give me some stuff like this once. What a horse's behind that clown was, and he was married! I mean, a little too familiar for my taste. I mean I'm not like, I mean, what an ass."

Mill's eyes went to the sheer thing on the hanger and back to Jane. "Come on Jane, I don't want to know. Yeah, maybe this is nothing, it's probably just somebody's stuff, but we have to tip off Henderson anyway. There's nothing like good old sex when it comes to murder. Right now it's just a hunch. It's nothing solid. But due diligence and all that .. at least it rates checking."

"Nothing? Yeah, sure! Like, what other explanation Mill? You're right. What a jerk. A little love-nest all of his own and right under Natalie's nose. You're right,

Henderson needs in here. Like you just said, I see murder motives all over the place."

Mill said, "Maybe, but remember, we don't know yet. Right now it's just somebody's stuff. Maybe you're right, maybe Schmidt's friends come to visit once a month. We don't know anything yet."

"Yeah, right, Mill, let's get out of here. This little love-nest makes me feel weird and it pisses me off too."

As Jane spoke a light but audible knock came at the front door. Mill and Jane traded glances. Jane whispered, "Answer it or hide and see?"

Mill said, "Answer."

Jane and Mill clambered down the steep stairs in time to see the door slowly swing open and two young ladies come in. One wore plain clothing, the other wore skin tight stretch pants and a tight fitting top.

Lois Feine said, "Oops! Hello! Who are you?"

Jane said "Agents Mill and Paine. Who are you?"

"Agents? Like detectives?" She looked at Swan. "Umm, I'm Lois Feine and this is my cousin Swan. We're neighbors."

Jane said, "And what brings you to this little house?"

Swan answered this time, "I'd guess the same thing as you. We're looking into something. What are you two doing here? Do you have a warrant or anything?"

Jane said. "Okay, fair enough, but I asked first and we're official."

Swan said, "Well .. well okay, umm, let me think. Umm, there have been rumors around the neighborhood for years about this place, about maybe Mr. Schmidt and Mrs. Webb meeting out here, and since, well, the recent event, we thought we should take a look. I'm not into squealing on people's personal business, I mean it's their business, stuff like that happens all the time and its nobody's business, but, you know, Dr. Schmidt and all and maybe someone should look. The two of us talked about it and, and, well, here we are."

Lois continued, "My grandmother was just telling Mrs. Schmidt some odd stuff about the Holocaust and saying other really weird things just a little while ago, like twenty minutes ago and it got Swan and me thinking about if maybe someone killed old Schmidt and, anyway, we decided to look."

Jane said, "Huh, that's really interesting, I know what you mean. We're not the regular cops you know, and we're doing the same thing as you. We're just looking into everything. So what do ya' say, give us all the dirt and we'll see if the regular cops need to come out here and look or if it's just nothing."

Swan said, "Agents? Like FBI? Why FBI?"

Mill said, "Because there might be a national security angle to all this. Just might. We don't know. We need to be sure there's not. But the Schmidt's suicide or whatever it was is the local cops' business, not ours. Like Ms. Paine said, just checking to be sure. So come on, what do you guys know?"

Swan said, "You sound like this guy I know. He was really smart and he said he had some big secret assignment for a job this summer and he wouldn't talk because everything was some kind of national security secret."

Lois hesitated then said, "You're, um, you're Mill and Paine huh?"

Jane said, "Relax guys. Help us and maybe Mrs. Webb too. If this place is nothing, and that's how it looks, we'll just lock 'er up and leave. But c'mon, let's get some good old dirt. We want in on the fun."

Swan spoke. "Look, our Bubbie, well, great aunt, was being weird talking about hating Germans right to Mrs. Schmidt. But we figure this place is the real motive if Schmidt was killed. Before Mrs. Schmidt calls the cops on Bubbie, we thought we better check things out and maybe call the cops ourselves."

Jane said, "Seems reasonable. Your Bubbie was talking about hating Germans?"

Lois said, "Well yeah, but she's way too old to shoot old Dr. Schmidt. Look, we really don't know anything, but once when I was little, I was playing outside and kind of came exploring through the woods and ended up over here. It was maybe nine years ago, a long time ago anyway. Then I saw Mr. Schmidt come out here and kind of look around like a kid that was about to be guilty of something, then he went in. He didn't see me. Then I saw Mrs. Webb come from the other way. She looked around too. She looked just like a kid I saw shoplift candy one time. I was scared by that and ran home. I told my Mom and she said they were probably just painting pictures or talking or playing cards or something and that I should forget all about it. After that, I watched for lights to turn on and off at night and stuff. I can see this place from my bedroom window, and they did. I told Swan about it a couple years ago. She was visiting and we were smoking, umm, when .. anyway, I told her about it cuz' it was kind of a laugh. But now, with what happened, we decided to peek in here and, after we saw what was in here, then decide if we should tell the cops, or not."

Jane said, "That all makes sense. Okay, have a seat. Let's go over what you just told us."

Swan sat on the edge of a chair and said, "I think I'm actually glad we bumped into you. It's just that when we were at the party that German couple talked to me. And they kept asking me about Mr. and Mrs. Schmidt, I mean I hardly know the Schmidts, I don't even really live here, I'm really just visiting, but they really kept going, is Schmidt the old man's real name and all that kind of thing. Then Mrs. Schmidt just told Bubbie, that she wasn't married to Mr. Schmidt at all and Schmidt wasn't her name either and suddenly Bubbie said she knew it all along and it all started me thinking. And you guys are here now. Something's wrong. Okay, it's your turn, what's going on?"

Mill held his hands up. Then put his finger to his lips to signal quiet. In a moment footsteps could be heard. The door opened and a woman walked in.

"Oh, hello Mrs. Webb" said Lois.

Sally Webb had a clear plastic rain hat and poncho on. She jumped at Swan's voice then looked from face to face, then said, "Oh boy."

In The Garden Cabana

"A garden, you know, is a very usual refuge."

Alexander Hamilton

Val Tessler could see Schmidt's yard from his second floor windows. Schmidt's yard was far bigger than any of the neighbor's yards. Maybe it should be called an estate, not a yard. From those second floor windows, it looked more like a city park with the other, lesser yards spaced one by one around the perimeter. Today, the rain and haze obscured most of that, except that Val Tesler had made out more than the usual comings and goings at Schmidt's guest house.

Normally, Tesler's yard would be considered very big, two acres counting some woods on his land, but it did not compare with Schmidt's. Tesler's yard sloped away from his back patio and down to the wooded area where there was a stream. Perhaps the steam should have been a border between the two yards but was not, instead, it meandered through Tessler's and then Schmidt's.

Val's Wife Claudia had a big garden at the back of the yard not far from the stream and the woods. The soil was very good down there and Val had rigged an electric pump that would sprinkle water from the stream at the flick of a switch. Claudia's garden always thrived. Claudia's biggest challenge had been deer, the deer's friends the rabbits and an occasional groundhog. The deer and rabbits seemed to think vegetables were like chocolate bars and lettuce and Swiss chard was ice cream. The groundhogs liked anything at all that was subterranean. But Val had solved all that some years ago. The solution was tall chain link fence that also extended three feet underground. It was painted forest green and it had low shrubs around it. It had fancy wrought iron gates too. The fence was not as unattractive as it might have been. Plus there was a nice paver-block walk that led to the gates Best of all it kept the deer, rabbits and groundhogs out.

The garden was Claudia's retreat. It was her favorite place.

The 'Garden Cabana' was a big screened room that was located some distance from the house. It had red brick that matched the house. The bricks made a short wall and then brick columns held up a real shingled roof. There was a patio made from the same pavers that led to the garden and it had an outdoor brick grill. There were electric lights and even an overhead infrared heater. The cabana and patio could serve for entertaining on pleasant summer evenings.

This day, Claudia sat bundled in a winter coat inside the cabana. She looked toward her garden and listened to the patter of rain on the roof. Claudia's harvest was already in. Or more exactly, the part she called her American garden, tomatoes, corn, beans, all the American crops had been harvested and the plants were in decline. But her 'old world' garden was still going strong. Cabbage would be good even after the snow flew and her prized swedes, or rutabaga as Americans called them, actually improved with two or three frosts. The beets were small enough to still be tender and good to use now, their beet greens, swiss chard really, would be good too. Claudia thought, if the rain stopped, she might dig a few beets later today.

Klavdiya Tesler, had called herself Claudia so long she had almost forgotten anything else, but at quite, chilly, rainy times like this, she remembered Russia. Claudia could even remember the war, although just barely. Her real father never came back from the war. Then her mother remarried a doctor who had a good position. He was a fine man, jovial, strong, smart, fond of vodka and fond of children. He was cheerful and seldom drunk. Claudia had no complaints. Mostly, her childhood had been happy. Claudia had even met Val through her jolly step-father. Still, Claudia sometimes wondered how things might have been with her real father. She did not like the Germans who invaded Russia and brutalized the people and changed so many lives for the worse. It was Germans who cost her a real father. Yet Val was vehement in his hatred of Stalin. He probably hated Stalin more than Germans. Claudia supposed the textbook facts proved Val was right. She thought about that. She even remembered Stalin's arresting all the Jewish doctors in Moscow and having them shipped off to the Gulag or even shot for an imagined plot of trying to poison Soviet leaders. That was just before Stalin's stroke. Some stroke! Everybody knew Lavrentiy Beria had poisoned Stalin. At least Beria lived long enough to declare that the 'Doctor's Plot' was a fake and have some surviving Doctors released. That was just before Beria himself was shot on orders from Malenkov and Nikita Khrushchev. Lucky her Doctor step-father was not Jewish or he would have been in the Gulag. Stalin distrusted doctors and hated Jews. A Jewish doctor didn't have a chance with

Stalin. Claudia chuckled to herself as she recalled that Stalin distrusted doctors so much that he had himself treated by veterinarians.

Claudia knew the history, yes it condemned Stalin. But it seemed to her that the German invaders were more evil than Stalin. Millions and millions died fighting Germans. And when they invaded and drew near Moscow, they brutalized even innocent civilians. Claudia's mother kept a pistol handy at all times in those days, just in case. That was a habit she passed on to Claudia.

The cabana's screen door opened and Val Tesler came in. He stood brushing rain off his light jacket. "Clyde Webb just phoned. It looks like all the cop cars and action at Schmidt's is bad news. He says Günter shot himself last night. That sure seems funny. He didn't seem dejected or anything at the party last night, he seemed pretty normal to me. Don't you think so?"

"Claudia looked up with a frown. She was silent."

"Claudia, c'mon, Günter was good neighbor. You even enjoyed his party last night. He's dead; can't you let his German roots go even now?"

"So full of himself. Such a typical German. But yes, it's sad. Too bad for Natalie. What do you think it would take to replace these screens with sliding windows? I like it out here. It would be a nice quiet place to sit in the winter if there were windows and better heat."

"Claudia .." Val sighed, "Claudia, why must you always bring that pistol down here. We've been here twenty-five years and you have never needed it." An old Smith and Wesson thirty-two automatic sat on a little table near Claudia. Next to it was in milk crate full of garden tools, dry and unused today.

"There is talk of rabid raccoons. I saw three raccoons in daylight last week, I told you about them. Healthy raccoons do not come out in daylight. Plus last night Sally Webb told me she thought she saw a bobcat in the woods. Sally Webb says she is an American country girl so she would know a bobcat when she sees one. And I saw a couple men walking through the woods last month. I'll keep my thirty-two with me, thank you."

"Claudia, we had no reason to dislike old Schmidt and lots of reasons we should like him. You should speak better of the dead. And think of Natalie. She will be alone now."

"Natalie, oh yes. Have you ever spoken to her in Polish? She answers in perfect Polish. But, of course, I never asked that woman what she was. You might think I was impolite. Polish .. Pah! Not even a real Russian."

"Klavdiya! Stydno!" Tesler used a Russian word for 'shame.' He put his hands on his hips. "What has come over you? You're impossible when you get like this. The poor man is dead."

"Windows, I think maybe simple storm windows would do. The place is not really insulated anyway. But a good electric heater and storm windows might make it comfortable enough to sit and watch snow. It is so pleasant here. It would be nice this winter."

Claudia's brows knitted. "Who's this?"

Tesler turned and saw two men in business suits approaching through the rain at a fast pace. Both carried umbrellas and one carried a clip board that he held close to his chest.

Tesler pushed the screen door open and the two rushed in stamping their feet and folding umbrellas.

"Thank you, excuse us, we tried your front door. When we looked, there were cars are in the garage, so we looked back here. I am Detective Brown and this is Detective Marino." Brown held a badge up, but his eyes were fixed on the Smith and Wesson thirty-two. "Why do you have a pistol out here?"

Tesler answered. "Rabid raccoons, it's just in case."

"Discharging a firearm is illegal around here and there are animal control people."

"We've never discharged it around here and don't expect to, but I think I'd rather face firearms charges that rabies treatments. It's just a precaution. We won't fire it unless something really threatens us. Now what can we do for you?"

"Do you mind if I unload it? I'll give it right back."

"If that would make you comfortable, of course."

Marino scooped the little gun up, pulled the clip out and checked the chamber. Then he sniffed at the barrel and then, after looking at Brown, he replaced the pistol where it was, but he put the clip on another table.

"Okay," said Brown. "I'm afraid there's been some trouble at Dr. Schmidt's house and we need to ask some routine questions of the neighbors." Brown looked at his clip-board and produced a pen. "We'd just like to ask a few routine questions."

Claudia said, "You mean the old Kraut blasted himself? That's the talk."

Tesler said "Claudia! .. Gentlemen, I'm afraid my wife never cared much for Dr. Schmidt."

Brown looked at Marino then said, "Please state your names?"

Claudia replied even spelling out 'Klavdiya' as Brown wrote.

"You have lived here a while?"

"Twenty-five years or more."

"And you knew the Schmidt's well?"

"Of course, they have been neighbors all that time."

"Were you present at last night's cocktail party?

Tesler said they were.

"Did you speak to, or did you know a Dr. Shaw? We are having trouble finding or even identifying him. Can you help us there?"

"Shaw? No, I did not speak to any Dr. Shaw, did you Claudia?"

"Val, he was that Turkish, Arab kind of a man. You remember, he was following Schmidt around half the night like a puppy dog. What Arabs see in Germans, I'll never know."

Brown wrote something.

"Mrs. Tesler, do you know this Shaw? Did you speak to him? Can you tell us how to reach him?"

"No, I never met him before. We did not speak more than an introduction last night either. But he wanted something from Schmidt. I can't imagine that there are such a large number of Dr. Shaws, did you try the phone book? Why not call and ask each Dr. Shaw if they were at the party?"

"You mean you presume Shaw wanted something because he followed Dr. Schmidt around and spoke to him a lot?"

"Yes, he wanted Schmidt's attention all night and he kept talking to him. Val just told you I was never a fan of Schmidt's. We tolerated each other and were polite, but that was for the sake of the other neighbors. I do not like pompous people like Schmidt. But last night, I almost felt sorry for him. He couldn't shake Shaw."

"Hmm .." Brown took more notes.

"You describe Shaw as small and Arabic."

"He wasn't dark, just medium, like those Chaldean people from Iraq or something, you know, dark eyes and all that. He looked Arabic to me, maybe upper fifties in age, average size. Otherwise, he was pretty nondescript."

"Okay then, when did you arrive at the party?"

Tesler said, "About five."

"You went together?"

"Yes."

"Did you have that pistol with you?"

"No, Claudia keeps it in her night stand at night and only takes it down here to the garden when she has seen raccoons and such. Raccoons are nocturnal but they have been wandering around in daylight which indicates they are sick."

"When did you leave the party?"

"About seven."

"The others came and went about the same time?"

"I'd say so. I can't say if others stayed after we left, but mostly, I think, we were all leaving at about seven."

"Did you notice anything unusual last night?"

Tesler said "Well, there were a couple new students from Germany who I understand were going to stay at Schmidt's. Nice kids. We only said hello to them, but they seemed polite."

"More Germans." said Claudia.

"Yes, and anything else? Anything out of the ordinary?"

"Umm, no. Just that Shaw guy."

"How did Dr. Schmidt seem? Was he normal would you say?"

Claudia said, "His usual self-important self."

Tesler said, "As I said, I'm afraid Claudia never cared for Schmidt, but he seemed normal to me."

"Then you came back here?"

"Yes."

"Directly?

"Yes. Actually, we drove. We could have walked, but driving is better for us after dark, it's too easy to trip or have trouble in the dark. It was not really dark that early, but it's our habit to drive even short distances in the evening in case things run long."

"Then did you hear or notice anything out of the ordinary later? I should say after you came home?"

"No. We had a leftover dinner, watched the TV and then the news and went to bed. Nothing unusual happened."

"Did you see any unfamiliar cars?"

"Umm .. no."

"Hear anything?"

"No."

"Here is a list of those Mrs. Schmidt remembers from the party. Do you remember anyone else who might not be on the list? "

Tesler looked at the list, then handed it to Claudia. "No, I think that is all I remember."

"I agree," said Claudia,

"Thank you very much. If you think of anything that seemed out of the ordinary, please phone me. That happens sometimes, people think about it and something occurs to them later. Even little things sometimes help us. Here is my card. There is also a chance we might want to test your pistol. I will phone or come by if that is needed. And please keep that thing safe and do not return the clip to your gun until we are fully out of sight. Again thank you and excuse us for barging in."

The two men left with their umbrellas, almost running.

Val turned to Claudia. "Those were not questions about a suicide. Something's up. And your dumb gun almost got us in trouble. But something bad's up. I'm calling Clyde, maybe if they stop there, he can get something more out of them."

Tesler departed in haste. Claudia resumed her survey of the garden and listening to the patter of rain on the roof above. She considered the little streams of water that fell from the roof and passed in front of the screens. She inhaled the rain freshened cool air. And then she reflected on childhood in Russia again.

At the Police Station

"Get the facts, or the facts will get you. And when you get them, get them right, or they will get you wrong."

Thomas Fuller

The meeting room was too small. A local police chief and three police officers crowded around a table. The forensics team sat in chairs dragged in from other rooms. There were a few others Jane did not recognize leaning against walls or standing. Then Jane noticed Clarence, the Detroit FBI man, notepad and pen in hand, standing against the back wall. He was as silent and dour looking as he had been at the airport.

Henderson was in the front of what looked like a school blackboard. He held a marker. He said, "Okay, let's review what we have so far, figure out what we still need and then we need to agree on action steps for each of us. I want to use a timeline for an outline. I've put a preliminary on the blackboard starting at four pm yesterday. At four pm Kuhn's Catering shows up. Betty Kuhn owns the business, Alex heats up hors d'oeuvres that they get at Gordon Food Service. Then he parades around the room serving wine while Betty offers the hors d'oeuvres. Betty bought the business from Alex about five years ago when he wanted to retire. She really just took over the customer list and contact names. But Alex still helps out when Betty needs a hand. Real name Aleksander Szczepanski." Henderson read the last name one letter at a time. "Goes by Alex Panski, nick name in the trade is Alka-Seltser Panski." That drew a chuckle. "We've been aware of Panski for a long time. He had connections to the underworld. He'd cater for what used to be called 'The Polish Mafia' when there was a Polish mafia in Hamtramck. That's nineteen-fifties. He just seemed to be around catering every time there was a dead body of someone whose name ended 'ski.' In those days, he was one of the 'usual suspects.' But nothing ever stuck to him. Panski might have been a real tough actor. The last thing we have is this . Immigration asked us to help find him in .. 1978. I guess he has a good lawyer because he's still here. Keep this guy in mind.

"Anyway, half an hour later, make it four-thirty," Henderson marked the blackboard "the new students show up, Hans and Helga Hoffman. They were driven in from Metro Airport by Colebrook Dean of Students. His name is James McIntyre. They're getting situated in their rooms as guests show up for five pm cocktails. Old folks are always early to parties, always! So make it four-forty-five here on the time line." He put another mark on the timeline. "Mrs. Schmidt is in the servant's quarters that they now call the gate house with the kids, Dr, Schmidt is greeting guests. McIntyre talks to a couple of Schmidt's neighbors on the way out and then he splits."

Henderson turned from the board. "Here's the guest list according to Mrs. Schmidt. I've included the addresses we have so far." Henderson slid papers onto the table and they were passed around. "I'll comment on it, I already mentioned the caterers. McIntyre's Dean of Students at Colebrook School. He was only there a minute. Four Feines are neighbors next door. Mrs. Feine, first name Sylvia, her twenty year old daughter is Lois, twenty-two year old niece Swan and Sylvia's aunt also goes by Sylvia but real name Selde. They all call the old lady 'Bubbie.' The niece, Swan, also named Feine, is in grad school and hanging out at the Feine's till she gets an apartment or some such story. Swan's folks are retired, sold their local place and now have place in Charlevoix and another in Fort Lauderdale. Mr. Feine died of an odd-ball skin infection, septic shock took him out, that was two years ago, but he was insured to the very eyeballs so Mrs. Feine is reasonably well off.

"Mrs. Hubchic is a widow - lives in Grosse Pointe. She's a long time friend of several of these people. Mrs. Schmidt says her first name is Bohuslava. She prefers Mrs. Hubcheck. We have not contacted her yet. Neighbor Dr.Veniamin Tesler, retired pediatrician, called Val by friends. Telser's wife, umm, Klavdiya, called Claudia by neighbors. They were married in Russia and came here forty years ago. They carry an automatic pistol around the yard. The pistol's an old Smith and Wesson thirty-two automatic and might be the right caliber for the hole in Schmidt. They say the gun's in case of rabid raccoons.

"There was a Dr. Shaw. Mrs. Schmidt didn't know Shaw. We still need to identify Shaw and contact him.

"Clyde Webb, he's probably seventy years old, with Sally his thirty-some year old trophy wife. They live across the back fence.

"I put a pizza delivery kid's name on here too. That's Jason O'Neal. They called for pizza later. Jason worked last night, but they have three drivers and they don't keep track of who drives which order. The guy we spoke to was guessing it was Jason. Jason's cell phone didn't answer but he works tonight so we'll pay them a visit and ask about it."

"The new German kids appeared at the party too. They mainly hung around with the Feine kids.

"We have spoken to all of them except Shaw, Hubchic and the pizza kid. Nobody heard or suspected anything. The interview sheets are here if you want to look. Everything was normal.

"Anyway, the party only goes on till seven. Remember, these guys are old, so that's probably normal. Then it breaks up. There's no dinner. By seven thirty everybody's gone. The German kids are still in the main house. Betty Kuhn says she had things put away and the catering truck out of there before eight." Henderson turned again and filled in the blackboard timeline.

"Mrs. Schmidt says the German students were polite and even walked the last old folks to their cars. After everybody beat it, they sat around and talked and then Dr. Schmidt ordered pizza. Mrs. Schmidt says pizza came about eight-thirty. The kids ate up then said they were tired, because of their travel. They cut out to hit the hay about nine. Not surprising, nine'd be about two in the morning German time. Mrs. Schmidt hits the bedroom and watches a movie on the tube. Günter Schmidt stays downstairs, we don't know doing what, till eleven forty-five when Schmidt calls Washington for help and says, in code words, send help, the boogie man is here. The initial estimate of forensics and the coroner agree that he's dead by about midnight. Nobody heard a thing. There's a single small caliber hole in his chest. We need to wait for an official opinion on that, but I'll guess less than a nine millimeter. The coroner says the path looks nearly straight on. No burn marks so the gun was at least a few feet away. The coroner won't have an official report for several days. We haven't found the bullet yet, there's both entry and exit wounds so it isn't in the victim. We need to look again. This time I think we should grid the room off into one foot squares and find the bullet. As long as it's missing, it leaves open the outside chance the victim was killed elsewhere and dropped where we found him. Besides, we need to know if it's a match with Schmidt's gun or the neighbor Tesler's gun. We have not lifted the police cordon and we can't till we find the bullet or we're sure it's not there. I request the crime scene team stay on and search again in the morning. You may have to do the search grid thing."

"The telephone company has already confirmed a land-line call to a two-zero-two area code from Schmidt's home, that's Washington D.C. area code. That was at eleven forty-five. That supports the call to Washington for help and two plus two says Schmidt was in the house when he places the call. You Washington guys, here's the number he called. Please confirm it. That's a requested action step. Please confirm it's the contact number you mentioned. And we want the tape of the call to confirm that it's his voice, not the boogie man's. Anyway, Washington calls Detroit FBI, they call Bloomfield cops at three-thirty and they send a car, Officer Kelly doesn't know it, but Schmidt's already dead. Kelly, by the way, is in court today. He'll be back later. At seven-eighteen Mrs. Schmidt calls Bloomfield cops, not nine-one-one but the regular cop-shop number, and asks for an ambulance. We found the number on a list of numbers she keeps by the phone so that makes sense. At least we have that call on tape. Officer Kelly, still cooling his heels in the car, responds. He enters the house, recognizes the problem, and within two minutes calls for assistance. Kelly checked for pulse and breath only. He says he did not move Schmidt. Schmidt's on the floor next to his dining room chair. We can't tell if he was seated or standing when he was shot. A gun's on the table, but it's not been fired and it's a nine millimeter anyway. I think that's a shade too big for the hole in Schmidt. My opinion only. Plus, we've got an Agatha Christie spin, Mrs. Schmidt says all the doors to the room locked from the inside. Mr. Mill here correctly points out that that little fact argues for a shooter that is familiar with the house."

"Anyway, the phone company says no other calls went out last night, just the pizza place and that Washington area code."

"The obvious first guess is that the boogie man is the new students. We checked them for gun powder residual. Negative, but that's never conclusive. They're too young to be personally from Schmidt's mysterious past anyway. On the other hand, they showed up and Schmidt called his buddies in Washington saying he saw an enemy. This Dr. Shaw guy is the only other new face. We need to find him.

"I'd like the county to look for Dr. Shaw. Deputy?" A man nodded and circled something on the list of names. "You may need to contact the other guests again to see if anybody knows him."

"Anyway, we have a couple holes just where we don't want them, besides the one in Schmidt I mean. What was Schmidt doing in the dining room in this part of the time line, three hours from eight forty-five and the eleven forty-five phone call, apparently with his heavy artillery on the table in front of him. He must have expected trouble. Who's the boogie man or what was it he saw? The students? Shaw? Panski's a good guess too, but he's catered there many times before and would be no big shock to Schmidt. What's the dark secret from Schmidt's past? And obviously, exactly what happened after his call for help.

"Like I said, I'm asking forensics crime scene to take another pass for the bullet.

"We sure need to know about Schmidt's dark past too. I'd want our Washington contingent to press for release of this top secret dark past stuff. We really want that stuff! It's the biggest hole we have in all this. Get on that and get an answer please."

"Finally, I'd like to know who speaks German here because just a moment ago, the coroner sent us a present we missed in Schmidt's pants pocket. It's a note written in what looks like German. It might be a break or a figurative black spot. It sounds like the German kids so far."

Smith said, "I spent a couple years in Germany. Long time ago so I'm rusty, but let's see."

Henderson handed Smith a piece of paper protected in plastic.

"You looked for prints?"

"Yes, nothing at all, not even Schmidt's."

Smith took the paper. "Small handwriting, printed, not script, looks maybe feminine to me, neat, elegant, quite small. Then he read; "Bitte wir mussen sprechen' .. umm .. 'we must please talk' … or maybe; 'please, we must talk.' Next line; 'twenty-two,' it's written as a number, 'Treffen wir im kuche ab zwei und zwanzig uhr' .. um 'kitchen.' Make that line, 'ten PM, your kitchen,' that's guessing number twenty-two means European style time. You guys have a handwriting guy handy? Let's find out who wrote this."

Mill said, "Can I peek at that?" He got his magnifying glass out and squinted at the paper for some time. "Hmmm, weird. Not natural looking. Not like I'd expect. I'd guess someone's covering up his natural handwriting. I agree, we need an expert."

Henderson said, "Okay, I'll get it to Forensics for a serious once over.

"Maybe the kids didn't go to bed but met Schmidt at ten," said Henderson, " Detective Brown, maybe McIntyre can get us some handwriting samples. Don't ask the kids if they wrote the note yet. Also, Brown, see if you can find out who at the party, besides the kids, speaks German. But I'll bet half of the crowd at that party does. They're all European. And now that I think, find or get a sample of Mrs. Schmidt's handwriting too."

"And guys, I need to look into Dr. Schmidt's past using normal law enforcement channels. We know you say there may be a matter of secrecy and security issues, but nothing has come out of Washington yet and I have a murder. I will certainly keep you Washington guys informed. But we have a murder case and the motive seems to be in this man's mysterious past. We need to use all the resources we have. That means regular FBI and the rest."

Jane looked and Clarence seemed to be writing something. Jane had burped at the dinner table on purpose once when she was in middle school and the look from her dad made her feel the way she felt now. "Please keep us posted. Like I told you before, we have asked that all pertinent information be released, but you're right, there's nothing yet."

"Okay," said Henderson with a more matter-of-fact tone than Jane expected, "Additionally, these guys spotted a love nest or some such thing in the guest house behind Schmidt's and they also caught a rumored tryst or something between old Schmidt and Sally Webb. We'll be aware of this and note anything that relates to it, but for now anyway, this angle is not our main investigation. For one thing, Schmidt was older than creation and that argues against this sort of thing. The fact that the guest house is in plain view of both Schmidt's house and Webb's means that love triangle motives for murder seem unlikely. Plus, you don't call Washington over a jealous husband or wife. So this angle is plan 'B.' Due diligence means we'll check it, but it's not our first focus right now."

Henderson went on, "We can't use silence from Washington as an excuse. We go ahead and solve this. I mean to talk to Mrs. Schmidt again and probe the past. I'll ask if she has a voice tape of Schmidt to compare his voice to the Washington tape I want from you guys. I'll get some handwriting too, maybe Schmidt wrote the note himself. Like I said, I want your tape to ask her to confirm his voice. I'll probe for suspicions about the guest house and Webb, but only gently. Okay, next meeting here in two days at ten AM unless something comes up first. The stuff I just mentioned; do it guys. Action! Action! Let's get it done and someone arrested."

Everybody started out but Jane beckoned to Smith and Mill to stay.

Jane said, "I'm with Henderson. I say the neighbor liaison thing is just background noise. Look, I went into that secret room and I think the files in there are pertinent. I think Schmidt, or whatever is name is, was guarding them. They're old and yellowed, but they look like lists of names and financial records, but nothing's in English. I don't even think it's all German. I think the files are the key. If this is National Security maybe we should impound them or something."

"Grab them out from under the noses of the local cops on a murder investigation?" Smith said, "I wouldn't even want to ask legal about that one."

Jane went on, "I phoned Dorsey and told him what I thought. I asked that he requested urgent action from the White House. We need to know what we're doing! Dorsey may or may not send a truck to impound the stuff, we'll see. So what did you see Smith?"

"Well, first off, I'm pissed! You guys held out on me. I wanted to see that hot little apartment and you guys didn't call me."

"Typical male," said Jane.

"Okay, okay, the guy I saw at the morgue is probably the guy I dragged out of the east alright. It's been a while, but I think it's him. No surprise there. And the cops are right so far. We don't know if Schmidt was standing or sitting, but I say probably standing, 'cuz he kinda fell back more than he would have if he fell out of the chair. Also the straight bullet trajectory argues for standing because seated, the trajectory would be down a little and maybe from the side a little because of that big table. So I'd say it argues against someone he knew well or even those kids. An old German man would not stand up for kids. Maybe he'd stand for a lady or maybe a stranger or intruder. I like the idea of some lady he knew because he didn't even pick up his gun. I say a lady. Not the kids. The secret meeting in the kitchen is a wild card. I have to think about that. That's my take so far anyway."

"Mill?"

"Well, the killer left by either the entry door or the kitchen door, flip a coin, I can't tell. The fact that the entry door's knob is cleaned of prints argues for that way, but the killer might have come in that way and out the other. Anyway, it looks like it was cleaned on purpose. But that may be meaningless. The maid could'a cleaned it five years ago and nobody's touched it since. The door's always left open so nobody would.

"Mrs. Schmidt says she came in that way to check on Schmidt, still no prints. That's odd. But that Mrs. Schmidt didn't leave a print is still possible. People don't always leave prints, especially dried up old people with no oil in their skin anymore. But I think maybe she knows something she's not saying. Maybe. Make that a strong maybe.

"Killer got in or out the windows? No way, too high up. Back to the entry door, if you latch it and hold the latch with a credit card or something as you close it, you can get out and leave it locked. Or if you have the key of course. The kitchen door will lock itself too, but it takes a little care when closing it. The killer is someone who has been in the place before, knows the place and planned what he did. That's not the students.

"The hidden room had not been entered before the cops got in and they just peeked. There's way too much old dust on everything in there. The footprints on the floor were an easy read. You nearly screwed up the foot-prints though Jane. I didn't see any secret passages, but another look wouldn't hurt, I mean we have a secret room, so why not a secret passage? Anyway, maybe I'm with Jane. Schmidt was guarding those papers. If so, it means Schmidt thought somebody else knew where they were. So Mr. Bad Guy, or Bad Lady, came in looking for them or something hidden in them, and then plugged Schmidt. But the killer didn't actually go in the secret room.

"Anyway, my conclusion is we're looking for someone who's been in the house and knows his way around. Not someone new. I also would take a flier that Mrs. Schmidt knows or suspects something she's holding back."

Jane said, "Okay, but if Mr. Bad Guy from the past has been around all along, Schmidt wouldn't have made the emergency call. Maybe the new Mr. Bad Guy has a local accomplice who knows the house and doors. The new Mr. Bad Guy was probably at the party. That says maybe this Dr. Shaw guy or maybe the kids or maybe even some other German speaker recognized somebody and tipped Schmidt with that mysterious note. More than one shooter? A Mr. Bad Guy and an outsider? Would that make sense?"

Mill said, "Yes, that would make plenty of sense. An accomplice, that's pretty unusual in real murder cases, but it could fit and explain plenty here. I like it Jane. Two shooters, one's local and knows the house, the other's the person that alarmed Schmidt and made him phone for help. It fits."

Smith said, "I say you guys get on the phone and chase Dorsey to get the dirt before Henderson blows a fuse. Definitely get something, anything to Henderson before he cuts us off. We need to know what he's doing. I told him my story at the morgue, but it didn't make him happy. We need to toss him something more to stay in the game, and I don't have any more. Anyway, I want to see the old lady before Henderson pounces on her and alone would be better. If it's the same lady I dragged out of the Russian zone, and I bet it is, she'll remember me. I bet I can learn a bunch from her. It looks like a car rental place down the block. I'll rent a car. Mrs. Schmidt should be home by now, so I'll go over to the house. We'll all share the car later."

Jane paused. "Okay Smith, I don't have any better plan. Let's do it."

Smith said, "I was thinking, that office where I picked Schmidt up back when. It had file cabinets everywhere. Old wood file cabinets. It's a long time ago, but I remember that part. I wonder if it's the same stuff that's is in those files. But I have no idea how the stuff could get from the Russian zone in 1946 to here now. I sure didn't move it."

Just as Smith started out, Henderson reappeared and beckoned to Jane. "Some lawyer just called. Moore's his name. I don't know him. He said he does work for the school and McIntyre asked him to talk to the German kids. The guy said he wants to meet with me after lunch, the day after tomorrow to review some things they didn't say earlier, whatever that means. He told the kids not to say anything more to us for now. He says after we meet, he'll probably endorse a complete re-interview with the kids. I asked for an earlier meeting, but he said he needs to call the German consulate and a bunch of other stuff first. I made noises about picking the kids up at any time, but he wouldn't budge. Actually, my read is he's okay. I think McIntyre caught him flat footed and he's going strictly by the book till he figures out what's up. I imagine you'll want to be at his meeting."

"Thanks," said Jane, "We were afraid you guys were getting impatient."

"I am impatient, and I'm serious. I want you to twist arms and get us something and do it soon. And oh yes, about your love nest, don't get me wrong, I don't pooh-pooh it. People are always getting murdered over women. I'm not forgetting it, but Schmidt was really old and he didn't call you guys in Washington because of a jealous husband. So get me Schmidt's past! That's number one. That's the key. Do it!"

Jane felt Henderson had gotten past his frustration and although blunt, he was almost friendly now. She decided to call Dorsey one more time and e-mail him again too. "Agreed, I'll call again." she said. Through the window, Jane saw Smith hurrying away. He had his cell phone to his ear.

The Second Murder Scene

"Death is the solution to all problems. No man – no problem."

Joseph Stalin

The Kingswood Inn was so close to the police station that they could have walked, but Henderson took Mill and Paine in his car anyway. It was in the ritzy part of town, but the Kingswood itself was old and tired. Henderson said that in Detroit's auto boom days, The Kingswood was a terrific bar and restaurant in a great old country style building. Top auto execs used to hang out at the bar where many an important auto company decision was made. He said that about 1960, the Kingswood moved a block south and added hotel rooms. After that, it was never the same place. Now it felt more like just an overblown, past its prime, overpriced roadside motel.

Jane left a message at the desk for Smith to call when he checked in, then Jane found her room. It was on a lower level that felt like a basement. In fact it really was half below ground. The window looked out on the tires of parked cars. Dorsey didn't answer his cell so she left him a message asking for extremely urgent handling of the request for the secret information. Then she met Mill in the restaurant for an early meal. The restaurant announced itself as a seafood place. But when one is from the east coast where good seafood is really fresh, the midwestern version just does not measure up. Jane thought about steak but then ordered 'Whitefish Marquette.' Whitefish was, she thought, a fresh water fish, so Jane hoped it had a better chance of being good here in Michigan. 'Whitefish Marquette' turned out to be fish with mushrooms, truffles, celery in some kind of lobster-wine sauce. The meal was expensive and the whitefish was good, she had guessed right on that, but there was too little fish and too much Marquette. Mill had almond salmon and he said it was good too. Then Mill walked Jane to her room and followed her in. Jane was amused to notice that Mill made a point of leaving the room's door wide open. Mill sat in the single chair, talking more about the money trail he had been chasing in Washington than the murder case. Jane slouched on the bed studying a truly awful art print on the wall. The print was an old mill with an out-of-round waterwheel. Next to it was another print; this one was modern art drip style. She wondered who on earth would have chosen these prints and who had put both in the same room.

"Mill, who was General Tso?"

"Umm, you mean Sun Tzu or General Zuo? Sun Tzu, dates way back, like 600 BC or something. He's a mythical figure who probably didn't really exist at all. He was kind of a Chinese King Arthur. His book, 'The Art of War,' is advertised like it's really old. But the book is really a 1970's compilation of a few third hand fragments and plenty of new writing. Only bits of it have much of a provenance at all and none of it within a thousand years of when he's supposed to have lived. People are always quoting the book. Personally, if I wanted to study war, I would want to read books by real generals who won real wars. The other guy, General Zuo, let's see here, he was a 19th century Chinese military leader, a bloody son of a bitch. He was on the winning side in the Taiping Rebellion. The Taiping Rebellion was a hell of a bloody affair in the 1850's. Millions killed, a real horror show. He's the same Zuo was also in the war that first lost Viet Nam to the French. Why do you ask?"

"General Tso Chicken."

"Oh, that stuff, that'd be General Zuo, but the stuff was invented in New York in about 1975. Chinese carry-out places like it because it's cheap and easy to make and they think it lasts forever under warming lights. It doesn't. The chicken gets hard and breaks tines on those stupid plastic forks. Anyway, I get the hint. Good Night Jane." Mill closed the door as he left. Smith still hadn't been heard from.

Jane thought this trip was going to take longer than expected and she had only packed one change. She wondered about calling a cab and finding some late night place, a Walmart or something, to get more cheap stuff to get by. But instead, she checked e-mail on the extra-small laptop that fit in her overnight bag. The real estate man said her Mom's little house had been shown. Then she watched some news headlines on the television. She knew Mill would be up and ready to go by five so she went to bed.

Her rest was short. The room phone rang. "Paine, we have big trouble," it was Henderson's voice, "I'm afraid it's Smith. He's been shot. Found by campus police at Colebrook."

Jane was half asleep but adrenaline and a sinking feeling woke her up. "He's okay, right?"

A pause, "No."

"What is it?"

"It's bad. Colebrook campus police think he's dead. "

Jane felt sick. She tried to clear her head for a second.

"Come and get us."

"He was found by campus police at Colebrook. I'll pick you up."

Jane paused to let her head clear a little more and think. She needed to dress, call Dorsey and Mill, Mill first so he can dress. "We'll be in front in five minutes. I have to call Washington."

Jane had no idea what Mill's room number was and the front desk didn't answer for what seemed like hours. She thought, 'Jeez, they just connected Henderson with me, where'd they go?' Then keeping the room phone to one ear she found the outside number on a brochure and dialed that on her cell .. busy .. as the phone rang and rang Jane fumbled, she had Dorsey's cell number on her cell somewhere .. finally, "Guest service, how can I help."

"This is an emergency, John Mill's room. Emergency!"

Long pause, "We have no Mills. Could it me Milt?"

"It's John Mill, no 's', he checked in with me, try what you have as Milt."

"John, yes, sorry, one moment."

More interminable ringing, "Umm, hello."

"Mill, Smith was just shot, meet me in front as fast as you can, in front of the lobby I mean, that's where Henderson is picking us up."

Jane did not wait for a reply, she hung up and dialed Dorsey on her cell phone. She got voice mail again. "Jim, they're shooting up the town, Smith was just shot. We don't know a thing yet. The cops are coming to get us right now." Then Jane yelled, "Get me what we're dealing with! Get whatever the White House is hiding. We're getting blind-sided and we're getting shot. Hurry!"

Mill was already in front of the Kingswood when Jane got there. He had a big black flashlight in his hand. Jane wondered where he got that thing. Mill had everything.

"Where did you say they were?"

"I don't know, at Colebrook, the school, Henderson's taking us there, he said he's picking us up."

The two stood under the roof of the oversized drive-through entrance. Looking into the dark and rain, nearby street lights seemed like glowing fuzz-balls. Except for vague rain noise, it was quiet. Then tire noise could be heard, a car with glowing headlights curved in from the road. It was a marked police car and it was being driven fast. It made splashing noises as it came. It stopped in front of them.

An man rolled down a window, "Paine and Mill?"

"Yes."

"Hop in."

Before Jane could move, Mill jumped in back, behind some kind of wire barrier. Jane got in front. The car moved even as Jane was closing the door. At least inside the car, it was warm. Jane noticed that the driver was in coat and tie and he was not Henderson. "Name's Marino, I was at the meeting this afternoon. This looks like bad stuff. Henderson's already there."

Less than a mile down the road the car turned onto a divided drive with a strip of grass and a few trees in the middle. Marino slowed as it approached a guard shack. He turned the red and blue flashers on. The light fog made the colors visible from inside the car. A gate went up. A window in the guard shack cracked opened and a man's hand poked out and waved them through. Then the window shut. Marino turned the flashers off. Now the headlights showed a very big lawn and the drive curved gracefully through it. After some distance, the drive ran down a hill and then became a narrow, curbed street. It ran over a small, narrow bridge and between brick buildings that seemed to be built too close to the street. The officer turned right at a corner that Jane thought was both blind and tight.

Finally, Marino said, "He's in front of the art museum." His tone suggested that he thought Jane and Mill knew where that was. A left turn complete with squeaking tire noise took them past a small wooded area, past a parking lot and finally to a drive around a big pool or goldfish pond. The car stopped short. "Henderson said he's on the steps." There was a very wide stairway that started by the circular drive. At the top, lighted statues of naked ladies and men stood in some sort of fountain. In the misty air, the lights formed ghostly halos around the statues. Behind the statues was a nineteen-thirties modern building. Apparently, this was the art museum. On the steps, a man was setting up what looked like a floodlights on tripods. Jane thought there was lightning for a moment, then, she realized that a photographer was taking flash pictures.

Henderson must have been waiting for them because he was there and talking as Jane opened the car's door. "I feel awful, I'm too upset to think right." Henderson was wringing his hands. Jane had never seen anybody really wring their hands from anxiety before. She thought that was only in movies. "Oh man, what a situation. He's over there, you can look, but don't touch anything yet. We're just starting. Be careful where you step, don't kick stuff around." Henderson walked with Jane and Mill. "The campus police spotted him an hour ago on a regular walk around. The campus police are mostly volunteers, parents of students and some other neighbors and stuff. Usually two or three of them walk together. But this time it was just one guy. He's in the car over there."

Jane watched Mill walk ahead very slowly scanning the ground with his flashlight as he went. Then the photographer held his hand out to signal Mill to stop. After a couple more flashes he said "Okay."

Mill examined the first step with his light. "This footprint is headed away, you saw this?"

Henderson said, "We think it's the campus cop who spotted the body. He says he crossed the grass was half way up the steps when he saw. Then he turned ran back down two steps at a time. The muddy footprints agree with what he said. It's been raining so if there were any earlier footprints, we can't find them."

Mill nodded and started slowly up the steps again leaning low and very carefully scanning each step with his light. Mill passed Smith's body and kept climbing, then near the top he knelt down. Then he called out, "Did you guys spot this?"

"Not yet, what is it?"

"Bullet." Mill pulled the magnifying glass from his pocket with his free hand. He looked at the bullet very closely without touching it, then he said. "Maybe a thirty-two? It's kinda smooshed over. It's hard to tell. Bigger than a twenty-two, smaller than a thirty-eight. Looks like a thirty-two." Mill resumed his flashlight sweep. "Here's another one."

There was the sound of a generator starting and then floodlights flickered on.

Mill abruptly put the flashlight away and turned back toward the Smith's body. Smith almost looked like he was taking a rest. He was half seated and half slumped back and to one side a bit. Beside him was a Smith and Wesson thirty-eight revolver.

Mill looked carefully at the gun but did not touch it. "Looks like all five rounds were fired. Looks like he got all five shots off then sat down after he was hit. Or maybe he sat and fired while seated. The old guys used to like to fire from a seated position. That's what they used to teach."

Mill wiped rain off his magnifying glass with something out of his pocket and started examining Smith's body. But the main thing to Jane's eye was the amount of blood. There was a lot of blood. The rain might have made it look like even more, but there was an impressive amount anyway.

A truck arrived. It was the State Police Mobile Forensic unit. Henderson told Jane, "I'll be back in a minute."

The photographer resumed shooting, apparently to take advantage of the new lighting.

Mill got out of the photographer's way. He walked back to Jane. "Help me remember, a thirty-two's the same as a seven point six-five millimeter right? I think it's the round that Hitler used to kill himself. Maybe Archduke Ferdinand got it from a seven-six-five too, but those Browning FNs came in different calibers. Hitler was a Walther PP. That was seven-six-five for sure. Seven-six-five -thirty two - same thing .. "

"Guns that killed Archduke Ferdinand and Hitler? Mill, one of our guys was just murdered. I'm not sure I want a history lesson right now. What's with you?"

"Well, both were automatics. Smith and Wesson made a thirty-two automatic too. The point is, those are all automatics and automatics eject brass when you fire them. But I haven't seen any brass. There wasn't any brass at Schmidt's house either. Revolvers don't eject brass. Not many revolvers are thirty-two's. Starter guns for races are revolvers and they are usually thirty-two's but they'll only for blanks. Wild Bill Hickok used thirty-two revolvers, but those were cap and ball antiques. But there's an odd-ball revolver I think. It's a slightly different round, but still it's a thirty-two. Now help me remember, an odd-ball Russian revolver that has some really weird spring action that locks the wheel in place and keeps it very quiet. I mean when there's a silencer it's real, quiet. Real, real quiet. And it's a thirty-two or a seven point six-five millimeter which is the same thing. I think it was the gun that the Bolsheviks used to murder Czar Nicholas and his family."

Jane said, "I have no idea what you're talking about. Are you onto something? I mean this trip just got really serious. You're talking about Wild Bill Hickok. Smith is dead. Are you onto something or are you just being totally weird?"

"A Nagant I think. Umm, made in Belgium for the Czar at first, then Russia started making them too. Russia made a ka-jillion of 'em over the years. They're

100

real weird, the part that turns also moves forward and back so the wheel can seal up tight to the barrel for each shot. That's why it's as quiet as a pin if it has a silencer. No gas escapes between the wheel and the barrel. Action's complicated as hell."

"Mill, you know that? You know about Czarist pistols? Someone's shooting up the country side with a Czarist revolver? When was the last Czar? C'mon."

"They're actually common and cheap, Russians made 'em forever, all the way through both wars, even after. When the Soviet bloc broke up, floods of then came here as surplus. You can still buy 'em cheap. The silencer's illegal in most states, but it works like crazy because of the tight barrel seal. It'll fire thirty-two, but there's also a round that's special made for it that has a weird expanding neck that adds even more to the seal and makes it dead quiet."

"Okay, okay, I'm starting to buy it. Real quiet huh? And nobody heard anything when Schmidt got shot at the house."

"Kinda underpowered too. That could explain Schmidt's smaller wound."

"I buy it too." It was Henderson's voice. "You're right, the quiet gun is a Nagant. One of our guys brought one to the range. With a silencer, you can't even tell when it goes off, it just goes 'click' like it's not even loaded. Just 'click.' I say a Nagant with a silencer was the weapon both here and at the house. I'll bet forensics can confirm it from those bullets."

"Henderson," said Mill, "It's raining and that makes the blood run all over the place. But does this all look like it came from Smith? It's running all over the place but could that area over there be where Smith nailed his assailant? I say have the forensics guys take lots of samples. "

Henderson nodded, "They'd do that anyway, but I'll get them going before this rain screws everything up. Plus I'll tip them to look for brass. If there isn't any, it'll support your Nagant theory."

Then Jane said, "Mill, let's think. Smith said he was going to see the old lady, Mrs. Schmidt, but he turns up here instead. Did Smith know something? Was he kidding us, hiding something he suspected or knew? Was he holding out? He seemed to leave the cop shop in an awful big hurry. Or maybe he learned something from Mrs. Schmidt? Or maybe she led him here on some pretense and shot him with an antique revolver. Is she the common denominator? Maybe she was mad at the old man and shot him too. But if they drove here together how did she get home? I assume that's Smith's rental car over there. We need to confirm that. Or here's another theory; The new students are the secret agents, he went to the school to confront them but they're shooting up the town. But an antique gun? I say not the style of kids."

Mill said, "I go for a new theory, we haven't got the foggiest idea. We're clueless. So for starters, let's find out if Smith really rented a car and let's find out if that's it. The cops should be able to trace the plate to a rental outfit right now."

Jane said, "I agree with your theory. We're clueless. We need more info. Did Smith see the old lady? We need to know that. And I wonder if the cops have talked to the guy at the guard shack? Did he see any comings and goings?"

Mill said, "My flying guess on what little I see here is Smith was here to meet someone, but that someone started shooting. I'd guess he took a hit or two then returned fire and emptied his gun doing it. I bet he hit the assailant but he was nailed too many times to walk away. I'm just guessing, but that's my read on what I see. But why? Was he holding out on us about something he knew for some reason? The old lady told him something? So far, I dunno."

Jane said, "Yesterday we said the stuff in the hidden room was the key. I want to look at more it closely. But Mill, I think that's more your kind of thing. Plus, let's talk to the old lady and confirm that Smith saw her. So step one, as soon as it's morning, let's go to the old lady's house. Here's another thing, this will bring out every cop in the state plus half the FBI plus every news reporter for a hundred miles around. We need to move fast before they muddy everything up. Hey, wait a minute, if that's Smith's rental car over there, let's get the mileage right now. Like you said, if they haven't already, let's have the cops run the plate right now and find out. The rental company should know what the mileage was when Smith took the car. I'll see if the forensics guys will dust it first then we can look. Smith had a cell phone, remember, he was calling someone, let's get that as soon as the cops will let us and see who he called, maybe he made more calls. Mill, what else should we look at here?"

"We'll need the key to that car to make the odometer light up and if it's the right car, the key'll be in Smith's pocket. Rental papers'll probably be on the front seat or in the glove box. If Henderson will approve our fishing in Smith's pockets, let's find his cell and see who he called and when."

Henderson said, "I'm still right here listening to you guys, and nah, don't do it. But I'll have the forensics guys take keys and cell phone to the van right now for prints and stuff. I'll give you your answers in a few minutes. In fact, you guys come into the van, at least it's not raining in there and it'll be easier for me to eavesdrop on you."

Then Jane looked toward Smith's body and back. "Mill, did you bring your gun? I'm scared."

"Yes .. and yes, scared makes perfect sense."

A Betty Boop voice said "Poop-boo-be-doop-squeek!' Jane pulled her cell phone out; "Paine here, just a minute, I'm putting you on speaker phone, we're at the scene and you're talking to Mill and State Police Lieutenant Henderson. It's Dorsey, our boss."

Dorsey's voice was strained, "What the hell's going on? Give me the rundown."

Mill spoke, "We last saw Smith this afternoon at a cop-shop meeting. After the meeting Smith figured Mrs. Schmidt might remember him and maybe give him something to go on. So he rented a car and headed out to see her. Smith was just found shot full of holes, not at Schmidt's house, but at the local school, shot dead on the steps to the school's art museum. That's where we are now. We're going to check Smith's cell phone to see who he called and stuff. We'll e-mail you a summary when there's something to summarize. We're just starting."

"Yeah, I spoke to Smith by cell phone right after your meeting at the police station. He was headed for the old lady's house. Shit! Let me think for a minute. I should come out myself. This is going to be a mess. Go ahead with what you're doing.

103

I'll need to round up more resources. Controlling the fall-out of this thing is going to be a political mess."

Henderson spoke, "Dorsey! This is Henderson, State Police. We really need your secret scoop from the past. We very seriously need to know what this is all about. Two people have been shot and one of 'em is yours. Not good buddy! Get me these damn secrets and I'm not kidding!"

Long pause … "Understood. Understood. Springing anything is probably going to involve either the Secretary of State himself or the Attorney General or both. So far, either they can't find anything or it's so hot they won't tell me squat. So maybe I should be in Washington after all. But your message is received. Shit, I should be in D.C. and pound out the politics and get whatever it is. Crap, what a situation!"

Mill was unfolding a note, "Here's the number that Schmidt called before he was blown away. Can you confirm this is the emergency number you told us about?" He read a number.

"That's the number who called?"

"Schmidt, just before he was shot. The emergency number you told us about. Need to confirm it."

"Hang till I get a pen .. okay number again?"

A minute later, inside the forensics van, it was, at least, dry. Henderson asked forensics that Smith's cell phone be inspected right away and that they get millage information from the car. Then, Jane Paine and Mill mostly tried to stay out of the way in the bustling space. The rain got harder and made noise on the metal roof. There was a flash of light in the windows that might have been the photographer's flash again, but this time, a boom of thunder confirmed that it was not.

Tesler's Story

"One man's death is a tragedy, a million men's deaths is a statistic."

Joseph Stalin

Natalie Schmidt sat in an Adirondack chair on the porch in front of the big, discordant house. Her favorite knit blanket was on her lap. The shadow of the house was on the drive and lawn before her. Birds sang in the clear, chilly morning. Years ago, this was a favorite spot but Natalie Schmidt had not sat here for a long time. Natalie was starting to feel chilled and thought of going in, but instead, she just pulled her blanket up and over her shoulders. She sat reflecting. What now? What about this great big house? The students, if they stayed at all, might help out for now, but then what? Time passed, and then she heard voices.

"Good morning Mrs. Schmidt. Isn't it nice this morning?" It was Val Tesler speaking. Clyde Webb and Sally were there too.

Sally carried a big picnic basket. "I have a coffeecake. And we have coffee and hot water for tea in these thermoses. May we join you?" Clyde Webb carried a cooler. Val Tesler had three thermoses.

"How nice to see you. What a nice surprise to see all of you. And you have brought your own party!"

Sally said, "Let's sit right here on the porch, or is the shade too chilly for you?"

Natalie thought it was chilly, but she said, "Oh, this old knit thing keeps me warm enough. Let's stay."

In a moment Sally Webb had spread a small table cloth on one of the rustic tables and cut coffeecake onto paper plates, each with a brightly colored plastic fork. She even produced a small vase with a flower.

"Oh, how sweet of you," said Natalie, "Even a flower, how elegant. What a nice party. I was just thinking my way into a funk about, well, about everything. I was afraid of what I must do today, make arrangements you know, and I was thinking about the future. I did not sleep well. This is very thoughtful and it's just the right medicine. It will make things easier."

Sally said, "I wish you had come to our house when I asked you last night. I hated to think of you alone. But I want to help out today. We'd all like to stay and be with you today, and I'll help make arrangements about Günter. "

"So many people are so helpful. At times like this, you find you have friends. Mrs. Hubchic drove all the way from Grosse Pointe, and the Feines were so nice to me yesterday, and here you all are today. One learns we are not alone. Yes we do. Bubbie Feine, what's her name? Selde? Selda was funny yesterday. She wanted to talk about the old days before either of us came here. Those days were not so nice for either of us. It was funny that she thought of that yesterday. "

Dr. Tesler said, "Oh, I imagine there are some real stories in this neighborhood. My own father had some. Stalin's boys sent him for a Siberian vacation. After they let him come back, his tales were really something. Solzhenitsyn talked about all that. Stalin killed maybe ten million in the Gulag, but my father came home."

Ally poured coffee and put pieces of coffee cake on paper plates.

"My Dad had been in charge of a Penicillin factory. Not much more than a laboratory really, and Stalin wanted production doubled every month. Penicillin was new then. But that rate of increase was impossible, so he was sent to the Gulag. Then, two or three others got his job and, of course, they did no better. In fact the bad products that they rushed out killed about as many people as they helped. So they brought my father back home and gave him his old job again and they sent the other guys to the Gulag instead." Tesler chuckled.

Clyde Webb said, "I thought Solzhenitsyn put the number Stalin killed over seventy million."

"Oh, that's probably for all of Stalin's handy-work, the purges; Ukraine, Poland, German relocation, exterminating Trotsky's boys, the Gulag were only part of it.

Seventy million would be no exaggeration for all of Stalin's work. But for the Gulag alone, that'd be way high. Today, we'd give Stalin's marks for diversity. He'd murder anyone. He had no qualms about killing Poles, Lithuanians and Estonians, Ukrainians, you name it, and after the war, of all things, Jewish doctors, plus anyone, anywhere who so much as spoke German."

Clyde Webb said, "Yes, my family knows a little about that German part. My Dad had a story too. Say Doc, I read 'The Gulag Archipelago' when it was new. It was long, but it was good."

Natalie said, "We were not fans of Stalin when I was younger. I guess we didn't need a book to know."

Tesler said, "The Communist system needed fear and terror to exist. That's what Communism thrives on."

Natalie said, "That's true."

"It was a good book. But I do not think Solzhenitsyn's gallows humor and irony comes through in English. Natalie, do you read Russian?"

"Well, no. I understand a little bit but those Cyrillic letters throw me."

Val Tesler said, "In Russian, Solzhenitsyn is spooky and it's close to poetry. The man chose his words well. It doesn't come through in English though. I thought of trying to translate it myself once. I wanted to try to get the black feel of it across. I started, but about a page and half in, I realized I have no gift for that kind of thing." Tesler took a piece of coffeecake. "Stalin kept records of the Gulag, but they were all destroyed at the last minute just as the Soviet Union fell, so we'll never know how many died. Solzhenitsyn's book was almost lost too. What was the name of the lady they tortured to find the manuscript? She killed herself after she spilled the beans, but there turned out to be two more copies."

"Your father went to the Gulag?" Natalie said, "Bubbie Feine was in a concentration camp, it's odd how we have been neighbors so long but we only talk of this now."

"Yes, he was there almost six years. They took him before I can remember, but I sure remember his coming back. That was an adjustment for my mother. After he was rehabilitated, that's what they called it when they fix your record, we were given a new house, things were good then. As for me, I was sent school to be a chemist. That part got me into medical school here."

Tesler paused and looked thoughtful, "My father called the experience and the place, umm, it translates to, umm, 'meat grinder.' I think that was the common name for it really. Stalin liked to have your wife arrested and let you worry for a while, then they'd arrest you in the middle of the night and brutally interrogate you, make you stand on your feet for twenty-four hours or just beat the daylights out of you and say your family was in trouble and tell you they had arrested you daughter and put her in a cell with ten syphilitic male felons or even sometimes they'd have you interrogated by a naked woman! I guess that one usually worked, ha, ha, ha! Many confessions to political crimes were made to naked women! Leave it to Stalin.

"They seldom bothered with trials unless Stalin wanted a show. They just shipped you in an unheated cattle-car to a camp in the arctic parts of Siberia, or a camp building a dam or a railroad. Your clothes and all your stuff was taken and you entered the work camp naked. The idea was forced labor, but it was really just brutality and starvation. There were too many prisoners for the amount of work so losing a few didn't matter. They didn't care about that. You only survived by your wits and by cheating others. My father was educated and so he got engineering work on a rail-line. So I guess he had it a little better than some. But cooperating with the authorities and living a little better was risky. Inside the Gulag there were always murders, tit-for-tat murders and violence against sukas. In that context, 'suka' means those who cooperated with the authorities. During World War II, Stalin promised to pardon all the prisoners he sent to be in the army. After the war, no surprise, he reneged on his promise and sent them all back to the Gulag. There they were called stukas and got the worst jobs or got murdered. You had to pick your friends with care inside that system. Murdering one another was a popular pastime.

"What was that guy's name? Umm .. Naftaly Frenkel .. what a sweet man he was! He was still around when my Dad was there. Frenkel was in the Gulag for smuggling when he cooked up the idea that you should be only be fed if you put out enough work. He sold the idea to the camp commandant. So there got to be a work quota and if you couldn't keep up, or you got sick, you just died of starvation. This great idea got Frenkel put in charge at the camp. He had incoming prisoners grouped as fit for hard work or fit for light work. You better hope you were fit for hard work, because light work didn't get you enough food to live. Even then, any day you were only fed after you made that day's quota. His ideas sure got work done though. Nice sweet guy! Ha, ha. Stalin was so impressed he promoted Frenkel and put him in charge of all railroad construction. Frenkel did great because his labor was free and the other railroad building guys had to pay workers, if call you that kind of thing competing in Soviet Russia. Frenkel was still around and my father met him. Anyway, my Dad survived in okay shape. Probably because he was an engineer and Frenkel and his boys needed engineers. Still, it makes me angry thinking about all that. And get this, that Frenkel turkey was from Palestine and he was Jewish. How do you figure that? A Jewish Palestinian?

"But how did I get on that story? Natalie, let's talk and see what we can all do about your plans."

McIntyre's Office

We dance round in a ring and suppose, but the secret sits in the middle and knows.

Robert Frost

Jane and Mill had gotten back to their hotel rooms at four in the morning. Jane's room phone rang at seven thirty and it was Mill. "The rental car office opened at seven. I have a car. Do you need breakfast? I'll meet you in the hotel restaurant or we can fast food it."

Jane wondered if agreeing to fast food would buy her fifteen more minutes of sleep, but she said, "Hotel restaurant, give me twenty minutes." Then Jane quickly showered and put on her only change of clothes.

Jane knew from experience that hotel restaurants are slow at breakfast time. That always seemed odd to Jane. The 'necktie convention' men, that is to say the businessmen wearing business suits who frequent hotels on weekdays, were always in a big rush. If she ran a hotel she thought she would put on extra staff and have very fast breakfast service. That, she imagined, might attract more of those high paying business customers. At any rate, Jane suggested to Mill that the buffet might save time. So they talked over lukewarm hotel breakfast fare gotten from cafeteria style steam trays.

Mill thought it would be bad form to get to Schmidt's looking for Natalie before she was even up. Then he said, "The hotel has computers and internet in the library room. I found an old write-up on Schmidt and I found a few news articles about a financial gift for a big addition to the art museum I guess we saw last night. We probably passed the school's dean, a guy named McIntyre's office, on the way in last night. It's here on this map. Remember, Henderson said McIntyre was at the party and he's the guy who came by yesterday and picked up the Hoffman kids. I found some other stuff too. It's not much to work with really, but I printed anything that seemed even slightly interesting. So let's be efficient and detour by McIntyre's office before we go to see Natalie Schmidt."

"Christ Grindstone, the library room? You must not sleep at all." But Smith's murder, she knew, demanded urgent action and Mill had been on the ball while she slept. So Jane added, "Are you okay?"

"I got a couple hours sleep, I'm okay."

Jane looked at Mill's papers. He was right. There wasn't much to go on. But a fat gift for an art museum addition meant money. Maybe that meant something. Schmidt's curriculum vitae said that he was educated in Europe. Apparently the forged diplomas Smith had made had flown all these years. Nobody had ever checked. And it said Schmidt was advanced to acting department head in 1960 when the regular head had a heart attack. The position was made permanent in 1961. That, Jane thought, meant Schmidt was a competent, or at least a politically astute administrator. Mill was right, the key to the murders did not jump from these papers.

Jane's hunch about the buffet was right. They were on their way before others had even been served.

The way to McIntyre's office was past the same guard shack as the night before, but now the gate was up and the guard seemed to be reading a newspaper. Cars drove through without even slowing. There was the same long winding drive through what must have been twenty acres of mowed grass, then, at the place where older buildings were so close to the road, Mill made a tight turn into a narrow drive between them. The alley was so narrow that Jane wondered how anyone could get out if the car stalled. Mill parked in a small lot behind the buildings.

Mill seemed to know exactly where he was going. He led Jane back through the narrow alley and to a door in the front of the building. Inside was a coat rack, a couple upholstered chairs, a table with what looked likes several copies of the school's newspaper and there was a desk with nobody sitting behind it. The desk was positioned so it seemed to guard a hall that presumably led to offices.

Jane was preparing to call out 'Hello!' when the door they came in opened and a rather mundane man of unclear age entered. The man looked around and then said, "Have you been helped?"

Mill said, "Mr. McIntyre?"

The man looked around again as if looking for the desk's captain, then, not seeing anybody, he said, "Yes, how can I help you?"

Jane said, "Mr. McIntyre, this is Mill and I am Paine. We are agents from the Department of Justice. May we come in?"

Jane held up a badge.

McIntyre looked at them in silence for a moment, then he said, "If this concerns the Hoffman students, I'm afraid you will need to see the attorney I have arranged for them. His name is Moore. I can provide his card."

Mill said, "Mr. McIntyre, this may or may not concern the Hoffmans, but it may concern you. If you would like to call an attorney, please do so at once. But the matter is urgent and we would like to talk now."

McIntyre frowned at Mill and Paine and remained silent. At this point, a middle-aged woman entered. She looked at the standoff and stopped in her tracks.

McIntyre turned his gaze away from Mill and Paine and toward the lady. "Miss Gordon, I think the meeting room is not booked this morning unless you put a class in there. As soon as you are settled, please print the latest version of the construction ledger, the one you set up on Excel, and join us with it."

"You two may come in. The books will show nothing of interest, but if you like, Miss Gordon can provide whatever documentation you require."

McIntyre led the way a couple doors down the hall to smallish meeting room with a very big Danish Modern table. The table was fat in the middle and tapered to narrow ends. It had chairs of matching style. The table was too big for the room. McIntyre made an undignified skipping crab-walk and squeezed between widest part of the table and the wall to get to the head of the table where he sat down. "Have a seat."

The backs of the chairs leaned generously backward. Jane sat in one and leaned back. That turned out to be much too far back, so she sat back up on the edge of the chair. She noticed McIntyre sat on the edge of his seat too.

McIntyre smiled, "Everyone does that on the first try. But hey, the chairs keep meetings short."

Mill sat straight at first, but hearing that he leaned back. "Huh, not bad! They'd work great in a bar after a few drinks." He sat back up again.

McIntyre smiled again, then he said, "We use what I call checkbook accounting here. When our construction manger tells us a construction benchmark is completed, we check the work out and take photographs of it and then sign off that the work is really done. Then we release payment. It's all done with a single bank account. When the consortium releases money to us, it goes in the same account. It's a simple system and eliminates any co-mingling of funds with anything else. You will find everything in order. Nobody has his hand in the till."

Mill said, "Mr. McIntyre, our interests may be a little different than exactly that."

McIntyre paused again. "Urgent? Is this about Schmidt? This is about Schmidt isn't it. The police have talked to me, I told them all I know about the demise of Dr. Schmidt which is just about nothing. You can just talk to them can't you? This really is a bit inconvenient right now."

Mill said, "Mr. McIntyre, there has been more than one violent act and we need to get up to speed on what this violence is all about. We need to do this quickly. It is rather urgent."

McIntyre sighed, "Violent? I thought Schmidt killed himself." He paused, "Well, okay, sure. Will I need a lawyer?"

"Are you guilty of anything?"

"Of course not."

Mill went on. "Then probably not. I presume that after Schmidt was found, the Hoffman students phoned you and asked for your help because you are dean here. Is that right?"

"Look, I'm not talking about the kids. The gift of an addition to the school's art museum came from a consortium and the head of that consortium is a Mr. Hoffman. Those kids, who I only suspect, but do not know to be his, applied for admission to our school and to make the story short, I personally met them at the airport and welcomed them. Naturally, when the tragedy came to light yesterday, they phoned me probably because I'm the only person they knew at all here,. That's how I won that little prize. I referred them to our attorney, Mr. Moore. That's about all I can say. For that matter, that's all I know. Now, because they were apparently at the house when the tragedy occurred, I think you should direct anything else to Moore. He advised them, and he advised me as well, not to talk to the police about any of this unless he is present. I feel the term, 'the police,' probably includes you guys. I will, however, be pleased to show you the financial records regarding that gift. That, I feel, is outside of anything directly concerning those students so I will offer that."

"Very well, I would like to look at that material." said Mill, "Stories in the press say this gift came from a consortium, a German consortium. This is hard to understand. Can you tell us about that?"

McIntyre hesitated, then, he spoke in a more stiff and formal, maybe defensive tone, "Considering the amount of money involved, they have been remarkably vague about who, exactly, they are."

Mill waited, but McIntyre remained silent.

"Can you give us their name at least? And a contact name and number?"

"I have the feeling I should consult our attorney."

"By all means, but perhaps you can give us their intentions in making this gift?"

"They support education and fine art."

Mill sat in silence for a moment but McIntyre said nothing. "Mr. McIntyre, do you suspect anything unethical is going on?"

"No."

Jane felt that some defusing of tension might help. "Mr. McIntyre, how on earth did they get this beautiful table into this room? I mean there's no way it'd fit through that door."

McIntyre took the bait at once, "Good question. I have a photo of this room from about 1955 and it's right here. It's my bet it was assembled right here in the room. Even at that, the top would have been a problem to get in, so it must have been joined right here. Either that, or the room was built around the table.

"The better question is how to get it back out. It's too big for this room and we have several places where it would be much more useful, but we would hate to cut the table up and try to re-glue it. We're actually thinking about shoring up the ceiling joists and temporarily removing part of the wall. The truth is, the repair of the wall would be easier than fixing the table. The punch line is, this table and the chairs were designed by Finn Juhl. The school actually commissioned the design. So they're way too valuable to risk cutting anything up to move out of here. Every year I throw five thousand dollars in the budget to temporarily remove a wall and get the table out of here, and then just at the last, it gets cut because something more important comes up. But one of these days we'll find a little money and get it out of here."

Mill spoke, "Finn Juhl? Holy cow. Jane, that's the guy who brought the Danish Modern trend to America right after World War Two. Juhl was doing furniture from what, the thirties or so and into the fifties or sixties? But this building must be older than that."

McIntyre, "I don't know how the table landed here. Schmidt was one of the last guys who might have known. We still have the paperwork. If I recall, it's from 1948. At least we know it's authentic. But why's it in this room? If it was meant for this room, somebody, sure blew the measurements. But I don't think you are here to take a class in furniture design.

"Look, I will admit that the whole affair of this gift has been so surprising and so casual that at times I have been ill-at-ease. It was not the normal way things happen. But as far as I can tell, it is all on the up and up. As far as giving you names and contacts and stuff, I am going to have to ask our attorney about all that. Public information is in our press releases. I'll ask Miss Gordon to supply copies of the press stuff for now. But I don't know if I'm at liberty to disclose competitive prices and all that. You could follow up on specifics after I talk to our attorney."

Mill said, "It has been my experience that when a reasonable adult is ill at ease about something, when his sixth sense says something is wrong, it usually turns out that something really is wrong. Just what has put you ill at ease?"

"Oh, not really ill-at-ease exactly, that's too strong. I miss-spoke. The gift and it's terms have been remarkably, remarkably unexpected, generous, and free of complication."

"Sir, there is more than one way for things to be wrong with easy money. Easy money sometimes implies something less than obvious is going on."

Miss Gordon entered the room and started McIntyre's funny crab walked beside the fat part of the table. McIntyre spoke. "Miss Gordon, these people, Mr. Mill and Miss Paine, are here from The Department of Justice and they are looking into what they characterize as 'some violent acts.' They seem interested in information about the gift of an addition to the art museum. Would you please advise Mr. Moore that they are here. Do that right away. Without Mr. Moore present, we will not discuss the Hoffman students at all, but we will open our books regarding the gift. I would also like you to supply the press packet to them, the big one we circulated last month."

Miss Gordon reversed her crab walk. Then she asked for business cards from Mill and Jane and then she left without giving McIntyre the manila folder she carried.

"Mr. McIntyre, how did you choose your contractors? Did the gift givers express a preference one way or the other?"

McIntyre said, "Oh, I see, you suspect a come-back or kick-back on money from contractors, or that they're laundering cash. No, I think not. Actually the gift giving consortium did not express anything about preferring one contractor or another. We used an architectural firm that we have used in the past to draw-up a bid package. That package included a plan and other requirements. It was approved by the consortium with no changes. Then we competitively bid the job. The same architect helped us evaluate the bids. There were three bids as I recall. The architect looked especially for loopholes in the bids that might lead to cost overruns and that sort of thing, and then a contract was awarded. We have also retained the same architectural firm to act as a construction manager."

Mill said, "Would you be so good as to ask Miss Gordon to supply me with the names of all of those firms and any subcontractors and so on? I would like to review that area if you don't mind. I would also like the same information about the gift giving consortium."

"Mr. Mill, I'll tell you what. I'm unclear on law here. I have no issue with your requests but I do not know what we are at liberty to disclose and what we are not. I'll ask Mr. Moore to advise me or better, be present at a future meeting. I'll call Mr. Moore, our attorney, and I'll ask how soon he can be present."

Jane asked, "Mr. McIntyre, did an investigator named Smith see you or call you yesterday or ask for an appointment?"

McIntyre looked surprised. "An investigator or agent named Smith? No, not any kind of investigator named Smith. One of the consortium men, a Mr. Smith, called and said he wanted to come out to take photographs of the building to confirm progress. That happens sometimes. But no investigator named Smith."

Mill said, "I very much expect the police will contact you soon. They will have similar questions. You might pass that along to Moore. Please understand that we are not the police, we are looking into a topic related to what they are doing, but not the same thing. Please excuse us if we are vague for now. But there is urgency and your help will be appreciated."

"I see."

Dr. Shaw's Office

No crooked leg, no bleared eye,
No part deformed out of kind,
Nor yet so ugly half can be
As is the inward suspicious mind.

Queen Elizabeth I - Written in her Psalter - 1554

The Doctor's office opened at seven and Mrs. Hubchic had the first appointment. Dr. Shaw's waiting room was typical. It was shared by three other Doctors. There were chairs, magazines, a counter where one wrote his name on a clipboard and then a lady behind the counter blotted the name out with a marker. Another lady in a blue lab-coat appeared. "Mrs. Hubchic .. Hubchic."

Mrs. Hubchic was directed to "Room four, on the left." The nurse, if she really was a nurse, took temperature and pulse and blood pressure, "Have you fasted this morning? We'll take a little blood sample now." Then the nurse stood with her clip board and asked in a cheery voice, "How are your bowel movements?"

Mrs. Hunchic wanted to say, 'Do you mean how are my bowel movements or do you mean how am I? As for me, I'm dried up and old! What do you think? Do you offer prune juice prescriptions here?' But instead of saying anything like that, she just said, "No problems." Why did that particular woman always ask that question? And why was she so cheery about the subject of bowel movements?

Then came the usual, "The doctor will be right with you." That usually meant a twenty-five minute wait.

Mrs. Hubchic considered a three year old Bride's Magazine, a Mechanic's Illustrated with part of the cover torn off and an Economist opened to a story about elephant DNA research. She opted instead for studying a chart of the human circulatory system that was on the wall.

But this time it really was only a minute and there was a knock at the door.

"Good morning, Mrs. Hubchick."

"Good morning, Doctor Shaw."

Shaw eyed a clipboard, then flipped a page, then looked up. "How are we feeling? Anything new? Any changes?

"As far as I know, things are fine, except, I'd like you to look at this little spot on my arm. It's not like these other brown spots. It's only been there a month or so and maybe I need to see a dermatologist and have it taken off."

"Okay, let's take a peek." Shaw looked and ran his fingers over an area. Then he produced a magnifier and looked again. "Yes, I think maybe we need to have someone look at that one. I'll have them give you a referral on the way out or better yet, there are a couple good dermatologists up one floor from here. Maybe you can just take the elevator up a floor and make an appointment. Sometimes you can even just walk in. Both of the Doctors up there are good. We need to check and see if it's a little beta cell carcinoma or something like that."

Mrs. Hubchic wondered why doctors and their staff always said 'we' and why everything was 'little.'

"They'll probably want to take a little sample and do a test. These usually don't amount to much but we should take care of them. If it's a carcinoma, they'll just sort-of scrape it away. Those usually come from our long term accumulation of sunlight, exposure over our life-time. They are not dangerous if we get right after them. But set an appointment. If we let these go for a long time, they can be trouble."

"Now let's see," he looked at the chart again, "Nothing has changed much. Your last blood test looks good all the way around. We're still on our blood pressure medication? Blood pressure's up just a shade, but nothing to worry about yet, we'll check again next time you come. Keep up the multi-vitamins too. But overall things look good. We're pretty healthy."

Shaw put a stethoscope to his ears and started the usual routine, "Deep breath .. " When he was done he said, "heart and lungs sound fine," then he wrote something on the clip board.

Mrs. Hubchic said, "Doctor Shaw, did the police call you about what happened to Dr. Schmidt?"

Shaw paused, "Why, yes, in fact, just a moment ago."

"I gave them your office number when they bluntly asked me if I knew you, I thought covering that up would be the worst thing. So I gave them your number and said I had introduced you and Schmidt."

"I see. Thank you."

"Did I do the right thing?"

Shaw paused again, "Of course."

Shaw put the clip board aside, then he sat on a little wheeled stool. He looked into his lap for a moment. "Mrs. Hubchic, I have enjoyed the chats we have had. We all seem to have a story, don't we. The genocide in Ukraine that so interests you, and with such good reason, was a revelation to me. At least the incredible extent of it was. I thought the story of my family's history in Palestine and what happened to us might strike you just as your story affected me. That is why I spoke of it, perhaps with too much anger. Yes, people I know have an interest in the events in which Dr. Schmidt seems to have been involved. To speak clearly, the relocation of Zionists to Palestine, I'm afraid, still fosters resentment. Finding a man who was involved in that right here in Detroit was quite a surprise. So yes, I have acquaintances who I thought it better, not to mention any of this to."

"The rumor is that the police do not think it was suicide. Neither do I. Did you, or your friends have anything to do with what happened?"

"No. Of course not. When I met him, I found him pleasant, even sympathetic, and we even agreed to meet later, later in the week that is."

"Doctor, we have spoken about Stalin and how he starved the millions of us in Ukraine. But, did you know that ten years later, many of the self-same men who barely survived the Ukrainian starvation set out to kill all Poles in our midst? That was mostly in Volhynia. They are Catholic; we are Orthodox, is that something to kill over? But common Ukrainian men, working men, every day men, formed armed bands and set about killing anyone who was Polish."

Shaw was silent.

"One day when I was very young, my parents brought me inside from play and made me sit quietly. The next day I was told some neighbors had moved away. Today I wonder. My parents are gone so I cannot ask what they knew. But I wonder.

"In Ukraine, there are monuments and crosses here and there and even a little wall in Berezovka with Polish names on it. I have seen all this when visiting my family. The Ukrainian people are honest enough to allow these monuments and they even cooperate with the research to learn the truth. Polish people in Ukraine were massacred, maybe fifty thousand, maybe a hundred thousand and massacred by people who themselves had so recently been victims of Stalin.

"Doctor, as they say, there are no coincidences. If Schmidt helped Jewish people flee to Palestine, that's what some say anyway, you and your friends and family may have reason to hate that man. You met him and now he's dead. Did you or your friends have something to do with that?"

"No. I am sure. Nothing."

"If the police ask me more, shall I tell them I am aware of your more radical friends or shall I try to keep quiet?"

"Mrs. Hubchic, tell the police the truth. Dr. Schmidt led me to think he would even consider a humanitarian gift to help with the refugee camps. Even before I spoke to him I did some looking into details of how that might be done. I thought he might be generous, but would not want money to find its way into radical hands. That turned out to be the very subject we expected to talk about later. Humanitarian money to help refugees in camps - yes. Money for rockets to shoot at Israel - no. Schmidy, I believe, was a man of peace and reason and he had sympathy for the Palestinians now suffering in horrible camps."

"But you personally did not kill him that night?"

"No."

"Nor your friends?"

"No."

"Thank you. I absolutely believe you. I would hate to think my personally introducing you led to his demise. I felt I had to ask. Doctor, where oh where will this sort of thing end?"

"I understand. I understand why you ask me. And I take no offense. End? It will not end. It never has. We must just do our best to keep the memory of it all alive, to tell the truth and hope for education about the truth. Lets us hope truth will win more souls than ignorance and hate. It will not end till we find justice. That has not happened often."

Mrs. Hubchic stood to leave, but as she passed out the door, she saw that Shaw was dialing his cell phone.

Back to Schmidt's House

"This is not a clue ... or is it?"

Anonymous
also
Bart Simpson's Blackboard
Attributed to Nancy Cartwright

"Hey Mill, pull in here!" Jane spotted a sign on a shop that said "Miner's Boutique." She remembered that her overnight bag was empty, she had no change of clothes or underwear or anything else for tomorrow. "I'll really rush, but I gotta get a couple things."

Jane did rush. She found plain black slacks her size, and a colorful blouse and she didn't even look at the prices. Then she charged into a big lingerie department that seemed to fill half of the store. And there, his thick glasses pushed up onto his forehead and holding a pair of thong panties inches from his face, was none other than Patrick O'Neal.

"Hello Patrick. This neck of the woods must be home for you?"

"Oh Jeez!" Patrick jumped just as he had in the Washington office. He adjusted his glasses. "Oh! Hi! Wow, you scared me, what are you doing here?"

"Same thing as you I'd guess."

"Oh, ha, good one. It's the present you know, just the present you know." Patrick O'Neal placed several garments on the table. "Hey Jane, you know my folks live just a half mile from here and classes are starting at Oakland U tomorrow. My girl friend is in town too. So here I am gift shopping. What brings you here?"

"Sorry, security you know, I can't say. Besides, I'm in a big rush. See you later."

"Yeah, me too, I'm in a rush." Patrick sheepishly picked his selections up again. "Think this is enough? Bye."

Jane burst out of Miner's. Mill was outside the car half sitting on the hood. "Girls need stuff you know."

"No sweat," said Mill, "Only eight minutes, that might be a world record."

Jane threw her bag on the back seat and got into the car. "Patrick O'Neal was in there."

"Patrick O'Neal? You mean the intern from the office? Hmm, yeah, I guess I knew he was from around here somewhere. But in there? Does he work in there now or something?"

"He said he was getting his girlfriend a present, he had a fistful of skimpy underwear."

"Huh, well I hope he knows her well."

Moments later they drove past the odd mailbox and up the wooded brick drive to Schmidt's house. There, as before, was the big forensics van at the big porch, and past that, the garage with many doors. But unlike before, two garage doors were wide open. Mill parked. "C'mon Jane, what's up in the garage? Let's see."

The inside of the garage was big, shadowy and too dark to see much, at least until Jane's eyes started to adjust to it. A furnace sat against a far wall. Not an overhead garage heater but a regular forced-air furnace like a house might have. It had long, round ducts that extended overhead, octopus-like, around the garage's open rafters. Every few feet, a round heat vent faced downward. There were lights with big round reflectors up there too. Jane saw wheeled tool boxes, hydraulic jacks, an air compressor and all manner of other garage stuff and everything was neatly lined up against the walls. And there was a faint but familiar odor. Jane thought it was like an old pickup truck she had been in, although she couldn't remember when, exactly, she'd been in an old pickup truck. Maybe that part was another old garage or, at any rate, someplace or other she only half remembered. Whatever it was, it was garage-like and not really unpleasant.

124

But more obvious than any of this were several cars. Some were clearly antiques with streamlined headlights mounted on the front fenders. And a couple of the cars were monstrously big.

Jane called into the shadows, "Hello?"

"Hello," "Hello," two voices answered.

Clyde Webb advanced out of the dull interior, "Hi there, I'm Clyde Webb, this is Dr. Tesler. We're nosy neighbors butting in here to look at the old cars. Who might you guys be?"

Jane's eyes had not adjusted enough to see where Tesler was, so she showed a badge to Webb, "We're Paine and Mill, we're federal agents, sort-of detectives. We're here to check and confirm some stuff."

"Hmm, Department of Justice. I didn't know Schmidt was of interest on a federal level. This is about Schmidt I take it. So, well-then, what stuff is it you'd like to check? Can us nosy neighbors help you out?"

"Well maybe we'd like to talk to neighbors, but that should be later." Jane thought getting to Natalie soon was way more important than getting into exactly why these guys were here and time lost on a long interview. So she changed the subject. "Wow! What is that?" Jane faced a gigantic old car.

Webb turned, "Pretty amazing huh? I guess Günter Schmidt really liked old Mercedes Benz cars. He used to tinker with them all the time then get them out for Fourth of July parades and the Woodward Dream Cruise and stuff. But we haven't seen them for a few years and being nosy neighbors, we decided to poke in here and see if the cars were still around.

"Really, we were visiting and trying to console Mrs. Schmidt. She's inside right now. My wife is with her. Those two are, well, they seemed to be getting on so we kind-of broke off and just wandered out here."

Jane said, "Look at the size of that thing!"

Mill spoke, "I think that's, what, now let me remember .. it's a Mercedes Benz all right, I think they called it a 770 Grosser? I mean how German can you be? A 'Grosser'! What a name! I think they made two models, big and bigger. This has to be bigger. They didn't build many of these beasts, probably not even a hundred. They were mainly special Nazi parade cars. Hitler or Himmler or Herman Goering, guys like that would stand in the back as they paraded along with Nazi troops goose stepping all around. Just look at this thing! What a picture! I bet this car saw some history."

Clyde Webb gazed at Mill for a moment, "Yeah, I think you're right. 'Großer' .. that's German for bigger, or in this case, huge. Actually, Günter told me a little about it. He got this monster after the war when the US Army auctioned Nazi stuff they had seized. He told me he had an agent bid a thousand bucks or some such low price at the auction in Berlin and he was surprised when he got it. Then he got the bad news. Shipping it here from Berlin, or wherever it was, cost three times that amount."

The huge car barely fit in the garage. Its front featured lots of chrome, lights, horns, trim, all rather dull with age, or maybe they were tarnished real silver. There was a hefty front bumper and a tall chrome grill that leaned back at a jaunty angle. The grill was topped by what looked like a modern Mercedes Benz emblem. The hood and engine compartment were very long and had spare tires inside smooth molded cases on each side. The car had a slate gray cloth or canvas top, perhaps it had been black long ago. The top was fraying where it was tight over its frame and at the rear, the sides of the top had big, graceful "S" shaped chrome hinges on the outside.

Door handles were near the front, not the back of each door. Jane tried the driver's door. It swung heavily, but freely backward 'suicide door' style. The seat was leather and it showed its age. The corners were turning to dust and cracks showed all over, but the sitting areas had newer looking leather pads that looked intact enough. It took two big steps to get up and in. The steering wheel was huge and was of some kind of fine wood. A floor gear shift handle had an extraordinarily long arm that disappeared past Jane's feet under the dash. Beside that was another lever that Jane figured was a parking break with a hand release. Looking around, Jane saw the back seat area was over-sized with leather seats at the very rear. In the middle there was another row of seats. These seats were smaller and apparently could be folded down, maybe to make a short platform to stand on during parades. A chrome bar passed side to side and looked like it was intended to be a hand-hold for standing up. Imposing as the car was, Jane somehow expected the inside to be even bigger.

Jane grabbed the giant steering wheel and went, "Doot-doo-doo-doo-do-do" to the tune of 'The Flight of the Valkyries.' "C'mon you guys, aren't you supposed to be goose stepping along?" Jane smiled, then the thought of the horrors that surrounded the Nazis who might have ridden in this car. Then she thought of the sober business she was on.

The passenger side door opened and Val Tesler, seen at last, climbed in. "Look at the size of that steering wheel. That's for leverage! No power steering on this monster."

Clyde Webb said, "I wonder what this thing is worth now? It's not a real practical car to run to the market, unless you're into bulldozing the other cars in the parking lot, but maybe it has historical value to a museum or something."

"Hard to say," said Mill, "Nazi era stuff is funny. It all carries a nasty stigma. It could be worth ten thousand, or it could be a million. If you could prove it was the very car used in such and so a parade on such and so a date, it'd be worth more, or, maybe less. Nazi stuff is funny like that."

A smaller car was parked next to the big Mercedes Benz. Mill said. "I think that's, a 170. It's a pre-war design. Somehow the tooling survived the war so they put it back in production after. The 170's carried Mercedes Benz for a while till they could get newer designs out."

A third old car had fenders that were streamlined as if they belonged on a Flash Gordon space ship and its roof swept down in a long curve all the way to a rear bumper. Mill nodded at it, "A model Stromlinie I think, or something like that anyway. Very cool. There's one I wouldn't mind driving to the market."

Jane got out of the big car and watched Mill. He spoke in a normal tone, but he was opening doors, kneeling down and looking close, and moving rapidly. "Lincoln Mark IV, about 1975, "big, isn't it, almost Grossen sized." There was a

127

newer and smaller Lincoln next to the big one. Mill moved quickly and even pulled his magnifying glass out a couple times. Then Mill wandered away and looked in cabinets and a big wheeled tool box.

Jane saw that Webb was watching Mill too. "Ms. Paine? You're Paine right? A reasonable person might assume that the fact that you are here implies something is amiss. This is related to our loss of Dr. Schmidt's isn't it."

"Well yes it is, but I'm not in a position to say more. Mr. Webb. If I may, were you at last night's neighborhood get-together? I think you were, weren't you?"

"Why, yes."

"And Dr. Tesler was too?"

"Well, yes."

"And just now, were you looking for anything in particular besides old cars out here?"

Webb stood silent for a moment. "Looking at these old cars was something to do while Sally, my wife that is, spent some time with Mrs. Schmidt with whom she is close. They pretend to be more distant than they are when others are around, but they are, in fact, very close."

A door in the back of the garage opened and a past middle-aged woman appeared. Webb spoke to Jane in a lowered voice. "That's Mrs. Tesler, Claudia Tesler. Val Tesler's wife."

Val Tesler emerged from the giant Benz and closed the door. "Claudia, let's doddle on home. We have a couple detectives here and they should .. detect. Clyde, You're coming too?"

After they left Jane asked Mill, "What do you make of that? What were they looking for?"

Mill said, "I don't know. But ya' see these floor drains? They're all in a row. There should be one more under the Stromlinie, but where the drain should be, there's a sheet of plywood on the floor. Maybe it's to keep dripping oil from going down the drain. Maybe it's a hole for a bucket for changing oil or something. But plywood wouldn't be the style of an old German guy like Schmidt. I think the plywood might be hiding something. That's the only odd thing I've spotted. As far as these cars go, they've been sitting here idle for a long time. They're dusty inside and door hinges need oil and stuff like that. It's the same thing with cabinets and everything else except for the new Lincoln over there. That one's been driven recently. But mostly, this place is a ghost town. Stuff hasn't been touched in a while.

"It could be that Claudia Tesler was behind that door using a bathroom or something. Or maybe not. Maybe Webb was right, maybe they were just being nosy and looking at the cars. But I'm with you, I think they were out here looking for something. To do a real search we'll need more time, some idea what we're looking for and either Mrs. Schmidt's permission or a warrant.

"But ya know what, we really need to talk to Natalie Schmidt. We'll come back here later." Mill paused. "On the other hand, we're here now. Let's do a super quick look around, especially let's peek behind that door where Mrs. Tesler came out."

Jane was not at ease entering places without permission, without a search warrant, not even in hot pursuit, the more so because she had no idea what she was looking for. But she was also aware that two murders demanded extra measures.

The door Claudia Tesler came out of opened to a short hall. On one side it was open to lead past some kind of utility room that included counters and a washtub. Behind another door was a very small bathroom. Mill put his hand on the toilet's water closet. "Not cold, same temperature as the room, it hasn't been used lately. Sink's dry too, not used for a day or more."

Jane still felt uneasy. She felt they were trespassing. But she followed Mill and watched his hurried examination.

The short hall led to a two floor apartment. A cursory tour of the apartments revealed quarters where the new students had obviously just taken up residence. Suitcases were open and only partly unpacked. A refrigerator was on, but empty. Mill repeated his check in a bathroom next to the bedroom. "This one's not used either." Then Mill said, "Nothing surprising." Then he opened a door in the lower level. Flipping lights on revealed a musty hall, almost a tunnel, with a few windows to the yard on one side only. The windows were between cabinets and closets. More doors to storage closets lined the other, windowless side. At the end were stairs that climbed to a closed door. A peek behind that door revealed a larder or pantry and the kitchen in the main house. Mill quietly closed the door and they returned down the hall. Mill peeked inside everything as he went. There was folded linens, towels and blankets, many services of dishes, tarnished silver serving platters, canned goods that looked decades, a tarnished silver punch bowl with cups, three wooden boxes of equally tarnished silverware, cleaning supplies, several boxes of light bulbs, a small tool box, an old vacuum cleaner, several boxes of Christmas decorations and three dusty toilet plungers.

Then to Jane's relief, they headed out. As they passed though the apartment, Jane noticed that the two floors of rooms were actually large and rather luxurious. Chairs were real leather, tables had marble tops. The apartment was nice, or, at any rate, it was nicer for sure than her little house. That a place this nice was obviously intended to be servant's quarters, rankled her in an odd way.

The garage doors had no electric openers; they had old fashioned pull ropes. Mill yanked them down one after the other. They made a rattling noise as they came. Then Mill pushed them tight against the ground by hand. Jane wondered if they could be locked, the simple handles on the outside did not look like they latched at all.

Natalie Speaks

"Information's pretty thin stuff unless mixed with experience"

Clarence Day

Jane Paine and Mill proceeded to Schmidt's big incongruous front porch. There they met two forensics men loading their equipment into the van. They addressed Mill. "The bullet was in a groove in a carved part of the paneling. We should have spotted it yesterday but we missed it. Anyway, finding it takes one variable off the table, the victim was shot there alright. And the bullet looks the same as last night's bullets. It looks like you were right last night. I checked a reference book and it looks like last night's bullets are compatible with a Nagant. We haven't really proved the Nagant angle in the lab yet, but off the record, it looks just like a sample we got from one of our guys who owns one. Off the record, same gun here and there. The bullet was in a spot that says the victim was standing, not seated. We left a piece of yellow tape on the wall if you want to look yourself. So that's about it for us right now."

Jane rang the bell and soon Sally Webb answered. Sally's first words were in an impatient tone, "More of you?" Then she became more polite. "Okay, please come it." Sally asked Jane and Mill to take seats in the large foyer and said she'd get Natalie. They stood to wait anyway. In spite of the nice, if chilly day, the big foyer or entry hall or whatever this room was, seemed too dark and too big, but Jane could see in the next big room, the morning sun was streaming in the windows and making bright outlines and shadows on the floor. When Natalie appeared, she sat down. So did all the rest. After Sally made polite if formal introductions, Jane did the talking.

"Did a retired man named Smith visit you yesterday; it would have been late in the afternoon?"

Natalie said, "Oh yes, Mr. Smith. We spoke for a time and then I remembered him from many years ago. That was a great surprise to see someone from so long ago. But I imagine you knew that he came here. Yes, he was here."

The big foyer's paneled wood walls and floor added a curious reverberation that made voices sound more alive than normal. The room was big, dark and drafty, but it was a warm draft, not chilly. Apparently the heating system was on. People seemed too small for this room or, Jane thought, maybe the room was too big.

Jane asked, "What did you talk about?"

Natalie looked surprised. "Have you not spoken to Mr. Smith? We spoke of everything, even the weather, but then we talked about the old days. After some of that talk, he seemed excited. He said he would return and left in a great hurry calling someone on his cell phone as he went."

"Do you recall what you were talking about just before he left? What you said that might have excited him?"

"Is there some problem? Have you not spoken to Mr. Smith?

"Well, yes, there is a problem, but first, please remember what made Smith excited."

"Well, alright, we spoke of coming here and things even before that. You know Günter was from a good Prussian family and was wealthy, but the money from home could only be sent here a little at a time. That seemed to interest Mr. Smith. Then we spoke of the new art wing at the school and Dean McIntyre. When I mentioned that Günter had maintained contact with his friend, Franz von Papen, till Franz died of course, when was that? Sixty-nine or so? Anyway, Mr. Smith seemed excited by that. We were talking most about the addition to the museum but the name Franz von Papen seemed to set him off. I think that surprised him. What is the matter?"

Mill spoke now, "Franz von Papen? The former German Chancellor and man behind the Reichskonkordat? The Cicero spy contact?"

Natalie said, "My! That's all true I suppose. He was a well bred gentleman and a friend of Günter's although he was not Prussian. He was once Chancellor over all of Germany you know. But yes, that was the man."

Sally Webb sat up a bit straighter. Her eyes narrowed and she seemed to study Mill and Paine.

Natalie seemed to look Mill and Paine over too. Then she went on, "Yes. You probably know from Mr. Smith that Günter's old name was Otto Guderian von Below. Like all of the Junkers, he had half a dozen more names he never used. But he was Otto Guderian von Below. The Guderian part was the same family as General Heinz Guderian. Heinz was a cousin and Günter was on friendly terms with him. Otto von Below, the first Otto von Below, not Günter, and Fritz von Below were World War One Generals and retired by our time. Nicolaus von Below, bah! He was one of Hitler's yes-men and an oberst in the Luftwaffe. That's a colonel I think. All the von Belows were cousins, but in spite of the same last name, rather distant cousins."

Mill spoke to Jane, "Guderian was the German General behind the idea of blitzkrieg war. Later he was the chief of the war against Russia. He was an important guy. He had a son with the same name who was a big NATO officer later.

"Natalie, your name is not Schmidt either?"

"Oh no, no. Mr. Smith did not tell you I am Natalia Paderewski. You do not know this?"

Mill said, "Please tell us, it's a bit unclear to us."

"Well, I worked in the Polish underground against the Communists. Günter was Prussian, I suppose that is German to you. He and his .. associates .. opposed the Communists just as we did. That is how we came to work together. Since you do not seem to know all of this, I will tell you. Mr. Smith invented our marriage and that bit of fiction suited Günter, or I should say Otto and me. Right after the war, when the Russians occupied the area, the Communists' hunt for Germans and their hunt for the old Polish underground put us both in difficult positions and you might say, that brought us into close contact. I should perhaps not be so open about all this, but everything is so long ago. I have always assumed Mr. Smith took care of any immigration issues for us. We had no papers you know, except those I know very well Smith made for us. I hope that will not be a problem for me now, so many years later."

Jane spoke again, "Mrs. Schmidt, what is in those files in the hidden room behind the dining room? Are they connected to those old days?"

"Oh those, Mr. Smith asked about those too. They are records of some kind. Günter preferred that I not study them as they related to his work and personal business. But I believe some of them pertain to money assistance given to refugees. There were so many refugees in those bad days, so many dislocated people."

"Mrs. Schmidt, may we look in the dining room once again and at those records? And we may want to maybe walk around a bit too. And maybe look inside your out buildings?"

"Yes, of course you may. That guest house as you might call it served as Günter's private study. I have not been out back in years. Sally tells me you have already seen it. Sometimes Günter also met people there. Ha! Even I call him Günter now. It was also Otto's private study. He liked to be alone out there sometimes. He had his private things and some private business there too. You may look more of course. But now will you explain? What is the trouble?"

It was Mill who spoke, "Mrs. Schmidt, I'm afraid Mr. Smith was shot last night and he did not survive. The police will, no doubt, also want to talk."

Natalie did not seem shocked. "I see. I am sorry and hope I did nothing wrong. And Günter then, not a suicide?"

"We think not."

Natalie seemed not surprised at all. "So it has followed us here. The old days are not as far gone as I had hoped. This makes me very sad. If we killed a Communist, they would kill one of ours. Tit for tat, tit for tat. But what a price. It is the old days again."

Sally Webb, who had been quiet, quickly stood up. "I'll make coffee."

"Be calm Sally, I have seen all of this before. Perhaps if all this can be resolved, I may finally come to understand much that I did not before. I have wondered about much for many years and understanding some of it would compensate me a small amount."

"What sort of things puzzle you so?" asked Jane.

Natalie sighed. "It is hard to explain to someone who did not live in that world. It was different then. I was an underground courier, little more. Günter dealt at a much higher level and had access to much money and influence. But I never understood all that, nor did I want to. He never made things clear to me either. My view was simple. The Communists had brutalized my country and murdered my people, and I did my part to fight back. That meant I carried messages and sometimes packages for those who resisted the Communists. I seldom knew what the messages meant. There is very much I never knew. That is how it is underground. In fact, knowing too much will usually put you at greater risk. Life is so .. ironic."

Jane said, "We would like to know all you can tell us about those days. I would like to try to understand. May I spend today with you?" Jane saw a very slight thumbs up from Mill. "I might also help with whatever arrangements you must make. May I impose if I promise to help out too?"

"Oh my! Help? Sally and Mr. Webb and others have already done so much. But certainly. Why not? If you feel those old days might matter in what is happening, then yes. I would like to talk."

Mill signaled Jane with a tilt of his head. "We'd like to look at those files now but Ms. Paine will be right back."

Jane said, "I will be back shortly and try not to intrude too much."

Natalie said, "It would take a year to tell it all. It would make a book. A poor book I'm afraid. But I will be pleased to answer questions. I am too old to dance now."

In the file room Mill showed uncharacteristic excitement. He said, "Too old to dance? Bull, she's dancing. This is deep Jane! von Papen! Holy cow! And Guderian! Did you see how she looked at us when she said von Papen? And that set Smith off! That means something.

"Jane, von Papen was Chancellor in Germany before Hitler. And he's the guy who screwed up and got Hitler into power. Let's see, von Papen was a super Roman Catholic, a Papal Chamberlain. That means he had access to the Pope whenever he liked. He was even a Papal Knight. And when he wasn't busy being Chancellor and Catholic, he was into spies and sabotage. He was even under indictment for espionage in the U.S. when he became Chancellor in Germany.

"It was von Papen who was behind the Reichskonkordat, that's the agreement where Nazi Germany and the Vatican, the Catholic church really, got in bed with each other."

"Whoa!" Jane said, "Reichskonkordat? Nazis and the Catholic Church?"

"The Reichskonkordat, yeah! The treaty between Nazis and the Vatican. The public parts of the agreement weren't really so bad. The Catholic Church got to continue collecting church tax in Germany. That means Catholics could sign up and give part of their income to the church. The Reichskonkordat guaranteed the church that all kinds of stuff like that would continue under the Nazis. But really, that public part was only what had been done in Germany all along. It should have been no big deal. But its political impact was huge. Before that agreement, Nazis were mostly seen as laughable wack-o's whose power would soon pass. But Nazis striking an agreement with the Vatican? The Catholic church-state? That had to be taken seriously. That agreement made Nazis look respectable and legitimate.

"Later, we learned there were extra secret clauses. That was bad. It was a real bombshell. It was really bad for the Vatican. The secret part said Catholic Priests and other church-men were exempt from the German military draft. Only, there was no German draft. The treaty of Versailles forbade it. What the secret part of the agreement really meant was the Church, The Vatican that is, knew that Hitler was planning to violate the Treaty of Versailles. They knew that he had already started building his war machine. The fact that the Vatican kept these clauses secret looked bad for them. It said the church was playing along with Hitler and the Nazis. That part was a big, big mistake. It put the Vatican way, way too close to the Nazis. The Spanish Civil War, where the Catholics and the Nazis were bedfellows again didn't help with the way things looked either.

"Now this might be the punch line, there's rumors that the Nazis gave the church a huge pile of money and land to get them to sign the Reichskonkordat. Like really huge amounts of money. That part has never been proved very well, but the rumors about it have also refused to die.

"If Schmidt or von Below or whatever his real name is, was involved in any of that .. wow! No wonder it's all secret. If that's what we bumped into, Dorsey won't get us any data at all and the next thing we'll know is this stuff is impounded never to be seen again." Mill was already looking in file drawers.

"Jane, what did Smith figure out? Think Jane. The coroner's first guess is Smith was hit late at night, so he didn't go straight to the school from here. The car had about sixty extra miles on it. Where was he? And he called Dorsey three times! And a bunch of other numbers too. I wonder if Henderson's tracked those down yet. I wonder if one was this McIntyre guy. Why not us? Why didn't he call us? The turkey! Smith knew the score, or part of it anyway, as soon as he heard the name von Papen. Man, I smell Reichskonkordat money. Does Dorsey know more that he's telling us too?"

Jane said, "Yeah, Mrs. Schmidt or whatever her name is, said von Papen set Smith off. Run this von Papen guy by me again."

Mill stopped shuffling in the file drawers. "Umm, Franz von Papen, German diplomat, spy-master, Chancellor, head of a political party called The Catholic Center Party and super plugged into the church. He was close pals with a couple popes. Let's see here, Papen was military attaché in the Germen embassy in Washington right before World War One. He was a beginner at the spy business then. He kept paying people to become saboteurs and spies and stuff and he kept a receipt book to show all the expenses to his bosses in Germany. But the FBI took a look in his luggage and found the receipt book, check stubs, names and all. The FBI figured out that he was plotting to blow up railroads and The Welland Canal. When the war started in Europe, before we were in it, he went to Mexico and offered to give Texas back to them if they'd join the war on the German side and attack us. When he got back to Washington, we indicted him for plotting sabotage. He had diplomatic immunity, so all we could do is toss his butt out of the country.

"Next he went to work anti-British activity in Ireland and he had a hand in an anti-British revolt in India too. After the First World War, he headed his political party in Prussia. He was an insider with all the Prussian aristocrats and even pals with the German President, von Hindenburg. Later, about 1932, Hindenburg made von Papen Chancellor, a year or so before Hitler. The Chancellor had the real power, even though the President appointed him. Can you imagine? He was German Chancellor at the same time that he was indicted in the US. He appointed what was called 'The Monocle Cabinet' for all the monocle wearing Prussians aristocrat pals of his that he made ministers of this and that. Then von Papen legalized the Nazi paramilitary SA. No doubt he was hoping that would buy Nazi support for himself and his party. But things didn't work out and he was forced to quit. He was replaced by, let's see, some General .. by General Kurt von Schleicher.

"Schleicher did no better and it was not a year after that when Papen used his influence with old Hindenburg to maneuver Hitler into the Chancellor's office with himself as vice-Chancellor. He figured Hitler was such a political amateur that he'd be the real power. That bright idea sure did not work out and Papen regretted the mistake ever after.

"By 1934 Papen had seen enough. He gave a rip roaring speech in public attacking Hitler. Just then Hitler ordered 'The Night of the Long Knives.' Hitler had anyone who was politically inconvenient for him, murdered. The included von Schleicher, the last Chancellor and Ernst Röhm, head of Hitler's own paramilitary SA. It even included von Papen's secretary, his speech writer and other pals of Papen's. Those guys were shot dead right at their desks. Papen himself was put under house arrest in his home and his phone cut off. Number two man to Hitler, Hermann Göring figured Papen's contacts at The Vatican might come in handy and somehow talked Hitler into letting Papen go. So instead of murdering him, Hitler made Papen ambassador to Austria and later ambassador to Turkey. In Turkey, von Papen was the German contact for the famous World War Two spy, 'Cicero.' Then Hitler let Papen come home and he showered medals all over him.

"Von Papen was pals with the Pope Pius, um, Pope Pius XI. That little acquaintance came in extra handy right in the beginning, when Hitler first came to power. Von Papen is the guy who negotiated the Reichskonkordat between Nazi Germany and the Vatican and he even signed it for Germany. That little agreement, by the way, is still in effect today. This part is important, the rumor is serious money changed hands on that one. The Nazis gave the church a serious pile of money and land as some kind of settlement, or to be blunt, as a giant bribe to sign the Reichskonkordat. But the bribe aspect has never really been proven.

"After the war, von Papen was tried at Nuremburg along with the top Nazis. He was one of only three guys who were acquitted. When we let him go, the Germans arrested him themselves and convicted him of 'crimes against peace,' but he was out of prison in a few years. After that, Papen was pals with the new pope, Pope John, no, it was another Pius, umm, Pius XII. Pius XII made Papen a Papal Knight. Then von Papen tried to re-start his political career. But that didn't fly. By then, the German people had seen enough of his act.

"Von Papen was a slippery old fox, as slippery as they came. A real, what did Natalie just say? A real dancer. And Papen's personality was, by all reports, super-pompous. He was old royalty and he wanted everyone to know it. He even lived a great whopping-sized castle. He was a self important aristocrat type and he was true to the stereotype. But once in a while, he was also a real bone-head boob. Like when we caught him spying or when he promoted Hitler to be Chancellor."

"Jeez Mill, you should rent yourself out as an encyclopedia, I never heard of this dude before. The Nazis gave the Church huge money to sign an agreement? How much does it take to bribe the Catholic Church? And this guy was the connection between the Nazis and the church?"

"The bribe's a rumor. But it fits. Now think Jane, Smith would have know all this from back when. Von Papen was really well known back then. So what did Smith figure out? And why would Schmidt keep this stuff, these papers all these years. Never mind how he got the papers here. Was this insurance? Protection of some kind? Or maybe just a smoke screen? And he asked Natalie not to snoop? And she says she didn't? Sure! At any rate, judging by Natalie's remarks, it sounds like Schmidt didn't retire from whatever he was up to when Smith put him here. This is good and deep."

"This Guderian cousin, what about him?"

"Um .. Guderian .. Prussian German General of World War Two, weren't they all Prussians? He wrote a book 'Achtung - Panzer!' Ya' like that name? 'Achtung - Panzer!' That means 'Watch out! There's tanks!' How Prussian can you get? His book had a huge influence on German 'Blitzkrieg' warfare. Blitzkrieg, 'lightning war,' that's fast moving attack led by bunches of tanks and aircraft. The idea is the speed and fire power of concentrated armor and aircraft throws the enemy into confusion so they have no time to organize a proper defense. It's like Civil War General Nathan Forrest's quote, 'Get there first with the most' only modernized to World War Two with fast moving tanks instead of Forrest's cavalry."

"Oh." Jane said.

"But hold on, Guderian became head of OKH, that was the German General Staff, that was headquarters for the war in the east. OKW ran the war in the west, OKH ran it in the east. That made Guderian a really big shot. Hitler had political generals like Keitel and Jodl who's job was to agree with him, but Guderian was may have been the biggest real general. Guderian, like all the old-line General Staff guys had no use for Hitler. He thought Hitler was a bad joke and he had plenty of shouting arguments with Hitler. But Hitler knew he needed real military generals to run the war, so he put up with Guderian's shouting at him. But HIlter finally fired him just days before Hitler killed himself."

Jane took this in. Then she started looking in the FILE drawers.

"Look Jane, Smith probably figured something out. Then he must have accidentally tipped somebody off and got himself shot over it. I'm not personally that fond of gun fights. We need to be real cautious now."

"Jeez!" said Jane. "And whoever that is, maybe, already knows we're snooping."

"You have your little Glock pistol?"

"Got it. Do you think I'll need it?"

"I hope not. But keep it handy, and loaded."

Then Mill said, "I think this stuff is in Polish and some of it in German, and this part is something screwy I don't recognize. It's financial records of some kind I think, part of it anyway, and it looks like some lists of names. It reminds me of those airline manifests, only hand written in languages I don't read. Aid for refugees Natalie said. It looks like that could be it to me.

"Look Jane, we're leaving finger prints all over the place and messing up any that might be here. We can't read this stuff anyway. Let's see if Henderson has a resource to read this stuff. If we ask Dorsey, I bet we'll lose it. He'll impound it"

"Risky for us, but agreed. I mean we work for Dorsey, not Henderson and this is undercutting Dorsey. Still, we should use resources available and that's Henderson. Dorsey hasn't called or e-mailed back. I mean, we shouldn't wait. I'm sure Dorsey's up to his ass with politics and with Smith getting shot, but c'mon, he's leaving our butts out in the breeze. He should at least call. I say call Henderson."

Mill closed the drawer he was looking at. "But I want to think first. What did Smith realize and did it get him blown away? Let's not make the same mistake. I want to walk the property anyway and see what's out back, see the student's quarters, sponge up anything I can find. I want to think before we call Henderson. Just a hunch, but I want to look around. Remember the love nest? There may be more surprises. I want to digest all this and think before we make a wrong move. In the mean time, why don't you go back and sponge up Natalie's story.

Shawesh's Decision

"In The Evening Of Life, We Will Be Judged On Love Alone"

St. John Of The Cross

Dr. Shaw lived in a nouveau riche subdivision. The sub had been a huge old estate and farm till the seventies when the place was divided into building sites. But recession set in and the whole area sat almost empty for a decade before new home buyers came and built big, garish houses.

Dr. Shaw sat in an oversized upholstered chair. He was talking to a young man who sat in a dining room chair that was pulled up in front of Shaw. Shaw's daughter sat beside him in another straight chair, hands folded and looking into her lap.

Shaw's daughter had brought this young man around before. Shaw liked him. He was a medical student. That was good. He was respectful, had good manners and dressed conservatively. That was all good too. But he was not Muslim and he was not Palestinian and that was awkward.

This meeting had quite a different tone than earlier visits.. This time his daughter had not called, the young man himself had phoned asking to meet. Shaw was getting the picture. This was serious.

The young man had apparently thought carefully about what to say. He had explained his typical mixed American roots, Italian, Irish, and English and he said both of his parents were Roman Catholic and that he too embraced that church. There was only one reason to explain all this and Shaw was becoming uncomfortable. Perhaps he should have listened more carefully to those inquiries from Palestinian friends with eligible sons. Perhaps he should not have encouraged his daughter to go not only to college, but even to graduate school.

After reviewing his own family, the young man, respectfully and eloquently, expressed sympathy for Shaw's loss of his wife to cancer, now fully ten years ago. Shaw was impressed and touched by that courtesy.

"Dr. Shaw, your daughter tells me that Shaw was originally a Palestinian name. I'm afraid they don't teach very much about Palestine in American schools."

Shaw knew the young man was really asking Shaw if he objected to his daughter marrying an American Catholic. Shaw had still hoped his daughter might spare him this situation, this sharp fork in the road. She could be introducing an educated Palestinian, perhaps the son of a friend, instead of bringing on this uncomfortable situation.

This young man was Catholic and he was as American as apple pie. Shaw wanted his daughter to become American too. In that way, he was a very pleased and even proud. In that way, a better choice could not be made. An American medical student, a doctor to be, and a polite, well bred American. But in another, Shaw was unsure of his mind. He was, in spite of his western dress, American home, and highly educated daughter, still a Muslim and he was proud of it. This was tricky.

Shaw knew he must welcome this young man without reservation and help make a happy family for his daughter, or he must lay down the law to his daughter. Equivocation would be the worst answer.

Shaw's thoughts turned to early days with his wife, then he thought of his daughter as a baby and then he thought of her as a little girl. Shaw reflected on the two of them, he and his daughter, both making a life after he lost his wife and she, her mother. This sort of reflection, Shaw now supposed, was universal at a time like this; memories of a child now grown to adulthood. Had he done his best? Had he been a good father? Mistakes? Yes, many, but never of the heart.

Shaw was amazed that this young man had the insight to offer condolences for his wife at this particular time. That was the part that actually moved him. That was important.

Shaw needed a moment or two, so he spoke mostly to postpone.

"Shaw? You ask about Shaw? Well, first of all, my people do not have surnames exactly. We have a whole string of names and they can change. For example, 'Abdul' is not exactly a name, it means 'servant of' and 'Abdullah' means God, so Abdul Abdullah means servant of God. 'Kunya' means father of first son and we follow it with the name of that son. We do not add Kunya to our name till we really have a son. So the name Kunya Abdul Abdullah literally means Father of a first son named Servant of God. But when we come to western countries, we westernize our names."

Shaw knew he was just talking about nothing. He was talking as if he was from Palestine, but he was really born in Canada.

"Shaw is Americanized Shawesh. Shawesh is as close to a surname as we have. Our family started in Jerusalem, in Palestine and the family is now wide-spread."

The young man said, "Yes, Palestinian, what does that mean today? Is there still what we would call a country of Palestine?" The question seemed overly simple; maybe the young man was just as anxious as Shaw to postpone the real subject.

"Well then, Palestine is the area between the Mediterranean Sea and the Jordan River. It has been so since the time of Rome, even before. It is a place and it is also a country.

"We were part of the Ottoman Empire for centuries and our Sultans were in what is now Turkey. But we were always Palestine. In the early nineteen hundreds things became very confusing. There were Turkish coups and counter-coups, constitutions, and suspension of the constitutions, fundamentalist movements, and our own movement because we wanted to separate from Turkey and the Sultans. Then World War One came along and Turkey lined up with Germany. We wanted to throw off their rule and that grew into 'The Arab Revolt.' The British, who were fighting the Turks too, wanted to exploit that, so they sent military people like Lawrence of Arabia.

"In Turkey, groups like 'The Young Turks' led that country in the murder of Armenians and Kurds and ethnic Greeks. That genocide was very complicated and far from as one sided as westerners say today, but Turkey still tells only a one-sided version of it all. That's not really honest.

"Here's an irony, the Allies negotiated peace with Turkey at war's end, but we who fought with the Allies weren't invited to the table. Palestine was taken from Turkey, but handed over to Britain. We had nothing to say about it.

"Well, to move on. Zionism is a Jewish belief that God gave the Holy Land to Jewish people. But that land is really Palestine. Zionism became a serious movement starting in about the eighteen-nineties. That part's another long story. Zionist Jewish people started coming to our country in pretty good numbers about then and our tradition of religious toleration had us welcome them. But in 1909, they formed an armed militia. They had an attitude that the land was theirs and we didn't matter. That part was difficult for us to accommodate. In 1937 our disagreement became a bloodbath of rioting and then it turned into civil war.

"The British called us a protectorate, but there was no protection for us when we were being shot in our own homes. Then we demanded self-determination instead of decisions from the British Foreign Office. All the British did was set quotas to limit the arrival of Jews. That didn't work at all.

Shaw knew he was straying from the real subject, namely his daughter's future.

"Well, in 1946, I think it was '46 anyway, the British got together with the Americans to decide our fate. Once again, we were not invited to the table. Why Americans got a say in this is a good question. "The Anglo-American Committee of Inquiry," some inquiry! President Truman didn't get the problem at all. All he knew was there were millions of Jewish people displaced by the war in Europe and he just wanted to dump them all in our country.

"The British, at least, had a little bit of a clue. But they just washed their hands of the whole mess and tossed it to the United Nations. Mind you, the United Nations, they didn't ask us. Anyway, in 1948, the UN voted for a Jewish enclave called Israel located inside Palestine. It was to be subject to our approval and it would come under our laws. But just then we were attacked once again by Zionist militia. Again, our civilians were murdered. Even European vacationers in hotels were gunned down. We fought back and were winning for a time. But arms and money and men flooded in to help Israel. Much of the money for these so-called Israelis came from America. Somehow, and how ironic this is, much old German world war two weaponry fell into their hands. Our neighbors, that's to say all the old Ottoman states, declared war on the new Israel, but that was too little and too late."

" 'A land without a people, a people without a land,' that was their slogan. Some view of things! We were not people?

"My uncle was killed in the rioting in 1937, my grandfather was a man of position, but he lost his land and home in 1939. My father and mother fled in 1947 just before the war. I had an uncle who died in that war. We do not see justice here. Palestine is our country. And we are angry.

"Well, my folks fled to Honduras. Why Honduras I do not know, but many Palestinians got a new start there. Then my father went to Canada. My father, like me, was a medical doctor and medical doctors went to the head of Canada's immigration list. Then we moved here, to Michigan in 1959. I was born in Canada. When we came here, Shawesh became Shaw.

"And now the CIA and FBI keep an eye on me because I keep family contacts in Honduras and Palestine. I'm afraid I see that part poorly. Yes indeed, something should be done about it.

Shaw sat for a moment. Had he too much? He had better moderate. "We are American now. We have become, as they say, 'westernized.' I have taught my daughter that, all people everywhere are the same. All have strengths and beauty and all have weakness. But like all Americans, we have a story. I want my daughter to be American. I celebrate that, but I would not like my daughter to forget our story nor forget our religion."

Shaw knew he had not answered the hidden question about marriage. But he felt he had been honest. A metaphor in the form of a history lesson, he thought told his honest feelings.

So Shaw waited for the young man to speak. But the young man waited too. This unexpected silence became tension. Shaw's daughter remained statue-like. The tension needed to be broken.

"Why have you come here today? This is not idle curiosity about Palestine. Is there something else?"

"Sir, yes, of course. You surely know your daughter and I are very much in love. We see, perhaps as lovers always see, ideals and dreams. We think everything can be as we would hope. We are, no doubt, blind to realities. But we are practical too. My school is going well and I will start an internship in January. Not here. It will be in Houston. As a Doctor to be, I think I will have good prospects. I know we are in love and foolish and blind, but I think we are realistic too. I came to learn your thoughts. But yes, if now is the time to ask for your blessing, I ask for it. And I promise to love and honor and protect your daughter with all my strength. And if you will bless this, I have come to ask if I may offer this ring to your daughter." The young man produced a small jewelry box from a pocket.

The room was silent. Shaw looked at his daughter, her head respectfully bowed. But now she trembled and he thought he saw a tear. She looked so like his wife many years ago. And he could tell she knew very well what this meant. Shaw's culture and heritage, maybe his religion put aside replaced by new hopes and new dreams.

Shaw stood and walked to a window. He looked out. He might ask what religion any children might be. He might ask what the Catholic Priest thought. He might ask and ask. But he must not ask. A thousand problems came to mind, problems naïve young people would never think of. But he must not equivocate with questions or make further conversation. He must not say 'have you thought of this or that.' He must support this with his heart and help solve the problems unseen by young people, or reject this out of hand. This young man had done well. He had respectfully heard Shaw's reservations disguised as a history lesson. He had not argued. Then Shaw admitted to himself, that rejecting this could not be. It was too late. Perhaps they would do as they pleased regardless. He thought for whole moments. Do not equivocate. Do not postpone. Support honestly, or reject. Then Shaw took a deep breath.

Shaw turned and said in a stern voice, "Daughter, do you concur?"

A meek "yes" was the answer.

Shaw, to his own surprise said, "Your mother's spirit is happy."

Then he faced the young man and in a booming voice he hardly recognized himself, said, "Welcome my son! Welcome! You have my whole heart. I bless this. Welcome! This is glorious. If you are to be married before your internship, we must plan now. How can I meet your parents? Dinner, here, soon. Ask them at once. Yes, I am pleased! Welcome son!" Then for reasons he did not know, tears came.

For a moment, he feared such a dramatic outburst was ridiculous. But the sight of the young man, rising to his feet to embrace told Shaw his tone was exactly right.

The Hen Party

"Old friends pass away, new friends appear"

Dalai Lama

When Mill headed out of the house, Jane checked in her purse. She pulled her small-frame Glock 27 out and checked it. She put a round in the chamber and made sure the clip was full. Normally, Jane didn't like carrying that thing around, especially with a round ready to fire, but what happened to Smith made things different. Next Jane dug around and found her spare clip. She checked to see that it was free of lint and other stuff from her purse and that it was full too. Then she put the little gun and the spare clip in the purse's side pocket. She even checked a couple times to be sure the gun pulled out freely with nothing catching on it. Then Jane closed her eyes and tried to review her handgun training. Keep the gun in front of you, hold it with both hands, left hand over right hand, thumbs forward. Only your finger tip on the trigger, not the first joint. Take your time and aim at the center of mass. Passing a test at the range was one thing, but this was another matter. This was not comforting at all. She wished Mill was closer, but her pride, plus the sense that she must do her job, would not let her chase after him. Then she went looking for Natalie and Sally Webb.

"I'm back! Mr. Mill has excused himself to look around out back. I think he'll be out there for a while." Jane sat down with Natalie and Sally Webb.

Sally Webb said. "Natalie, may I make tea?"

Natalie watched Sally disappear then she put on a disapproving expression. She leaned toward Jane and hissed, "Her! Sometimes she drives me crazy."

Jane ignored the remark and started, "Natalie, I had an Aunt Natalie. I really liked her. I remember when I was really little I'd visit her and we'd make arrangements out of the flowers she grew in her garden, and she showed me how to make paper hats out of newspapers. She could always make me smile."

149

"Oh my! You had a big family?"

"No, oh no, I was an only child, but I had great folks and a really nice Aunt Natalie. They had a sense of humor and we always had lots of fun. There were neighborhood kids too. I was very lucky. I had a happy childhood."

"You grew up here?"

"Yes, well, in Washington DC anyway. My folks left me their house and I still live there. I'm what you might call 'home grown.'"

"Oh, your parents are gone? I am sorry."

"Thank you. Yes, I lost my father several years ago, my mother, just a year. That makes me sad, but we had so many good times. So I can remember with a smile. I was lucky."

Natalie looked very pleased. "Indeed, very few people have such good luck in that way. Those who do seldom know it till it's too late. Good for you."

"Oh, I knew it all along. And I remember so much with a smile. But, well-then Mrs. Schmidt, my job is to get to the bottom of all this trouble. So first thing, will you take me back before my time? Was it East Prussia or Poland in your days there?"

"Oh my, I think I would rather have happy stories of paper hats from your childhood right now. But, well, I suppose you must do your work.

"Well, tell me about your time. Tell me about your family. It might help me understand what's going on."

Natalie hesitated for a rather long time, "Well .. okay. I was Polish, or rather, I spoke the Polish language and we were Catholic. The place I lived was taken by Russia. But never mind if the land you stand on is Poland or Russia or Lithuania or Germany or Prussia or Ukraine or Memelland. You are Polish if you are Polish. They even used to say it was a race.

"A thousand years ago, when Viking women still wore horned hats and guys like Ivar the Boneless were busy plundering places like the Faroe Islands, Poland was already Christian. Poland was powerful and fought and beat the Ottomans, the Tartars from Siberia, Norway, really, we handled all comers. By the fifteen-hundreds Lithuania joined us and we even elected, elected mind you, our kings. But over time, constant war wore Poland down and in 1795, German Prussians on one hand, and Russia on the other took Poland apart. Poland just didn't exist for a century after that.

"Now then, how many places make goofy looking concert pianists into Prime Ministers? Hold on for that. And yes, that part ties to me.

"Poles were not happy to be ruled by Germans and Russians and we kept making a stink to get our country back. Then in 1863, the same time your civil war, we had the 'January Uprising.' That started out as local resistance to being conscripted into the Russian army, but many big-shots and leaders jumped in, many working men joined, and the next thing you know, it was a general uprising and war for independence. But Russia sent a huge army to handle us. It took them a year, but just about everyone involved in the uprising ended up shot or hanged. On leader was named Jan Paderewski. Jan was wealthy and he had enough pull to get tossed in prison instead of hanged. At the time, Jan had a two year old kid named Ignacy and when Jan was arrested, Ignacy's wealthy aunt adopted the two year old. Ignacy turned out to be a music prodigy and he was sent to learn piano from all the greatest pianists of the time.

It was Ignacy who became the famous pianist. He had a big mop of frizzy red hair that he waved about while he played. He looked like he shared barbers with Albert Einstein. And his wife was an honest-to-goodness baroness. Ignacy's concert tours had him traveling the world with his pet parrot who made conversation with him in Polish."

"A Polish speaking parrot?"

"Oh yes! And quite a smart parrot. If you came to see Ignacy, the parrot would say, 'Have a drink!' If Ignacy practiced piano, he would say, 'My how beautiful!' .. 'Napić się! .. Dobra wódkę! .. Piękny.'"

Jane laughed. "Oh my! A long haired concert pianist traveling with a parrot and his Baroness wife. There's a picture. And then what?"

"One day at a big concert, before Ignacy came on the stage, a little boy ran up and played chopsticks on the piano. The crowd booed and shouted, but Ignacy sat down beside the boy and told him to play on. Then he joined in and made it sound beautiful. Then the crowd cheered and laughed and cheered. That's the kind of man he was. He was a good man."

"Oh, what fun. I hope the parrot said 'Dobra wódkę! Piękny.' "

 "Well, Ignacy settled down in California in 1913, only a year before the fist war started in Europe. He bought a big estate and took up making Zinfandel wine. I guess he took up drinking it too.

"Ignacy had argued for restoring Poland all along and during the war he got the ear of your President Wilson. Wilson was a megalomaniac. He spoke of 'self determination,' but he seemed to think the self in that phrase was himself. Well, Ignacy and some others managed to sell the idea of Poland to Wilson and that became one of Wilson's fourteen points for ending the war. Wilson even took Ignacy Paderewski to Versailles to hammer out the war ending treaty. And Ignacy did all right for Poland, or, I suppose better than his parrot might have.

"But things were as simple as that in Poland. For one thing, it had been illegal to sell land to Poles for a century. If you were Polish, you could only sell to 'The Prussian Settlement Commission' and that commission would only sell land to incoming Germans and Prussians. That was usually a group we called 'The German Barons.' In the east of Poland, the Russians just stole our land. So by the time Poland was restored, half the population was not Polish at all. It was German, or Russian or Czech .. you name it. So there were ethnically and politically driven coups and counter coups, new constitutions and suspensions of constitutions. It was terribly violent and many people died. Also, Wilson had insisted that there be a Poland, but he did a poor job of saying just where it was. The Wielkoplska area, still occupied by Germany rose in violent revolt to join Poland. In Upper Silesia there was supposed to be a vote, but Germans and Slavs rioted instead and killed each other over being German or Polish.

"Nor did the war really end in 1918 for us. Poland fought wars with Ukraine, Czechoslovakia and bloodiest of all, the Russian Bolsheviks. Our neighbors were all in bloody chaos too. When the Czar fell and the Bolsheviks murdered him there was no stable government. Russia was in civil war, Germany was defeated. So the whole of Eastern Europe found itself in civil wars, wars over where borders should be and wars between ethnic groups. North of us, when Lithuania was having a civil war between ethnic Germans and everyone else, they were at war with the Bolsheviks too. Finland had a bloody civil war too. Finland threw off Russian control, voted against socialism, then, the losing socialists or I should say communists provoked a short but terrible civil war. Almost the same story in Latvia. The same in Czechoslovakia. Ukraine was a complete bloody mess. Through it all 'German Freicorp' forces did not hesitate to wade into the fights. Freicorps were groups of German soldiers returning home who kept their arms,. Fortunately, those groups usually fought against the Bolsheviks. Fortunately for Germany, they took out Bolsheviks trying to take over in Germany too. All this was, of course, only a preview of worse that was to come twenty years later in my day.

"Well then, in Poland, Ignacy found himself in the middle of all of this and even Prime Minister for a time.

"You remember that I said Poles are those who speak Polish and are Catholic? Well what about the Jews who lived in Poland? A man named Roman Dmowski had also been involved in restoring Poland. He was popular and had a big following with many votes. And he said Poles were strictly Catholic so Jewish people were not Poles at all. Jews could not be citizens in Poland. Jews had no rights and, according to Dmowski, could not even own property. And, in spite of objections from people like Ignacy, that idea became our policy. It seems to me that was very stupid. That drove many young Jewish people into the arms of the Bolsheviks and inside Poland, into the Communist underground."

Jane was very surprised to hear Jewish people could not be citizens in Poland. But she just said, "Tell me what happened to you! How do you fit into all this?"

"We're almost there. My last name was Paderewski and here's the connection. Ignacy Paderewski's mother died when he was not a year old. His father, Jan Paderewski, was the Jan who was tossed in prison. Many years later Ignacy's

153

father Jan finally got out of prison and he married again. My Mom was one of the children with his new wife. So my Mom was half brother to Ignacy, but she was a good deal younger and he was long gone anyway. So I am connected to the famous pianist, Ignacy Paderewski, but I'm not connected very closely. On paper's he's a half uncle, but in fact, I never even met the man. The family was not very interested in my mom or me because she was unmarried."

Sally Webb returned with a big tray with a tea pot, coffee urn, cups, lemons, honey, cookies, cocktail napkins, and a bottle of Luksusowa vodka. "Try this! It's honey, lemon and a splash of vodka in strong tea. It's like krupnik. My grandmother loves it! It's good."

Natalie smiled.

Jane poured herself coffee and took a cookie.

"Now tell me Jane Paine. Paine, I think, is French. Are you a peacock or a pagan? That's what the name Paine means in French you know. Paon, peacock, paien, pagan. In my opinion, you would make a better peacock."

"Natalie, you speak French?"

"Oh no, only a very little. But I think names are sometimes fun and Paine, I think, is French."

"I always thought my name came down from Irish, but maybe it's French. I'm American, all mixed up with different roots. All that was so long ago, I am not even sure what all the roots are. But if it's French, I'd guess I'd rather be a peacock."

"Ha, ha! Yes, you could be a peacock! You should dress all colorful! You would be so very pretty!"

Jane felt insulted. Then she thought of Mill's remarks about vanity. She put the issue aside to consider later. "But peacocks probably make poor investigators. We must be a bit more subtle you know."

"Bah! Be brash! Be a peacock, it's more fun. Ask Sally! She can be a peacock now and then! It looks like fun! I wish I still could. Or maybe she's a coxcomb. Or are coxcombs only men?"

Sally said, "But coxcombs are not so good, they're all show and no stuff. And I do think only men can be coxcombs. And aren't the showy peacocks the men too? The girl peacocks are dull. But what would I know? Natalie, you know I am just a country girl, just a hayseed. I don't know very much. After all, that's what pagan means in French, doesn't it. Its literal meaning is un-baptized, but the French nuanced meaning is rustic, or maybe rustikal or hinterwäldler in German, maybe wiesniak or prowincjusz in Polish. Say, aren't Bauer and Wiesniak sometimes names, just like Paine? But what would a country girl know? Now that I think of it, I had a neighbor named Paine, that was in the hills in West Virginia of course, where we went bare-foot all the time. "

Natalie laughed heartily. "Good for you Sally. You win! Very good." Natalie laughed more. "You know far more than me. But tell the truth Sally, you have been known to dress to show off a little. I've seen it myself. You should encourage Jane. How else is she going to catch that Mill fellow?"

Jane smiled at Natalie's obvious pleasure, but then she said, "Oh come on, I want to know about Poland. How did things happen in Poland? I'd like to hear about the old days."

"Spoil sport! Oh, well, let me see, it was not so interesting."

"Well then, tell me about Dr. Schmidt. If he was German, how did he avoid military service in the war?"

"Avoid the military? Oh he didn't, not at all. He held the rank of oberst, that is a colonel, almost a general. And he was attached to the general staff and he worked directly for General, Gehlen. Otto, I should say Günter was of good Junker family. When the war started, there was need to increase the size of the military at once. He was given a temporary rank right away, he did good work so his rank was made official. His Guderian and von Below family certainly did not hurt with that part. Günter was the General Staff expert, chief of intelligence really, on Poland."

'Gehlen?' Jane thought to herself, 'Gehlen?' The guy Mill talked about? The intelligence guy we recruited after the war?'

"It make more sense to know politics then. Hitler hated all the old-school Prussian professional officers. He only liked the hand-picked political generals who told him only what he wanted to hear. Hitler's yes-men, his political generals stayed in Berlin. The old General Staff, the real military leadership, kept headquarters outside of Berlin, in the city of Zossen. They couldn't stand each other.

"That separation become a game of power. The professionals knew Hitler was a military fool. But the political Generals played up to Hitler and told him he was a genius. As the war went bad, Hitler became more dictatorial and ordered more military mistakes. Then the division between political and real Generals became deeper. The real generals saw no answer but to assassinate Hitler. They tried more than once and but for bad luck would have got him. And this would be funny if it were not so serious. The British had an excellent plan to kill Hitler while he was taking his daily afternoon walk, but they decided not to do it because the colossal mistakes he ordered helped the Allies. They rightly figured his military incompetence was a great help to the Allies.

"Anyway, Günter's rank got him a staff car with General Staff flags on it and a driver, good quarters and everything that went with all that. But mostly he worked near his home in Danzig because that was almost inside Poland anyway. He was called to Zossen to report now and then, but mostly he stayed in the east. Hitler's eastern headquarters called the 'Wolf's Lair,' was actually inside Poland. But Günter was seldom called there.

"Oh my! So did Günter know Hitler?"

"Oh no, Günter was assigned to collect military information for the General Staff. Hitler relied on his intuition more than facts. Even Hitler's political RSHA intelligence men like Walter Schellenberg had to be careful what they said near Hitler. Schellenberg knew the score, that the Allies were gaining strength and Germany was losing, but even he could never get the truth past to men who surrounded Hitler.

"Günter made accurate maps showing roads and crossing points in rivers and rail lines. He reported, as best he could, enemy military movements and so on. This meant he gathered information wherever he could including reports from interrogations of captured prisoners, and when he could, from the underground as well. That sometimes meant contacts with friendly or at least anti-Soviet underground organizations.

"That sounds really exciting!"

"Exciting? That word, I think, is a romantic word. Really, it was, well, it was all very bloody, and frightening. It was a treacherous, hate-filled time all around. The murder and violence was .. frightful."

"Well then, what about you?"

"Well .. alright .. my Mom's family was wealthy and had influence. But my Mom brought shame on the family and she was cut off from all that. Still, the family was kind enough to use their influence and arrange a job for me. That was inspecting women's working conditions. I traveled around Poland looking at factories and shops and wherever women worked and I checked a list of requirements. No more than so many hours work every week, sanitary conditions, width of aisles and fire escapes, that sort of thing.

"By then, the Polish Communists were a real threat. They had already formed soviets, that's local councils to run things and wanted to put us under Stalin. So I used my official travel to be a courier for the patriotic underground that wanted to save Poland and keep Poland our own country. It was an anti-Soviet underground. When the Russian army invaded in 1939, I was arrested and spent some very unpleasant time in a very dark room.

"Later, after the imprisonment, when I had been forgotten by the Communists, I rejoined and even headed a secret cell. Finally I was a candidate to the overall committee that communicated with our legal government which by then was in exile. There I met Zofia Kossak-Szczucka? She was an underground member and she formed' Żegota.' That was 'The Polish Council to Aid Jews.' And how ironic was that? It was us, more than the Bolsheviks who tried to save Jewish people. The Nazis, of course, caught Zofia and took her to Auschwitz."

Jane thought, 'Wow! Where's Mill? He'd know about this and know what to ask now.'

Sally made Natalie another spiked tea. Jane noticed Sally was more generous with the vodka this time.

"Those were very violent times. Terrible times. The communists murdered us whenever they learned who we were. They murdered innocent people they only suspected. And the Russian occupying army was worse, raping and murdering ordinary Poles.

"Yes, Germany invaded Poland first. The Nazi 'General Government' under Hitler's man Hans Frank forced Jewish people into ghettos, hanged them in the streets and tried to exterminate them in concentration camps. The Nazis thought little better of the rest of us either. Nazis took our property and killed us too.

"Russians or Germans, in Poland we got the worst either way. The German Wehrmacht, their military at least, mostly followed rules of war. Oh, they were German like the Nazis, but there was certainly a difference.

"Then Germany invaded Russia itself. They drove the Russians right out of Poland. Later, Germany lost terrible numbers of soldiers in Russia. Stalingrad was a bloody disaster and they lost a whole army at Leningrad. After that, back came the Russian army. We'd seen the Russians and knew what brutality was coming. So those of us who had fought communists had to make friends wherever we could. I knew of Otto, that is to say Günter only by reputation and rumor. We had never met. The Germans had brutalized us and meeting a German officer was a bad idea. But we both had contact with Żegota, that is the organization saving Jewish people, and that was not so German. When things became more and more desperate, I, of necessity, risked meeting him. We hated the Nazis and their SS and Gestapo. But the men of Wehrmacht, that is the old-line German Military, and Günter was one of those, were, at least, not Nazis.

"In an underground, information is the medium of exchange. Information is the currency. Information is used like money but it is worth more even. A tip that the enemy plans a raid saved lives. Pay back for the tip might be another tip, a contact name or some such. Doing this, I developed closer and closer dealings with Günter. We had much that was useful to each other. I even helped him get messages to our government in exile. The oncoming Russians gave us common cause and soon we were working closely together. We found we trusted each other and we found we were fond of each other.

"When the war was obviously nearing an end, the Russians identified Günter. They judged him a spy and marked him for death. The Russians had again listed me as a fugitive and now marked me for death too. In the so called civilized places like Holland and France, women who collaborated with Germans had their hair cut off and were marched naked through the streets where crowds pelted them with rocks. Often worse happened to them. In the east, it was worse yet. To collaborate with a German meant a terrible death. So now my life depended on hiding and escaping. There was no protection for us anywhere and time was not on our side. Günter finally managed a way out for us. But you know all about that."

Jane asked, "Those files in the other room, did you have those when you two were in Danzig or Poland or Prussia or whatever you were?"

"Those? By the end, we were hiding in Konigsberg. That had been the capital of East Prussia once. It was a hundred miles by car from Günter's home in Danzig, a hundred miles the wrong way for us. It was almost in Russia. If the SS or Gestapo caught a German officer racing for Germany, they would say he was fleeing duty and would shoot him on the spot. Going that way was out. Günter thought the Russians would not look for us in Konigsberg, besides Günter had some old contacts there. Getting there was not so simple. The roads were reserved for the retreating German army. They stayed on roads except when they slaughtered a farm animal for food or destroyed things just to keep them from the Russians hands. The fleeing people trying to stay ahead of Russian murder and rape were not allowed to use roads at all. People fled for their lives, even on foot through woods. And we were headed the wrong way. Heading the other way, toward Russia, took some doing, even in a staff car with flags.

"It was bad when the Russian army took Konigsberg. Few women escaped the brutality of the Russian troops. Men and even children were just murdered where they stood. Anything the Russians wanted was pillaged. We managed to hide in the Swedish Consulate until the worst had past. That was illegal because Sweden was neutral and not supposed to hide refugees, but Günter used old connections to get us in. There was a close call. The Swedish Console asked the Russians to post a protective guard. And the Russians actually did it. Of course that wanted to search the building first. That was a close call. We put blankets over ourselves and hid in under coal for the boiler.

"Oh yes, you asked about the hidden papers. We left those behind when we ran for Kaliningrad. Later, Otto, I mean Günter said they would cast us in a good light with Americans if we were ever questioned. Some of those papers even go back to Żegota.

"Then how on earth did you get them here?"

"Oh, Günter simply paid a mover. Well, not so simply. In those days the Russian military occupation made anything like that complicated and illegal. But Russians were as corrupt as anyone else, more corrupt really, and so with some political pull and some money .. anyway, they got here."

Jane spoke, "Natalie, do you think anyone from those bad old days is still around? Would anyone still hold a grudge against you or Günter after all these years?'

"Still around? Oh no. Hold a grudge? That's different. People can hold a grudge about having their land taken or about ethnic cleansing and ethnic hatred, about losing their freedom, the Palestinians are probably still angry about Jewish people we sent there. All that kind of anger can go from generation to generation for a very long time. But I doubt many people from those days are still alive and none remembers us."

Jane said, "Some of the papers seem to be in German, some in Polish, maybe you could help me understand what they say."

Then Natalie said, "Oh heavens, c'mon Jane. I'll just show you and explain. Sally can help too. She's better at this stuff than she admits."

Sally said, "I don't really speak anything but down home hillbilly English, but let's look." Sally picked up the tray and followed.

The Third Dead Man

"With death comes honesty"

Salmon Rushdie

Outside was pleasant. The little sunken yard with its short wall was pleasant even if the cement seats looked hard, cold and moldy. Mill spent only a minute there. Then he hiked to the flat gray bridge at the edge of the yard. He guessed a worn track in the grass was from the occasional passage of a lawn tractor. He followed the tracks and they led, as expected, to the half hidden shed in the woods. Back here, under the trees, it was darker and it was quiet. Peaceful or gloomy? Mill decided gloomy won. Mill heard the sound of some creature and Mill felt a nervous prickle. A squirrel or chipmunk? No, something much bigger. A raccoon? No, raccoons are nocturnal. Maybe it was a deer or a person. It seemed to be running away in any case.

The garden shed had a Pennsylvania Dutch hex sign over the door. That was another style that went with nothing else in this place.

The shed was bigger than it looked from a distance. Mill lifted a latch on the shed's barn style doors and one of them opened freely. It was dark inside but Mill could see a refrigerator. It was humming. There was a microwave oven on top of it. Odd, thought Mill, maybe grounds keepers brought their lunch. But that also meant there was electricity in the shed. Mill fumbled around for a light switch and he found one. A light did come on.

There were the expected yard tools and an expensive looking lawn tractor with a cart attached as a trailer. In a far corner there was a rototiller that looked like it had not been used in a decade. A couple bags of fertilizer were on a shelf and gasoline cans on a higher shelf. Mill winced. He knew that if gasoline spilled into high nitrogen fertilizer it makes a low grade explosive. Above was a small heater. Little good that would do in this un-insulated place.

The expected smell of cut grass and gas was there, but something about it was off. Rakes, shovels and more tools hung on the walls. There was a five gallon bucket on the floor and a tool box that was open. But something was wrong. Then it registered in Mill's brain. He was looking at a man's foot sticking out from behind the tractor. "Oh crap!" he said out loud. He backed away a step, then, he rushed forward. There was no doubt now. A man lay on a blanket mostly behind the tractor. He was an old guy, his head was at an odd angle and he looked quite dead.

Mill moved quickly and felt for pulse. There was none and the guy seemed cold. He had no matches or lighter or any other way to check for breath, but he was sure the man was dead. Mill quickly fumbled out his cell phone and dialed nine-one-one.

"My name is John Mill, I have a dead body in a shed behind Günter Schmidt's house .. it's a man. .. No, I don't know the address. Günter Schmidt's house, the old professor from Colebrook School. No it's not him, it's an unknown body. Call the State Police, they were here just this morning and they know the place. They'll know where I mean. But send an ambulance now. I'm sure he's dead so no siren needed. … No I'm not going to run around and hunt for an address. I'm well behind the house in a shed. Do not send your guys to the door of the house, I'm around in back. Have them go around the side of the house and come straight back. .. Look the guy up, Günter Schmidt. Günter and Natalie Schmidt's house. I'll be here waiting, but I'm hanging up to make another emergency call. ..Yes, my name is Mill, no, not Mills. Mill, no 'S.' Sorry, I'm hanging up because I need to make an emergency call to an interested police lieutenant, but I'll be here and I'll wait. Tell your ambulance guys to look for the guy near the woods out back, sports coat, bow tie."

Mill clicked off. Henderson's card was already in his hand. He dialed again. "Henderson, We've got another body. You better get to Schmidt's house right now. Different this time. This guy's been hidden in the shed out back. I can't identify him. I called nine-one-one already. .. He's dead all right. .. My fingerprints are already on all over. I checked for pulse and breath and stuff, otherwise everything's as found it. It's out back near the love nest. The tool shed or yard shed, whatever this place is. I'll control the ambulance guys and keep 'em from messing everything up till you get here, but please get yourself and forensics over here. .. No, it was dumb luck, just snooping around."

Mill looked back at the dead man, then turned and surveyed the area. Now that he looked more closely, obvious auto tire marks came most of the way up the path that led to the shed. It looked like a car had backed up the path as far as it could. There were footprints too. All was obvious. Why hadn't he noticed all this before he entered the shed? That stupid deer must have distracted him. But how did a car get in this back yard at all? The slope around Schmidt's house was too steep and narrow and there was that little stream too. The little flat bridge would never handle a car. It must have come the other way, from the neighbor's place past the guest house. There should be auto tire tracks all the way. Whoever drove must be familiar with the area and the yard. Just like Schmidt's killer, this killer was familiar with the place.

Then Mill heard voices from the direction of the guest house. He pushed the shed's barn door closed and hurried down the path. It was Lois and Swan Feine. "Oh! Mr. Mill, is Jane Paine with you? Are you looking in the guest house again? We'd like to talk." It was Swan speaking.

Mill stood still so he wouldn't mess up footprints or tire tracks any more. "Please stay there. Ms. Paine's in the house talking to Mrs. Schmidt just now. Can I help? But please stay where you are, we have a big problem here and I don't want you to come any closer. Don't put prints in the grass."

The Feine girls look at the grass. "A big problem?"

"Just keep back please."

"Well, you see, this is all getting very serious and we thought we better be totally truthful with you guys. We want to tell Ms. Paine some stuff."

"That will be fine, but don't move any closer. Don't walk on the grass. Go around the long way."

Swan spoke up, "No, I don't need Ms. Paine, talking to you is all the same to me. I don't care. I just want to say what we told you about Mrs. Webb was true as far as it went. We did think something was up. But there were others who visited the house too. They would park at Webb's and come in that way. We're not so sure it was all so romantic after all. Maybe some kind of business meetings or something was going on. There were other people there even Mr. Webb. But here's the deal, the things you probably spotted upstairs are really mine, not Mrs. Webb's if that's what you thought. And I'd like to get them out of there unless they're evidence or something. The real reason we were there the other day, was to get that stuff out before it was found."

Lois spoke again. "You see, Dr. Schmidt even told us about that upper room once. He joked about it. He said he put it together when he and Mrs. Schmidt were younger and now he thought it was funny to have a getaway so close to home. He told us they never even used it. When we watched for the lights, that seemed to be so. Nobody went upstairs. We sneaked up there one day and thought it was a gas just looking around. I think Dr. Schmidt was onto us though because the next time we sneaked in, it was locked. But we figured out how to unlock it by quickly twisting a paperclip back and forth in the key hole. I saw some guys do that with a lock at school and we tried it. We got pretty good at it."

Swan, "Anyway, the stuff up there is mine, not Mrs. Webb's. I have a boyfriend who gives me stuff. That's all. I don't want to say more unless I have to."

"I'm glad you told me. It might be important. Thank you. And we may need to talk more about everything you know and you saw. But I'm afraid now is the wrong time. There is a big problem here and all hell's going to break loose in a minute. It would be a favor to Jane Paine and me if you'd stay off the lawn or better yet, go to Schmidt's house and see Ms. Paine, but go another way, not through here, and repeat what you just told me to Ms. Paine."

Just then, two men and a woman and a gurney appeared at the side of the house. They were coming at a near run. "Uh!-oh!," said Swan. The girls didn't leave, they stayed and watched. Mill waved at the flat gray bridge at the yard's edge and one man and the woman handling the gurney detoured that way. The other came straight across the foot bridge.

Mill went back near the shed. Watch out! I think those car tire tracks are murder evidence. There's a dead guy in there. I'm going to open the door to keep your fingerprints off. Mine are already there. One of you guys carefully come up and check for pulse and stuff. Then just wait. The cops are on the way."

164

Lois, just visible in front of the guest house, held her hand over her mouth. Swan just stared.

One of the attendants pulled a two way radio off his hip. "Dispatch, some guy here says the cops are already summoned. Please confirm. He says he's got a dead guy in a shed and doesn't want us walkin' around on the yard. Says there's murder evidence. This guy might be screwy. If the cops are not en route already, please get them."

Mill held his badge up and said "Federal Agent, not screwy." Then he tried to step only in his previous foot prints and then opened the door again. One attendant came forward taking great long strides, then he produced a stethoscope. He carefully leaned over the body and listened. Then he felt for pulse. He opened the man's eye with a finger and turned a flashlight at the eye then away. Finally he held a lit match under the dead man's nose. "Nothin,' he's seriously dead."

The attendant returned the way he came actually walking backwards with big steps. Then a second attendant, the woman, repeated the long stride walk and felt for pulse too, but she did not continue the vital sign check. "Cold as a stone, he's been dead a while." She did an about face and walked away with big strides.

Mill said, "Okay, now please stay well back till the cops get here". At the same time the attendant's radio squawked "Affirmative, cops are probably in the driveway now."

Then Mill noticed Jane looking out from the house windows. He could barely see her through the trees. He came down the path and made a small circular wave meaning to say, keep Mrs. Schmidt busy and inside for now. Jane evidently understood as she nodded and moved on.

Mill said, "This is almost certainly a murder. My name is John Mill, I'm a kind of detective. I called you guys and the cops too. The cops, I think, are going to take some time here before you can move the body. I suggest each of you ask for one of those statement forms, write down what you saw, and then leave for a while. Otherwise you're going to waste the whole afternoon sitting around."

"Nope," said the attendant with the radio, "In a case like this, policy says we're stuck till the cops release the body. Less paperwork that way. Might cost us a run or two, but, in the end, it saves no end of pain in the ass paperwork. One run at a time, finish it out, then the next one."

"In that case, sorry for your trouble, but I needed somebody besides myself to say he's really dead. It wouldn't do for him to be alive and die after I found him just because I didn't call for you. I knew he was obviously dead, but I have to follow rules and take precautions just like you. Sorry."

"Understood, that we understand. But who the hell are you?"

"I'm a Federal investigator named Mill, leave it at that for now and please don't tell any news guys about me. The cops will know me and why I'm here. There's an investigation underway and I don't want news guys onto me yet. For now, if you have to say anything, just say the authorities called you or something."

"And those girls?"

"They just happened along. I told them to stay put."

"And that lady you waved to in the window?"

"My partner, she's looking after a little old lady who we don't want to upset."

"Mister, you better be right."

"I am."

"Is this investigation related to that suicide here a couple days ago?"

"What do you think?"

"And why did you think there'd be a dead guy in there?"

"I didn't think there would be, it was a total surprise."

Mill's phone rang. It was Jane. "Mrs. Schmidt hasn't noticed anything yet. I heard the ambulance and told her I was going to the can. She's in the secret file room with Sally Webb. What's up?"

"Found another one, another dead guy in the shed out here. Henderson's on the way. If you're doing any good up there keep it up. We'll have to tell Mrs. Schmidt, but it's probably okay to delay that, especially if you're doing any good with her. By the way, the Feine girls are here with a minor bomb shell, they say it's their fancy underwear in the guest house, not Mrs. Webb's."

The phone call was followed by an uncomfortable silence. It was not five minutes, but it seemed longer. Finally two uniformed policemen appeared. They were coming the same way as the ambulance attendants. Henderson followed with an unknown man in a highly tailored business suit plus rubbers protecting his expensive looking shoes.

As they approached, Mill held up a hand. "Hold it. Dead guy's in there. Notice the car tracks and footprints. Don't mess them up. Henderson, I turn this over to you. I was just snoopin' and found him."

The sounds of a bigger vehicle arriving could be heard. "Forensics van," said Henderson. "Spatz, this is Mill. I was just telling you about him. Mill, Colonel Spatz is from Lansing. I'm being booted off I guess. He's taking over."

Spatz was tall, he wore a business suit that must have cost a couple thousand, his lower jaw very wide and he obviously spent many hours in tanning salons. Mill thought that level of vanity needed to shed the tie, unbutton his shirt and load on ten pounds of gold chains. Mill wondered how much time Spatz spent looking at himself in the mirror. 'Narcissus himself,' Mill thought.

"Henderson, Henderson, you're not being booted. Nobody's unhappy with your work. We just want an appropriate level of attention here. That's what I'm for. Now what have you got for us Mr., um, Agent Mill?"

"Dead guy in there, I don't know him. Tire tracks and footprints, looks like he was moved by car and dumped. Haven't looked at the body for gunshots or anything. He's on a blanket. I'd guess the blanket was used to drag him in there."

Spatz raised his eyebrows as if to say, "And?"

"My partner Jane Paine is in the house interviewing Mrs. Schmidt regarding how she and Mr. Schmidt came here and asking about their lives before that. We think that might shed light on the murders of Mr. Schmidt and Agent Smith. Smith relocated Schmidt in forty-six so the connection may go way back. Mrs. Schmidt seems forthcoming about all that, so in order to put Mrs. Schmidt more at ease, with another woman instead of a man, she is being interviewed by Ms. Paine. In the mean time, to satisfy my curiosity, and to take one last pass for clues, I was simply looking around and happened to nose into the shed."

Spatz looked at Mill and said, "Nose into the shed, huh?" Then he remained silent with his raised eyebrows.

Mill recognized Spatz's silent interrogation trick. It was a respectable old method for suspects, but he did not care to be on the receiving end of it. He didn't care for the nose remark either. So he pointedly turned to Henderson and ignored Spatz, "After I point out my footprints and stuff to your forensics guys, I think you and I should join Jane and Mrs. Schmidt. There may be important data up there."

Spatz was still silent and raised his eyebrows yet higher and now he tilting his tanned head a bit. Mill almost laughed at this, but held himself. Then he picked up the slightest smile on Henderson's face. "I got-cha Mill. But is it a rush? I need to get these guys going. That'll take half an hour at least."

"It may be important. You should be there."

"Good, okay where did you step, what did you touch, what did you do? Show us inch by inch."

Odd Meetings

"Information is not knowledge"

Albert Einstein

Mill heard Jane, Sally Webb and Natalie Schmidt or rather Natalia Paderewski before he found them. They were giggling like much younger people. He heard Jane's voice say, "Oh, but I have never been married! How would I ever know about that sort of thing?" Then he heard gales of giggling.

"But I have never been married either! How do you suppose I ever found out?" That was Natalie's voice .. more laughter.

"Oh, when Clyde and I met, I was still size six."

"You have been size six since you were twelve. You're just too tall." More laughter.

When .. well, Jane, you know I am married. One day I asked Clyde to help me at the store with lingerie .."

Mill found them in the secret room. They sat on folding card table chairs around a small table. Jane had coffee, Sally and Natalie had tea. There was a plate of cookies and little plates and cocktail napkins in front of each lady. Natalie's hand was on Jane's arm and she was still giggling."

"Am I interrupting?"

"Oh no" said Natalie. She sounded and even looked younger than she had earlier. "We are just having girl talk. I haven't had such fun in a long time. I have even asked your Jane to move out of that smelly hotel and stay here to protect me! To protect ME! Ha, ha, ha .. Sally is giving Jane pointers on sexy clothes and maybe I'll give her some pointers on handgun use while she's here. Who would protect who?" All three giggled again. "Oh, I know! I'll protect her from your advances in that hotel!" .. more giggles. "Protect me Jane? Do you know the difference between a Blyskawica and a karabin przeciwpancerny?"

"A what?"

"See, one is a machine gun, the other an anti-tank rifle." Natalie laughed hard. She seemed to think this was extremely funny.

Jane said, "Okay, but do you know what a Glock is?"

"Oh yes, it's a composite pistol! See, I got you! I knew that one. I bet you have a little lady sized one. Pull it out of your purse, I see that bulge. Pull it out and I can give you some pointers!"

On the table was a tea kettle, lemon, honey and Luksusowa vodka. Mill thought, 'Vodka in tea? Yuk! Well, maybe with enough lemon and honey.' He looked back at Jane.

Jane gave him an almost imperceptible side to side turn of her head. He took that to mean she was not drinking. Or not drinking very much anyway.

"Oh come in." It was Natalie again. "I'll tell how we made Blyskawica machine guns in secret right under their noses. Sally will get you another chair?" She waved her hand past the file cabinets. "All this, this is what you want to know? You don't want to know about machine guns or dressing Jane sexy? This old stuff is long lists of names and accounts, just as you thought. There are four sets of lists. First, those Jewish people who applied for aid and relocation. Next, manifests and lists of groups of people who were relocated to Palestine. They are in groups that went together. Then there are lists of expenses and accounts for each group. And finally there are reconciliations. Estimates of costs and for delivering these people compared with actual costs all reconciled for the people who paid for all this. How's that Mr. Detective? And we did this all in an hour. Sally even helped. She was reading German to us. Will you hire me now? Maybe Sally too? Or do you suspect I knew everything all along?"

All three ladies laughed.

"Is that what Mr. Schmidt was doing before you came here? Moving Jewish refugees to Palestine?"

"What a party pooper. Everything is just business for you Mr. Mill detective. You don't want to know about our guns? This is not enough for now? Well yes, that and many other things. Yes, it was an underground railroad out of Poland and into Palestine."

"Do you also know where all this money for that came from?" Jane waved her hand as if to tell Mill to leave so Mill said, "If you'll excuse me, I'd like to meet with Lieutenant Henderson in your foyer or maybe out on the porch."

"Oh, the police again, you're no fun at all. But of course, go to your meeting."

To Mill's surprise, Sally Webb stood and said, "I'll bring coffee."

Jane rolled her eyes Sally's way, it was a 'Get her out of here' eye roll if ever there was one. Mill grinned back and said clearly. "I'll be up front in the foyer or maybe out on the porch. Coffee'd be great!"

Mill found the Feine girls talking to Henderson on the porch. Spatz sat there too. Mill sat down.

He also noticed that Swan wore some sort of low cut crocheted top. It left little to the imagination. When he saw her earlier at the shed, her clothing had escaped him. Now, at close range, Mill thought Swan's modesty would benefit from adding some underwear, even the immodest underwear he had seen in the guest house under her present attire. He decided he better look at Henderson, not stare at Swan. He sat down.

"I just told Lieutenant Henderson it was my stuff in the guest house, it was given to me by my boyfriend." said Swan, "And, well, we've been doing some thinking. Bubbie, that's our great aunt, said some mighty odd stuff about Germans. But I don't think she's shoot Dr. Schmidt over it. Besides, she came home with us that night. And I don't think Mrs. Schmidt would shoot Dr. Schmidt over Sally Webb.

171

We're not really so sure anything was happening anyway, just that they were meeting out there and not always with those other men."

"I gotta go," said Spatz. "See you at the shop."

Lois spoke. "That night we just talked to those two German guys who just showed up. They gave us their cell phone. It was a screwy European phone number, but it worked. And they said that McIntyre guy was at the art museum the night your friend was shot. They said their uncle wanted them to give a report about McIntyre. He wanted to see if his hand was in the cookie jar. That's the way they put it. They said, all this shooting confirms something's wrong and their uncle is on the way. They also say their uncle's calling the German Consulate and their State Department or whatever."

Swan, "I can't believe it, the German guys, Hans and Helga say they're going to stay here in this house anyway. Just like nothing happened. They say they should be here this afternoon and invited us to bring our friends over and all meet tomorrow just like nothing's going on. And one more thing, that Dr. Shaw guy, he has a daughter I know in school. She's Muslim and she's hooked up with some Catholic guy. We're all taking bets on where that's going and if the Catholic guy will live to tell about it. But she, that Muslim girl, keeps asking us all about Dr. Schmidt. Like, how did she even know that we knew him. Then her Dad was at that party, then Schmidt is dead."

Mill said, "You've watched that guest house you said. Tell us what you saw."

Lois; "Oh, that. Well we told you the truth. Sometimes Sally Webb and Dr. Schmidt seemed to meet a little more secret-like than looked exactly right to me. But other times there were more people. Mr. Webb was there for sure and sometimes an old husky guy too and sometimes other men."

"Would you recognize any of them?"

"I don't think so. We were kinda far away. But maybe. On one or two times, there was a whole bunch of them. All men but Sally Webb were usually there. The other funny thing is they usually came from the direction of Webb's house."

172

A big arts and crafts style door opened and Sally Webb appeared, rear end first pushing the door open. She had a tray and coffee, cream, sugar and some cookies. She put the tray down, started pouring and said. "Cream? Sugar?"

"Black, thank you," said Mill. "Me too, and thanks." said Henderson.

Lois looked up at Sally. "Thanks, but we need to go." She looked at Mill. "The cops have our cell numbers but we wrote them down again so you won't have to look them up. We'll do whatever we can."

As the Feine girls left, Sally sat down. "Those two little snoops. Always looking out that bedroom window of theirs. They even keep binoculars there. Oh well. So who do you think done it? Old Bubbie Feine? She hates Krauts. Natalie? Schmidt was, no doubt, a pompous old ass who should have been shot. Me? Sorry, nothing there. I actually liked the old stinker. How about the German kids. But why? What's the scoop?'

Henderson laughed. "Can't go there. Thanks for coffee."

"Then you Mr. Millnose. What do you say?"

"Same answer."

"Mind if I smoke a cigarette? It's a beautiful afternoon. Your girl Jane is good by the way. I was even having fun. I learned more about old Natalie and old Schmidt in an hour with Jane than I learned in ten years living across the back fence." Sally exhaled a big cloud of smoke.

Mill, "Were you in the habit of meeting Dr. Schmidt in the guest house?"

"Sure, and I know those kids told you that. Ha, some clandestine meeting, I made coffee for those jokers, just like now. I put on a short skirt and tight top and made coffee."

"Mr. Webb was there?"

"Sometimes."

"You acted as hostess?"

"Yes, I guess that's it."

"Why didn't Dr. Schmidt have Natalie act as hostess? Why you?"

Sally looked at Mill. "I flatter myself that I'm younger and dress sexier. Old Schmidt was a sort of low grade lecher. But, for sure, I know I'm not that young. I think the real reasons were first, Natalie didn't want to be bothered and next, I think Schmidt didn't want Natalie to know everything about his money dealings, and next, I don't speak German, and last, I'd do it just for the asking."

"Natalie Schmidt just told me you were reading German in there. Which is it?"

"Oops! .. Okay, I get German just a little. But I'm not very fluent. Mainly, I can read an accounting ledger in German because I've been a secretary in an American office to a German outfit and I needed to be able to do that part. Some stuff I worked on was in German. But it was just headers to columns of numbers and stuff. Reading a column of numbers is not the same thing as reading or speaking German. I still say I don't really speak German. Not well anyway."

"And Schmidt had secrets from Natalie, but not you?"

"Like I said, I don't really speak German."

"Who were these guys?"

"Krauts. Business. Finance. Like I said, I don't speak German. Now and then there'd be an American or two or three as well. Hell, that old Polish catering fart was even there once in a while. But for business, they spoke all German. It was about investments and stuff I think, and I think it was big money.'

"Do you know names? Could you identify any of them?'

"Mostly, I think so. Names? .. let me think. I'm good at names when I see them face to face. I'll try to make you a list of the names and stuff I can remember. Give me a couple hours or a day."

"Please, whatever you can tell us, descriptions with names, anything. And Mr. Webb? He was alright with this and dressing sexy?"

"Hell, he was behind it. He likes me dressing sexy. He thought it was fun. I'd show him what I was wearing and he'd always pick something even skimpier. He didn't even like bras. Well, I guess he invested a bunch in improving these," she looked down "so he wanted 'em noticed. Mostly I'd play along so long as I didn't look like an out and out hooker. If he didn't come along himself, he'd ask if the old guys liked what they saw and smile when I said I caught so and so stealing a peek at a sheer top or something. He thought it was fun. He even bought me one of those silly German , what does the Saint Pauli beer girl wear? A low cut dirndl, that's it, a dirndl with a really low top and really short skirt."

Mill looked at Sally. Today she was the image of a conservative suburban house-wife. Her clothes were expensive, but not showy, not exactly over-dressed, and not particularly sexy, just good taste and expensive looking. She had plain sweater, maybe cashmere, over a nice blouse and nice long pants and good, but flat shoes. Mill was mildly disappointed.

"And Natalie knew you were there serving coffee and pouring drinks and looking super-sexy?"

"It was no secret."

"And why did you do it? What's your angle?"

"I liked it. I'm bored. I still like people looking at me. I mean half a dozen men pretending not to stare .. it was kind of a kick for someone past her twenties, it was kind of hilarious from my point of view. Clyde doesn't exactly take me to the disco to show off you know. It made me feel younger and sexy and like I hadn't missed so much when I was a teenager after all. And besides, I'm not totally sure I'm so attractive really, and it was kind of like being re-assured. And after a couple drinks, did they ever stare. It was kind of a gas for my ego."

175

"More important though, I understand my job. I'm 'the trophy.' I'm Clyde's ego. For that I get to live here in style far beyond my means. I'm not from money. I'm 'country,' if you know what that really means."

"My first marriage was a horror show, I was a teenager and I was the whipping boy and I was the bread winner too. To say the least, we didn't have much. After that disaster, I went back and finished high school. I really did finish school, no G.E.D. for me, I took the real classes and did it. And I have two years at community college too, mostly in English, and I have an associate's degree. And I don't sound like West Virginia any more, do I? I'm as proud of that school and improving myself and my speech as you guys'd be of a PhD in astrophysics."

"And now my job is trophy-wife to a rich guy who loves me. That's not so bad at all. Look sexy, work out to keep in shape, do what Clyde wants, which is never anything too bad, be polite to everybody, fawn all over Clyde in public, and I get to live really, really well. They say trophy-wife job security falls off fast as you get older. But so far, I think Clyde's still very well pleased. He's a really good guy. He's a good, good man. The best and kindest man I ever met. And I mean that. Our arrangement works great. Trophy wife is not like prostituting yourself for money or anything because we're both happy with the arrangement and it works great for us."

"Job security huh, did you shoot either of those guys over that or for any other reason?"

"Nope."

"Was anything funny going on with Schmidt?"

"Ha, true, I did like the self important old ass. Funny stuff? Nah."

"Would Clyde have liked something funny?"

Sally glared, "No. He likes me just a bit sexier around men than is totally polite. But that's showing off, showing what he has. I think that anything funny, as you put it, would be way, way off limits. I'd lose my position as trophy wife over that.

Besides, do you know how old that man was? And, by the way, some things are off limits for me too."

"There's a bottle of scotch and a bottle of vodka on the counter in the guest house. Which is yours?"

"Trick question you turkey. Just ask me straight. Don't be so cute Mr. Mill. Yes, the booze was ours. Sure, we kept our favorite bottles there. Sure we shared a drink now and then. That doesn't mean anything. Ask Swan why she kept her underwear upstairs and picked the locks when her boyfriend is in town. She thinks we didn't notice. That'd be a better question."

"Fair enough. Do you own a gun?"

"Yup, a little Beretta automatic. I keep it in my night stand. It's totally legal. I bought it used years ago while I was married to the red-neck ass. It was two week's pay, tips and all back then. He was violent and I seriously thought I might need to shoot him. I lied about my age when I got it and I guess nobody checked. Clyde has an old army forty-five too. It's someplace or other in the house. Want to see them?"

"Maybe."

"And, by the way, old Bubbie Feine has a gun too. I met her when I took lessons at the range. She was taking lessons too. That was just coincidence and that was long ago and we had both forgotten. I didn't know her then. We remembered when we were talking about it at one of Schmidt's parties. I don't know why on earth she got that thing. That was a dozen years ago or more. She was in better shape then. I think she'd break her osteoporosis filled wrist if she tried to shoot that thing now."

"Do you know who shot Schmidt? Do you think it's Bubbie Feine?"

"No. Hell no. Not Bubbie Feine. She'd like to blow a hole in Schmidt all right, she hates krauts that much, and with good reason I suppose, but she'd have done it long ago if she was really going to do it. Not now."

"So who did?"

"Hmmm, it's someone new. I'd say the German kids or that Dr. Shaw. They're new. If anybody else did it, they would have done it years ago, but you guys are the detectives, not me. I'll let you two have your meeting. I know Jane wants me out of there, I saw her secret message to you, but too bad, I just gave her half an hour, now I'm going back. But don't worry, I'll really just back her up and keep Natalie just drunk enough to open up, but not so drunk she falls asleep. I'm good at this game. And I'm on your side. I like Jane's act and I'm a team player. I may play sexy for lecherous old men, but she plays life-long pal to little old ladies to a tee. In that department, she's way better than me. I'm 'in your face.' She's cute and disarming. Don't worry, I know how to keep out of her way. Let me know if there's anything I can do. I want to find out who blasted old Schmidt as much as you do. He was a real pal in his old fart kind of way and I owe him anything I can do. Count me in if I can help."

"The list, give us names and anything about who met Schmidt. Who were the guys in the guest house meetings. Anything you know or remember. That's what we want."

"Okay, okay!"

Sally squashed her cigarette on a plate and took the plate in with her. Mill rose and held the big door. Henderson stood too. Sally said, "I'll type up a list of names and data and give it to Jane tomorrow. I think she really is going to be a house guest here tonight." Then she disappeared into the house.

"Wow .. wow!?" said Henderson. "Do you believe her?"

"Well, partly. Not totally I guess. She weasel worded plenty and she didn't give us the names of the guys in the meetings right off the bat although you can bet she knows them all. She wants to check something with someone first. She plays brassy but really, she's not brassy, she's cagey. Did you like the recovery on not speaking German?"

Henderson said, "German? If she's as 'country' as she says and finished high school late, I bet her German is weak. Otherwise, I agree with you, especially about not giving us the names right now. Also, I mean, some men like to show their wives off to other men and all that, but the guest house meetings still don't feel right to me. That's too much. Besides, what were they meeting about anyway? And who are these guys? And Bubbie Feine has a gun, that's weird and interesting. And why did Sally make sure to tell us that?"

Mill said, "She's cagey and smart. She's working with someone. And I guess I'm not totally buying the country girl thing. There's more here."

Henderson; "Anyway, here's what I have so far. First, last night, Smith phoned Dorsey's cell three times, he phoned McIntyre's office then McIntyre's cell. Then he phoned, of all people, Alka Seltzer Panski. Second point; you were right, but you didn't know how right. There's blood of not two people, but three people on the steps at the school. Smith must have winged his assailants. I wonder if one was Alka Seltzer and I wonder if that's him out back in the shed? Point three, Dr. Shaw, lives in West Bloomfield. He's in our files from a couple informal FBI inquires to us and one from the CIA. He has Palestinian and radical Muslim connections all over the place. They think he's somehow connected to the terrorists in Gaza who fire home-made rockets into Israel. And he gives lots of money to Palestinian relief funds. There's nothing we can find exactly illegal on him, but there may be plenty that's scary hidden just out of sight."

"Last, as far as handwriting on the 'meet in the kitchen' note, no match yet, but no handwriting sample from the kids yet either.

"Okay, what do you have?"

"Dorsey's playing hard to catch with the big secrets from the past. But if you've worked in Washington, you know that's typical. Or he's been told to lay low and clam up. You have no idea how screwed up and paralyzed Washington can be. Maybe you can use your pal Spatz for a frontal assault. Demand information from both the Secretary of State's office and the Attorney General's office. But, of course, I didn't suggest that. That said, the files in that secret room look like financial records for moving Jewish refugees or displaced persons to Israel. That fits with what little we know about Schmidt. But they're in German and it looks like Polish and some stuff I don't recognize. If you have guys who can read that stuff, I'd get them in there fast. Dorsey or State Department impounding the stuff wouldn't amaze me so move quick. Again, I didn't say that. Also, Schmidt was in contact with Franz von Papen, a real slippery cat and spy master of those early days and he had access to big, big, Nazi money. Jane's pumping Natalie for anything she remembers now.

"Natalie, by the way, knows her guns and she's teasing and suggesting she can handle them. And I bet she's right, or at least she could years ago. Jane is no sharpshooter. That one's an overmatch. Natalie knows guns. Ya think maybe she blew old Schmidt away over Sally?"

Henderson said, "Maybe we shouldn't close the doors on that kind of thing. Maybe the motive is from 1946. But maybe it's not. That's a long gestation period for a murder. 'Cherchez la femme'! What does that 'cherchez la femme' mean anyway?   Look for the women? Beware the woman? Something like that anyway. Don't rule out these love triangle ideas just yet. When people start shooting each other, look for the women. That or look for drugs or money. Hate is another reason people kill each other. There's an ethnic thing in this neighborhood. It comes out reading the interviews. Half of 'em go back to World War Two and all that turmoil and they still hate. Keep an open mind on that Mill. Your Smith was around in 1946 and he's dead now. That argues that the motive goes back that far. Or maybe he just put the wrong two plus two together and stepped on something that blew up."

Mill said, "I'll go with Schmidt's past too, not love triangles. I bet Jane'll dig some clues out of Natalie. .. Cherchez la femme .. hmm .. Alexandre Dumas?"

"Mill, you're ridiculous. Nobody knows that without looking it up."

"The only femmes we have are the Feine girls and Sally Webb, unless you count ladies over eighty. And Sally's the only one that seriously belongs in a Dumas novel."

"And Jane Paine."

"Oh yeah! Jane. She is a femme, you're right. Sometimes I forget that. Ya think she did it?"

"And Helga Hoffman."

"Oh yeah. Now that you mention it, there are more femmes than I thought. But Dumas meant more like watch out for what women make men do, less watch out for the women themselves."

The sound of a car approaching stopped the conversation. A big sedan stopped in front of the forensics van. Henderson said, "McIntyre and the Hoffman kids."

McIntyre was first out of the car. "You're the police? You're still here?"

Henderson rose. "Yes sir, I'm afraid there has been a further incident and we are here again. Mill, what are you anyway? This is, uh, Agent Mill from Washington."

"So I see. Actually, we have met." McIntyre paused, "Henderson, the Hoffmans would like to resume their residence here. Is that appropriate?"

"I'd say it's up to them. We have no objection."

By now the Hoffmans were getting out of the car.

"Hello Lieutenant," it was Hans. "Still here?"

"More trouble I'm afraid."

"Oh? What?"

"We'll have to tell you about it later. We're just starting on it."

Hans looked at Helga and then back. "Okay."

Mill spoke, "Mr. McIntyre, I was about to phone you. It would be good to continue our meeting. There's a few things I don't understand."

"I'll be happy to meet, but at the moment, I am under instructions to speak only with an attorney present. Mr. Moore said he would contact you, or I can provide his number. But please make your appointment through him. I'll be happy to open our books and provide whatever financial data you want. But Moore should be present and advise me."

"Is this the same Mr. Moore who is advising the Hoffmans?"

"It is."

"There is no conflict there?"

"If Moore feels there is a conflict, he will refer the Hoffmans to another firm at once. But for the moment, it's Moore."

"I see. Henderson, you have Moore's number?"

"I do."

"Then I will phone him very shortly."

With that, McIntyre beckoned to the Hoffmans and they entered the house.

Mill said, "Financial records? He'll show me financial records? Why financial records? He's got something to hide there?"

But the meeting had another surprise. Swan and Lois Feine returned coming back from the same way they had gone.

Lois said, "We were, well, like Mrs. Webb just said, we were snooping and I overheard about Bubbie's gun … "

Henderson said, "Snooping? And what?"

Lois went on, "Bubbie kept that gun in a chest of drawers in her bedroom. When Mr. Schmidt was shot and she had that funny talk with Mrs. Schmidt, afterward, I looked for it. It wasn't there. So I asked Bubbie and she said she decided it was stupid to have it around the house and she just took it to the police station and handed it in. She said that was years ago. You can check. I'm sure it's the truth."

182

Mill said, "Quit snooping. Especially, on us. That can get you in real trouble. This is a real murder and we're not playing games. Okay? We could get you in big trouble right now, but just cut it out. Okay?"

"Okay," said Lois.

Henderson said, "The local cops tag and keep an inventory list for suspicious guns for evidence. But turn-ins? I hope whoever was on the desk didn't just take it home. Besides, local police station? Which one? State? Sheriff? Bloomfield Hills? And years ago? I'll try to find out but don't hold your breath."

The girls said nothing. But they also did not leave.

Webb's Story

"Give sorrow words; the grief that does not speak knits up the o-er wrought heart and bids it break."

Shakespeare - Macbeth

Another car pulled in front of the forensics van. Clyde Webb got out. "Hello. It's Henderson, right? Say, I saw a bunch of action out my back window and my wife Sally is here. I figured I'd better come around to be sure things are okay."

Henderson said, "This is Mill, he's from Washington looking into a couple things. Mrs. Webb is inside with Mrs. Schmidt and an associate of Mill's. I'd say everything is fine in there. In fact, it sounds like they're having a party and we weren't invited. But I'm afraid you're right, there is more trouble."

"Hello Mr. Webb", it was Swan Feine. "Say, umm, it's lucky to see you. Something funny happened yesterday and I wanted to ask you something. Ya see, Bubbie and Mrs. Schmidt were talking about when Bubbie was in a concentration camp. Bubbie never really talked about that before. I thought that was really odd that she waited till now to talk about it because Natalie's German husband just died and all. I mean, why talk about that stuff at this particular time? Then Bubbie was really angry with me, like she seemed to, well, to sympathize with some pretty mean things Mrs. Schmidt and Mrs. Hubchic said about Jewish people. Then Bubbie said Mrs. Schmidt wasn't really German and then Mrs. Schmidt said Bubbie was right. Well, some time back she said you weren't German either. What's the deal there?"

Clyde Webb looked puzzled, "That does seem like a funny topic for just now."

Henderson made motions to stand but Mill waved his hand as if to suggest he stay seated.

"Well," Clyde Webb seemed at a loss for a minute, "Well, Bubbie's right. Webb is usually British. It was shortened from Webbber when we came here and that's usually German. But my family's from Hungary. Confusing enough?"

Lois spoke, "Mrs. Schmidt had quite a story about Poland. She thinks in Poland, Jewish just about means Communist and she says Communists were worse than Nazis. What about the Warsaw Uprising and all that. Communists were worse?"

Web said, "Well, I never thought of the partisans, that's the Communist paramilitary, as particularly Jewish, but maybe some were. I was a kid then and didn't pay any attention to that angle. But what they did was horrible. They were some bad guys all right."

Swan said, "Bubbie was angry with me. I left the room when they said bad stuff about Jewish people, then Bubbie was mad as hell and said I missed some real history.

"Girls, I might have some sympathy with Bubbie on that one. You don't get that stuff first hand every day. There are really important lessons to learn from what happened. Too much is forgotten or it's simplified so much it's meaningless."

Mill spoke: "Vertreibung, were you were caught in that? You're Swabian then? Danube Swabian?"

"Huh? Well yes. Nobody knows about that these days. My goodness!"

Lois said, "Hungarians were plugged in with Hitler weren't they?"

"Oh boy, that's pretty complicated."

"Okay, so what did happen?"

"Well, let's see. We were kind-a like Finland. We didn't think Nazis were so hot, but events roped us into the same side of the war as Germany. That all turned into a huge debacle. In Hungary, we got it from all sides."

Swan said, "Okay, so what was it all about?"

Webb flopped into an Adirondack chair. "You really want this? You guys better sit down."

"Look, in Hungary the language you spoke was a big deal. Really, it's a big deal everywhere, even now. Back then, in Hungary business was always conducted in German. Schools were taught in German. If you wanted to get ahead in Hungary, you better speak German. Hungarian was common, but if that's all you spoke, you'd be stuck in menial labor at best."

"Sounds like a typical bourgeoisie, proletariat thing to me," said Swan.

"Well, you're close. 'Bourgeoisie' is a Bohemian word that means middle class or trade person. Bourgeoisie doesn't really mean rich ruling class. It means artisans and trade people. But Marx and the Communists took the view that these people were the evil who held others down and they needed to be exterminated."

"No, that's not it." Said Swan.

Webb continued, "Well, anyway, Mr. Mill mentioned 'Danube Swabians.' Well, way, way back, German speaking people from Baltic areas expanded into other lands. That was like one-thousand years ago. We went into lands that became Hungary, Bulgaria, Romania, all those Balkan places. Wars with the Ottoman Muslims had their ebbs and flows, but around 1790 or so, the Ottomans, that's the Muslins, pretty much got driven out by locals and by us. Then German speaking people really flowed in to fill the void. The main route for us was down the Danube River valley. We became miners, engineers, trade people and such all up and down the Danube. "Danube Swabians, German speaking middle class people who lived in places along the Danube.

Just before World War Two along came Hitler. He carved up Czechoslovakia and he gave a piece of it to Hungary. Annexing part of Czechoslovakia was a mistake even if the people in that region where 'Hunkies.' That put us politically way too close to Hitler. When the war started Hitler strong armed us into marching our Army into Russia and Yugoslavia. That was nuts. That's picking a fight with an elephant. Soon enough, politics at home got peace negotiations started but Hitler caught on and sent German SS and stuff into Hungary to take over. Good-bye

Hungarian Democracy. German SS controlled the Government, not us. They drafted even more of us into the war machine and kept us in the fight against Russia.

"The Nazis promised Swabians, German speakers, that was us, special status. That was especially if we could trace real German descent. Some special treatment! The truth of that was we were ordered to move out of our homes to make room for men from German SS and such. Meanwhile, the Partisans figured anyone who spoke German was totally with the Nazis and tried to kill us, families and all, over it.

"When the war turned against Germany, Russia invaded Hungary and they had no sense of humor at all. Between Nazis, Germans, Partisans and Russians, we just couldn't win.

"At the end of the war, President Truman, Britain's new Prime Minister Clement Atlee and Stalin met at Potsdam to work out what came next. Truman and Atlee were new and inexperienced and way over their heads trying to deal with the likes of Joseph Stalin and Molotov and they ended up handing Eastern Europe over to Stalin with a red colored bow tied around it. Another thing was what Stalin called 'democratization.' Democratization turned out to mean ethnic Germans all over Europe including us Danube Swabians lost citizenship and property in our countries. We had no rights to anything anymore.

"'Vertriebung der Deutschen,' throw out the Germans. They seemed to figure German speaking people only followed the Nazi war machine into countries like Hungary. Sometimes that was true. But most of us had been there for centuries. 'Vertriebung der Deutschen,' that meant all ethnic Germans had to go. That turned into the biggest forced population movement in Western history, ten-thousand times the size America's Indian trail of tears. Millions died. That's mostly forgotten now. 'Vertriebung der Deutschen,' the removal of the Germans. That was a rugged time if you had a German name or spoke German.

Webb became quiet.

"Swan said, "Okay, so what happened to you?"

Webb voice now had an edge, "My Dad had a college degree in physics with major study in electrical engineering. That got him a good job. He worked in a factory that built Turán tanks. And that, I guess, got him out of the military draft. When I was little, we lived in a really big house, but the Germans took the place for their own use and made us move out. Then, I suppose my Dad's position building tanks helped get us a little house by ourselves. That was by no means normal. Most people were packed into places like sardines in a can. Our place even had a garden and a few chickens out back. When things got bad, that little garden and an egg or two from the chickens was sometimes the only food we had. Well, somehow we survived the war with our family together.

"After the war ended a few others came to our house one night. I was sent to bed early but I heard what they said. They talked about the coming expulsion, the vertriebung, and they talked about whether we should go into hiding or risk getting shot. But hiding was no answer. We needed to get away.

"Just a few days after that, before we could move, a military truck showed up in front of our house and a bunch of soldiers jumped out. I've never known if they were army or police or partisans. My guess is they were partisans. That's, because their uniforms weren't much at all. But they sure had guns.

"They banged at our door so hard I thought the frame would split. They made us get in the back of their truck and not so gently either. We were not even allowed to get any of our stuff from the house. We only had the clothes on our back. We were taken to a train, not one with coaches, just with boxcars. We had to climb some kind of makeshift ladders and get into a boxcar. There were lots of others, especially lots of women with kids whose husbands, I suppose, had not come home from the war. Then they closed the doors and we rode in the dark for most of a day. When the train stopped a door was thrown open. We were told we were in Germany and we were ordered out. There was nothing there. There was no train station or anything. It was just a field. There was not even a road or farm in sight, just nothing.

Webb paused again and sighed.

"I remember looking out of that boxcar. They had not brought those ladders along and it seemed an awful long way to the ground. I was afraid to jump, but a soldier started pushing people out, so I jumped anyway. When I landed in the gravel under the tracks, I hurt my hands, and skinned my knees.

Webb looked down at his hands.

"Then the train left, women were crying and some men too. I had never seen that sort of thing, grownups crying I mean. It came to me that we had no food, no place to sleep that night, not even a place to get inside if it was cold. Even a kid started to get what this all meant. But milling around did nothing, all we could do was to start walking down the track. Not all came at first. Some just stood there. We had lost everything. And there we were, walking down a railroad track with nothing at all.

"We didn't know it then, but we were very lucky. Many more died all over Europe from the brutality, from starvation and exposure, or they were just plain murdered. Now it's politely called 'The German Relocation.' How polite! It was genocide! And being thrown out was not the worst. Many were dragged off into slave labor camps."

Swan fidgeted, but was this time she was quiet.

"We walked for a long time. I remember how walking on the gravel under the tracks was hard, but walking off the right-of-way, which was all overgrown with weeds was just as bad. I remember being thirsty and wanting to stop, so my father carried me for a time, then he put me down and said I must walk, like it or not. We finally came to a river. There we drank by lifting water in our bare hands. After that, the tracks followed the river for a long way. Finally, we came to a road and we could see a few houses. My father and some of the others went to ask for help.

"The place they dropped us turned out to be twenty miles south of Dresden. That city had been bombed to smithereens just when it was full of fleeing refugees. Now the countryside was still full of what they called dislocated persons. There were millions and there was no food. There was no shelter. People roamed to find whatever they could just to stay alive. It was not a good place to be.

"At any rate, a lady from one of the houses we saw said we could stay in a barn, just a shed really, for that night. She had a little farm. The Russians pillaged almost everything during the war, but their Army must not have come exactly this way. She was out of coal for heat and that sort of thing, but the place was still in workable shape. The lady said her husband had been taken into the German army and he had not come home. She had not heard from him and was very worried. I think she was also worried about the all desperate dislocated people in the area and she welcomed some civilized looking company just in case. Then my father told her we would help on the farm and, as soon as we could, we would pay her too. I remember her looking at us for a long time. I remember I was very hungry. Then she left for a while and I wondered, what now? But she came back to that shed with some sort of thin grain soup. I was very glad to have that soup. That was our new start.

"My father knew nothing about farming, so, after a couple days, with the farmer lady's agreement, even her urging, my father set out for Dresden to see what he could do. It is odd how real distress can make trusted friends overnight or a a couple days. Just that little time and we were friends.

"Along the way, my father saw some electrical linemen working. My father had never really done that kind of electrician's work, still, he pretended he was an expert on power lines. The men told him people with skills like his were much wanted and told him where to call in Dresden. So he found a job right away.

"Back in that farm shed, we were very afraid because there were so many desperate people around. Some of them walked the road right in front of the farm, plus we heard nothing from my father for a week. But that farmer lady shared what she could with us and my mother did all she could to help on the little farm, doing even a man's work. I was given chores too, like, there was a little cast iron stove inside the hen house. It was there to keep the chickens warm at night. I had to get the ashes out of it in the morning and spread them on the road. During the day, I hunted for scraps of wood or paper to make a fire. Then in the evening, I built a new fire for the hens. My mother and that lady became close, sharing their worries and the farm work and finding a way for us to get along. I know I learned a thing or two about cooperation and work. That lady was very kind to us in the most important ways, but she also expected us to pull our own weight. There was no nonsense. We all worked and we worked hard.

"Then my father came back and we all had a little celebration, even the farm lady joined us. Then he moved us to a single room he had rented in Dresden. Naturally, we walked there.

"After that, we always remembered that farmer lady and we went back often and helped with some heavy work. My dad gave her a little money or a few things she needed. Then, that winter, her husband finally got back. He had been a prisoner of war in a British camp. He too became our friend. We visited them or sometimes they came to see us and we always exchanged gifts. We had a little money, not money really, just occupation scrip, and they had some fresh milk or eggs or produce. That was funny. We didn't buy anything from them, but we gave each other gifts. Hard times can sure make a bond. It was like we were the same family.

Webb paused again. He looked distressed. He did not seem to talk directly to Swan and Lois at all now.

"Starvation, sickness, exposure or just shot by the Communists. Today's kids could not even guess. Those who survived in Hungary faced Russian tanks again in 1956. Thousands who only wanted democracy were imprisoned, hundreds executed for no reason but wanting democracy.

"A-hem .. anyway," Webb seemed to remember the girls now, "Dresden was in the Russian zone of occupation and so, as soon as we could, we went west. We landed in the American occupied zone. We did not leave too soon either. The border was shut after that. Life was not happy in East Germany after that.

"The American denazification program meant that anyone who had been a Nazi party member or belonged to the SS or anything like that was to be fired from their job as soon as someone with the right skills could be found to replace them. So again, my Dad quickly found electrical work.
Now he worked with some American military officers supervising restoration of electric power. With their help, he applied for US immigration. There were complications, like we had no papers of any kind plus he needed an American sponsor. But one of the officers liked him enough to sponsor us. Everything took time, but in 1950, we came here. My father went to work for Ford Motor

Company as an electrical shop superintendant. Later, he was promoted all the way to Vice President in charge of electrical maintenance programs.

Lois said, "Did you still keep in touch with that farmer lady?"

"Mrs. Bauer. Isn't that funny? Bauer means farmer in German. A perfect name. The Bauers, yes, as a matter of fact, we exchanged Christmas cards and things like that. Now and then my folks sent money and some clothes and things that were hard to get in East Germany, not that getting stuff into East Germany was so easy. Isn't it funny, just living there for ten days and some peasant soup .. that meant everything.

"Mr. Bauer died some years ago. They had moved to Berlin by then. I went to the funeral and saw Mrs. Bauer. That's .... or I should say that was just about the time I met Sally."

Swan said, "That story's sure different than what we leaned."

Mill cut in. "Mr. Webb, you speak German then?"

"Well, I did, as a child, as German was spoken in Hungary anyway. Real Germans, I guess, thought I sounded kinda rustic. I've been told you're finally American when you tell jokes in English or dream dreams in English. I guess I've been American a long time now. My German's probably pretty rusty."

Mill continued, "There were some meetings, Lois, Swan, please excuse us. That means beat it, and it means no snooping or eavesdropping this time."

Swan said, "But we want to know all this, will you guys tell us later?"

"Sure, if I can, but you guys scoot. This is official stuff."

And the girls did scoot.

"You want to know about that crowd at the guest house out back I assume."

"Yes, that's right, what was that all about, who were those guys?"

Webb sat in silence, then said, "It seems to me that Dr.Schmidt was bringing large amounts of money into this country. I think that's what it was about. I am not sure if what they were doing was exactly illegal, but it seemed to me Schmidt did not want to attract attention to it either. My guess is stocks, land, or other valuables would be purchased in Europe then titles transferred here at low prices and then they'd be sold again at full value. I think it was that sort of thing. There were also comments I recall that were something like, 'The usual deposit was made on time.' I was not privy to all of that. It was not exactly kept from me, but it was not all explained either."

"Why were you involved? Why Mrs. Webb?"

Webb paused once again, "That was never clear to me. At first I thought it was just social. Schmidt asked us over to meet 'old friends.' Later, I thought he wanted us for other reasons. It seemed to me he did not want to be alone with those guys and we were there as a sort of hint that there would be witnesses if there was trouble. There was other odd stuff, like they asked if they might park at my house instead of Schmidt's because the walk was shorter. It's not that much shorter. Why did they really want to park at my place? It was never explained. They were pleasant enough to me and mostly acted like it was just normal business. Nothing was exactly kept from me, but I didn't butt in either. Also, it did not take an eagle eye to tell that between them, the pleasantries were a little forced."

"Who were they? What names."

"They were German and they went by first names. That was funny too. Just first names, let's see, Gert, Axel, Desi, they called Günter Schmidt, 'Otto.'"

"German?"

"Mostly, not all, but your question about names, let me talk to Sally, she knows them all including last names. They'd pay her a little fee to be like a secretary and arrange hotel rooms for them or answer a phone now and then, get or send a fax, that kind of thing. She knew them well enough and knew their names. I'll ask her."

"And a phone?"

"Yes, they paid for an extra line to our house, it was for a FAX machine."

Mill looked at Henderson who nodded.

"Sometimes Mrs. Webb would go without you. Why was that?"

"Oh, Günter asked if he could 'borrow' her. That was his term, 'borrow.' It was sort of a game for us. Sally would play like a hostess and try to get them a little drunk then get their attention by leaning over a little too much with a low cut top on or something like that. She likes to play-act like that just a little. She has an odd kind of vain streak in that way, a funny quirk in her personality. But it's joking and fun, not serious."

"May I ask, what was Sally's maiden name? Where is she from?"

Webb seemed to ponder longer than the simple question required, quite a bit longer in fact. He looked across the yard at nothing. The he said, "Dorman, she had an earlier marriage, but kept her maiden name during that disastrous affair. From? She was an army brat. They lived all over. She told me her Dad, was originally from West Virginia. Her past is all mixed up."

"Why not Natalie? Why did Sally act as hostess and not Natalie?"

"I don't know. Maybe Sally was a better hostess. Maybe Natalie didn't like to be a waitress and hostess? I don't know the answer. Schmidt's always catered parties here in this house. I think hostess is not Natalie's calling. She's a nice lady, but I don't think she could fry an egg. It's just not her thing I guess. And Sally didn't mind. She even had fun doing it. That's my guess anyway."

"Mr. Webb, does Mrs. Webb speak German?"

"Oh sure!" Webb paused and looked like he was trying to remember something, "Well, I should say a little anyway. I think she took a German class in that community college or something like that." He paused again, "I speak to her in

German as a joke now and then. She doesn't always get it. If we went to Germany, I think she could order off a menu and ask for the ladies room and stuff like that. Not much more."

The Pace Quickens

"Fast is fine, but accuracy is everything." - Wyatt Earp

Clyde Webb went into the house to see how Sally was doing.

Mill spoke to Henderson who was still there, "This isn't all straight. Something's being covered up here. Sally says she can't remember all the names, Webb says she knows them all. They have a phone line these guys pay for. I bet a good look into Sally Webb née Dorman would get us a surprise or two."

Henderson said, "I agree. When you started asking questions, Webb didn't like it. This, I take it, means an action step for me, find out about Sally Webb née Dorman. I'll look at records of that phone line too. That might take a proper warrant."

Webb reappeared, now with Sally. Her demeanor was totally different than earlier. Her sweater was no longer worn but now thrown over her shoulder, several of the buttons were open on her blouse and she had an arm around Webb. As they walked, she moved with a fluid and youthful, even slinky gate.

After their car started to move down the drive, Mill said, "What was that? A magical transformation or what? She's right on one part, she sure knows her trophy wife job! Should we laugh or be envious?"

But just as the car disappeared five sharp cracks were heard. Mill and Henderson were on their feet at once. Then there was the sound of metal on metal and breaking glass.

Henderson said, "That's a gun.", but Mill was already running, his Glock 20 in hand, and he was several steps down the drive.

Henderson grabbed his little radio, "You guys get up in front of the house NOW! In front of the house, shots fired, and call for assistance." Then he was off at a sprint too.

An engine roared and was followed by the sound of tires throwing gravel.

Mill yelled, "Get a car! Get a car and chase his butt! I'll handle this part!"

Henderson turned on his heel and sprinted for his car. He called on his radio again, "Shooting suspect vehicle leaving Günter Schmidt residence at high speed, request assistance, request intercept. I'll have a description in a minute."

Mill reached the end of the drive to find Webb's car with a front wheel in the ditch. The windshield was shattered, and Sally was already out of the car, leaning in the driver's door looking at Clyde.

"He's bleeding, but I think it's only glass cuts, but call for an ambulance anyway, he's stunned."

Henderson roared up in his unmarked sedan, Sally pointed which way and Henderson, tires squealing, was off without even slowing.

"I've never seen Clyde act like that! When the guy stared shooting, Clyde charged him with the car and even whacked his car a little. He almost got him too, the guy was out of his car. His driver's side rear will be banged in."

Mill stuck his head in the car to look at Webb, who waved a hand, "I'm alright, I'm alright", but he was obviously not completely alright.

Mill pulled his cell phone out to dial, realized his gun was still in his hand, he put that away and dialed 911.

Next he turned to Sally, "What kind of car? What plate number?"

She said, "Crap! I forgot, I didn't get the plate. Black Crown Victoria. Big guy, over six feet, overweight, fifties, suit and tie. Nothing else remarkable about him." Then Sally stood quiet looking puzzled.

"What? What? Tell me."

"I might have seen him before. I'm trying to be sure. I'm playing it again in my head. I think I've seen him before."

Mill dialed his cell again, "Henderson! Black Crown Vic, left rear banged in. Fifty year-old male, over six feet, overweight, business suit."

Clyde put his feet on the ground through the now open door and tried to stand. "Good thing the air bags didn't fire. I'd be a pancake." Then he said, "Oops!" He sat back down.

"Did he crack his head? He's acting goofy."

"Can't say. I thought I was either dead or taking a ride head first through the windshield myself. I didn't watch him . "

 Mill looked Webb over.

"Who was the guy shooting at?"

"Both of us. I'm sure of that. He was shooting one way then the other. If Clyde hadn't surprised him and charged at him, I think we'd be dead."

"An amateur, a pro would make sure the driver was down, then get the passenger."

Sally made a guttural noise, "Uggg."

Footsteps were heard. It was one of the crew from the ambulance who had been waiting to remove the body behind the house. He was breathing hard but managed to pant out. "My partner's getting the vehicle and bringing the equipment".

Mill said, "Look at this guy's head, all I see is glass cuts, but he's acting goofy like he hit his head. I think it's a concussion."

Webb spoke up, "I've got an official report for you guys. Did you ever hear the phrase 'get your bell rung?' Well it really does ring. Wow! Ding-a-ling! Wow! Sounds like a telephone."

The medic said, "Yes sir, I've heard that. Now just sit there mister, I think you have a mild concussion but in case you cracked something inside there, we want you to move nice and easy. We need to take some care." The paramedic's face was very close to Webb's and he was looking at Webb's eyes.

Mill spoke to Sally, "Are you okay? You're too calm, you're not in shock or something are you?"

"No, not in shock. After what my ass-hole first husband would do to me, this is kind of thing is old hat. He'd put a gun to my head and shoot a blank, damn thing burned me. This one was easy compared to what that jerk did. But thanks, I'm okay, not in shock or anything. But look buddy, find out what's going on and arrest somebody. I'm not so okay that I want to make a habit of this stuff."

More footsteps, this time it was the whole forensics team.

Mill said, "Whoever's in charge? This is Mrs. Webb. Get a detailed statement from her. Henderson's in pursuit of the suspect who's in a black Crown Vic."

Moments later, sirens could be heard and at the same time, Jane Paine appeared, walking slowly with Natalie on her arm.

Natalie addressed Sally even as she was writing her statement on a police form, "Sally, you're all right?" Natalie looked Sally over closely. "You're really all right?" Thank god! And Clyde?" She finally looked his way. "Oh, I am sorry, I hope we did not bring this on you. Is Clyde alright?"

A second ambulance came into sight and came to a bumpy stop beside the Webb's car. After a very brief conference, Webb was moved with care into the ambulance. Sally was ushered to the front seat.

Jane and Mill distanced themselves from the commotion. Mill spoke quickly, "Dead guy dumped in the shed out back, shot somewhere else, best guess is it's Alka-Seltzer Panski. And there's three people's blood at Smith's shooting scene. My guess, Panski was nailed and the other shooter just got winged and dumped him here when he died. Oh yes, Smith got the same kind of bullet that killed Schmidt. Also, there's been some kind of secret money meetings in the guest house, Schmidt wanted Sally Webb there and sometimes Clyde. Clyde Webb thinks that was to be witnesses if something went wrong or something like that. That makes the Webbs witnesses and probably accomplices to whatever went on there. They can identify the bad guys and my guess is this shooting was an attempt to shut them up before they do it. I'm not one bit sure about the Webbs. It's ninety-nine percent sure they're hiding something. Sally in particular may be deep in this. Henderson's going to check her background out. Now you talk."

"Natalie was way more active in the Polish underground than she lets on. She was a courier, like she said, but she was a member of some underground leadership committee or some such thing. I think she may have been a real nasty actor in the anti-communist underground. Schmidt had access to money and political influence. She was the rough neck. Between them they made some kind of high powered communist hating team. It looks like Schmidt was shipping refugees, Jewish no doubt, out of Poland and headed them for Palestine. That'd make Schmidt some kind of international hero, especially as a German himself, but there is some kind of big secret they're keeping, so nobody knows about it. Hey, which side of the war was Palestine on?"

"Oh jeez, now you're the one who wants history while bullets are flying. Officially, Palestine was on our side. It was a British protectorate after all. But the Palestinians were mad as hell about lots of stuff, especially about Jewish people pouring into their country and trying to take over. So there was a lot of sympathy there running for the Axis powers. The British tried to keep the Palestinians happy by setting quotas for the number of Jewish people coming into Palestine, but the quota was way too high to suit Palestinians ideas. It didn't work. Far more than the quota allowed got in anyway. Hitler's pal Mussolini had been throwing Muslims, north African Muslims that is, into concentration camps since the nineteen-twenties, but that part didn't seem to worry the Palestinians much. That quota bright idea resulted in horror shows like a shipload on Jewish refugees being intercepted by the Palestinian's pals in Turkey and, because they didn't have proper papers, they were just pushed out into the middle of the Black Sea without fuel or food and set adrift. So yes, Palestine was officially on our side, but the reality was, it was a huge mess and they were mad as hell about Jewish people arriving in massive numbers."
"Interesting .. next point, Natalie thinks meeting that Dr. Shaw at the party upset Schmidt. Also, she doesn't know who invited Shaw to the party.

Mill said, "Henderson says Shaw had radical Palestinian ties. And it looks like Schmidt was sending the refugees there? Palestinians are still sore. Hell, they want to eradicate Israel. The whole beef about Israel comes from in those days, namely, they think Israel, if it exists at all, should be a Jewish enclave or ghetto ruled by Palestine."

They were silent for a minute.

"Look Jane, I think we both should stay in the house with Natalie. I'll take the car and check out of the hotel. Mind if I just throw your stuff in your bag? I promise not to peek at your underwear, I saw enough of that out back. Give me your room key."

"I agree, but give me your key, I'll do the check us out part. I want you here. We have a crazy man shooting up the neighborhood and if it comes to that, you can handle a gun better than me.

"Okay, agreed. But let's hope Henderson catches him first."

One of the forensics men appeared. "Henderson found the car in the parking lot of the seminary up the road. He thinks the suspect is on foot. If the suspect had another car there, or an accomplice there, Henderson thinks he was close enough to have seen it. Two local police are already there assisting and more are on the way. One of our guys is heading up there in a minute to go over the car. The plate's already identified it as a rental from the airport. The rest of us stay here for the situation out back and to look at things right here with the Webb's car. Obviously, no way it was that Nagant this time. For one thing, no silencer and loud as hell, for another, way too much destruction in the car, this was something heavy like a forty-five. Another thing, the Nagant shooter hit the target every time. This guy missed every time. This is a different bad-guy."

"Right, said Mill" And tell ya what, my guess is our Nagant man is in the shed out back."

More from Natalie and a Job for Kids

".. and in the end, it's not the years in your life that count. It's the life in your years."

Abraham Lincoln

Mill walked Natalie back to the house at the slow pace of old ladies.

"I had heard that the Blyskawica machine gun was secretly made in Warsaw right under the noses of the Nazis and even used in the Ghetto Uprising."

It struck even Mill as odd to be talking about firearms history at a time like this, but it took the edge off the situation somehow and Natalie seemed to be in a mood to talk.

"That is true. The Nazis and Russian both invaded Poland in 1939 and our government had to flee. There was more than one underground then. But the common cause of throwing invaders out meant we pulled together as best we could. For obvious reasons, cooperation had to come in baby steps. We had been murdering each other the week before. By 1942 we were 'Armia Krajowa'! That's Polish for 'Army of Our Country.' The see-saw way the war went made things confusing too. When Germany invaded Russia, they chased the Russians right out of just about everywhere. Then it seemed we had mainly Germans to fight in Poland. But when the war went the other way, oh my! When they came back, Russian brutality knew no limits."

"Let me see, it was forty three when Germany lost big-time at Stalingrad, forty-four when the German army surrendered at Leningrad. Those were terrible affairs, especially for civilians. More died there than from the atom bombs. After that, The Russians advanced to the Polish border, but then they stopped right there.

"Some of my countrymen were fools. 'Akcja Burza,' that means 'Operation Storm,' was a plan for the Polish Armia Krajowa to take control of Poland away from the Germans and take over ourselves. The plan was this; we would suddenly rise all across Poland and take the Germans by surprise. Then we would hold on till the Red Army arrived to chase the German forces back to Germany. It was all agreed in secret and carefully coordinated with the Red Army. So, just as planned, Armia Krajowa seized control with a sudden uprising, but the Russians double crossed us and did not come in to support us. Instead of chasing the Germans back to Germany, they halted the Red Army at the border to let the Germans with new reinforcements take care of us. And take care they did. The Red Army that had promised us aid and cooperation, just waited for the Germans to exterminate us. As usual, the worst of it was in Warsaw. Only when Armia Krajowa had much weakened the Germans, but gotten destroyed in the effort, did the Red Army resume its march into Poland. Nor did the Red Army just pass through. The Russians took all of Poland, made half of it Russia and set up their puppet communist government for the other half. We, or some of us, were naïve then. The ranks of Armia Krajowa included the Communists. Why else would any Pole expect the Red Army to back us up then leave us politely to have our own country after the war? I for one, and many like me, saw through it all along and even warned others of the Russian treachery. Of course, they did not listen.

"We were double crossed again when the war ended and the Allies did not insist that Russia pull out of Poland. Then, Armia Krajowa members, even those who had helped the Red Army, were made criminals by our Communist so-called friends. Then it was made even illegal to study or write about, or even talk about the anti-communist part of the resistance. 'Główny Urząd Kontroli Prasy, Publikacji i Widowisk,' the government office of sesorship, took our documents and destroyed then. Our leaders arrested and tortured and sent to the gulag to die. Stories of resistance against Germans were allowed, they exaggerated and romanticized. But the truth of resistance against the brutal, double crossing Russians was buried. We were called Jew killers and Nazis. That is why so much is taught about our resistance to the Germans now, but those of us loyal to our legal government, those who fought for a free Poland have been forgotten.

"The Blyskawica, oh yes, we made it ourselves. They were small and fired nine millimeter rounds. We made almost a thousand of them. They were good and they were deadly. Most of them were made in a metal fence shop near Warsaw."

By now Mill and Natalie were seated on the porch. Several police cars had arrived and the two of them watched the action as if it was just theatre.

"Mr. Mill, what do you think this killing and shooting is all about?"

"Well, I am unsure. I think the answer lies in the past. Perhaps Palestinian radicals found Schmidt at last. But I think this is more likely, there was a lot of money involved back then. There may still be much money involved. I think maybe the old organizations are finally breaking down. I might guess new-comers are eyeing the money and want to eliminate the old timers."

Natalie said, "That seems reasonable to me. We are all very old now. Did you know that von Papen was given rank in the Turkish Army? And he was also Ambassador to Turkey during the second war. He spent time in Cairo too. He had contacts throughout the mid-east. And he was very close to all that Nazi and Catholic money."

A moment passed as Mill took this in. Mill knew all this, but why did Natalie mention it. Then, Natalie said, "Mr. Mill, how does money move underground? I wonder. Günter, or Otto could be a hard, an overbearing man, but on important things, he was a kind and good man. He was involved in helping desperate people escape the Nazis and the Communists too. But now we see violence again .. the money part must be tied to it somehow. I have seen violence before. I know its face."

Mill said, "Please go on. Tell me what you think."

"I have spoken to your Ms. Paine. It was mostly silly girl talk. But in silly girl talk we can say things that are hard to get across in plain English. I like your Miss Paine. She has gained some insight."

"She is hardly my Ms. Paine. She holds higher rank than me."

"Oh! ha, ha! How times change. Good for her! In my day, that could never be. I apologize for any embarrassment. She holds you in the greatest esteem Mr. Mill, rank or not. Perhaps times do not change as much as they seem."

"I hold Ms. Paine in highest regard too."

Natalie eyed Mill closely, "You know she teases you out of affection for you."

"Please, I am here at the behest of Washington to make sure we meet any outstanding moral debts to our old friends. I think Dr. Schmidt and you were friends and perhaps even heroes. But I know too little. I am still too much in the dark. Help me understand."

Natalie sighed, "Relationships are important in insight Mr. Mill. Very important. Do you think the weather is nice? When you grow old you notice small things like that more. Small things like this pleasant moment right now, they are of value. A new friend, a nice day, yes even in the middle of terrible things, there are pleasant moments.

Natalie sat looking at trees and the sky, then said, "Mr. Mill, when there is confusion and fear all around, even your friends will deceive you. Even those who want your help, hide behind a ruse because they are unsure of you.

"You want to understand? Somebody just tried to shoot Sally. That is a fact I must now take into account. Mr. Mill, who are you sure of? Jane? Henderson maybe? If you were in my shoes and had seen what I have seen over my life, who would you trust? In the past, the answer has seldom been the authorities. But someone shot Günter and someone is shooting at Sally now and it does not seem to be you or Jane. Are you following me?

"I think, Mr. Mill, the past, Günter moving refugees and Franz von Papen and your remarkable knowledge of history will get you to the answers to all this given much time and study. But that will take far too much time. That is the long road to today's truth. The shooting has started and I am unsure who is shooting and I do not know exactly why. But when shooting starts, shortcuts are called for.

"Do you like autumn Mr. Mill? I think September is my favorite month. The weather changes, it is fresh, not like spring, perhaps, but ripe like the farm fields with crops coming in that I can remember. Real autumn is not far away. Relationships and friendship do matter.

Natalie sighed again, "I think back, how I wish I knew and understood better. The price of all this has been too high for me. And those questions closest to my heart can never be known now.

Natalie spoke firmly now, "Mr. Mill, Money, you should consider the money a bit more. Consider fine points of history less. And mostly we must both question who we trust.

Then Natalie took on a far away expression, "To know the fate of loved ones, the man I was to marry," she paused "to be satisfied that they knew of my love to the end. Possibilities like that are gone forever now, I know that. But any small part of it, even small bits of it would be nice. And justice, I want justice. I want to think good can win, that deceit and terror and evil can be beaten. The debt of honor you speak of? I do not care about any debt owed me. But things like finding who shot Günter and why, that would be a kindness to me." Natalie looked into space, a far away expression on her face. The she said, "I trusted none, Mr. Mill. I have learned that."

Now Natalie spoke more loudly, "Mr. Mill, listen to me. It's the money. Okay? It's not old hate. It's money. Mr. Mill, do people ever hold back or mislead because they have not decided who to trust? Do people always trust authorities?

 Mill said, "Natalie, just what are you saying? Please be more clear?"

"Mr. Mill. This gunfire says very soon things will become clear. The gunfire is making things clearer to me now. This will all play out very soon. The action has begun and cards will now play face up. That's how it goes. I have seen this."

"Natalie, what are you saying?"

"I am saying that I am not yet sure what is going on yet. I am saying we trusted nobody. We did not trust you. I think there is danger for those I care about so I must now decide quickly. Perhaps others need to be more forthright now. And I am saying money is the root of all this. More? It does no good to tell you what I myself am unsure of, what I suspect but do not know, But now I trust you enough to say, deal with today. A lifetime ago means less. That is what I am saying."

"Please Mrs. Schmidt. Why make me guess? Say right out what you want me to know!"

"I have."

"Hello Mrs. Schmidt." It was Swan and Lois Feine.

Lois said, "We're just being nosy. I mean, we want to ask, what now? This whole affair has become so .. unusual."

Mill just said, "Look guys, someone just took a pot shot at the Webbs. But it looks like they're okay." Then he turned and looked at them for a moment. "I'm real busy with Mrs. Schmidt, but maybe there is something a couple nosy aspiring detectives can do after all."

Swan and Lois looked at each other.

"I think the bad guy, whoever he is, is familiar with this neighborhood, and even this house. He keeps making moves like he knows his way around. He's been here before. He knew about the shed out back and, when he headed out of here, he knew to pull into the seminary and where to scoot out on foot. Now if Mister Bad-guy is running away from us, he'll head to a shopping mall or someplace where he'll get lost in a crowd. That's what the cops chasing him will assume, so they'll try to get between him and the nearest public places. But if he is as desperate as I think, and a nut-case like I bet he is, he'll come back here to finish his business. We'll see more of him and very soon."

Swan and Lois looked at each other again, this time with big eyes. Natalie nodded and said. "Yes, he will.".

"Now, if you were at the seminary hiding in a window-well or someplace like that, and you wanted to sneak back here on foot without being seen. How would you come?"

Lois said, "First, I'd wait for dark. Then I'd follow the back lot lines or the steam back there. Mostly it's wooded back there and unless there's a full moon or something, it's pitch black too. It'd be easy to sneak through back there unseen."

"And if you two were going to watch for this jerk, where would you set up your look-out?"

Swan said. "To catch him coming that way, I'd put a string across his path to trip a light or camera. Or I'd just watch out Lois's window just like we watched the guest house."

"Which house is that? How far?"

"Next door," Lois pointed, "The view up this way looking out my window is really good. Our house is sort of diagonal to this place and we have a great view of everything out back."

"Do you guys have my cell number? It's here on my card. I'm going to be at this house tonight. Set up and watch, but no funny strings and lights, just call me if you see or hear anyone. The description is a big, fifty year old man in a business suit, but descriptions are never reliable. Anyone headed in from the direction of the seminary, call me.

"The cops can't post a guard?"

"Sure, but we're smarter than the cops, aren't we. Besides, they'll think he's running away and they'll be half hearted about guarding this place. They'll, probably post just one guy here and put him at the front door. I think this guy is desperate and will do something stupid. He'll come back. Do you have Helga and Hans' number?"

"Sure."

"Get them in the act. They have a good view out their window too. I can't talk to them unless there's a lawyer present, but you can. Wait a minute! Did they write their number for you?"

"Yes, they both wrote it."

"Man! We're in luck! Do you have what they wrote it on with you?"

"Yes, they wrote it twice, once for each of us. That's why they both wrote."

"Let me see, I want to look at their handwriting …….. nope, no match at all, they didn't write the note."

"What note?"

"Oh, they found a note in Schmidt's pocket and we haven't figured out who wrote it yet. But you guys go set up for your surveillance. This guy may not wait for dark, he's desperate."

"Cool! Scary! Cool!"

"This isn't a cool game guys, we have a wack-o with a gun. Don't be stupid. Don't take any chances. Just watch out your window, don't get in his way, just lights out after dark and watch out the window. Then tip me off if you see anything or even if you just think you see something. In fact, let's put my number on speed-dial on both your phones and let's even test it to be real sure."

McIntyre Again

"No man pleases by silence, let me please by speaking briefly."

Ausonious

Mill watched the girls leave. He looked at Swan's crocheted top, it had been too reveling form the front, and going away, most of her back was bare. The truth was, Lois was prettier. But Swan always stole the show. He decided he should think about the irony of that and his disapproval of Swan, but he'd think about all that later. He didn't really like the answers that popped in his head just now and he didn't have time. Then he heard Natalie chuckle.

"Youth," she said. "You should see the expression on your face. I can read your thoughts. Swan will not learn any time soon. And in my old age, I'm not sure I don't say, 'good for her.'"

"I was just puzzling, that's all."

"Yes, I know, Swan Feine is an immature, self absorbed fool of a child. But fun is only fun. As for me, I think I'm all for her outlandish styles."

"Well, maybe, but in the longer run …"

"Posh! That kind of longer run never happens … "

The big arts and crafts door swung open and McIntyre appeared. Mill had forgotten that he had entered with the Hoffmans even though his car was obviously still right where he had parked it. Mill really wanted to talk to Natalie more, but McIntyre spoke.

"Mill, that's your name?"

"Yes."

"I was just thinking. Those were gunshots weren't they? Anyone hurt?"

"Nobody was hit. Maybe a concussion when a car went in the ditch."

"Okay, I don't like this. I'm going to ignore my lawyer. I have nothing to hide and people are getting shot. So let's talk right now. If anything I can say will contribute to ending this nonsense I want to say it. I want to go first, then you can ask questions. But first thing, I have a question or two for you, or at any rate, I want your opinion on some stuff."

"Okay."

"You probably know, the monetary gift for the museum addition came to me. I'm the Dean at Colebrook. That means I'm chief money getter. And you probably know by now that twenty million bucks fell out of the sky for no good reason to build that museum addition.'

"I didn't exactly know that, but okay, go on."

"Yeah, this German consortium just came to me, not the other way around, and poof, twenty million. Usually I have to buddy up to ninety year old ladies, put their dead husband's name on a building, play up to them and after ten years of that, we finally we get a hundred thousand bucks when they die. But this time, would you like twenty million? Fine! Here it is. My question is this, in your detective world, what's that kind of thing about?"

"Mr. McIntyre, I really have no idea in your case. But here's some rules of thumb. When an intelligent man gets surprised in his own field, somebody else is running the show. Somebody else has an agenda. When there's a surprise, you can count on that. There's another agenda. That also means you're not on his team or else you'd already be in the know. That's politics and life in the real world. Surprises mean you're not in the driver's seat, not even on the team. In this case, my wild guess is that the someone pulling the strings was Schmidt.

Natalie may have been watching birds or the sky, but she nodded and Mill noticed.

"Next, pennies from heaven mean a trap. Someone is drawing someone else out and will pull the carpet out from under him as soon as he shows his cards. If you're playing with, say, billions, and you want to nail a small-fry who might have his hand in the till or is up to some other kind of no good, you might lay down twenty million to bring this guy out into the open. In military doctrine, that's called a scrimmage line. If you think the enemy is hiding behind a hill, you send just enough force up the hill to tempt the enemy to fight. That makes him expose himself and his position. The enemy will blow his cover over your small potatoes scrimmage line. Then, when you know exactly where he stands, you pull your small potatoes scrimmagers back as fast as you can and you'll know how to commit your main force and annihilate him. That's basic military doctrine. So what I read in your story is this, it's big money and some upstart is making trouble. Some big actor is drawing some small actor out into the open to see what he's up to. Someone's tempting someone else with money and planning to change the whole game and whack him as soon as the other guy shows his cards. Some big cat is going to eat some mouse. The twenty million is the cheese in the mouse trap. It's all about changing the rules of the game after the bad guy has committed himself."

"Interesting, interesting, so I'm being used, the school and me that is, as cheese in a mousetrap, as a pawn in a bigger chess game. And I don't even know the players or what the fight's about."

"Right."

"Let me think about that. It feels uncomfortably correct. "

Now Natalie remained still.

"The game may be money laundering or some such thing. When lots of money moves, there's lots of ways to skim a bit. If there's enough, even just holding it for a while is very profitable. But I don't know yet. Mr. Big Cat might not have known exactly what, but he smells something he didn't like. If Mr. Big Cat was Schmidt, he might have tempted more out of hiding than he bargained for."

McIntyre said, "Oh boy, I don't like that scenario. I never did knew where Schmidt got all his money. I think you're right and I don't like it."

Natalie said, "Gentlemen, I would like to use the phone, do you think I can reach Sally at the hospital? Sometimes they make you turn your cell phone off there. I want to check with her. See how Clyde is doing that is. Then I will come back."

Mill turned to McIntyre, "Okay, now I'm serious. I need to know some stuff. Did a Detective named Smith phone you a couple nights ago?"

"Umm, no, not a detective named Smith, but a Smith from the consortium did. He said he wanted photos of a couple details of the project to send back to Germany. He said the committee wanted them for their files and to confirm a couple technical points, but he said it was trivial and he'd take care of it. So I just called our contractor and asked him to give Smith access to the sight for photos. Another thing, Smith wanted to know was if anyone else from that German committee was in town. That seemed like an odd question because he was one of them and I'd think he'd know before me. I remember that part."

"Okay, who was on that committee? Did he ask about anyone in particular?"

"No one in particular, just was anyone in town? Guys on the committee? It was remarkably casual for the amount of money involved. I have some phone number and stuff at the office, but let's see. There was one guy I only knew as Gert. Then there was a Hans, Hans Mueller, a Mr. Keller, Jan, a man named Jan, not a lady, a Ms. Dorman, let's see, a guy named Desi who was only there once or twice, and a couple others. Miss Gordon will have all the names because she made the hotel arrangements for the lot of them when they first came. After that time, their Ms. Dorman handled all that."

"A Ms. Dorman? Really? Dorman?"

"Yes, I remember her. Short skirt type. Dressed like a twenty year old, but she's not twenty. She just took notes, spoke German half the time, a secretary I think."

"And this Smith guy?"

"They mostly used first names in meetings. He might have been an older guy I think.. That was funny too, because most other Europeans I've worked with are more formal and use last names. Like I said, pretty much everything about this has been way too casual. Smith was maybe Jan or Desi .. I can't remember."

"Who are the Hoffman kids?"

"The same Ms. Dorman called me and asked if I could help place them in our school. Of course, I did. I just asked them the same question inside right now and they just told me Hoffman was Hans' uncle. If not Schmidt, Hoffman may be your big cat about to eat the mouse. He seems to be in charge of the consortium or in charge of the money anyway. Hey, do you think I'm at risk of losing the grant money? If we're cheese in a mousetrap, what happens when the mouse is caught?"

"Can't say about that, but shooting and murder is not a good sign. If your books are clean as you say they are, you're probably okay. I'd guess our mister big has flushed his problem out just as he planned, unless mister big was Schmidt, in which case it didn't go as planned. Mister bigs seldom figureF problems will start shooting. Whoever he is, he'll use authorities now that it's become violent. Real big-bucks guys don't like blood. He'll play it straight now. You've heard that Hoffman is on the way?"

"Yes, the kids told me."

"Then he might be our Mr. Big. But my hunch is still Schmidt. My guess, Hoffman is a mouse about to step in a trap. I think that fits better. Now then, how about an appointment in the morning to see that list of names and look at the books, and please try to get Moore there. We need permission to talk to the kids."

McIntyre said, "You're on, come over, how about at nine a.m. I can't speak for Moore or the kids. That's not up to me. But I'll call Moore now, I have his cell."

Mill said, "Now that bullets are flying, everything's going to come out fast. Am I going to find out that your hand is in the cookie jar? "

"Nope. Everything's clean and simple, just like I said. Money into a checking account, and money out of the account to pay the contractors. And the contractor bills are all legit. They all check out, we confirm each step of the work. We have records of it all. We even attach photos of each step."

Am I going to find Hoffman's got a stake in any of your contractors?"

"I'd seriously doubt it. The bidding was legit."

Mill, "Oh yes, was this Ms. Dorman at the party in this house the other night?"

"Hmm .. I was only there a minute and these two ladies talked my ear off. Huh .. umm, maybe. I'm not sure. Now that you mention .. hmm .. now that you mention it, one lady looked like .. I didn't get a good look .. I just can't say for sure."

Natalie had returned so quietly Mill almost overlooked her. She cleared her throat and when Mill looked, she was smiling and he thought, maybe nodding her head like before.

Before Mill could ask Natalie what exactly that meant, a forensics man appeared. "Thought I should tell you, Betty Kuhn just phoned-in a missing person report for Alex Panski. He's supposed to help her set up for a catering job tonight but he didn't show up. Someone told her he was not home last night either. She says she phoned around area hospitals because of his age, not there either. In view of his age and all that, the cops accepted the missing report earlier than we're technically supposed to." The forensic man looked intently at Mill, evidently to be sure Mill caught the importance.

Mill said, "Thanks, and how's stuff going out back?"

"We're not totally sure yet, but we're getting there." Then the forensics man said, "The description fits."

"Un-huh. Thank you very much," said Mill.

The forensics guy left.

"Okay, your turn, what did that mean?" said McIntyre.

"That meant that we have identified another problem connected to this. These forensics guys can't always officially express their hunches, so they make it a guessing game when they want to tell you something unofficially. It really means, 'Don't hold me to this and don't say I told you, but it looks like xyz and I'll be able to prove it later. This kind of thing is usually very helpful and gets you answers before the official channels move. Normally, they're right."

Natalie said, "Panski? The past really is returning."

A car pulled up driven by Jane Paine. When she got out she opened the trunk. Mill rose. "Excuse me, this'll take a second." Mill took two overnight bags out of the car's trunk, then he returned and sat again leaving the bags beside him.

Big Answers

"The problems are solved, not by giving new information,
but by arranging what we have known since long."

Ludwig Wittgenstein

"Mr. Mill, I think after the spiked tea and the excitement, a nap might help. Will you excuse me?"

Jane thought Natalie did look tired. "Mrs. Schmidt, you do look like a nap might do you some good."

Natalie added that she hadn't slept well last night. So Jane walked with her to her bedroom and even helped remove Natalie's shoes and, when she reclined on top of the covers, Jane put a throw blanket over her. "Can I get anything? Shall I come back in an hour?"

When Jane went back out in front, McIntyre was gone. Everyone was gone except Mill who sat on the porch, still beside the overnight bags. He seemed to be in deep thought.

Then the ambulance left, with the apparent remains of Alex Panski. Then the forensics van left and one by one, the police cars left.

Jane spoke, "Okay, what now?"

Mill, "Damn, and I was just getting somewhere with Natalie. She wants to say something but for some reason can't decide to do it. After this nap, I think you need to be her long lost friend again and get it out of her. But for sure, we're finally getting somewhere. I don't know where yet, but the pieces are coming together."

Jane; "Okay, then for starters, you seemed real interested in this Ms. Dorman. What's that about?"

217

Mill went on, "Sally Webb is Ms. Dorman. Dorman was her maiden name. We already knew she attended those secret confabs in the guest house and I'm totally sure she's not saying all she knows. I think she wants to check with someone before she says anything more to us. I'm sure of it. She knows plenty, but she's taking directions from someone else. Clyde's covering up too. He wants to tip us off, but he's afraid for Sally. Everyone wants to tip us, even Natalie, but they're waiting for a green light. Taking it further, there's more than one team playing here and neither team's exactly sure how to handle us. I have a hunch Sally needs to check with Natalie. For that matter, Natalie just phoned Sally at the hospital. Natalie said it was just to check how thing were going with Clyde Webb, but that's bull. So what's she really checking on? It'd be nice if that was the green light for Sally to talk to us."

"Hmm .."

Henderson's car pulled up with a squeak of the tires and Henderson jumped out as if in a hurry, "Look guys, Spatz has called in a whole army. I've got to fly into the cop-shop to control him. What a jerk! He's talking to the press and even talking himself up to the Governor like he's saving the day. So the tables are turned, now you guys have to carry the investigation-ball while I try to control the politics. Things turn around I guess. But keep me well posted."

Henderson went on, "But here's some quick information before I split. First, we lost the joker in the black Crown Vic. The local cops are still sweeping the area, but he's gone. The car was rented under a false name too. He used Franz non Papen as a name. Some joke on us huh?"

Mill said, "And the hand writing on the 'meet in the kitchen' note matches nobody, not even the kids."

"Right, how'd you know that? And the State Department and Justice Department and the White House? Nobody there ever heard from Dorsey. It'd be one thing if they told us to bag off. But total denial, and we are a police agency, not good on that front."

"Next, you guys didn't follow up. You were supposed to check that emergency phone number. We just did your part for you. That Washington area code number

Schmidt called, we assumed it was the secret code-word number? No answer on that number at all. So here's the atom bomb. Are you ready? The number Schmidt called is the residence of a certain Jim Dorsey. And in the last year, he called that number seven times. And he called a certain D. Smith who lives in Miami even more times."

There was a short silence.

Mill said, "Let me guess, every time he called Smith, a certain D. Smith flew to Detroit."

"We don't know that yet, but it's worth checking. Now then, Sally Webb? Her story checks so far. Sally Dorman was married when she was sixteen in West Virginia, divorced a year later. She went missing for several months after the divorce was filed. That part's still blank. Anyway, the cops had her husband questioned and he was suspected of murder. But later, Sally Dorman held a sales job in an industrial sales office up here. She did really well by the look of it. She even worked there for a couple years after she married Webb. So far, things check. Except this tid bit, the ex-husband went missing and hasn't been seen or heard from since. "

Mill interjected, "And except she was missing for a few months and she accompanied the German Consortium to Colebrook School calling herself Dorman and acting as their secretary and speaking German."

"The secretary thing could be honest enough. It's not illegal to hire a local lady with office experience to help out."

Mill said, "Unless you lie about speaking German and hide how much you know, and your husband covers too. Withholding information from authorities during a murder investigation is not okay."

"Okay, okay, agreed, but that's your ball to chase for now. The Dorman name, that could just be an old 'doing business as' or something. Anyway, she looks mostly clean, well, partly clean to me."

Henderson went on, "And that Dr. Shaw? We just talked to him again. He was invited to the party by Mrs. Hubchic. She told him Schmidt might be interested in Palestine and the plight of innocents in refugee camps. When we spoke to Shaw he said Schmidt turned out to be very sympathetic and asked Shaw to come and see him later this week. Shaw says Schmidt wanted to talk about peace initiatives, American policy and financial aid to camps, whatever all that means.

"One more, are you ready? Jason O'Neal, the pizza kid, remember him? His big brother Patrick is here going to college but he spent the summer on an internship at The Justice Department, 'The Office of Independent Investigations.' The kid just got back. Your intern is brother to the Pizza kid who was here the night of the party."

Jane's phone went, 'poop-boop-a-doop - squeak!'

"Hello, Oh, Hi Jim!" Jane frantically waved her hand in the air, put her finger to her lips as if to say 'keep quiet' and pushed a button to turn on speaker-phone.

"Look Paine, the politics back here are way too thick, I've got to call you guys back to Washington. The Attorney General says no-way on all this. It's secret, period."

Jane looked intently at Mill and Mill rolled his hands around in some kind of keep-him-talking sign.

"Let the local cops chase the murder thing, but you guys pull out right now."

"Wow Dorsey, and we were just melting the local cops a little. They were pissed at first, but we're just getting to them. And I feel we owe Smitty something too. We can't just leave this."

"Head out now. Don't even talk to the cops. I'll fix all that later. Fly out commercial, I've don't have a military plane up my sleeve this time. Is Mill there?"

"No, I left him at the mall to shop for underwear, we're not meeting till dinner-time."

"Where are you?"

"I'm at Colebrook School waiting to see some dean named McIntyre."

"Make your excuses and split .. now! Don't even see him. And cell-phone Mill and get him out too. Have you talked to the cops today?"

"Just early this morning. Nothing since then. They were looking for a Dr. Shaw who was at the party the night of Schmidt's murder."

"Tell Mill this. Tell him I solved his money trail mystery. It was nothing but cash for a check cashing outfit. I have the files with me. I'm in Miami now. You guys have earned a day or two off. When you get back, take a couple days, no, take three. When I get back, I'll have a couple good field assignments for you guys. I promise. Good job guys, but the politics won and we lost this time. Get out of there fast, preferably now, certainly by tonight. Don't even talk to the cops. Not a word. Politics demands it."

"Okay, okay, if that's an order. I don't like it for Smith's sake, but if that's it, okay. We'll go. But I've got to get back to the hotel for our stuff. My computer's there. I'll make air reservations and confirm to you from there."

"No, you don't need to call me, just split before I'm eaten alive. We stepped on national security this time and we're definitely called off. Cell phone battery's low. Gotta go. We'll talk later."

"Bye."

Mill said, "Wow Jane, I didn't know you were such a masterful liar. Good work!"

Jane looked back at Mill. "Dorsey's in on this for sure isn't he."

Mill just said, "Yup."

"And Smith was in on it too."

"Yup, Desi, one of the guys at the meetings, Desi, a certain Deasmumhnach Smith … and Henderson, when you and Smith were at the morgue to identify Schmidt, did Schmidt still have his pants? Could Smith have slipped that 'meet in the kitchen' note into his pocket?"

Henderson said, "Crap! You're right, his pants and clothes were in a bag sitting there and I remember Smith getting them out and looking them all over. I thought he was looking for a bullet hole or something, but even then I thought that was a little odd."

Jane said, "And Mill, that financial wild goose chase you were on in Washington is really this very case. Probably spooked Dorsey and caused all this."

"Yup, didn't cause it exactly, it was going to happen anyway, but it spooked them into premature action."

"And Dorsey sent us out here so he could destroy the money trail evidence while we were gone."

"I'd say so."

"Kind of insulting, he thought we couldn't figure this out? Send us right into the middle of it?"

"No, he knew we'd catch on, in the end anyway. He was just buying time. He and Smith probably meant to run to Brazil or something. It was just a delaying action till they could scoot."

"And he looked beat-to-shit that morning, not cuz he was up chasing old records all night, but cuz he just drove or flew in from here."

"Drove probably."

"And Alka-Seltzer Panski was the shooter till Smith nailed him. A fight over the spoils or something?"

"Looks that way. Dorsey carries an old style army forty-five under his suit coat and a small-frame forty caliber backup on his back hip. The first shooter used an antique from Russia with a silencer. Panski's a good guess as shooter."

"And it was probably Dorsey who dumped Panski in the shed."

"Probably."

"And we're not leaving as ordered are we."

"Hell no. That was probably Dorsey taking pot shots at the Webbs just now. Sally says the shooter was a big guy, fifties, business suit. That was Dorsey. He's probably under a manhole cover at the seminary right now. "

"Great," said Jane.

"Patrick O'Neal, what's his angle?"

"A courier or something."

"Hold it, I saw him in that boutique today. He is around here somewhere. Think he's with Dorsey now?"

"Maybe. But what the hell was he doing looking at ladies' underwear in a boutique if he's busy being an accomplice to murder? Maybe he's just a dupe of some kind."

Then Mill said, "Henderson, can you have one of your guys drive our rental car to the cop shop? I want it to look like nobody but Natalie is at home. And can you get back-up with guns in the house with us?"

"Sure."

"Can you build the case up from this? I think we've got the outline."

"It's enough to work with. It's easier when you know where you're going. And it all sure fits."

"Jane, we have to call the justice department fast, then we have to set up for a little house party. I think we can expect a visit from our soon-to-be former boss and rather soon. And Henderson, if I were you, I'd keep the Webbs out of their house and I'd put some of your guys in there instead, preferably with lots of big guns. Put a protective guard on the Webbs themselves, if they're still at the hospital or wherever they are. Dorsey wants to eliminate witnesses and the Webbs, especially Sally, are number one on Dorsey's list. And obviously put Dorsey's name and description out. Six two, fifty-nine years old or so, two-forty pounds maybe, graying, wears business suits. I say he lost you guys by doubling back and, he's likely on foot and in this neighborhood right now. He's desperate, so he's dangerous. He carries two guns, a forty-five under his jacket and a small-frame forty on his hip. Okay, go and deal with Spatz but get us some back-up."

"Screw Spatz, you guys are right, I'm calling every resource I can find and right now. We need to find Dorsey and protect everyone. I'll deal with that clown Spatz later."

Squealing tires announced a new arrival. A well used sedan with a pizza sign on top halted.

"What now?" said Jane.

 Patrick O'Neal emerged from the passenger seat and a smaller, younger version of him, obviously his brother, got out of the driver's seat.

Patrick moved his glasses up and down as if trying to see and be sure. Then he said, "Swan told me you were probably here. Look you guys, what's going on? What's with snooping up our stuff out back in the guest house? What Swan says is really weird. What are you guys doing here?"

Henderson spoke, "I'm police. Look at this badge."

Patrick raised his glasses to his forehead and, in a comical way, leaned and looked very closely at the badge.

"You're Patrick O'Neal? We have an emergency here and you need to tell us the truth and right now. It's really serious."

Mill interrupted, "Patrick, are you pulling any shit with Jim Dorsey?"

"Huh? What kind of shit?"

"Did he tell you to cover him and say you were in the office with him late the other night?"

"I really was in the office the other night. He wanted to find an old file."

Jane spoke, "Tell the truth Patrick. Dorsey's involved in some really, really nasty stuff and you need to be truthful. If you're in with him, the time to bail out is now."

"You mean Dorsey in Washington? Man am I ever out of it! I don't get what you're talking about."

The sound of a telephone ringing came from inside the house.

"Jeez!" Jane said. "I'm jumpy. That scared the hell out of me."

Henderson spoke, "Patrick, Jason, listen, there is a police emergency right now and it's bad. I have to leave. I want you two to keep your mouths shut. Talk to nobody except these two and me till I can interview you. If you want, you should find a lawyer, but keep still to everybody else. Except these guys I mean. I am very serious. But I have to get to the police station right now. I'll be in touch."

Patrick said, "Jeez! Okay. Jane, will someone tell me what's going on?"

Dorsey's Close Call

It is better to run back, than run the wrong way.

Proverb

Dorsey's arm was throbbing where Smith had winged him. He was furious at himself for missing the Webbs. When he parked in the seminary, he could hear tires squealing and an engine racing not far enough behind him. He was being followed. This wasn't the plan. His plan was to drive into the seminary, park, walk through the grounds and then up a road to the hotel where he left his car. There wasn't supposed to be someone in hot pursuit. Now he'd have to think fast. Dorsey knew very well he couldn't out-run younger men on foot, even with a head-start. He was too old and overweight for that. So he fought the impulse to run.

Dorsey leaned over into the rented car and used his jacket to make quick swipes at the steering wheel, gear shift and keys for finger prints. Then he wiped the door handle. He could hear that pursuing car. He didn't have much time.

Thirty year's effort and a luxurious tropical retirement in extradition-free Vanuatu was at the end of the rainbow, and now it was at risk, big risk. But he imagined he could still pull this off if he could just buy a couple days time. But first he had to get out of this fix.

He had to think. Think! And he still had to fight that panicky urge to run. When you lose your breath from running, you just burn energy huffing and puffing and then you can't keep running or do much of anything. It just makes you a sitting duck. Move quickly, but conserve your heart rate and breath. Don't run. So think! Okay, what did he learn about hiding way back in Boy Scouts. Climb a tree, that's oldest and the best trick in the book. That worked back then. Guys searching for you look at the ground. They don't look up. Boy scouts taught him that many years ago. What's his name"? Robert Baden-Powel, the scout founder, made climbing trees into a big deal. McIntyre's scout master he thought so too. One time he had even dropped out of the tree into the middle of the boys searching for him and cried 'Got 'cha!' That was valuable information right now.

Good information, but he knew he was way too old and out of shape to start climbing trees right now. Besides, his arm hurt like hell and if whoever was in pursuit had a scout master like he had, he'd know enough to look up, not just down. Dorsey knew he was wasting valuable seconds.

Make up some other plan, he thought. But don't run. There, in front of him, was a little stone building. To avoid footprints in the grass, Dorsey rapidly hurried a longer way around to a sidewalk that led back to the little building. Inside he saw some kind of stepped table with candles burning on it, some Roman Catholic pray-for-the-dead thing he thought. There was a possible hiding place underneath the candle covered table. But it was not good enough. That was the first kind of place somebody would look. He backed out of the building and closed the door. Now Dorsey could really hear that car coming. Time's up! It's got to be trees climbing, or running or set up an ambush and start shooting. What a choice!

Dorsey eyed the steep slate roof on the little building. It came quite low on both sides, only three or four feet from the ground, so with adrenaline inspired effort, Dorsey pulled himself up onto the roof and quickly walked, his hands on the steep roof for balance, to the peak. He looked around. Good luck! A big tree branch was right there. Hands and feet still on the roof, Dorsey sat on the branch without slipping, and then scooted back on the big tree branch in a sort of sitting position. He scooted his way all the way to the trunk. The thick leaves and big trunk afforded pretty good camouflage here, but standing and struggling for balance, he got his behind up on an even higher branch, then pulled his legs up, adjusted himself into a ball and sat on the branch as close to the trunk as he could. He was trembling from the effort and he was breathing hard, but this was a really good a hide-out. This was great thinking. Maybe he'd get out of this jam after all.

Dorsey sat, .. hmm .. a red oak .. a big one .. gotta be way over a hundred years old. Why that came to his mind at a time like this, he did not know. It must be some subconscious thing to help him deal with panic.

Dorsey heard a car door open and rapid footsteps. It sounded like only one person. The steps halted and he heard a man's voice. It was hard to make out, but Dorsey heard something like "on foot, don't see him yet." Then, through the leaves, Dorsey could actually see the man below, although just barely. It looked like he had a cell phone or radio in hand. Then the man put the object in a pocket and produced a big pistol instead. The man approached the door to the little building and shouted "Police! Come out with your hands up! Now! Now!" Then the man threw the door open and, with his gun held in front of him, and charged in. A moment later the man came back out, still holding his gun and looking around. But, sure enough, the man never looked up.

Dorsey's injured arm ached. The palms of his hands hurt from holding tight to the tree trunk. His behind hurt. And the effort of climbing up here still had him breathing more heavily than he liked. But he held on and tried to pace his breathing with big, slow quiet breaths with his mouth wide open. He tried to keep as quiet and still as he could. His plan was working.

Now the man below was even less visible through the leaves. Dorsey could just make out that he was jogging away. Then the man seemed to be scanning side to side with his pistol held in front of him, but he kept his head down all the way. Just like the scout master said, he never looked up at all.

When Dorsey could just barely hear the man's footsteps, he slid as quietly as he could to a lower branch, then a lower and lower. Dorsey thought he heard the man halt. Dorsey froze. After a minute Dorsey thought he heard the footsteps continue. Dorsey finally dropped as silently as he could to the ground. Another kid's game came to mind. Neighborhood kids used to hide from each other behind a backyard shed. The trick was to figure which way the kids hunting you would come and then, go the other way and run like hell. Now Dorsey, as quietly as he could, moved back toward the parking lot carefully keeping the little building between himself and where the man had jogged off. When he had crossed the parking lot, the man was totally out of sight and out of earshot. Now Dorsey moved through some trees to the road, then across the road and, staying as low as he could, he made his way along a shallow ditch on the far side of the road. It led to a little bridge over a small stream. The bridge looked like it might afford a hiding place. But underneath was wide open on both sides. No long term hiding place there. Dorsey heard another car and saw the reflection of police-car flashing lights. Dorsey ducked under the bridge, getting his shoes wet. Dorsey remembered the little stream at Schmidt's place and figured this was the same one. After a moment, staying as low as he could, he made his way up the stream in the direction of Schmidt's. Then, once at a safer distance, he walked upright, following the stream through wooded area. He moved slowly to keep his breath and he stayed as quiet as he could. And he kept a sharp lookout for anyone at all.

At length Dorsey picked out what looked like an out-of-sight place in the trees and he sat and rested. He thought to himself, one crisis down. That was way, way too close. If the cops were quick getting dogs to track him, his goose was still cooked. The walk through the stream would slow the dogs down, but the cops weren't stupid. They'd follow the stream. He just put that out of his mind to figure out what next. At least, he had a few minutes now. So what next? Think! Think! Retirement and a life of ease versus life in prison was in the balance. Stay ahead of the curve, keep the initiative. Don't let them take the initiative. Stay in control. Now think! Something had to be done very soon and done just right. It can all still be saved. Should he work his way back to his car by some roundabout route? Then what? Make a get-away? Nah, that'd just postpone the inevitable. He had to stay pro-active. An outline of a plan formed in his mind. It would be tricky and probably bloody, but it was way too late to be squeamish about that. It would tax all his skills, but it might just work if he made every move just right. Two more days, that's all he needed. Dorsey reviewed each step in his mind. Yes, just maybe he could still pull this off. Then he looked around checking for people again .. nobody. He listened .. nothing. Dorsey got his forty-five out removed the empty clip and, replaced it with a full clip.

Dorsey looked and listened again. Nothing? Oops, not nothing this time. Dorsey just barely heard something. Through the trees Dorsey saw movement. Dorsey rolled onto his belly and looked very carefully. There, just in barely view, was an older lady. She stood looking in his direction. He could not tell if she had actually spotted him. She slowly removed gardening gloves and then, to Dorsey's surprise and alarm, she picked up an automatic pistol and looked his way again.

Dorsey very slowly and very carefully took aim with his forty-five. The sound of a shot would bring his pursuers for sure. Shooting right now was a very bad idea. So he froze and waited.

The lady seemed to scan the woods. Then she moved quickly away keeping the pistol in one hand. She looked over her shoulder every few steps.

Dorsey took a deep breath. Would the lady call the cops? And what did she have a pistol for? Dorsey decided it made no difference as far as what he needed to do. He'd proceed as if she was never there. He would just carry out his plan anyway. He looked around again, listened again, then pulled his cell phone out of a pocket and dialed.

Big Trouble

"I like a man who grins when he fights"

Winston Churchill

"Don't make a sound or I'll blow your brains out. And good evening girls." Lois and Swan had just come into Lois's bedroom. They froze. "I've seen you two peeking out that window often enough and thought I'd see what the view is like. It's very nice. Are these your binoculars? A nice pair, but they're supposed to be for bird watching, not for spying!"

The big man had a big army style gun pointed at the girls. He had a white shirt and tie, but he was dirty all over and his left sleeve was rolled up and a blood stained towel was wrapped around his arm, held there with duct tape. He looked haggard and white.

"Oh shit." Swan said.

"We can help you. Let me help with that injury." Lois said.

"Very good, 'We can help you' line, just what you're supposed to say. You must have learned that one in school. Get on the same side as the intruder. But 'Oh shit' is the wrong answer. That belittles the intruder and might make him mad. Besides, I said keep quiet. So keep quiet. Don't make the intruder mad. I will blow you guys away. Now, the truth is, you two are both going to help me. We're going downstairs to receive Mrs. Schmidt who I believe is on the way now. I have just spoken to her on the phone and she seemed most amenable to coming, since I told her the alternate was blowing your collective brains all over the walls here. She is most willing to make an exchange. Herself for you two. You! Are you Lois? You'll need to let her in and make sure nobody is with her. And remember, I'll have this gun at the temple of your cousin Swan. You are Swan right? So Lois, you'll do this without a mistake. Open, look around, you are so good at that sort of thing, looking around I mean, then get the old lady in and close the door. If anybody sees you from the street, tell me, if she has any hidden company, tell me that too or there will be blood all over the place. But my guess is she'll be alone. Shall we go downstairs now?"

....

Mill's cell phone rang. "Hello …… Hello? …" His brows knitted and he concentrated, he hit speaker phone to make it louder.

".. hello Mrs. Schmidt, please come in. We were expecting you. Is anybody out here with you? No? Good. Come in quickly please."

Jane saw Mill's face darken. She had never seen him show emotion this way before. "They must be at Feine's, Lois must have hit speed dial. Paine! Call nine-one-one. Get cops ambulances, everything." Mill was nearly ranting, "Jeez, let's see, umm, he'll lock the front door, gotta surprise him, sneak in the back door, back door …" Mill was down the narrow back stairs and out the lower door at a dead sprint.

Jane, called nine-one-one and ran as fast as she could at the same time. She caught up with Mill at Feine's back door. He was on his knees with some sort of pick in the lock and his hands were shaking. Mill spoke but Jane didn't know if he spoke to her or himself. "The joker came in this way and he broke the damn lock. I can't pick it cuz it's broken. Damn it, open! Catch you turkey, catch the tumbler! ……… There! Finally, the door did open. Then Mill, held his 10 mm Glock in front of him. He moved into the house with an uncharacteristic smoothness and cat-like stealth that Jane had never seen in him. Jane forced herself to put alarm out of her head and she tried to remember all of her training. She held her smaller Glock with both hands and kept it in front of her. Then Jane followed Mill as quietly as she could.

....

Natalie stopped when she was half in the door, she saw Bubbie Feine seated on the couch and Swan seated next to her. Lois's mother, Sylvia Feine sat in a chair. "I will not advance a step more till you let all these people go. You said exchange."

The big man took Natalie's arm and threw her into the sofa next to Swan.

"First, a question or two, where are those two so-called detectives from Washington? You've been talking to them." The man pointed his gun at Swan and pulled the hammer back till it clicked.

"Swan closed her eyes."

Lois said, "I haven't seen them in two days. I think they went away."

The big man said, "Bullshit! Don't lie."

Natalie spoke, "Tell him nothing! Nothing!"

The big man fired his gun. It was ear splitting. The shot was close to Swan, but not right at her. "Try again. Where are they? Holed up at your house? Next one blows this girl away."

Natalie said, "Let these people go. They said they were going to their hotel and the school. That's what they said. Try there."

"Hmm, maybe." the big man said, "That jives with what Paine said on the phone. Okay, you two girls have been watching the guest house for years. Who have you told about that?"

Swan said, "Nobody."

The big man pulled the hammer back again … click! "Bullshit!"

"Okay, okay, okay, we told the cops. Did you shoot Dr. Schmidt? Are you the one?"

"Ha, ha, ha, funny. I'm asking the questions, not you. But the joke is this, no, I didn't."

． ． ． ． ． ． ． ． ．

"Freeze!" yelled Mill, "Drop it!"

233

Jane saw Dorsey wheel around. He seemed to be moving in slow motion. Jane saw his gun jump. He must be firing. All Jane's training was instantly crystal clear in her head. 'Fire at the center of mass!' She looked over her sites and followed the center of the man. He still seemed to be moving in slow motion. 'Don't rush, aim with care, be steady. Don't snap the trigger, slowly increase pressure … ' When Jane's gun fired, it almost surprised her. Jane re-aimed, but Mill's voice entered her thinking, he was yelling, "Stop shooing! Stop shooting!"

The form of Patrick O'Neal flew head first into view. He took Dorsey's gun hand and pushed it straight up in the air with both of his hands. O'Neal's momentum slammed Dorsey into a wall. Dorsey's gun flew free. Then Dorsey and O'Neal slid down the wall to the floor, O'Neal was punching Dorsey's face all the way. Behind them was an area of wall, now caved in from the impact."

Mill's voice was shouting "Stop shooting! Cease fire! Stop! He's down! He's hit!"

O'Neal was quickly on his feet, but Dorsey did not rise. He was in a sitting position, his back against the wall. His shirt showed blood around his belly. His pants around his thigh was bloody too.

Mill's voice was still shouting. "Hold up! He's shot. Hold up! He's down!"

Jane realized she had heard three deafening shots in very rapid succession, looking around, she saw that the room was filled with smoke. Mill was charging forward and kicked Dorsey's forty-five away, then Mill grabbed Dorsey and rolled him on his side. Mill grabbed a smaller gun from a belt holster on Dorsey's hip.

Patrick was breathing hard and screaming. "You were going to shoot Swan you piece of shit! You piece of shit!" Patrick was red faced and shaking, tears were pouring from his eyes. An incomprehensible "Arrrgh-ahhh!" came from his mouth, then he took several deep breaths and some mixture of crying and roaring came next.

"Anybody else hit?" It was Mill's voice again. He was on his feet again and he was looking around. Nobody answered.

Jane saw Dorsey slowly roll back to his sitting position. "Huh, huh, huh," then he managed a shallow breath then an "aaaargh." came from him. He obviously had the wind knocked out of him and was trying to recover his breath. Then he put his hands over the bloody area in his belly. He made a guttural, "Aaagh.!"

Next Jane saw that Natalie Schmidt had a small automatic in her hand and smoke was rolling from its barrel.

Jane heard her own voice, "I think I hit him, ohhh! I never thought I'd …" Jane stamped her foot. "Ohhh!" It was her own voice but she didn't know where the words were coming from..

Dorsey looked down at his gut, and bloody shirt, then at his thigh. But his breathing and his speech was surprisingly normal, "Holy cow." He took some deep breaths. "Jeez .. Don't out-number me or anything. O'Neal, what the hell are you doing here? Hey guys, this hurts like hell. I'm hurt guys. Call nine-one-one."

Swan curled up with her arms around her knees and leaned on Bubbie, in the meek voice of a child she said, "Bubbie, Bubbie." then she too started to cry.

O'Neal, a bit recovered now, sat next to Swan and took her hand. He was still red faced, visibly shaking and out of breath, but he smoothed Swan's hand.

Bubbie Feine calmly said, "You young people were all very brave, you did well. You all did well. I am proud of my brother's grandchildren. You both were strong and brave. Now you may cry. Patrick, that was dangerous, but it was heroic."

Sylvia Feine's eyes were like saucers, she let out a very deep breath. "My God! My God! Oh, My God!"

Jane felt faint. She sat in a chair, dropped her gun on the floor and put her head down with her face in her hands. Then she managed, "Wow!"

…………

"Dorsey, you never could hit a barn with that thing. Now Dorsey, answer me." It was Mill talking in an unnatural, loud and rough voice.

"Jeez! Call nine-one-one. Get me a damn ambulance. Look at me, man!"

"Answer me before I put another hole in you to improve your memory!"

"You can't do this, where's an ambulance."

Natalie stepped forward, a broad grin on her face.

"Shooting them in the feet always worked for us in the old days, or in the testicles. No, I think feet for this one, he has no testicles." She raised her little automatic.

"Mill, take that gun away from her! That woman's nuts!"

Patrick O'Neal said, "Crap guys! What's going on?"

Mill said, "Dorsey, I think that woman is making perfect sense, so answer me. What's going on?"

"Answer him!" said Natalie as she pointed the gun at Dorsey's feet.

"Wow! .. Ummm .. Smith was shaking 'em down. It was Smith. You didn't figure that out? He'd been at it since the beginning. He's even become part of their damn German club."

"Were you were blackmailing Smith?"

"Yeah, yeah, in a way. But it was his idea, not mine, that I take a fee to cover him. We struck that deal when he was still at work. It was just teamwork. Jeez! Get me an ambulance, apply pressure to this bleeding or something .. and take that gun away from that crazy woman."

"Crazy? I think I'll shoot. Kneecaps are good too." Natalie advanced and pointed her gun at Dorsey's knee, she smiled again and aimed with one eye over the gun sights and pulled the hammer back.

"No! No! What? What else?"

"Why'd you shoot Schmidt if things were working so well?"

"I didn't shoot him, that doofus polack Panski shot him. Schmidt brought Panski in early as a guard or something or maybe for muscle if Hoffman's boys acted up or maybe just for show. I don't know. Panski was a mean son-of-a-bitch. I'll give him that. Hell, your crazy woman here can tell you about Panski. She trained him way back when, in polack-land."

"Okay, but why shoot Schmidt?"

"Look, apply pressure to this or wrap me up or something. Call nine-one-one will ya?""

Natalie said, "The man just asked you a question."

"Okay, okay! Why shoot Schmidt? I was against it. Smith and I figured those Hoffman kids were being sent in to take over for Schmidt. He was being retired. We knew we were next. But the biggest chunk of cash yet was just en-route. We thought we'd just kind-a take it, the whole works this time as severance pay. I was against that too. That meant leaving the country and for what, a couple million each? No. I said just call it good. It was a good run while it lasted, so now just forget it. But Panski and Smith wanted that last shipment. The only guy who knew the pick-up confirmation code here was Schmidt himself and if he was gone, they wouldn't be sure the cash did or didn't make it for several days. He was old as crap anyway, so Panski said he'd make it look like suicide or a break-in or something. It was really Panski's idea. Then you stumbled on the Miami money break-in-the-money-trail thing. That was really bad luck. That made a simple plan really complicated and really complicated plans never work. I wanted to drop the whole damn thing."

"Why was Schmidt in the dining room?"

"That was Panski's idea of a set-up. He told him they needed to meet after the party. That sounded dumb to me, but I guess it worked. Panski said he's have his gun out. He was right. Schmidt always had his gun out when he met Panski. Schmidt never trusted Panski."

"You were there?"

"Yeah, I was there. But Panski was the shooter."

"So why'd you blow Smith away?"

"Hell, he threatened me! He went screwy. He thought I was setting him up to take the fall while I split the country. He was running around like an idiot. He was only supposed to lay down a smoke screen to slow you guys down while I covered what you dug up in Washington. We didn't even have the main shipment yet. We only needed three more days. So I phoned Panski for insurance and set a peace meeting to clear Smith's head. But I guess Smith phoned Panski too or something. Smith sure was surprised when Panski started shooting. So was I. I think Panski just decided at the last minute to play along with me instead of Smith. Probably he was going to try to blow me away too as soon as we had the full shipment. I'd bet that was really his plan."

"Was there really a national security secret?"

"That's the only part that's true, but even that's only half-assed true. Smith and his pals dragged Schmidt out of the Russian zone alright and they planted him here. Then he arranged with the State Department to let him stay. There really was a secrecy order too. Truman signed it. I saw it. Don't ask me why. Jeez! Do something. I'm pumping blood out. Call a damn ambulance okay?"

"SO look, my guess is Roosevelt released some God-awful amount of money to get Jews out of Germany and Poland and put 'em in Palestine. He just pumped money into all the so-called underground guys. He only wanted a head count on how many Jews got moved. The Palestinians had no sense of humor at all about all those Jews coming into their country. If that scoop got out, that we were behind so much of that, it would have put our diplomacy on its ear. Maybe that's still true today, as if they don't hate us enough already. Hell, they know we're on Israel's side. What's the difference? But that was the big secret and Smith used it to cover the move of Schmidt and even threaten Schmidt. He got Schmidt official asylum here, but he never told Schmidt about it. So Schmidt was always a little afraid."

Natalie made a noise like "Pffftt! We knew about that." But Natalie lowered her gun.

"Then why?" It was Dorsey who asked this time.

Natalie said, "Because you moved our money. You did your job. That'll all."

Mill said, "Jane, see if you can find a bed sheet or something. Let's wrap this turkey up before he spoils the whole carpet."

"Sheets are in the linen closet. C'mon." said Sylvia Feine.

Jason O'Neal, the pizza delivery kid had appeared. His eyes were big and his mouth was open, but he said, "I had a first aid class, shouldn't we check for shock?"

Mill turned back to Dorsey. "What's the von Papen angle?"

Dorsey looked as if he was trying to get to his feet, but he promptly sat back down. "Ohhhh man .. hurry up will you? I think that woman's bullets busted my leg. When are you calling nine-one-one?"

"When I'm happy with your answers."

Natalie waved her pistol again, "'Doofus polack,' is that a nice name? I think the young man over there might like to put his foot in your testicles. Young man, have you any Polish in you?"

"Mill, look out for that woman! She's the smartest one in the club. I've seen her act. She scared the hell out of Panski and it took something to scare him. He warned me about her. She's crazy, dangerous like a mad dog. Panski called her mongoose or something. He said she deserved that nick name. Watch out, okay? Now take her gun, will ya?"

"Mad dog? How flattering," said Natalie. Then she hummed a tune as she aimed at Dorsey's feet again.

Mill said, "Von Papen?"

"Jeez, okay, von Papen was half code-name and half joke. I think Schmidt really met the man. Alright? Maybe he really was friends back when, but to us it was an inside joke, a call for a meeting or whatever, a call that said come for cocktails with Papen meant we'd meet in the guest house. That all started a long, time ago when Schmidt got mad and threatened to call his friend von Papen, as if that dried up old turd could do anything about anything. We just laughed about it. Then even Schmidt started to laugh. And so going to see Papen got to mean having a meeting. But the real guy, von Papen, wasn't involved, not that I know of anyway. But with these guys, you never know."

"Was Catholic or Nazi money in it ?"

"Schmidt and Hoffman knew about that part, not us. They held those cards close to the vest."

"What were Smith and you all about? Be clear."

"Money laundering, well not exactly laundering, money moving. The old money was all over the place in Europe. At first the job was a game mainly to hide it from the Communist governments. They thought they had claims on it. It was in banks and land assets of all kinds of stuff. The job was making that money hard to track and pop up clean and preferably in cash over here. That's what we were good at. It was a shell game with money. Buy museum art in Poland and sell it over here, that kind of thing."

"Sally Webb's part?"

"Her? Her job was to report back to Hoffman and confirm the money got here. She'd send a code word to Germany. Oh, she knew way more than she let on. She pretended dumb, but she was onto it all. She'd put on a sheer gauze top and parade those giant fake boobs around and a check on everything for the Germans. She was an ornament, but a smart ornament."

"And Patrick O'Neal?"

"O'Neal? What's he doing here? Ask him. He's right here."

"No, you tell me."

"O'Neal? I brought him in on his zip-code only. He lived here. It was just a flier. Maybe he'd be real useful to us. It didn't work. The kid's half blind and he's a straight arrow. He was useless to us. "

"Was he in the office at midnight like you said?"

"Yeah, yeah, he was. Ask him! I needed to find the Schmidt file that night and get rid of it."

Jane Paine and Sylvia Feine appeared with bed sheets and some bath towels, Jason O'Neal carried a first aid kit in a white box with a red cross on it. But just then the doorbell started ringing and there was thundering knocking at the door. Jane jumped and opened the door and paramedics and police poured in.

"Mill, if you didn't call for an ambulance, who the hell are these guys? You turkey, you lied to me. You did call. They were coming all along. You can't use what I said, you got it all under duress. Ohhhhh .. jeez!"

"I'm not the cops Dorsey. It's different rules. But they'll get the same out of you, after I tell 'em what to look for that is. If by some accident you live that is. They'll be a little more polite, but they'll get it."

……..

Henderson sat in one of the upholstered living room chairs and was reviewing the statement forms he had collected. "Mill, you didn't fire at all?"

"No, as he turned Natalie put one or two in his leg, then I saw O'Neil in the corner of my eye. I held off."

Natalie said, "Legs to take him down, that usually works. They usually spill their gun when they fall. If he didn't, I had a bead on the rest of him just in case. But I think Jane took care of that part."

"Natalie, you were quick. I'm impressed." it was Mill.

"A mongoose is supposed to be quick. But I think I used to be quicker. At one time I would have had him as soon as I came in the door."

"And that pistol, where did that come from? It looks like a war era Walther."

"You mean here in my sleeve? Oh, well, oh yes, where did I get it .. I've had it a while. Don't worry. The last owner didn't miss it. And now I even have a concealed-carry permit. I took the class. The teacher learned a quite a bit."

Henderson looked at Natalie, then back at his papers.

A photographer, the same man as had been at the scene of Smith's murder, had a big camera on a tripod. Bubbie Feine sat beside her brother's grandchildren. She repeated, "You two were very brave, I have seen strong men go to tears over less. I am proud of you, you too Patrick."

Mill said, "Lois got her cell phone on somehow and called me. That was really good work Lois."

Lois said, "I think I'm more scared now than when it was happening. I felt sick a minute ago, but I think I'm okay. I wish I could calm down."

Bubbie Feine said, "Natalie, that was something! It was terrifying! I thought you were going to shoot him again! I believed you and so did he! I have not seen that sort of thing in a very long time. That was good work. Did you learn that in Poland?"

Natalie said, "Yes, I suppose so. Never bluff, never threaten with a gun. That only works if you're ready to follow through. Does that get me in trouble with the police Mr. Henderson?"

Henderson said, "That may not be up to me. But he was threatening with and fired his gun, you felt the man had recently murdered, or been a party to murdering your common-law husband, and it was a very extreme situation start to finish, so I will not recommend any action. But Mill, it sounds like you seriously pushed the envelope afterward, but, the same goes for you. I'll argue to let it pass. But I hope you have a lawyer. Even if Dorsey survives, even if he's in jail, he'll probably sue you. And as far as I know, your interrogation method was a shade off exact FBI procedure. They may want to talk to you about that part."

Jane spoke. "I hit him didn't I."

Henderson spoke again. "Looks like Mrs. Schmidt got his legs a couple times at least and maybe you hit him in the mid-section. Trained cops only hit with about a quarter of the shots fired. But it looks like you guys did a lot better. Gut shots are very painful and they can be fatal. Even if he makes it through surgery we might not know for a while. Plus his arm is hurt. More than one hit anywhere makes it tough odds. Patrick, you might have saved him by getting in the way and stopping the shooting. If Mill had fired that ten millimeter, Dorsey'd be all over the wall. His game would be over. But Patrick, definitely don't do that again. Diving into the middle of a shootout is a really, really bad idea."

"Yeah, but he had that gun on Swan and I just lost it. I didn't think. I lost it. Man, the picture of that gun on my girlfriend. Wow, it keeps playing in my head. And he was the ass-hole who wouldn't renew my internship. I just blew up. Now I feel like an idiot. I need to relax for a while."

Henderson said, "Fair enough Mr. O'Neal."

Jane said, "Oh, I hate this. I hate that man, but I don't want him to die."

Henderson said, "Yeah, I understand. Believe me, I understand."

Bubbie Feine said, "Come and sit with us Jane, we are close now. Come and be with us. I wish to calm you and Patrick too. Sit right next to me." Jane did just that and put her hands over her face again as Bubbie smoothed her hair.

Claudia Tesler rushed in the door followed by Val Tesler. She addressed a uniformed policeman, "That man on the gurney, I'm sure he was the one in the woods I called about. He's the one. I'm sure of it."

Then Spatz burst in the door. "Henderson! What the hell is bungled up now?"

Jane looked up and saw Mill clench his fists. His face seemed to turn red, then blue, then white. Then he spun and shouted, "Shut up you egotistical piss-ant. I need to take a leak and I'm pissing all over you right now!"

Jane got on her feet as Spatz said, "Sir, maybe I'll have you arrested for showing disrespect to a peace officer."

Jane put herself between the two, "And your remark of just now is out of line. We are federal agents and we insist on decorum here, especially from a non-participant like you. I think a letter from the Attorney General addressed to your Governor commenting on your complete non-performance, your incompetent headline grabbing obstruction and your asinine attitude and noting your inappropriate remark made to those who just resolved a very dangerous situation is now in order. You need to think again."

Mill moved to the side as if to get around Jane, but Jane side-stepped and kept herself in the between the two, still facing Spatz.

Spatz raised his eyebrows and turned his head up, but he remained silent.

For a moment Jane was tempted to step aside. She wanted to see if Mill was good for his threat. But then the gravity of the events of made her rethink and so she just stood her ground and continued to glare at Spatz with what she considered her most disgusted expression.

Cocktails Again

"Telling the truth will be a revolutionary act."

George Orwell

One might think from looking at a map that Michigan was on the receiving end of those notorious cold winter winds that sweep across the Great Plains. But the big Great Lakes take hold of those winds and change them into dull gray overcast and their own kind of hard, humid, cold.

In Michigan, September starts out as the last of summer's dog days. September is warm, even too warm sometimes. Older school buildings that lack air conditioning throw their windows open in early September. But after that, late in the month, that Great Lakes overcast and rain will arrive. College students who run from class to class on big outdoor campuses might carry umbrellas, but they get wet anyway. After Thanksgiving, or sometimes Christmas, the rain becomes snow. It's not the pretty white New England kind of snow that covers rolling hills and fills meadows and woods and makes pictures for Christmas cards. Michigan might get some of that in the north at ski lodges and in forests, but in the south of Michigan near Detroit anyway, snow is the wet and sloppy kind that soaks shoes. After that, serious, numbing cold has its season. That part is in January and February. But that cold, gray Great Lakes overcast lasts all the way to spring.

This was a September day with the ominous feel that summer was over and winter would visit soon enough. Jane Paine and Mill were Natalie's guests in the big Schmidt house. They had adopted some lower level rooms including a study, or maybe it was a library, that had a desk. That room was their temporary headquarters.

Noisy rain pelted the metal casement windows. Outside, waves of rain could be seen crossing the yard, but that sound of rain on the windows and a draft of warm air from the heating system, somehow, created a cozy feel.

True to form, Mill had wondered why the heat was forced air, not steam. Steam would be normal for a place this size and age. Mill wondered about everything.

Jane entered the room as Mill hung up an old fashioned corded desk telephone. "Okay, that confirms Natalie's political asylum status. It dates from 1946. Better, they say they'll still honor it. So we can forget about that problem."

"Cool," Jane said.

"Next item, who was Schmidt anyway? Stuff is starting to fit. Let me run down Reinhard Gehlen again because that explains most of it. Remember, Natalie said Günter, Otto that is, worked for Gehlen during the war. Okay, the German military General Staff was made up of Prussian Junkers. That means big land owners. They were those monocle wearing guys with 'von' on the front of their names. Half of them had scars on their faces from saber drill when they were in school. The treaty of Versailles that ended World War One banned the General Staff. But what those guys really did was change their name to the 'Truppenamt,' 'The Troop Office' instead of General Staff and they carried on just like before. Gehlen was one of those guys. His thing was intelligence.

Okay, Hitler came to power in thirty-three. He wanted a rapid military build-up so he ignored the treaty of Versailles, restored the General Staff and told those guys to get to work building the military up. Hitler hated rich big shots. But he knew that he needed those guys if he wanted a powerful military in a hurry.

The Prussian Generals returned Hitler's sentiments. They thought Hitler was a ranting wacko peasant, just a loud and unbalanced ex-corporal. But Hitler gave back their old powers and gave then the green light. Hitler even murdered the leaders of his Nazi SA paramilitary to eliminate conflict there. So those guys held their noses and put up with him, at first anyway.

"Gehlen was a hell of a colorful character. During the war Gehlen was German head of military intelligence for the eastern front. That meant spying on Russia. He was a General Staff officer, not one of Hitler's Nazi boys. Anyway, when the war ended, Gehlen surrendered to us, but he did not surrender to our regular army, he surrendered to the Army Intelligence Office. There he showed us some serious bargaining chips like, for example, Germany's intelligence records. He's had all

246

those records put on microfilm and buried in waterproof drums up in the Alps and he told us where to look for them. He also tipped us where stolen Nazi war spoils like fine art were hidden. And his tips kept being right.

"When he surrendered, the army Intelligence guys checked with Eisenhower's Chief of Staff, Bedell Smith. Smith had been in intelligence most of his career. Smith knew Gehlen was no Nazi and had plenty we wanted. Then, imagine this; we rounded up Gehlen's old German intelligence team. We already had most of 'em in POW camps anyway, and we put them back to work only this time, working for us. Later, Gehlen claimed that was the seed that grew into the CIA.

"Now remember, Schmidt was picked up in a hush-hush, move in forty six. That's when Bedell Smith was rounding up Gehlen's old team. And we know Schmidt worked for Gehlen. It all fits. The idea was Schmidt would work intelligence for us.

Jane said, "Okay, but if Gehlen put his guys to work after the war, what was Schmidt doing here just playing school professor? Was it Natalie? Was Natalie a liability?"

"No. No way. Natalie was an underground contact, a bridge between Schmidt and the Polish underground. That's stuff Gehlen would like. A guy like Schmidt is retired and put on a shelf if his cover is blown. I'd guess what took Schmidt out was his activities relocating Jewish people. That made him known to way too many people. Natalie said the Russian were already onto him. His cover leaked like a sieve. So when Gehlen pulled Schmidt out, he knew enough just to to put him on the shelf in reserve. Schmidt probably gave Gehlen reports on what he could, but was no good for further underground work."

A loud gust made Jane and Mill look out the window at the rain.

Then Jane said, "You figure Schmidt's money came from old Nazi spoils? I mean if he worked for Gehlen and Gehlen knew where that stuff was .. "

"I doubt it. Spoils were a Nazi thing. Military guys might take supplies they needed and livestock to feed the troops and stuff like that, but not so much fine art and spoils. Gehlen's team was military intelligence. Not Nazi.

247

"The Money? There's Schmidt's own pre-war family wealth. Those Prussian Junkers with 'von' on their names had spectacular estates, and Schmidt's money could be as simple as that. Another option is money for moving Jewish people out of harm's way. That was really profitable for some. Even Heinrich Himmler had Jewish people moved out of Germany for money. He told Hitler he could finance the war doing that. One more choice is this. It's the mysterious money and land tied to the German Concordat with Vatican, the mysterious bribe money. We know some land and money really did change hands. That's part's not a secret. But much, much more is rumored. Von Papen was the point man on all that and Schmidt was pals with von Papen. Concordat money is be my bet.

"Do you think Natalie knows?"

"Oh yeah, she knows."

"Will she tell us?"

"Only if it buys her something. Remember, in her world, her old underground world, information was the medium of exchange. Information was like money. She'd trade her knowledge, but only for other knowledge or something else she needs. Otherwise, she'll just say nothing. That's how undergrounds really work. Think about it, she planned and measured what she told us. It was just enough to help us catch Dorsey. Now she'll shut up."

Sounds of creaky floors and voices could be heard above.

"That's everyone arriving upstairs? We better go up."

"Yeah, let's head up."

The narrow steep metal stairs were no wider than before. They called for single file. Mill said "Ladies first" but then, watching Jane's behind in front of him, made him reconsidered the etiquette of having ladies go first. Maybe, on steep, narrow stairs, men should lead the way. He decided he better consider that question later.

Natalie had invited the neighbors for cocktails. She included McIntyre, Mill and Jane, really everyone involved in the tragedy and everybody the tragedy touched. She even brought Betty Kuhn back to cater. Then, the young Hoffmans said they wanted to make an authentic German dinner for the crowd. That idea pleased Natalie. A plan that called for dining in the very room where Schmidt had been murdered struck Jane as a bit morbid. Any celebration just now seemed odd to her. But nobody else commented, so Jane put that feeling aside.

When Mill and Jane reached the top of the narrow metal stairs, the big two story foyer reverberated with the sounds of conversation, but it reverberated even more with the sound of the rain on the roof. The noise from the rain made Jane wondered if there was enough insulation up there. Still, the sound of rain and conversation plus the a fire in the fireplace made things cheery.

Betty Kuhn's hair was still sprayed in place to stay. It seemed, not a hair had moved since her last job here. Her remarkably short skirt, ample thighs, bow tie and cuff links were all intact and unchanged. Betty had a new assistant and he was much younger and more spry than old Panski had been. His vocabulary was more than just "Cabernet, merlot, chardonnay" too. He might even be said to present the wine with a flourish.

Jane spoke to Mill, "Don't German meals always have sauerkraut one way or another? Exactly what wine goes with sauerkraut? Shouldn't this guy be handing out beer instead of wine?"

Mill looked puzzled, "Huh, I never considered the question."

"Mill! There's something you don't know? Wow!"

"I think you're right, cabernet, merlot and chardonnay won't work at all."

Tonight Swan Feine dressed as garishly as ever, but decidedly not in Betty Kuhn's style. She had her revealing crocheted top on, but this time it somehow looked dressier. That may have been because of Swan's gobs of jewelry and her flashy belt, stretch pants and heels. Jane thought, no doubt undergarments for Swan's attire, if there were undergarments at all, were compliments of a certain Patrick O'Neal, the very O'Neal who clung to Swan now. O'Neal had a horrible looking green drink in his hand.

Lois Feine had no date and she said she wanted to see if she could help out in the kitchen. Apparently she could because she did not come back out.

To Jane's incredulity, Sally Webb paraded about outdoing the much younger Swan in the provocative department. Sally's risqué and gossamer-like attire was not only wrong for the rainy and cool season, it was wrong for the occasion, it was really wrong for any occasion save, perhaps, a bedroom with one's paramour. Clyde Webb sported a few new but small scars on his forehead. Mostly he was busy making drinks at the sideboard, but he wore a big foolish grin whenever he admired his wife, or whenever he caught someone else stealing a peek at her.

Mill had taken Jane's hint and approached Webb hoping to find beer. Webb said, "Tonight no rum punch, tonight, Jägermeister, 'The Huntsman.' Jägermeister's a term coined in Germany in 1934 for official foresters and such. It's a Nazi term, a little like 'Volkswagen.' It is the title given a forest officer. But thank goodness, nobody remembers the Nazi roots anymore. This stuff has all kinds of good herbs and stuff in it. It even has ginseng. It's good for you! But in Germany they call it Leberkleister because that sounds like Jägermeister . Leberkleister means liver glue! Ha, ha, ha! Jägermeister thinned out with gin and lemon makes a Silver Bullet. Can I make you one?"

Mill almost shuddered.

Sally Webb held the bottle of green stuff for Mill to see. "Look! The Cross of Saint Hubertus and Saint Eustace, patron saints of hunters," Then Sally rocked back and forth in rhythm as she recited.

> *"Das ist des Jägers Ehrenschild,*
> *daß er beschützt und hegt sein Wild,*
> *weidmännisch jagt, wie sich's gehört,*
> *den Schöpfer im Geschöpfe ehrt."*

"That poem means show honor to your wild prey." Sally smiled and wiggled. Webb grinned mightily at the resulting wiggly display.

A roar of hard rain on the roof made Webb pause in his drink making. Sally Webb said "Oooo!" and she wiggled again. Webb smiled again.

There was no beer on the sideboard. Mill took two mineral waters and returned to Jane.

Jane said, "Mill, is it just me? Sally's putting on a show, and she's helping Clyde push his gross green drinks, she's waltzing around with one herself, but she hasn't taken sip of it yet."

"It's not you. I noticed that too. But, for some reason, that doesn't surprise me. Something's up."

Sally, as if on cue, floated by Mill and Jane, and in a low voice she said, "Franz von Papen invites you to an afterglow tonight. Right after dinner. I left a couple umbrellas by the lower door earlier. Have your guns." Then she floated away.

Jane wanted to ask Sally exactly what that meant, but Sally was too quick. She was already across the room.

Then McIntyre came forward, "Have you guys heard anything? Do you think the gift to the school is at any risk?"

Mill said, "We haven't heard much, but it looks like the the gift was Schmidt's idea. At least it was his money. As you might guess, things are in quite an uproar right now, but I'm not aware of any changes."

Henderson was next. "You wouldn't believe the change in Spatz. Your guys from Washington are all over us, mostly telling us how to handle the press. They want to keep this a simple blackmail case and put a tight publicity cap on the rest of it. Spatz turns out to be masterful in that department. And he's even become polite to me. And he told me to bring you one of those portable urinals that guys with prostate trouble use. Humorous huh?"

Jane laughed.

Mill said, "Okay, okay, umm, tell him, him I send back a bound edition of 'The Hunter of Thespiae' signed by Nemesis."

Jane looked puzzled. The she smiled and chuckled politely. Then she said, "Okay, I give."

"The hunter of Thespiae is Narcissus, the guy who likes to look at his own reflection, and Nemesis is the goddess of retribution against arrogance. You're right, Spatz would never get it."

"Mill, c'mon, be nice."

Mill continued with Henderson, "Anything from the hospital?"

"You already know the bullet missed Dorsey's internal organs. That's lucky for him. Jane too I guess. Last I heard, he's hanging on."

Jane's smile fell off her face, "Oh man." but Val Tesler had already started talking to Mill on the topic of Memelland and The Council of Ambassadors. Jane looked around and noticed Swan taking two Silver Bullets from Webb. Patrick O'Neal stood nearby with an empty glass.

Claudia Tesler apparently noticed that Jane needed rescuing from Memelland and started a conversation about rutabaga. Claudia said they could be boiled, baked, used in stew, anything at all.

Forty-five minutes of awkward talk with people Jane hardly knew passed, then Hans appeared with a white towel draped over his arm and rang a silver bell to call everyone to dinner.

Jane noticed that O'Neal was now seated. He appeared to have fallen asleep. Whether that was a result of silver bullets or boring conversation was not obvious. Swan was rocking his shoulders back and forth. He seemed to come to life and wobble to his feet. Jane watched, a little concerned, but O'Neal smiled and seemed to regain himself.

Mill took a detour by the back windows while others filed into the dining room so Jane followed him. Mill looked out as if regarding the rain. It came across the darkening yard in waves. He also seemed interested in how it played on the glass of those old metal framed windows. He seemed deep in thought. Jane stood by him, in fact, she stood very close. Finally Jane said, "So you think I'm cute, huh, you like my curves and smile huh? But you say I need some vanity and to dress nicer and sexier huh?" Mill looked at her with a puzzled expression. Then Jane very obviously turned and looked straight at the immodestly clad Sally Webb. Sally was wiggling and dancing and making a general display of herself. Mill followed her eyes and looked too, then he snorted like he was suppressing a laugh.

"That'd be a sight to behold."

Jane said, "Jeez Mill."

As they turned to walk to the dining room, the small and quiet figure of Natalie was there. She said, "Listen carefully, some things will come to light tonight. But if things go wrong, there is a note that looks like an old love poem to me from Günter. It is taped to the wall behind my clothing in my closet. There is a vault within another vault under an old car in the garage. The alarm shut-off for those vaults is in my bedroom. The combination for the shut-off is the date the war with Germany ended. The combination for the second vault is Mrs Webb's cell phone number. If anything goes wrong tonight, show the poem and the contents of the vault to Sally Webb. Sally will know how what you find in the vault unlocks a very great deal of money. The secret room you looked in is, of course, only a diversion for treasure hunters like Hoffman and the kids. Forget that room. If all goes well, amnesia about what I just said would please me and probably people in very high places in your government. Now Mr. Mill, please take my arm and escort me to the head of the table."

Mill took Natalie's arm and Jane walked close by.

Inside the dining room, the table was set finely. There was no wild boar with an apple in its mouth, but there was a finely printed menu at each place. It had three columns, German, French and English. Jane counted seven courses. Each place had a little card too. Jane looked for hers as they moved toward the head of the table. Mill tapped Jane and in a low voice said, "Looks like you are matron, you're right next to Natalie, act surprised, honored and pleased."

Jane really was pleased and flattered. She smiled and said, "Oh my! What am I doing here? Oh, Natalie, thank you!"

Jane sat on one side, Bubbie Feine on the other. Next to Jane's surprise, was Sally Webb and then Clyde. Mill sat nest to Jane and Henderson. This all struck Mill as an odd deviation from formal man-woman-man-woman seating. Something was being said, but Mill could not de-code it.

Lois Feine and the Hoffman kids emerged from the kitchen, then Betty Kuhn and her new man flowed from the kitchen with wine and a first course of caviar potato cups.

"Ahh, service à la russe, how nice!" said Mill to Jane.

Jane looked at Mill blankly.

"Service à la russe, Russian style service, courses come from the kitchen one at a time. French style is everything's out all at once in a big display for the ego of the host, then it all gets cold."

"Mill, you know too much. I think you're just showing off." Then in a lower voice Jane asked, "Is caviar German? I thought it was Russian."

"Show off? Mill sat for a moment. "Horrors, that would be vanity wouldn't it! How feminine of me." Then he said, "Caviar Russian? You're right I guess. In Germany they'd spell fish eggs with a K, but putting 'em in a potato just has to be German." After a minute more, "Jane, The Germans surrendered to the West May 8, 1945 and they surrendered to Russia May 9. Truman didn't declare hostilities over till 1946 and congress didn't conclude peace legally till 1951. I wonder which date Natalie meant."

"Mill, now I'm sure you know too much. Everybody knows it's May 8, '45 .. I think."

After *the* Party

"The only free cheese is in the mousetrap"

American Proverb

It was very dark and quiet behind the house. The rain's drone was all that could be heard. Jane wondered how rain made that sound. It was so familiar, but what really made rain sound that way? Perhaps it was raindrops hitting leaves on trees, or falling into puddles on the ground or roof gutters pouring it into the yard. Whatever it was, it was a pleasant comfortable sound. In an odd sort of way, the umbrellas made the hurried walk through the rain with Mill feel rather cozy. Jane wondered at that too. She smiled her big toothy smile. She was headed into who knew what trouble. Sally had warned to bring her Glock. What danger was at hand? Yet it was still pleasant walking through the rain like this. They crossed the little arched foot bridge, then, lights could be seen coming from the guest house ahead. As if reading her thoughts, Mill said, "Jane, I wonder what mess we're about to step into. This should be real interesting."

Once up the steps, onto the porch and into the guest house, it was warm and dry and bright and cheery. Or so it seemed at first.

Jane did not notice people leaving the house early, but somehow, people were here before Jane and Mill.

Betty Kuhn was there. The remarkably short skirt outfit had given way to one of those out-of-style women's suits made to look like a men's business suit. The surprising result was, dressed this way, Betty, sprayed hair and all, bordered on attractive. Her new sidekick was here too. He was still in his tux. Now he had a tray of assorted dessert liquors and half bottles of dessert wine. There were petit fours on tables around the room and a carafe of coffee with cream and sugar on the bar. Another big tray of petit fours and other little desserts sat by the coffee. Sally Webb had donned something that looked a bit like a man's sports coat over her ridiculous gossamer clothing. Clyde Webb was here too. He sat sipping coffee. A bulge in his business suit jacket betrayed what Jane took to be an old army forty-five. In fact, as Jane looked around, there were bulges or closely held purses everywhere. Jane guessed everyone was armed. Eyes were on Jane and Mill and there was an uneasy lack of conversation.

Finally, Natalie spoke. "Please sit down Jane, sit down Mill."

Jane did not sit, she headed for the coffee and made a show of fixing a cup.

Mill sat.

Jane stood by the bar and took a little petit four cake then moved around behind the bar. There was a stool there that she perched on. Then she, with as much stealth as she could, put her Glock in easy reach on the counter behind the bar. Then she made a show of taking another little cake.

Betty's side-kick with the tray of drinks could not see the gun, but he obviously noticed Jane's move and smiled at her and nodded his head very gently. Mill's eyes too flashed very quickly at Jane then back.

Natalie was talking, "Mr. Mill, Jane, we have some business to do. I understand that information not extracted from suspects in the most polite and correct ways may not be used as evidence against them in prosecutions, so I have elected not to invite your police friend Henderson. What will happen now might serve to compromise his position. But, perhaps you may witness this, then coach Henderson appropriately."

Jane noticed that Mill sat on the very edge of his chair. He was very straight and alert.

Mill spoke, "We are not authorized to allow illegal activities or risk danger of violence. From your comment, I think perhaps I disagree and Henderson should come at once."

"Certainly, you should call him whenever you see fit. But perhaps it would be better for you to wait a few minutes. Betty has just gotten a phone call. That was about half an hour ago and our guest is running earlier than I expected. I thought I would have some time here to talk to you and Jane first, but we have already picked him up and he is on the way now."

Mill was expressionless and remained stiff. "We?"

"Leon has picked him up."

"Leon?"

"Leon works for Betty."

"Picked up who?"

"Mr. Hoffman, of course. Mr. Mill, I have learned by hard experience that silence is safety. I have learned that knowledge is power. I do not break silence cheaply. But tonight, I find I need to make a trade, information for a solution to a certain problem. I am taking your good will on faith. Because we are rushed, I do not have time to negotiate with you about that. Also, I would like you to know that it would have been much simpler, and no doubt a just thing to do, to extinguish a life in reprisal for my loss of Günter. But I now choose to leave that method in the past. What I do now is with faith that your system of laws can do the appropriate things. Do not let me wish I had employed the old system. That would have been much simpler and it would have been very effective in the eyes of Hoffman's associates. Allow me credit for going out of my way to make this arrangement tonight."

"Now, I would like the two of you to meet my granddaughter. Frau Doktor Salida Dorman Webb is my granddaughter. Salida means happiness and she has certainly been that to me. I am afraid that we never met the unfortunate young American named Sally Dorman. She was murdered by her young husband in West Virginia some time ago. Her body was never found so her husband was never convicted of that crime. But backwoods justice, being what it is, neither has he been heard from since. It was convenient to allow my granddaughter and poor Ms. Dorman's identity become .. confused. It was convenient for our needs here.

Sally is, in fact, my granddaughter. Her mother was born in Poland and was taken from me when I was under arrest. By the time I found my daughter again, she was happily married and living in Germany. Sadly, she died at too early an age, then, with her father's permission and Günter's money, Salida went to private schools in Germany and later, went to college in the United States. Salida is, in fact, married to Mr. Webb. But it was convenient for Hoffman and the others to believe Sally was the rustic American. Clyde has always been aware of all this and he has been most understanding. Mr. Mill, you are a good detective and I was impressed by you, but you missed these little facts. So did you Jane. But it should be obvious to you in retrospect. So that's one for Sally and me."

Jane noticed that Mill did not move an inch. His face betrayed nothing.

"No doubt you have surmised that Hoffman paid Panski to murder Günter. Evidently, your Dorsey did not fathom that part. That surprised me. Dorsey was not a complete fool. I thought he would, at least, understand that part. That's why Panski tried to shoot Smith and would have shot Dorsey. And now, Hoffman means to eliminate me. He has contracted Panski's replacement Leon to do that. Or so he thinks. Betty?"

Betty Kuhn spoke, "It has been Hoffman's habit to enter the U.S. by way of the St. Clair railroad tunnel, the old abandoned one, not the new one. He would contact me and I'd send Panski to pick him up on the American end. In fact, it was Panski who originally showed him the way through. The old tunnel is blocked off of course, but getting past that part through the ventilation system is easy. It is quite a hike through there, over a mile actually, and it's not easy walking, especially in the dark, then it's another quarter mile up the old rail bed to the pickup point on 16th street in Port Huron, but since Hoffman did not care to have customs record his comings and goings, this has been his travel method of choice. Leon picked him up over half an hour ago."

The man with the tray of petit fours smiled broadly.

Natalie spoke again, "When we speak to Henderson, I will provide him with the names of Hoffman's associates in Germany. I have spoken to two of them already. They had not yet made the connection that Günter was murdered, much less that Hoffman was behind it. But they were easily persuaded of the fact have agreed to provide the authorities with some very good circumstantial information when the time comes. And now, Betty, will you continue the story?"

"Hoffman asked to be picked up tonight. Leon was to stand by at the Amtrak parking lot near 16th Street. I told Hoffman that Leon was Panski's replacement and I told him that Leon could be trusted in all things. I gave him Leon's cell-phone number and told him to call when he was free of the tunnel. But just as Natalie predicted, Hoffman contacted Leon directly the same day. He wasn't so obvious as to use the word 'murder' but he offered ten thousand for what he called 'a certain kind of job.' We recorded the call. He also said 'to take care of Mrs. Schmidt so we hear no more from her.' Those were his exact words. We took the liberty of recording them. Leon followed our instructions and told him twenty-five thousand with fifteen up front. Hoffman agreed at once. Hoffman expects to hand Leon that fifteen in this room tonight."

Mill pulled his cell phone out of a pocket. "We need Henderson."

"Just a moment more Mr. Mill, consider that people very high up in your government do not want light shed on all of this. Consider also, the young Hoffmans. We need to ascertain if they were in on this and maybe couriers between Hoffman and Panski, or if they are innocents. I may be a brutal woman, but I do not like brutalizing innocent youths. Think about what you mean to do for a moment. Then you may phone Henderson if you need to."

Mill looked straight at Natalie for only a moment, then, he hit a speed dial.

Neither Natalie nor the others interfered but Natalie did say, "Ask him not to spook Hoffman, ask him to take his time."

"Henderson, it's Mill. Get to the guest house behind Schmidt's with some uniformed cops. … Yeah, I'm here and Jane is too. Something's going down, a trap set for an accessory to Schmidt's murder. No time to explain. No need for sirens and lights and don't spook anyone you see coming in. Keep the uniforms out of sight if you can. Come by way of Schmidt's house, not Webb's. And be careful, don't spook anyone you see. It's a set-up."

Natalie did not seem upset at all. She just said, "Now then Mr. Mill, now we must hurry."

Betty Kuhn moved behind the bar beside Jane and quietly placed another, bigger gun next to Jane's. Then she turned and tilted her head and smiled broadly at Jane. "Seems like a good place to watch the proceedings here, doesn't it?"

Just then noises were heard on the porch. The door flew open.

"Leon, please escort Mr. Hoffman in."

Loose Ends

"Peace and Justice Are Two Sides of the Same Coin"

Dwight Eisenhower

There was a very big man and he had the arm graying man twisted behind his back. The big guy shoved the other guy forward, then he bumped the door closed with his shoulder.

"We did okay till right here on the porch. Then he kind-a changed his mind when he saw the lights on and everybody inside. He needed a little persuading to come the rest of the way."

The smaller man wore an expressive looking leather jacket, dress pants that seemed tailored and incongruous hiking boots.

Natalie spoke. "Hello Herr Hoffman, it's been too long. I am afraid you need to know that nine people in this room are armed and you are only one of them. You need to place your hands on top of your head. Leon, let him go."

Leon shoved Hoffman into the midst of the others and quickly produced a pistol that he pointed at Hoffman. Hoffman stumbled and almost fell.

"Hands on top of your head. Now!" It was Leon this time.

Jane saw Hoffman's eyes dart around the room, he was frozen like a deer at the roadside.

Natalie's was hard now, "If you want to live through the next minute, do not try anything silly. Hands on top of your head."

Hoffman slowly put his hands on his head.

"Now then Sally, please remove his gun and see if he has brought us his fifteen thousand."

Sally stepped forward and removed a Colt .45 automatic from inside Hoffman's jacket. She placed the it on a table. She removed an envelope from the jacket too and peeked inside. "Money lots of it." She put the envelope next to the gun. Then she patted him down, starting with his collar and working her way down. She had obviously done this before. "Oops, another!" An smaller automatic was stuck in his belt. Sally checked Hoffman's crotch. "My, rather small, are you frightened or are they always like that?" She continued down his trouser legs. "Now sit down but keep your hands on your head and lift up your feet."
Hoffman did so, awkwardly. Sally pulled Hoffman's boots off. "Look at this! A twenty five caliber pistol. What did you mean to shoot with this? A chipmunk?" Sally then inspected his boot and tossed them across the room. "Okay, all clear."

Sally took Hoffman's guns and put them on the bar in front of Jane.

"Thank you Sally. Mr. Hoffman, you may relax. Coffee? A drink? You will need a drink very shortly."

Hoffman looked around the room again but did not speak.

"Mr. Hoffman, My Treasurer, Frau Webb, has prepared a report for us. Frau Webb, now that you have removed out guest's arms, will you tell us how things stand?"

"Why yes. I would first like to thank Mr. Hoffman's accountant, Gert Wiesenberg, for his cooperation and help in all this. As soon as we explained what has happened, he became most co-operative. He provided everything we wanted and made all this very clear."

Jane thought Hoffman now looked both exhausted and more even terrified. His eyes kept nervously scanning the room. He began to rise but Leon stepped forward and pushed him back into his seat.

Mill said, "Take it easy guys, take it easy."

Hoffman finally spoke, his voice was high and thin and he spoke in English, although with a thick German accent. "Natalie, there is some terrible misunderstanding!"

Natalie cut him off, "Oh no, we understand. No misunderstanding. Please continue, Frau Webb, go on."

Sally spoke again, "Well, to make short work of this report, the revenue from the hundred year leases on our properties is mostly intact. Mostly. There is only minor pilfering here and there, fifty thousand here, a hundred there, not so much really. And, Mr. Hoffman, you also used our money to make excellent purchases of expensive art inside Russia and then you skillfully paid officials off to obtain the appropriate export permits. You got them to Germany where their value was very high. Good work! Happily, Gert has already helped us take possession of our art. I am sorry, but you may not sell it now. We will sell that material and keep the profits. That was a clever way to move so much money out of Russia Herr Hoffman, it will help us very much. Next, we find our securities, the ones you are aware of, are nearly as we expected. And then we checked the money you hold for us in accounts in Switzerland and the Cayman Islands. Oh my! Mr. Hoffman, one withdrawal is just so obviously the same amount as you paid for your estate in Westphalia. And my word! That was careless of you. And fifty million more is simply missing. And Axel Braun, your corporate attorney, was good enough to share the curious information with us that fifty million in securities has just come into your personal possession."

Natalie spoke now, "Mr. Hoffman, Axel is taking the appropriate legal steps with the authorities to seize those securities and your estate. And Gert and Axel have also promised to assist with testimony and any further inquiries. Isn't that nice of them? So you see Herr. Hoffman,"

Natalie interrupted, her voice chilling, You see Hoffman, Killing Günter to cover your tracks has failed! There is no need to kill me either now! It will not help you now."

The room was silent. Hoffman looked at Natalie.

"But I am still curious, what made you think Gert and Axel would not notice any of this? Did you mean to kill them too? What were you thinking?"

"Natalie, what wild talk! This is surely a misunderstanding. Moving so much money is complicated and I certainly meant to deliver it all to you. Hoffman's eyes were darting around again. You know I must use whatever device I can to move your money, especially from country to country."

"Mr. Hoffman, I do not know that at all. All of our funds are perfectly legal and should be handled above board. As you well know, the days when your father helped us hide assets from the Soviets ended years ago. And now, perhaps you will explain why you had not one, but three pistols on your person? And exactly why did you offer Leon that twenty-five thousand?"

Hoffman was silent.

"Alright, Leon, please fetch the Hoffman kids. I think starting with them may loosen Mr. Hoffman's tongue. I assume they are your couriers. Let's maybe start by cutting a toe or thumb off Helga for Mr. Hoffman's benefit."

Hoffman suddenly spoke. "No, you don't need to do that. Those kids don't know a thing. Let's see if we can work this all out without them. Natalie, I still have an ace or two you know. Not all of your money got here so legally. Natalie, I can still hang you on that part. So let's do some negotiating."

"I think not, you were contracted to manage our funds including transfers into our accounts here. Minimize taxes and other problems? Yes. Break the law? No. That you chose illegal methods to do all that was not our doing. And if, for some reason, in the very near future, you are suddenly unable to relate your side if the story, oh well! I think you argue against your own self interests! Threats like you just made against me may shorten your life expectancy and that of those kids. Do not threaten me."

"Okay, okay, anyway I think tax considerations will hang you even without me. Natalie, you still need to be reasonable and negotiate. I can still help. Not threaten, no not me! I mean help! I'll make an offer right now. Let the kids go, keep them out of this, then I'll cop a plea and get everything off your back. How's that? Be reasonable. I'll take the rap for everything. How's that? But lay off the kids." Hoffman's voice was strained, "Kinder wissen nichts. Keine Notwendigkeit, sie zu verletzen. Ich werde zusammenarbeiten."

"I think I do not trust you. Leon, bring the kids."

Leon took an umbrella and left.

Jane watched Mill. He turned as if to watch Leon but doing so he put one hand behind the other. He used manual alphabet for the deaf to spell out 'bluffing' with his hidden hand. Jane wondered how he knew she had studied manual alphabet. That was in high school.

"Did your father never mention the Das Mungo, The Mongoose, to you?"

Hoffman said, "That was you wasn't it"

"How quickly you forgot. How soon we forget our parent's advice. You father would not have been such a fool. No Hoffman, I was never remembered for being reasonable or for negotiating. You sir, have murdered my husband. I am very, very annoyed about that. Would you like a drink? You, I am afraid, are about to need one or maybe more than one. This will not be pleasant for you or the kids."

"Okay, okay, what do you want? They do not know anything. If you were going to shoot me, you would have done that by now. And you wouldn't have done it in front of all these people. You want something. What do you want? You win. What do you want?"

"First of all, a couple honest answers please. That and you might even survive the night. Might. How did you communicate with Panski? Were the kids your messengers? Why did you put those kids here?"

"They're here to go to school. Das ist ehrlich That's the truth. Now please call what's his name .. call Leon back? I'll tell the truth. All of it."

"We'll see about that."

Hoffman sat silently for a long moment. "Okay. It was all set with Panski months ago. Yeah, the kids gave the 'go' order, but they did not know that they did it. The code was to ask Panski if he had Zinfandel when he was serving wine. I told them it was just an old inside joke of ours. When he paraded around with his tray, ask for Zinfandel. And that's the truth. You can shoot me or whatever your damn Polish resistance idea of justice demands. But the kids knew nothing. Lay off them. That's the truth."

"And our money?"

"Yeah, okay, in the beginning, your husband just slipped enough information to us, account numbers and passwords, that kind of thing, to handle the money a bit at a time. Just one item moved here at a time and no more information till it was delivered. We couldn't whack him before because we'd lose most of the money. But as time passed, he got careless and he trusted us. The amount of money we could get now made it worth the risk. Now call your goon back and lay off the kids. Okay?"

"I think we'll wait. Who was 'we'? Who else was in on this?"

"That clown Panksi, who else? Gert and Axel were starting to notice stuff and I was thinking of offering them real money to close their eyes. But that part hadn't happened yet."

To Jane's surprise, Mill spoke. "Hoffman, do you have a hand in the contractors for the school work or other angles working?"

"No, no, in the end we'd have needed McIntyre or some other insider. It wasn't worth it. It was too risky."

"The money, the Riechskonkordat bribe or relocating Jewish people or what? Where'd it come from?"

Natalie spoke, "Mr. Mill, Mr. Hoffman thinks he knows, but he does not know. But to pass the time till the kids get here, I offer a make-believe story. Suppose you were Franz von Papen and the Nazis gave you the job of secretly slipping an enormous amount of money and property to the Catholic Church to grease the skids for signing a big agreement. Suppose you were von Papen and you loved Germany but you actually hated the Nazis. The Nazis had even murdered several of your good friends. Suppose, when you met the Pope and the others, they were interested in preserving church tax in Germany and keeping their priests in Spain safe from the Communist murderers and keeping their church people out of any military draft. They were really more interested in opposing the anti-Catholic Communists than anything else and you knew that would make an easy agreement for anti-Bolshevik Nazis. You knew a bribe would only offend them and it would work against, not for making a deal. Suppose you quietly set that huge amount of money and land aside. You left an old friend in charge of it to divide up and hide in smaller amounts here and there and, you were able to strike the church deal hardly touching that money and land at all. Suppose the Nazis, being the thugs they were, assumed the secret payment had been made in some out-of-sight way because the deal went through and so they intentionally didn't look for the money. This is, of course, only an imaginary story."

After a minute Natalie spoke again, "Now as I think, I offer an epilogue to my story. Suppose the relocation of Jewish people to Palestine was funded from America alright, but it took much, much more money than that. Suppose large amounts of the Nazi money was used for that purpose too. Suppose that after the fact, the American government wanted their hand in the Jewish relocations and co-mingling funds with Nazi money and the implications of all that to remain unknown. Suppose the Americans decided to simply locate the parties involved in different places in America and then put blinders on everyone. Suppose that plan has lasted till today and even you are in the dark about it. Okay? Are you happy? Now I think you should drop it. Drop it okay? You see that's because this is only a bedtime story."

The door opened and Hans and Helga came in. They were followed by Leon.

Leon said, "They were kind-a having a party with some neighbor kids. Sorry, the other kids know these two are out here. It was that, or bring 'em all. Want me to go get the rest?"

"This will do for now Leon."

Hans looked at the guns on the bar, but said nothing about them. "Onkel! Wie bist du so schnell hier hin gekommen? Wir haben dich in zwei tagen erwartet."

Hoffman replied in English, "Hans, there is a very bad misunderstanding here. Mrs. Schmidt, I think, wants to ask a question or two. It may seem trivial, but it is very important, so tell the absolute truth. I'm afraid it is terribly important."

"Hans, your uncle is right, but I really have only one question. Do you remember the old Polish man serving wine the night you got here?"

"Sure, of course. He spoke us in German but his German was half Polish."

"Did you uncle suggest you say anything to him?"

Hans looked at the older Hoffman, "Sure, he said ask the old guy for Zinfandel, he said that was a joke here. Panski was his name right?"

"Did you do that?"

"Sure, he seemed pretty amused too. Then and he said, 'Sehr gut. Es wird passieren.' I remember that because I wondered if pouring cab instead was part of the joke."

Natalie turned to Mill, "What do you think?"

Mill said, "It's the truth. That's good for now. Get the kids out of here."

Jane slid her Glock back into a pocket, and then she spoke to the young Hoffmans, "Look guys, some really awful stuff is coming down and Dr. Schmidt's death isn't all of it. There's more and it's really kind-a bad. Look, let's go back to the house and hang out. I want to check out that wine if any's left. We'll need to call that attorney Mr. Moore too. We'll need to get him to come out right now. Do you have his cell number?"

Hans answered, "Yeah, it's on speed dial. But why? What's with the guns? What's going on?"

"I think we should all go back to the house now. Things are way too tense here right now. Let's relax and hang out. I'll talk to Moore and explain a couple things to him. I can't tell you guys much till the cops get more statements from you. Come with me, we'll hang out in the house. But it's seriously best to scoot and right now."

"Thank you, Jane," Natalie said, "I'll see you later, if I'm not arrested that is."

Hoffman spoke too, "Thank you, whoever you are, and thank God. Natalie, you will find me good for my word. But don't hurt those kids."

Jane hustled the Hoffman youngsters out the door.

"I have spared your life Herr Hoffman, and the kids too. Why I went to that trouble, I don't exactly know. I should have eliminated you at once and maybe the kids too. In repayment for that, tell the authorities the truth. And remember, those kids are still in my house and I'm still very, very angry." said Natalie.

As Jane walked out into the rain, she met Henderson and a two uniformed policemen coming in. "They're all in there. The set-up worked fine. Nobody was hurt. The situation is stable, but there's guns everywhere. I'd say handcuff Hoffman, he's the graying German guy in a leather jacket who you haven't met. Arrest him for having concealed weapons. I'm a witness to that part. So's Mill. Then ask Mill about the rest. You've got an accessory to murder in Hoffman. He's an accessory to attempted murder too. They've got him dead to rights in there. These kids shouldn't be involved so I'm taking them back to the house. Come down to the house to get their statements as soon as you have this place under control. I'm calling Moore for them. I'll keep them at the house till you get there."

Finis

Much later that night; Natalie and Jane and Mill stood looking out the casement windows into the darkness. The September rain played on the glass. Little streams of water slowly moved down the windows. Clyde and Sally sat nearby, each with a big cocktail.

Mill spoke, "Natalie, why did you not tell us everything at first? Why, did you continue the ruse about Sally? That made things harder for us."

Sally answered for her grandmother, "We didn't know what was happening at first. After all, you worked for Dorsey and you arrived with Smith. We didn't think we could trust you. I wasn't at ease with that part. I kept the Sally Dorman of West Virginia identity only to fool Hoffman and his pals. I never really misled authorities before. But we were in the dark and you might have been sent as reinforcements for the wrong team."

Natalie sighed, "Oh, it was so much like going back to Poland. I could trust nobody till I understood what was going on. I have lived these things before and I could not trust you, nor even trust the police at first."

Natalie was silent for a time. Then she continued, "My new friends, it is true that I have done very hard, even brutal things in my life, more brutal than you could guess. But I will say the truth; I have never sided with evil or selfishness. Günter and I helped many of those who were in trouble and who needed help. We fought evil and brutality, often the evil dressed up as a people's movement or a legitimate government or police or armed forces. I would ask you to believe that of me."

Jane said, "Then why us? What changed your mind? You have just met us, yet more and more, you trusted us. I understand why you would not trust at first, but then you did trust us. After all that has happened, why us? "

Another moment passed. "Oh, that was partly because I had just met you, because Hoffman would never guess I had trusted you. You were convenient. Hoffman was wily and dangerous till the last minute. I chose you as back-up, just in case more things went wrong."

They stood in silence moments more. Then Natalie spoke again, but now with a voice that betrayed emotion. "Really, it is more than that, so much more than that. You are not old enough to know. You see, one can never shed the terrible things of the past. One cannot become someone new. I am old now and I am not as hard as I once was. The past is still alive for me and I am so tired. I am so weary. Something you will have a hard time understanding is this, It was your humanity Jane, and you too Mill. I knew you were my friends.

"You act the stoic Mr. Mill, but you are no stoic. I can see that. Old people can see.

"Jane," Natalie sighed again, "Nobody can shed who they are, we cannot shed the past or even have it again. None of us can do that. I cannot visit the man I was to marry. I cannot sit in a park and hold his hand. I cannot tell him that I still remember. And I cannot have Günter here again either. He never understood how I appreciated him. He was gruff and arrogant and bitter, but he was a selfless and a good, good man. Günter was even a hero. I knew that. Nor can I forget my time under communist arrest and what happened there. In one way, it is all done, all done and all over. It is all gone and in the past, but it is all still with me. It is past, but it is who I am. One may not alter any of it. But one can know the truth. One must have respect for the truth … the truth, to see the facts, facts with dignity, to embrace the truth. You steadied me in ways you did not know. You are young and strong. Jane, your spoke of you parents. You told me they are gone, then you did not weep, you smiled. You smiled! That was so wonderful. You could never guess what that meant. I knew I could trust that. Smile Jane, your smile is so encouraging to me. You know tragedy and can smile."

Jane did smile, but for only a moment. Then she spoke, "Mill imagine, just imagine what we have touched here. All that sadness, all the terror, ruin, hate, all of that. I don't mean the textbook part, I mean the people." The contradictions of this September pulled at Jane. There had been some joy in it, a little fun anyway, but mostly it was tragedy after tragedy and tragedy revisited. "Oh Natalie all this is too real for me .. so many people over the years, it's all so sad. It is not all gone at all. No Natalie, it is not lost on me. Oh my, look at me." Jane began to weep. "It all still echoes."

Epilogue

The barbarism of the twentieth century strains the imagination. It mocks the proposition that we are civilized. Mass murder, brutality and war were the norm, charity and peace the exception. We should not forget. We should do better. - RK

Made in the USA
Middletown, DE
21 December 2018